PRAISE FOR *THE PI...*

'A deeply engrossing and authentic story, with such passionate realism you must keep reading.'

Jackie French AM, award-winning author and historian

PRAISE FOR *MEZZA ITALIANA*

'This is a memoir with a difference. Zoë Boccabella's story of her embrace of her Italian roots culminates in a dramatic event that brings into focus her entire family history. She's a charming and thoughtful writer with a vibrant story to tell.'

Frances Mayes, author of *Under the Tuscan Sun*

'Wonderful descriptions of relatives and other villagers, the countryside and the food ... This is a beautifully written memoir full of characters and places, which will appeal to the literary traveller, to people who already love Italy and to all those intending to visit.'

Chris Harrington, *Bookseller+Publisher*

'I loved this book! Zoë Boccabella has a vastly different story to the foreigner who falls in love with Italy. She has Italian blood running through her veins as the granddaughter of Italians who immigrated from Abruzzo ... There is much to love about this book. The wonderful characters, her fabulous Italian grandfather who takes his love for all Italian traditions to Brisbane and cherishes them till he dies. Her boyfriend who becomes the poster boy for all things Italian and the people of Fossa, a village tucked away in Abruzzo. I can highly recommend *Mezza Italiana*.'

Carla Coulson, author of *Italian Joy*

'This is a delightful book that is part travel story, part a very personal narrative of self-discovery, that the author Zoë Boccabella (*beautiful mouth* in Italian) shares with us ... It has everything – romance, drama, pathos and tragedy as well as many humorous anecdotes. A lovely tale that I can warmly recommend.'

Karen Brooks, author and academic

PRAISE FOR *JOE'S FRUIT SHOP AND MILK BAR*

'The strength of the book is the effective simplicity of the writing and the poignant immediacy of its images – old glasses, folded sheets and milk bar signs from another age that conjure the past so clearly for the author and the reader.'

Steven Carroll, *Sydney Morning Herald*

'The manner in which this book is written is absolutely beautiful ... a wonderful read.'

David Curnow, ABC Brisbane

'Writer Zoë Boccabella has delved into her family's own rich story ... pieced together from listening to three decades of her grandparents' incredible stories ... A great story that will connect with so many people.'

Natasha Mitchell, *Life Matters*, ABC Radio

'Zoë Boccabella has written a beautiful book ... it's a universal story and one that resonates across the extraordinary Italian communities.'

Jon Faine, *The Conversation Hour*, ABC Radio

Zoë Boccabella is an Australian author of both fiction and non-fiction. Her books have been much acclaimed, selected for literary and popular awards and sold internationally. Zoë's migrant ancestry and handed-down recipes influence her writing, along with subtropical Brisbane, where she was born and lives, as well as travels in Europe and Australia. With a degree in literature, communications and sociology and a Master of Philosophy, she's worked as a researcher, writer and media advisor for several levels of government, the police service, universities and freelance. Zoë also loves to cook, especially dishes from generations of women and men in her family and their varied cultural pasts, ingredients and spoken stories shared over the kitchen table.

zoeboccabella.com

Also by Zoë Boccabella

Mezza Italiana
Joe's Fruit Shop and Milk Bar

THE PROXY BRIDE

Zoë Boccabella

First Published 2022
First Australian Paperback Edition 2022
ISBN 9781867247562

THE PROXY BRIDE
© 2022 by Zoë Boccabella
Australian Copyright Year
New Zealand Copyright Year

Published by
HQ Fiction
An imprint of Harlequin Enterprises (Australia) Pty Limited (ABN 47 001 180 918),
a subsidiary of HarperCollins Publishers Australia Pty Limited (ABN 36 009 913 517)
Level 13, 201 Elizabeth St
SYDNEY NSW 2000
AUSTRALIA

A catalogue record for this book is available from the National Library of Australia
www.librariesaustralia.nla.gov.au

Printed and bound in Australia by McPherson's Printing Group

MIX
Paper | Supporting
responsible forestry
FSC® C001695

To my great-uncle, Vince,
with thanks for his gentle stories,
last of those from the Solano
family's Applethorpe orchards.

~

And for Soccorsa Misale, Antonio Carozza,
Francesca Rizzitano and Vincenzo Solano,
my trisnonni who, almost a century ago,
accepted with modest grace in hard times
that once Francesca and Domenico left
Palmi, Calabria, to migrate to Australia,
they could never see their children again,
or know their grandchildren.

Contents

Amore, dolore e peperoncini
non possono essere tenuti segreti,
presto si tradiscono.

Love, pain and chillies
cannot be kept secret,
soon they betray themselves.

southern Italian proverb

The Match

1939 ~ Palmi, Calabria, Italy

Clasping her father's arm at the church threshold, Gia looked down the aisle to her younger brother, Salvatore, waiting for her at the altar. The priest gave a nod and with gentle fluster the few wedding guests in pews stood up, her mother, Nonna, Taddeo's parents and family. Wall-candelabra smoke ghosted up the plaster, and the seventeenth-century crucifix behind the altar watched from its blood-red backdrop. Gia thought of Taddeo and what he might be doing in Australia just then. Yet it was impossible to conjure much substance of him or Australia from the still pictures she'd seen.

Angelo went to step forward but she baulked. 'Come,' he murmured, with his usual fatherly gentleness. '*Who falls in water doesn't drown, but who falls badly will.*'

She squeezed his arm and let him lead her onward, knowing she'd miss her father's quaint way of talking in verse and proverb, an unfulfilled storyteller who hadn't had the opportunity to learn to write.

Salvatore, as Taddeo's proxy groom, looked so swamped in their father's old wedding suit that Gia almost let out a nervous laugh. Drawing up close to him, she smelt the minty, sage waft of wormwood bunches their mother had stored with the suit to guard it from moths. His eyes met hers. There was a sheen on his forehead. Her own hands felt moist. She turned as Angelo stepped back. The bobby pins her mother had used with zeal to keep the veil circlet on Gia's thick curls prickled her scalp. *Many girls marry this way now*, she reminded herself. And they did, with so many young men gone.

The priest began and she stole a glance at her mother. If Gia had hoped for reassurance, Rosaria only gave her a pointed stare, directing her to concentrate on what was at hand. She didn't look over to Taddeo's mother but she knew the two women behind the arrangement would only be at ease once the nuptials were complete and she was on a ship to Australia. Marked out as old at twenty-three, she wasn't sought after for marriage. But neither was Taddeo with his shyness and the purple birthmark on his face. Not that Gia recalled him or the birthmark too well – he was five years older than her, and she had still been at school when he'd left Italy a decade ago.

Despite the sunny morning, she felt the coldness that the echoey interior of Santissimo Crocifisso still held from the night before, heard the scrape of stone dust when she moved her feet. Through the open church door drifted passing voices followed by a cart on the road outside. At once she felt a part and yet apart from it all. And as Salvatore awkwardly edged the plain ring onto her finger, they heard Nonna blow her nose loudly and Gia felt herself already separating from her life in Palmi.

Back out front of the church in the little square, Piazzetta dell'Annunziata, she was momentarily blinded by sunlight bouncing off the pale paving stones.

'*Congratulazioni*, Giacinta.' Rosaria kissed Gia's cheeks. 'You are Signora Poletti now …' and before Gia could digest this, Nonna, still crying, pushed forward for her turn.

'*Tante belle cose*,' she wished her, *many beautiful things*.

Taddeo's mother was next. 'Look after my son well and be sure he is content.'

Gia felt the ring on her finger, the slim gold band delicate but unyielding. Her gaze swept the small piazza hoping to see a few of the schoolchildren she helped teach, but of course at that hour they were in their classroom, as she usually would have been as well. Those passers-by who did happen to look over tarried between errands to watch the two families arrange themselves around the proxy bride for a photograph.

Gia wore her best dress. It was linen, a shade between summer sky and the mauve of the Tyrrhenian Sea their town sat beside. Apart from tiny embroidered flowers around the neckline, it was quite plain, fastened down the back with covered buttons so small they were almost impossible to the fingertips. The long skirt hung straight, slightly crushed.

Taddeo would tell Gia much later that at about the time she'd been in the church, he'd been sitting on the back stairs of his farm house in Stanthorpe unlacing his work shoes. His shirt sagged, sweat-dampened, and the dusk insect thrum promised early summer and the peaches ripening before they usually did. In socks, he'd begun up the steps of his timber house on stumps as a utility truck bumped along the track into the property.

Alfio drove and there were several fellows on the tray singing a Calabrian wedding song.

Pino, Taddeo's closest friend whose own orchards neighboured his, stuck his head out the passenger window. 'We couldn't let your wedding day go by without a bit of celebrating.'

And despite his worries, Taddeo smiled. He'd been content in his own company that evening but as Alfio got out a crate of tinkling bottles and Pino carried in a boiler pot, he knew they were right to mark the occasion. The stark kitchen felt cheerier as the men bustled inside.

'I'll just clean myself up.'

'Wait, let's do a toast.' Alfio wanted to get started on the table-grape wine he'd made.

Pino put the boiler of rabbit passata on the stove to reheat and fetched Taddeo's clean jars he used as glasses in the manner of one at home in the house of his friend.

'To the groom.' Pino raised his drink before Alfio could and the others clinked it.

Alfio, who'd married in Italy and brought his wife, Josie, with him to Australia, looked from the bare shelves to the living room's one easy chair. 'And not a moment too soon.'

One of the others laughed then halted.

In the bathroom, Taddeo splashed water on his face and stared in the mirror. He was married. To Giacinta, who he hardly knew. He blinked. Yet their situation wasn't so unusual, he strove to console himself, with so many more Italian men than women in Australia. He watched a trickle of water run down the side of his face. Immigration had allowed him and Pino entry permits as 'white aliens', non-British European migrants, because Pino's uncle in Ingham had nominated them and had cane-cutting work awaiting them both. It was only possible for

Giacinta to emigrate because she'd be reuniting with kin. Him. Taddeo blinked again.

He thought of the Stanthorpe church socials and sixpence dances at the Oddfellows' Hall that he and Pino had attended in the hope of meeting someone. The smell of the raw timber, tobacco and ladies' talc, and his own sweat. Pino's smoothness compared to the awkward way he held himself, conscious of his birthmark, neither of them having much luck with the Australian girls, who'd been warned off foreigners. Just one local Australian woman and Italian man had married. In town one day, Taddeo saw them being jeered at by both Italians and Australians.

'Look, we each have a house and farm now,' Pino had pointed out to Taddeo, as they'd driven home in Pino's horse-drawn cart, axle lantern swaying, after yet another dance. 'A girl and her parents hope for that. Let's make a pact to write home and see who might be interested in marriage.'

For, like Taddeo, Pino was unable to afford a trip back to Italy and most Italian families wouldn't let their daughters travel out alone and unmarried. This had left them with their only option being a proxy wedding, their brides, who they wouldn't really know, to marry stand-in grooms at ceremonies held in Italy while Taddeo and Pino remained in Australia. Pino's had gone ahead a fortnight before Taddeo's. His wife Serena, also from Palmi, was to travel to Australia on the same ship as Gia. Taddeo rubbed his face hard with the rough towel. The thought of Gia soon getting on a ship and coming closer and closer made him break out in more nervous sweat.

Buttoning on a clean shirt, he wondered if she'd had any second thoughts, knowing how pushy both their mothers were. The first real test of his promise to marry from afar was staying dedicated through the baffling torrent of paperwork required by

Italian and Australian churches and governments. But now the wedding had gone ahead, it suddenly felt very real.

'Here he is.' Alfio raised his wine before Pino this time as Taddeo returned to the kitchen, foggy with cooking steam and tobacco smoke. 'And here's to his bride!'

Propped on the table was Taddeo's only photograph of Gia. It had come with one of his mother's letters in which she'd told him Gia's mother had organised to have the portrait taken. They all drank again, Taddeo's eyes staying on Gia's face. The studio photograph showed her smooth skin, hair held back tight in a net, face serious, but he discerned a fervency to her dark eyes.

Pino cuffed his shoulder. 'Take heart, Taddi, all will be well.'

Taddeo forced a smile, thinking of the portrait he'd sent to her. How the Stanthorpe photographer had kindly directed him to pose side-on to veil the birthmark. On impulse, Taddeo had also bought one of the local-area photographs the studio sold. It was of an attractive brick house with portico arches, its garden a mass of roses. Nothing like his actual modest timber farmhouse on stumps. Perhaps anxious about his birthmark or his mother's need to boast of his success, when he'd sent his portrait to Gia he'd also slipped in the photograph of the better house.

Mauve Sea

Gia rolled out the last dough with her nonna's two-foot rolling pin and waited as her mother cut it into thin ribbons of linguine. Rosaria gave a nod – 'Well, that's the end of it' – and turned away, hiding tears, for it was Gia's last day making pasta with them, her last day in Palmi. In the morning, Angelo would take her on the train to Naples and from there she'd board the ship to Australia. Gia glanced over to where Nonna sat, head bent as though nothing was different while she went on mending one of Gia's shirts before it was packed in the luggage, but as she sewed her usually steady hands faltered, giving her away.

For all their sakes, Gia pretended not to see their damp eyes, just as she pretended not to have heard the neighbourhood whispers about her being a proxy bride, and the way it marked her out from those who'd had what they called a 'love marriage'. And as much as Gia wanted to raise her voice, she kept silent, for the sake of her parents and Nonna, and also Salvatore, who in his role as proxy groom had had even less say on her wedding day than she.

'The sea is giving a good breeze,' was all she felt able to respond, and, gathering up the linguine in flour-dusty hands, Gia carried it outside, as she had since she was a young girl.

All along the lanes, just outside doors, racks of pasta hanging to dry captured the salty currents funnelled from the sea up between the stone houses. She hung the last strands on their rack, spacing them evenly, and then stood for a moment feeling the gentle breeze in her hair, her curls damp from the muggy kitchen. Gia's gaze moved beyond the terracotta rooftops to the olive tree forest and mountain, Sant'Elia, to rest, as always, on the sea.

Water and sky melded hazy mauve. Costa Viola, they called it, the violet coast. Its jagged shores nestled between sea and steep slopes. In the distance, across the Strait of Messina, rose the spectre of Mount Etna, the volcano haloed by its faint cloud. The sea between was demure just then but Gia knew their Calabrian coastline had borne violent change where earthquake and tidal wave had gulped chunks of it just two decades before. Her father said old-time sailors barely recognised it.

She scanned the shore for him and Salvatore. Swordfish hunting season was over but she knew they'd be sitting mending the hemp nets they used for other catches like tuna and mackerel. The boats bobbled at shore anchor, distinctive with their forty-foot masts atop which a man would look out for the swordfish and steer, while below, out on a lengthy bow platform, another aimed a harpoon. Angelo held neither position – he was one of several who hauled the impaled swordfish onto the boat, and then its mate, for the fish usually swam in pairs.

'Signorina Giacinta ...'

Gia turned to see a girl from the little school. 'Why aren't you at class?'

'My mother says I must help her from now on.' Her hands too were flour dusty from hanging pasta to dry as she shyly proffered a paper flower. 'I made this like you showed us.'

Gia saw the prized paper had been torn in haste, its folds fragile yet strong. 'Oh, I'll treasure it.' She bent and kissed her cheeks. 'Thank you.'

The girl beamed. 'Goodbye, Signorina Giacinta.'

And in truth, it really was goodbye to that version of herself, Gia realised. She was a signora now, a wife, no longer a signorina. Signora Poletti. It sounded more like Taddeo's mother than her. Gia watched the girl run off to get home before her mother found her gone. She looked back to the paper flower in her hand. Her own mother had taken her out of school at the same age, despite her doing very well in her lessons. But Angelo, uncharacteristically, had spoken up to insist Gia stay in class, perhaps due to his own lamented illiteracy, she suspected. There followed nights of hissed argument, Rosaria anxious about them being out of step with the other parents and the girls Gia's age, and then louder quarrels when Gia later had finished school but pushed to stay on and give some of her time to helping the schoolmistress, with an eye to herself teaching one day.

It seemed all Gia's life her mother had done her utmost to constrain her to the lanes between home, church, the park and school – the same perimeter within which Rosaria and Nonna before her had been kept. Chiefly bound by what others might think. Rosaria rarely even let Gia go to meet the fishing boat, or put her feet in the sea as she longed to. And yet – Gia felt her wedding ring that Rosaria had chosen – soon she'd be able to sail right across the ocean.

Later, in early evening by the light of the kitchen fire, Gia again examined the photograph Taddeo had sent. She realised he'd posed in such a way that it hid his birthmark, but if only his face wasn't turned to the side she would be able to better see his eyes. It was harder to tell what he might be like as a person with him gazing off to the distance – just as his letters were always succinct, stilted, giving little away. As for the photograph of the lovely house with its rose garden, his mother had commandeered it before Gia could properly study it.

Nonna, shredding old bread into crumbs with her hands, saw her looking at Taddeo. 'You know, in Australia he will be your husband, but he will also be your mamma, father, brother, nonna, all of us.' From her apron pocket she pulled a tightly folded bud of paper. 'Here, take this. At your new house, sow them in a pot on a windowsill as spring starts.'

Gia understood it held the *Piccante Calabrese* seeds. Nonna's plaited strings of chilli hung all around the kitchen, even framing the arched window where the sea showed. 'Thank you, I will, Nonna.' She kissed her forehead, smelling the rosemary-scented olive oil that Nonna put in her hair.

'Oh, go on with you.' Eyes watery, Nonna lightly pushed her away, giving a gappy smile. 'And remember to brush away cobwebs with your left hand for good luck. And it is bad luck to sweep your house at night!'

Outside on their narrow balcony that faced the sea, Rosaria looked up from shelling peas as Gia came out to join her. 'You don't have to help me with these any more, Giacinta.'

But Gia wanted to. The simple act of slitting a pod with her thumb and gouging the peas out to fall in satisfying plunks into the bowl was comforting in the face of leaving the next day. Beyond the lavender dusk, lightning flickered on the other side of the strait, the storm some way off. In their mutual quiet, they heard from below children's calls echoing off stone walls in their last games for the day, final bird cheeps and, inside, Salvatore talking to Angelo and Nonna, his voice rocketing into his high laugh. Cooling air carried a hint of salt beneath sharper chimney smoke. Suddenly, Gia wasn't sure if she could bear to leave.

'I won't know anyone in Australia except Taddeo and Serena.'

'They're a good start.' Rosaria eyed her sideways. 'You can't come back, you know.'

Gia bit her lip and nodded. 'The ship's fare costs very much.'

'And think of the dishonour, for us and you, if you returned with the marriage failed.'

❧

The railway line followed the Calabrian coast, which meant the platform at Palmi's station overlooked the sea. Gia kept glancing at the water, seeking its calm as Salvatore, followed by Rosaria, kissed her cheeks. Despite her resolve, the tears came with her mother's embrace.

'Write to us when you get there.' Rosaria couldn't resist trying to smooth Gia's bulk of curls a last time.

'Here, Giacinta.' Nonna pressed a *cornicello* into her hand, the chilli-shaped amulet on a string. 'To keep you safe.' Gia felt Nonna's dry, thin lips swift on her cheeks before she too stood back.

Taddeo's mother stepped forward. 'You should have this back now.'

It was the photograph Taddeo had sent of the brick house with portico arches and a rose garden. From the sharp shadows it appeared a sunny place where she was going. Noticing the picture corners had wilted from it being much shown around, Gia shook her head.

'You keep that, Mrs Poletti. I'll see the real one soon enough.'

The picture was swiftly tucked away. 'You're very lucky Taddeo has such a house waiting for you.'

There was a blast of the train horn and Angelo turned from stowing the trunk on board. 'Come!'

Gia regarded Serena, who she'd be travelling with. She was crying a lot as she hugged her mother, sister and both her nonni in unison. Serena was considered the better catch – she was eighteen and Pino twenty-eight, as Taddeo was. Gia, five years older than her, was well aware of the southern Italian 18/28 custom that eighteen and twenty-eight were deemed the perfect ages for a woman and man to marry so the wife would still be young enough to look after her older husband in later life. *Yet who's supposed to look after the wife if there are no children*, Gia wondered, taking in Serena's more girlish figure as she climbed up into the carriage first.

Before following her, Gia peered up at the stone houses covering the hillside, the yellow-flowering liquorice bushes and the *fico d'india* cacti in fruit with rosy prickly pears. Then Angelo hustled her aboard and climbed in behind along with Serena's father to accompany the girls to Naples' port. Again, the train horn sounded. Handkerchiefs fluttered from those waving on the platform. Feeling the carriages start to move, Gia jumped up and stuck her head out the window to see her mother, Nonna and Salvatore one last time.

'Get back in!' shouted Rosaria in worry, then burst into tears and covered her face.

Gia plonked down as the platform slid from sight. She felt unable to speak. Angelo frowned towards the sea. Serena wept into her own father's shoulder. The morning sun made the sea appear a bluer shade of mauve, fading to aqua nearer the pale pebbly shore. All her life she'd breathed its salted air, sought to see its colour for that day's light – sun-soaked, rain-soaked, ceaselessly undulating before her, and after. Gia squeezed her handkerchief tight.

With a chapped boatman's hand, Angelo covered her pressed fists. 'Think of us, but not so often it makes you too sorrowful.' He sighed. 'But of course, *between the saying and the doing lies the sea.*'

Tears trickled down her cheeks but she wasn't about to raise her handkerchief and make him let go of her hands. 'Perhaps it is wrong for me to go so far away ...'

'No.' Angelo gently withdrew his hand. 'And you will be safe there.'

She looked at him quickly, aware he worried about Europe's fresh unrest. But Gia stayed quiet, for her father never spoke of the great war in which he'd served. A man who loved proverb and verse and who hated seeing the swordfish harpooned, along with its mate. Only hauling them in because it was all he was able to do. Gia regarded the sea again. For an instant, its glittering silence sang, then the train whooshed into a tunnel and all went dim.

Angry Spaghetti

1984 ~ Stanthorpe, Queensland, Australia

That summer, the chillies began ripening early. Rotund, peeking brightest red among leaves, the *Piccante Calabrese* were almost like cherries, heart-shaped but with a devil's kiss. Nonna Gia gathered them into her apron, ignoring the eyes on her back, and bustled inside to her kitchen table, letting them tumble from the folds of cotton. Her petite blade wrought red pools on the board. A rising piquant tang. Seeds set in smiles. Tiny teeth discarded with green-throated stems. And all the while, in the living room Dean Martin crooned from the 1950s stereogram.

A rush of olive oil into the pan. Garlic paling beneath the angry red of the nightshade sisters. Low flame, so as not to burn the sugars in the tomatoes, their sweet resonance stepping back for the heat of the chillies. With the sauce set to simmer, Nonna Gia hauled on a pot of water to boil and threw in handfuls of salt, for it must taste like the sea, always the sea.

14

Apart from those early chillies, that summer began much like the summer before and the one before that, ever since Nonno Taddeo had died and Mum finally got out of the typing pool at the City Council in Brisbane and into an assistant position in the building department. It had been decided that Nonna Gia and I would keep each other company during my school holidays and I still had a chip on my shoulder that no-one had consulted me in the matter. Perhaps it was okay at first – Nonna did spoil me more than Mum did – but at sixteen, thinking of my friends going to movies and to the beach together while I spent my holidays in the country felt like torture.

From Brisbane the highway ribboned inland, south-west past undulant country with grasses flaxen in the heat haze and cattle somnolent, eucalypt stags of lifeless branches on hilltops. I gazed out the car's side window, my Walkman headphones on and the tape up loud. The music like a wall around me as I refused to look across to Mum, even when her annoying crystal dangling from the rear-vision mirror swung light shards into my peripheral vision. Despite it being 1984, Mum still dressed like some seventies hippie in a long skirt, peasant blouse, a headscarf and feathers for earrings. Real feathers. It was embarrassing. My friends' mothers wore more normal things for their age, like trouser suits or dresses belted neatly at the waist.

On the tableland, the air became thinner compared to the humidity on the coast, and nearing Stanthorpe colossal granite boulders began to appear, glinting silver-bronze beneath the high sun. Soon after, we passed orchards, that drooped with ripening summer fruit, and then the first little houses on the outskirts of town. I was glad I had at least had Kentucky Fried for tea the night before. There wasn't even a McDonald's in town, just the bakery and some old milk bar with hamburgers.

'Come on, Sofie. Enough silence. We're almost there.'

I still didn't look over, even though I knew I was pushing it.

Mum drove into town past the post office clocktower and the hotel with sprawling verandahs before turning down the side street my grandparents had moved to after they retired and Frank, the only son, took over the farm with Connie and my cousins. Despite being the eldest, I don't think Mum had ever intended coming back to it. After she'd left and had me in Brisbane on her own, it'd always been just the two of us.

'Take those things off your ears now.' Mum jerked the car to a halt outside Nonna Gia's house. 'I know you can hear me.'

And as she got out, I did as I was told but sat unmoving, looking out to Nonna's neat lowset brick house with portico arches. Past the fence, the front lawn lay bare except for two chilli bushes and, by the front steps, a huge rosemary shrub, its mauve flowers attracting bees. *Where the rosemary thrives, the woman rules the home,* or so the Italian saying went.

Nonna Gia appeared beneath the portico wiping her hands on the apron tight across her tummy, dark eyes darting from Mum getting bags out of the boot to me still in the car.

'You hungry?' came her usual greeting, and I sighed and opened the door.

Mum slammed the boot. 'We called in halfway at the Aratula bakery.'

'Come on, I've got the pasta water on.'

The noon sun had bite. I noticed an old man sitting in the verandah shade of the house across the road. He seemed to be watching me but didn't wave nor look away as I looked back. Rolling my eyes, I dragged my other bag from the backseat and went inside.

◡

The plastic over the hallway carpet had been removed sometime after Nonno Taddeo died but Nonna Gia insisted everyone go barefoot on her cream shag pile. She did so with toenails that at sixty-eight she still painted bright red, the same colour as the chilli-shaped *cornicello* amulet she'd worn around her neck since leaving Italy forty-five years ago. 'My nonna gave me this the day I left Palmi to protect me and I've worn it every day since,' she'd told me time and time again. 'And when I'm dead, it will be yours.' I gave it about as much thought as all the times she'd told me thirteen was a lucky number in Italy, except to never set a table for thirteen, like the Last Supper, as that was unlucky. There was always some loophole.

I saw Nonna's eyes go to the feathers dangling from Mum's ears but she only said, 'I'll boil the pasta,' and went to the kitchen, and in a funny way I liked that about Nonna, especially as I seemed to seesaw between saying nothing and too much, never getting it right.

Mum put my bags in the front room across the hall from the main bedroom and hissed to me, 'Just drop the attitude.'

'As if I can't be at home alone while you work. Or go out during the day. It's not fair.' I slumped onto the end of the bed. 'All my friends get to see each other in the holidays.'

'I told you, next year, when you're in senior. We can tell Nonna you have to study.' She regarded me. 'Please bend a bit. This is probably the last summer you'll spend with her.'

'Elena!'

'Coming, Ma.' Mum turned back to me. 'It's only a few weeks until I'll be down for Christmas anyway.'

I gave her a hard look. As if that made being separated from all my friends feel better. She'd driven me down on her rare rostered Friday off but I'd noticed she had decided not to stay on for the weekend, instead heading back later that day.

Mum hurried out to the kitchen, leaving a linger of patchouli that was swiftly outdone by Nonna's strident 'meadow'-perfumed carpet deodoriser. Everything was spotless – the cream bedroom furniture, the apricot bedspread that matched the curtains made from a heavy Italian fabric. Also covering the windows were sheer curtains as well as venetian blinds, for Nonna Gia hated draughts, or people seeing in. On a wall hung the painting of a beach in Italy, its pebbly shore, mauve sea and mountains behind as foreign to the surrounding country Australian landscape as to the Queensland beaches that I knew. I hauled myself up.

Along the hallway, a spicy aroma of *arrabbiata* sauce pummelled my nostrils. Of course Nonna was cooking her angry spaghetti. As well as her fresh chillies, she also had lots of dried chillies from each year's garden harvest that she plaited onto string. It hung by the back door, not just to eat but to prevent the *malocchio* – evil eye – from entering. (And according to Nonna the chillies also deflected that evil back onto whoever was bringing it.) Zucchero, her black cat, stretched out on the lino and I immediately bent to pat him. Well, he was almost black but for a patch of white on his chest. That was one good thing about staying at Nonna Gia's, having a pet in the house. Mum and I were never allowed one in our flat.

'Sofie, wash your hands,' Mum said almost at once, plunking down ceramic bowls.

I glowered but did so. The tablecloth dulled the noise of each bowl landing. Nonna must have sensed the taut air between us but to her credit said nothing and served the spaghetti. I didn't want to hurt Nonna or bring her into it, I really didn't, but it felt like an impossible situation I was in – too old to be a child, too young to be an adult, not told things. All I could do was push back against what I felt I could. Even when I heard my own wrongness. I couldn't stand myself sometimes.

'It's too hot.' I sat back.

'Blow on it.' Nonna's order overlapped with Mum saying, 'Open another window.'

'I meant the chilli.' I rolled my eyes at them both and folded my arms.

'*Mangia.*' Nonna wound her fork. 'It's good for you. More vitamin C than oranges.'

I tore at a piece of bread instead, crumbs falling on the tablecloth, and avoided Mum's stare. But it was about much more than spaghetti or not being with my friends for the summer holidays. It was what wasn't ever spoken about. The thread sticking out from a hem and nothing to cut it with. Inviting and niggling until I didn't know whether to leave it or yank it, uncertain if it would come away cleanly or unravel all the stitches. It was about my father.

Nonna Gia got up. 'I cook you some plain pasta with cheese then.'

'Ma, she can have what she's been given.' Mum fired me a look.

'I won't have her not eating. She might get sick.'

Sighing, Mum took another mouthful. I remained silent but I did feel uneasy inside.

I kept up that defiance until Mum left to drive back to Brisbane, standing limp in her embrace as an earring feather brushed my cheek. Yet watching her small car turn the corner out of sight at the end of the street, I immediately felt a pang and regretted how I'd been.

'Sofia …' Nonna was already heading inside. '*Perfect Match* is starting on the TV.'

I glanced at the house across the road. The chair where the man had sat on the verandah was empty but the two front windows with drawn, dark blinds felt like eyes on us.

In Nonna Gia's living room, the long, low timber stereogram from the 1950s took up almost one wall, and an Italian coffee table with ornate lion feet crouched in front of the lounge suite. In shorts, I shifted on the plastic covering the lounge, feeling sweat forming beneath the bare skin of my thighs despite the cooler Stanthorpe evening on the tableland. Nonna kept the television up loud though she had good ears. A doily on top of the wooden set on legs hung slightly over the screen so the show host appeared to wear it on his head.

'Here.' She handed me a cup of coffee. 'I put in a bit of Tia Maria to help you sleep later.' And then she reached into her dress pocket and dropped in my lap a few chocolates from the tin she kept hidden in different spots, that I'd then secretly search for.

'Thanks, Nonna. I didn't mean to be a pain.' It was easier to say so to her than Mum.

'*Boh.*' She shrugged and kept her eyes on the TV screen.

We sat in the wan glow of the television and a slant of the fluorescent light from the kitchen. I wasn't sure if she truly believed Tia Maria in coffee would help me sleep later but I liked that she considered me old enough to have it. I sipped its bitter sweetness and, bored by the show, gazed at the two framed photographs on the doily atop the television.

Nonna and Nonno's only wedding pictures had sat there as long as I recalled, so long I'd ceased to really see them. Over on the good cabinet amid crystalware and bonbonniere stood framed photos of Elena and Frank as children; Frank in a ruffled blue tuxedo beside Connie in pure white; me; my cousins, Lena and Sam. Yet my grandparents' wedding pictures sat alone.

In one, Nonna Gia stood surrounded by her family outside a church that I knew was in Calabria. The other was a studio portrait of her and Nonno Taddeo, the black-and-white shot retouched in pastels, as photographers did in the late thirties. Nonno Taddeo had been one to speak little and Nonna Gia a lot, though I'd also seen her bite her tongue. Or perhaps I picked up on it more because I too was biting mine, knowing the silence I got if I even hinted at beginning to ask all the questions that I wanted to about my father.

'How old were you when you and Nonno got married, Nonna?'

'What?' Behind her glasses that reflected the TV, Nonna's eyes went to the photos and back to the screen. 'Old. Twenty-three. Don't you wait that long. Now shush.'

I slowly unwrapped another chocolate. Frank and Connie had had a big 1970s Italian wedding with four hundred guests where I ran riot with other children, but I'd long sensed a reluctance to talk about family weddings. Or any weddings really, especially when Nonno Taddeo was alive, considering he got up and went outside at any hint of Mum never marrying.

Looking again to the studio portrait, I regarded Nonna Gia's direct gaze and beautiful skin, cheeks plumped in a smile, while Nonno Taddeo solemnly peered slightly away as he usually did, both in shyness and to try to hide the birthmark on one side of his face. My eyes returned to the church photo. Something nagged at me but I wasn't sure what.

'Nonna, on your wedding day—'

'*Santa Maria*, talk, talk, why talk of that all of a sudden? Let me watch the TV.'

～

Nonna tucked me into bed and I let her, even though Mum hadn't for a decade at least. But there was something nice in the care Nonna Gia took as she moved along the sides, her flat palm pushing the sheet between the mattress and bed slats until it hugged me close, and I didn't have to pretend I was too old to need such comfort any more.

'Goodnight, *cara*.' She bent to kiss my forehead and the chilli amulet around her neck swung and nearly hit me in the eye.

'Night, Nonna.'

She pulled shut the curtains on the front window, blocking out the house on the opposite side of the road, but didn't close those over the side window.

Tucked in tight, I lay wedged on my back. The strip of light under my door vanished as she shut her bedroom door opposite. It was so quiet I could hear the clock ticking out in the kitchen. From a distance came the thunder of a semi-trailer that barely slowed as it roared through the main street at the end of ours. Then the cranky squawking of a nightjar overhead.

I pulled out some tucked sheet so I could roll onto my side. For a while I lay like that, unable to sleep. The clock ticked. Another truck rumbled through. I got up. Earlier, when Nonna was in the shower, I'd found the Quality Street tin she'd hidden in her sewing and taken a small handful of chocolates that I hid in my bedroom. I stared out the side window, past the open blind, as a strawberry centre flooded my mouth.

'Sofia?' The light clicked on and I squinted at Nonna Gia.

I should have known she'd have some sixth sense and notice I was up. Or likely she'd lain awake too, being my first night back, and had listened for any movement, quiet as I'd been.

Seeing the chocolate, she sighed. 'Oh, Sofia, don't let yourself be a cupboard eater.'

'What do you mean?' I said hotly.

'Eating hiding away like that.' Nonna scrunched the wrappers. 'If you're hungry, tell me and I'll make you something.'

She watched me get back into bed and didn't tuck me in this time. I felt I'd let her down but I didn't say a word as she left. I lay in the dark again. A dull chocolate fug hung in my mouth. When I was small, Nonna would hug me and say, *it'll all be right in the sunshine tomorrow, passerotta*, little sparrow. And, impatient as I was to be older, just then I wished to be a child.

❧

I awoke to 'Volare' blaring out in the living room. Sunlight poured through the sheer curtains and open venetian on the side window. *'Volare'. At this hour. Seriously.* Rolling over, I saw the bedroom door was ajar, as though Nonna had peeked in. Clatter emanated from out in the kitchen. From my doorway, Zucchero eyed the bed. I beckoned but he didn't move, perhaps knowing he faced Nonna's wrath if he got on furniture. Still in my pyjamas and slippers, I scuffed out past the stereogram with its lid up, record turning, Dean Martin singing of flying up to the clouds.

Fully dressed, Nonna Gia stood at the stove. 'You hungry?'

I sat down giving a shrug and reached for the coffee pot. 'I'll just have toast, thanks.'

'You can eat it with eggs.' She tore holes in bread slices and put them into the hot pan before she cracked eggs to fry in their empty middles. Glancing behind her, she added a pinch of something to the yolks, just a touch, and flipped the frying eggs and bread to serve.

I patted Zucchero who'd trailed in. 'I don't want to get fat.' But I was hungry.

'You don't want to look ill.' With satisfaction, she watched me tuck into the eggs and fried bread. 'And why do you straighten your hair? It looks better natural. You got your curls from your nonna. Elena got Taddeo's straight hair.'

'What about my father? He might've had curly hair.' I met her eye.

She got up and turned off the stereogram and began clearing the table. 'I need some things at the shops. Come up for the walk and tell me if there's anything you'd like.'

For a moment I didn't answer, but then it felt easier to acquiesce. 'Okay, Nonna.'

The old man across the road was back sitting on his front verandah. He watched us come out Nonna's gate and seemed to lean forward slightly as though to get a better look at us but didn't wave. And I noticed Nonna didn't call out hello to him as she did when passing another neighbour who stood watering their cannas. We came around the corner into the heart of Stanthorpe's main street. It was busy, being a Saturday morning, since the shops all shut at midday, and there were plenty of cars angle-parked and people about on footpaths avoiding the hot sun beneath shop awnings.

'Gia, *come sta*? And Sofie's here!' Josie, one of Nonna's friends, approached us with a shopping basket over her arm. She kissed Nonna's cheeks three times, pinched my face and abandoned English to speak loudly in rapid Italian dialect that I didn't understand much of.

Passers-by looked our way. I shifted my feet and then the bag strap across my chest.

'Nonna, can I meet you back home? Mum lets me go to town on my own in Brisbane during the day now.'

Distracted, she appeared uncertain but agreed and I hastened off, hearing my name amid Josie's Italian fading behind me. Out of their sight, I bought some Fruit Tingles from the newsagent and, tucking the lollies in my bag, crossed the road near the corner hotel. The liver-coloured brick building with 1915 on the facade, a second-storey, timber verandah and wide windows below wafted cool, beery air and horseracing belting from a radio. In its backyard, chickens pecked and chittered behind wire. I kept on past, uphill, away from the shops and people.

The small, deserted train station sat quiet. Its weatherboards were painted cream and well-kept, though I knew it'd closed more than a decade before. As usual the platform stretched empty. I sat on a bench and put on my Walkman, winding the mixed tape to 'All Through the Night', Cyndi Lauper, and the line in the chorus I related to. For I felt unsettled and like I had no past, not a proper one anyway until I knew more of those parts being kept from me. I turned it up, wishing a train might take me somewhere, anywhere. Wispy grass grew on the tracks. I turned to gaze at the town spread out below. Stanthorpe's roofs gleamed silver or were dull russet, their peaks jutting in between mainly European-looking trees. The pub's old brick chimneys and the clocktower of the post office stood proud over them all.

When I was little, it had seemed natural not to even question the situation I'd always known. Mum told me my father had died in an accident before I'd been born and it hurt her to speak of him. Nonna Gia and Nonno Taddeo, shamed by Mum having a baby unwed, wouldn't speak of him. Yet the older I got, the louder the silence felt. Some days it was like a hollowness within that nothing was able to fill, and on others a rising, almost primal need to know more.

After a time, I wiped my cheeks and crammed two Fruit Tingles in my mouth. Sugar and sherbet prickled and took over in reassuring sweetness. A dry, hot breeze shifted my hair that was longer with the curls straightened. I turned my Walkman up louder.

When I came in the back door, Nonna was making pasta dough, the kitchen table blanketed in flour. 'Good, you're home. You hungry? Come and make the pasta. Kneading shapes the chest. If you can make pasta and have a nice chest, you'll find a good husband.'

I went and flopped on the lounge. 'My husband might cook while I'm at work.'

'Oh, yes, of course he will.' Her gold hoop earrings swung as she rolled the dough.

Pushing my bag aside, I got up to put on the television and, as I bent, I suddenly saw in the wedding photos what had niggled the night before. 'Nonna, that chilli amulet you wear, you said your nonna gave you it the day you left Palmi and you've worn it every day since?'

'*Il cornicello*? Every single day since the day I left. It protects from the evil eye and ...'

'Then how come you've got it on in the wedding photo with Nonno but not in the one taken outside the church?'

From the kitchen, the rhythmic trundle of the rolling pin halted.

I carried in the studio portrait. 'See?'

Nonna Gia stared. First at it. Then at me. 'Well, that's just ...' She seemed to wrestle between two answers and then, somewhat resigned, sat down. 'Do you know, in all these years you're the first to notice that? Your Nonno Taddeo worried someone would eventually. Always worrying what people might think. But most often, people usually see what they want to see, or think they want to.'

'What?' Without thinking, I stood the frame in the flour, but she didn't get upset as she usually might have. 'I don't know what you mean.'

'Most don't talk of it. Of being a proxy bride, having a marriage arranged like that.'

'Proxy? A what?'

'Me in Italy on the wedding day, my groom in Australia. Do you know it was my brother, Salvatore, who exchanged vows with me? He stood in for Taddeo. I didn't really know Taddeo until after I got to Australia as his wife.'

'What?' My mind started to fill with all sorts of scenes. 'You and Nonno didn't even know each other? But ... why would you do that?'

'To be true, I didn't mind if I never married.' Her voice was soft. 'I helped the schoolteacher at the little school and wished to be a teacher myself. But my mother worried others saw more shame in me being a spinster than being a proxy bride.'

'Oh, Nonna ...' I frowned sadly and sat down with her. 'That's so unfair.' I'd never heard her speak of having wanted to be a teacher and I realised it hadn't really occurred to me that she may have hoped to be anything other than a housewife. Actually, I hadn't thought much about her life when she was younger at all. 'But how then? I don't understand.' I truly felt for her and without thinking put my hand on her arm, something I didn't usually do.

Nonna kept looking at me. Her lips twitched. 'Okay, I will tell you about what happened ...'

My eyes held hers, the past being so seldom spoken of in our family.

She nodded, almost more to herself, and stood up. 'Let me finish making this pasta and then I tell you first about the wedding day. And about Palmi. When it was time for me to leave.'

I stayed in the chair not wanting to move or seem uninterested, or too eager, or anything that might make her suddenly reconsider.

'But, Sofia, you need to see that what is true and what is thought to be true can run side by side, not meeting, staying just ahead of the creeping shadow.' She smiled sadly at my puzzled look. 'The shadow ... of *vergogna*, shame.' Nonna shook her head. 'But sometimes the silence can be pitiless, I know.'

And that I did understand.

Tutto nel Dente

The next morning, Sunday, meant having to go to Mass with Nonna. Dallying in getting ready, I wiped steam from the bathroom mirror and opened the cabinet for a cotton bud. As usual, Nonna Gia's Oil of Ulan sat on the shelf beside her Felce Azzurra talcum powder in its blue plastic bottle. Then it struck me to see Nonno Taddeo's shaving brush and half-used bottle of Pino Silvestre still there alongside, two years on, for Nonna was fastidious in keeping house.

I thought of what she'd told me so far about her and Nonno marrying by proxy. Of standing at the church door and looking down the aisle to her brother, Salvatore, at the altar. Nonno sending her a photo of a house that wasn't his. Leaving her nonna, parents and friends to be with a man she didn't know. It felt all wrong. Yet seeing her and Nonno's things remaining side by side was somewhat reassuring. There must have come to be some love between them.

With care, I opened the glass pinecone-shaped Silvestre bottle, aware how terrible it would be if I shattered it by accident. The spicy forest aftershave scent prickled my nostrils. I thought of Nonno at the kitchen table immersed in his newspapers, *The Stanthorpe*

Border Post, Il Globo, La Fiamma, The Courier Mail. His birthmark and thinning hair. How he was quiet, reserved, seeming content in retirement to be in the backyard vegetable patch most days. I'd come to think him very hard about Mum being unmarried and never allowing any mention of my father. But Nonno was gone. And Nonna had begun talking about the past.

La lingua batte dove il dente duole, she often said. *The tongue always goes to the sore tooth.* Sometimes it drove me mad, these sayings she had about different things, especially as she somehow got many to stick in my head without me even realising it. But that saying about the sore tooth couldn't have expressed any better the way my mind kept going back to what niggled. Perhaps Nonna knew that feeling too. I'd not thought much before of how hard it must've been to leave her family knowing she'd never be able to return to see them again.

I headed into my room, and from beyond her half-closed bedroom door across the hall Nonna, back to her no-nonsense manner, called out, 'Wear your pink dress I bought you!'

'It'll be too hot in church.'

'When God wants you to grow in life, he makes you uncomfortable.'

Did she really believe that? I heard short, sharp wheezes and knew she was lacing on the contraption that seemed to me a cross between a corset and a girdle. She wore it under her 'good' going-out dresses and it held her in like a tight salami from under her boobs to the tops of her thighs. It did the job, but in truth I preferred Nonna in her flowery house dresses with her plumpness relaxed, for I knew its squishy comfort from when I was little and buried my head into her tummy for a cuddle. Nonno had been standoffish about affection and didn't encourage it but Nonna fussed over all three of her grandkids.

'Hurry up, Sofia! Mass starts at ten.'

I came out into the hallway. The pink, long-sleeved dress with ruffle skirt was thankfully at least knee-length, considering the hot morning, although the synthetic itched. And to further please Nonna I hadn't straightened my curls, glad none of my friends could see me like this.

Nonna Gia emerged too, holding her purse. '*Santa Maria!*'

'What?' My hands went to my hair.

'You can't wear that!'

'You told me to!'

'No, that, *that!*' She pointed to the rosary beads I'd put around my neck along with several strings of plastic pearls. 'I gave those to you for your Holy Communion!'

'Madonna wears them.'

'You can't wear a rosary to church!' She gave my arm a twisting pinch.

'*Ow!* All right. *God.*'

'Don't say *God* like that, for God sake.' Her hand went to her forehead. 'And only one lot of pearls is nice. *One.*' Out front, the taxi beeped. 'And hurry, Sofia!'

In church, Nonna almost always situated herself for Mass in the same spot, about midway down the pews. A little closer to the back than the front, if I thought about it. Looking at the altar, I couldn't help picturing again her having to stand and marry her brother, sort of, when Nonno Taddeo was in Australia. How she didn't really even know Nonno then. It seemed a ridiculous decision, yet I wasn't sure I would've been brave enough to do it. I snuck a look at Nonna, her head held high, focused on the priest, looking her best for Mass.

I don't know if she supposed Mum and I went to church in Brisbane but we never did, and I didn't have the heart to tell Nonna that most Sunday mornings I usually watched music videos on TV while Mum lay in bed with a coffee and the crossword. Perhaps

Nonna never asked so she could assume we went, or maybe she was only concerned that we attended in front of people in Stanthorpe, especially for Easter and Christmas, which we did.

During the priest's sermon, I didn't listen much. In church I often played a game to myself, looking among the pews and wondering if any of the people were related to my father. The Australians, that is. I'd managed to glean some details about him. In the rare times Mum spoke of him when I asked, she called him Arro, a funny sort of name that I'd accepted as a kid. And I knew he was from Stanthorpe and was Australian, not Italian. Which possibly explained why my grandparents were funny about him, since Mum told me that in the sixties when I was born, cross-cultural marriages still weren't very accepted by either the Italians or the Australians.

My gaze darted among the pews. I fantasised that my father had a brother who looked like him so I could see a man who was almost him. I hadn't seen a photo of Arro as Mum didn't have any, she said, and I'd never found one all the times I'd gone through cupboards and boxes at home. Yet I still tried to recognise someone related to him. I guess I thought I'd somehow just *know*, naive and romantic as that was. When you hope like that, you start to think in all sorts of ways you otherwise wouldn't. I swivelled to see if maybe someone among the pews had a ski-jump nose tip like mine. No other Poletti had it, only me. But as I twisted back, I felt a covert jab from Nonna in my side and the game was up.

I didn't persist, for I knew my little game never ended well. The more I looked to no avail the more resentment crept in that I had to be like a detective at all. And then I would begin to think how much I hated Mum's stupid hippie clothes and the way she almost wore them in defiance, and Nonna Gia wearing that stupid corset-girdle thing, always about how people might be looking at them, at us. *The tongue kept going to the sore tooth.*

After Mass, and a seemingly interminable stint standing outside the church in the sun afterwards while Nonna Gia chatted to various people, finally her friends Josie and Alfio dropped us back home. As they drove off, horn beeping a few too many times, I noticed the old man was again sitting out on his verandah faced towards us, staring. I stared back.

'What is it with him?'

Nonna squinted. 'What? Sofia, don't, it's rude to stare.'

'Tell him that.'

'You want to eat? I make tin tuna and tomatoes with bread.'

We went in and I glanced back to see the man still watching.

'Make sure you take off your good dress and put on some house clothes.'

Nonna went straight to her room, no doubt to take off the corset-girdle that I was sure made her a bit cranky after a while.

By the afternoon, I needed some time to myself, and in shorts and singlet went out to the floral banana lounge on the back patio. Zucchero was already there and let me pat his tummy and the white spot on his chest. Nonna Gia once told me most black cats had that patch of white fur bred into them over the centuries to save them from superstitious people who'd kill them because they associated them with evil and witches.

'*Stupido.*' She'd shaken her head. 'The woman down the street from us in Palmi everyone called *la strega*, the witch, and she was a healer and very good. She pulled out Salvatore's rotten tooth when he was young and also got rid of a big boil on my father's bum. A good woman.' I must've had a certain look on my face, for she'd said, 'What? He couldn't sit down! We had no doctor or dentist nearby and couldn't have afforded one if we did!'

I put on my white sunglasses and the Walkman, moved
Zucchero off the banana lounge and dug out the last couple of
Fruit Tingles from the end of the roll that I'd hidden in my pocket.
After church that morning, I needed them. Just as I lay down,
I heard the laundry trolley screech along the cement path to the
Hills Hoist and Nonna Gia began getting the washing off the line.

I gave a sigh and clicked off the Walkman. 'Do you want some
help, Nonna?'

'What? You think I can't get in my own washing?'

It was easier to stay put when she was like that. Especially
knowing she'd dismiss any further offers in the way she indulged
all her grandchildren, even if I did feel a bit guilty. I switched the
tape back on, watching her. It was still a revelation to discover
she'd helped out at the little school in Palmi and had wanted to
be a teacher. It made me look at her a little differently, the proxy
matter aside, like I'd underestimated her in some way. And yet,
Nonna had worked hard as a mother and housewife, and on the
farm too, and there was a nobleness to that, especially if it was her
choice. It was just that ... it hadn't been.

My feet were well short of the end of the banana lounge and
I noticed my toenails, painted frosted pink and a little stubby,
were no match to Nonna's in elegant red. Even in her house dress
she looked well-dressed; the way she tied a faded scarf over her
head, stylish.

'G'day, Mrs Poletti.' A young bloke, perhaps a year or two
older than me, came striding up the driveway around the side of
the house.

I flinched in surprise and swiftly crossed my legs at the ankle,
squeezing them together to appear slimmer, especially along my
thighs that had always been a bit stocky. Furtively, I clicked off
the tape but left on the headphones to mask I was listening in.

He glanced at me and back to Nonna Gia. 'You right for me to mow shortly?'

'Thank you, I'll just get this lot in.' Nonna kept unpegging but when she saw me take off my headphones she hesitated and offhandedly introduced me to Tim Dinning as if she'd have preferred not to. 'Sofia is here on her *school* holidays,' she emphasised, no doubt to stress I was younger than him and therefore to keep a distance, which of course gave me the shits.

'Oh, right then.' Tim turned from Nonna unpegging her petticoat from the line to me pushing my sunglasses up onto my head. He grinned and I felt my insides flicker.

'Next year is my *last* though,' I countered.

He was wearing a Rip Curl cap, however even in the shade beneath its rim I could see the rich blueness of his eyes and a scatter of freckles across his face as he came closer. I'd always longed for freckles, pretty ones across my nose, but with my olive skin I had none.

'I'm doing your nan's lawn when I mow my granddad's place across the road.'

'That's your grandfather?' I didn't mention he often sat staring at us.

'Mum and Dad run the pub.' Tim glanced at my bare tanned legs still clasped closed.

The laundry trolley screeched loudly.

He looked back up. 'You might want to move that chair back when I mow, princess.'

At once I felt embarrassed for not helping Nonna but gave him a sharp look as I swung my legs over the side. Slowly and deliberately, I wound the headphones' cord around my Walkman before I stood up. He held my gaze, just a fraction too long, and I knew. He felt it too. Straightaway, that something between us.

He gave a short laugh and was about to say more but Nonna, watching on, halted with the laundry at the back door. 'Sofia! *Vieni qua!*' And I had to follow her inside.

Dean Martin again played on the stereogram – 'Come Back to Sorrento', crooned mostly in Italian. I could hear Nonna out in the kitchen singing along to the part about the beauty of the sea. Beyond the lace curtains, twilight's blush deepened, turning the sky mauve. While I was in the shower, Nonna must've given the coffee table a spray and polish with Mr Sheen. Its scent competed with the meadow-fragranced carpet. On top sat the latest *Women's Weekly* with the TV guide fanned beneath, both set at a certain angle to the cut-glass sweets dish, which was empty. And I was still to find the latest spot she'd hidden the chocolate tin.

Looking at the items placed just so on the coffee table I felt a sudden rush of affection for Nonna and wondered how we were ever going to be without her one day. I didn't mean to be morbid, but this had crossed my mind at times since Nonno Taddeo died at seventy-one. To me, her presence was so big it seemed able to stretch out and fill the void left without him, yet I couldn't imagine anything that would fill hers. And I feared that feeling, because all my life I'd known how it was to have that empty space. Once someone was gone, that was it.

Nonna had her apron back on and was slicing eggplant at the kitchen table. She looked up as I came in, her eyes going straight to my washed hair. 'Dry that or you might as well be asking for pneumonia.'

'But it's summer.' I sat down.

She pursed her lips and went on slicing. Dean Martin reached fever pitch and I found myself wondering when *Perfect Match* started. Zucchero lay elongated on the lino near the cool of the screen door and out in the backyard crickets kept up a steady resonance. I wanted to ask Nonna about Tim Dinning but I feared my face would give me away. She had a way of seeing the slightest hint of a blush or brighter eyes. And it hadn't yet occurred to me that one who looks for such things has usually learnt about hiding them.

Grateful for Nonna's heavy-handed curtaining for once, I'd watched Tim from inside, keenly observing his arm muscles as he'd pushed the mower back and forth. I liked that they were well-defined but not too big, as if they came from doing work or push-ups rather than lifting weights in front of a mirror. For the time being though, I couldn't let Nonna glean the slightest inkling of my thoughts considering she hadn't been too pleased about us just talking.

I casually gave Zucchero a rub. 'Are we having *melanzane fritte* for dinner?'

'We are.'

'Are you crumbing them?'

'If you help. It'll take longer otherwise.' She handed me the knife. 'Cut each slice about so thick, I'll get the crumbs ready.'

'Mum sometimes salts the eggplant slices.'

'No need. These don't have seeds in them so they won't be bitter.'

Over at the bench, she poured breadcrumbs in a bowl and, putting her back to me, added something to them from a little jar and mixed it in. I finished the eggplant and patted Zucchero again, pretending not to look at the array of jars that she'd chosen from. Nothing was labelled but I could guess which were salt,

aniseed, her dried chillies she ground to powder with her mortar
and pestle, saffron, white peppercorns she'd also ground herself,
cinnamon and fennel seeds.

I almost asked what she'd added, however I decided instead
to see if she might talk about the past again. Perhaps something
about my father might slip. *Tutto nel dente*. Again, it was all in that
tooth. But also, I kind of liked hearing about Nonna when she
was young.

'Did your nonna teach you to make crumbed *melanzane fritte*?'

'Crumbed! What luxury.' She returned to the table. 'My
nonna had to tear with her poor hands old bread into crumbs just
for the pasta.'

'The pasta?'

'To sprinkle fried on top. We never had cheese.'

She cracked an egg into a bowl and mixed it with a fork ready
to dip in the eggplant slices for crumbing. Making a fist, she
smashed the eggshell on the table. I looked at her.

'What?' She shrugged. 'If we throw out eggshells in halves
we'll be inviting in evil.'

I thought again of her calling superstitious people who killed
black cats because they linked them to evil and witches *stupido*.
How she'd defended the woman in her street in Italy who they
called a *strega*, witch, the healer who'd got rid of the boil on her
father's bum. Always that ambiguity, that fluctuation. *What's true
and thought to be true run side by side*. My eyes went to the *cornicello*
amulet hanging around her neck.

'I liked finding out you wanted to be a teacher, Nonna. It's not
fair you couldn't be.'

She looked at me quickly, twice, that old guard up, perhaps not
expecting me to be serious. In a way I'd surprised myself a bit.
I loved Nonna and she was like a second mum to me, however

we'd hardly spoken this way before, about the past, just between us. But then, in the last couple of years since Nonno Taddeo had died, we'd come to spend a lot of time together, just Nonna and me on our own, with me being there for my school holidays.

'I liked hearing about Palmi too,' I went on. 'What was it like coming to Australia?'

She dunked a slice of eggplant in the egg mixture then the crumbs. 'You like hearing about Palmi and that is nice, Sofia, but you might not like to hear all that happened.'

'Of course I would.' My cheeks coloured a little. 'I'm not a kid any more.'

She paused to look at me for longer. 'No, you are not.' With the back of her eggy palm, she brushed the side of my face and I felt a breadcrumb stick to my skin.

'It shouldn't be bad to talk about the past.' I brushed away the crumb. Nonna had to know I was talking about my father too, for she seemed to be contemplating what I said.

Again she plunged an eggplant slice into the mixture. 'Well, it is woman talk, Sofia, and it must stay between us for now.'

'Of course.' Her including me as a woman made me sit up a little straighter.

She picked up another piece of eggplant as she began to tell me more. With rising fervour, Dean Martin sang on.

The Bride Ship

'Gia, stop eating so much.' Serena leant in close so the other proxy brides at their dining table onboard the *Viminale* wouldn't hear, although a couple gave them amused glances.

With a slight toss of her hair, Gia kept chewing. How could Serena be such a killjoy when they'd never before had roast beef, or spaghetti in cream, let alone chocolate cake. In Palmi their food at home was so humble it was a treat to have meat at all, and usually that was sausage pork. The ship even offered *new* bread *daily*. At home her mother made them soak the hard week-old bread in water to eat it – nothing could be wasted. And poor Nonna with more gum than teeth.

Gia guessed there must've been hundreds of proxy brides aboard, all Italian, and by the look of their clothes most came from poorer families and towns like her own. Surely she wasn't the only one who thought the ship having refrigeration was an unexpected marvel. Fresh butter, meat, eggs and vegetables for all, and it kept coming, every day of the voyage. And while the third-class dining room ceiling was low, Gia decided the snowy tablecloths made it like the fine restaurants she'd glimpsed as they'd walked past on the way to the port in Naples. The kind her family could never have afforded to eat at.

Vilma, another joining a husband in Stanthorpe, cast a pointed look at the straining buttons of Gia's blouse. 'I guess it must all fit somewhere.'

'And a big mouth fits nowhere.' Gia heard her voice come out sharper than intended, causing others to look over. Flushing, she added in a hiss to Serena, 'Just because I haven't been seasick like you ...' But her skirt pressed tight at the waist, even with a button undone.

The ship photographer came over then. 'How about you all huddle in for a picture?'

⌣

In late morning sun, Gia and the other proxy brides gathered on deck after their daily English lesson. A slight breeze caused by the ship's movement quelled the heat and kept the funnel fumes streaming just above them, but the acrid scent still drifted down. There wasn't a lot to do but stroll, play quoits, sew or talk. As she got talking Gia discovered that, like her, none of them travelled as assisted migrants – their husbands had saved up to pay for the voyage just as Taddeo had. 'And I had to wait eleven months since my wedding day while he saved for the fare,' one bride told her.

'Did any of you know your husbands in childhood at all?' Gia asked, and only a few did but mumbled they were like strangers now, while most hadn't known their husbands at all.

'Gia ...' Serena murmured, beckoning her over to the railing so she'd stop.

Gia gave a faint frown but went to join her. She leant on the railing, watching foamy riffles trail in the *Viminale*'s wake. She never tired of being on the water, even as the glinting of all that restlessness beneath began to hurt her eyes.

'Are you thinking about meeting Taddeo?'

Gia glanced at Serena. 'Are you thinking of Pino?'

She almost blushed. 'I suppose his house mightn't be as good as Taddeo's since he didn't send a picture of it, but he works hard and sounds like a good man in his letters.'

Gia's hands tightened on the rail. 'I'll miss the sea.'

That Stanthorpe wasn't near the sea was one of the few things Taddeo had put in his letters, and just then it was all she could think to say to Serena. In that ever-widening distance between her and her family as the ship drew nearer to Australia and Taddeo, it was easier to ask others questions. She snuck another look at Serena. Gia hadn't known her well before they'd left and while her quiet dutifulness grated, since sharing a cabin she had realised she did like her. And coveted her straight, long hair. In the salty humidity, her own curls puffed out even more.

They heard some fuss among several women nearby and saw Vilma again showing the photograph of her husband, Carmelo. 'He looks like a film star, no?'

Hearing Gia sigh, Serena acknowledged, 'He is rather good looking.'

Vilma smiled. 'Where's your photograph, Gia? Or is he an old man or something?'

Gia remained mulish by the rail, not about to show Taddeo's picture with his head so deliberately turned. Although just then she wished she'd kept the picture of the fancy house.

'I'm going for a walk,' she told Serena, still eyeing Vilma.

Serena pursed her lips, knowing where she was really going. 'You shouldn't talk to sailors.'

'They're teaching me more English. Those lessons aren't enough.' Perhaps it was her extra schooling but Gia found learning English easier than Serena did. 'Besides, I'm a wife now and plenty of others are about.' She began to babble. 'You're so scared of the rule never to be alone with a man, you forget you're married and don't risk shaming your family now.'

Serena shook her head. 'You should always be a little bit afraid, Gia.'

'Of the sailors?' Gia's fingertips went to the *cornicello* at her neck.

'Them. The sea. Everything, all the time. That's what will keep you safe.'

Gia said nothing, but deep down she didn't want to be led by fear.

In the stifling closeness of Brisbane's sweet air and cries of reunion among the disembarking crowd, Serena clutched Gia's arm and again looked from the photograph in her hand to Pino on the wharf. Gia saw Taddeo beside him, his stance ill at ease. She faltered then steeled herself, following as Serena drew up to them amid the noisy throng. Pino at once embraced Serena, his grin wide, her cheeks pink. Gia and Taddeo looked awkwardly from them to each other. Taddeo clammed up but, at a nudge from Pino, he hesitantly leant in and kissed Gia's cheek. His face smelt of soap, like he'd vigorously scrubbed that morning, she thought.

Gia noticed he tried to keep his birthmark on the side away from her. It didn't look too bad, she decided, the grape-juice mark like a splash on one cheek below his cheekbone. She gave him a bright smile and saw his eyes move to her hair. Her hands went to smooth it down, just as Rosaria had often done. Gia had thought it neat, if a little wild considering the muggy air. But then she recalled her mother insisting that a net hold it tight for the studio photograph of Gia that had been sent to Taddeo.

'We have rooms at a boarding house,' was all he said, and as he bent to help pick up her luggage Gia quickly had another more determined try at smoothing down her curls.

'*No, I'm not staying!*'

They all looked around to the commotion as a woman refused to come ashore.

'*I don't know this man.* He doesn't look like the picture he sent.' She gripped a rail as her husband held his hat, head down. 'I want an annulment. Our aunts arranged this, not me!'

'He's got himself a live one,' Pino chuckled to Taddeo in English, thinking Serena wouldn't understand him, which she didn't really, but Gia mostly did.

Her eyes went to the back of Taddeo's neck as he walked just in front of her. It was reddened as if it too had copped a soapy scrubbing. He had the body of a labourer and she knew from his letters that it was earlier cane-cutting and then clearing scrub and farm work at his orchards that had given him some muscle. She let her gaze slip to the curve of his buttocks just visible beneath the loose trouser fabric. That very night, they must share a bed.

A frisson of unease darted in between her anticipation. When her mother and Nonna had helped put together Gia's *baule*, glory box, all Rosaria had told her of the wedding night was that 'men can be like a lamb or a lion in bed, and whichever you get, at times you'll wish you had the other'. Nonna had actually giggled, showing her gappy teeth she'd usually cover, and said, 'Lamb, lion or *donkey*.' Rosaria had hushed her in case Angelo overheard, but Nonna added, 'And I mean ass!' When they'd seen Gia's bewildered face it had only made the two of them cackle even more.

They left the wharf, hearing the woman still arguing, and Gia looked back, feeling sorry for her. Her eyes went to the half-built Story Bridge yet to meet in the middle, the tiny figures of workers climbing about its girders, then down to the Brisbane River that glistened in the morning sun. It smelt briny but, unlike the sea, it also had an overriding muddiness to it. The sea she'd loved all her life was already out of view, and within a short time, as they kept on walking up among people on footpaths, past buildings and with cars and trams trundling past, she lost sight even of the river.

'Hold yourself in a bit more.' Serena tried easing together the tiny covered buttons at the back of Gia's best dress that she'd worn on her wedding day in Palmi, but it was no use.

Gia's breath gushed out. 'What will I do?'

It was later that same morning and Taddeo and Pino were already downstairs waiting out the front of the boarding house.

'You're lucky I brought some pins.' Serena hastily retrieved them. 'The veil will hide them and afterwards you can put a shawl around you.'

'Thank you.' Gia touched her arm, having expected an *I told you so* for all her eating.

After each had their studio wedding portraits taken as newly married couples, Pino led them to a Greek café in the main part of town. Gia gazed about at the black-and-white tiles, art deco mirrors and chrome soda fountains that lent an alluring silver-screen ambience echoed in the nearby His Majesty's and Regent theatres she'd keenly noticed on their way in. Amid the kitchen clatter seeping through the swinging doors came aromas of sizzling steaks and fried fish. Louis Armstrong sang 'When the

Saints Go Marching In' from a radiogram near the row of booths. Gia couldn't help beaming.

'Four mixed grills and vanilla ice cream sodas.' Pino ordered for them all, apparently not contemplating that she or Serena might want to choose from the menu themselves.

Gia flashed him a look and almost said something but noticed Serena seemed content to concur. Taddeo too kept his head down. Yet after the ship's journey away from her parents' authority, Pino's assumption jarred Gia. Of course her father's word had held most weight – without it she wouldn't have been allowed to stay at school or help out the schoolmistress, but her mother had also been strong in having her say, as had Nonna. And ultimately Rosaria had overruled Angelo and convinced them all of the proxy marriage, if Gia thought about it.

'Let's go to a picture theatre,' she suggested, not caring if the others expected her to let Taddeo take the lead. 'We've never been before and—'

'They're in English!' Pino cut in with a laugh. 'You wouldn't understand a word.'

Gia bridled. 'I've been learning English on the ship.'

Pino glanced at Serena, who said, 'We had lessons but I found it hard to learn a lot.'

'Well, I found it not too hard,' Gia went on. 'And I had extra lessons.'

'From who?' It was the first time Taddeo had questioned her.

Gia felt her face warm. 'A Scalabrinian priest.' She didn't look at Serena, grateful she remained quiet, but cursed herself. Their first day together and already she'd told Taddeo an untruth.

But later, as they climbed back up Jacob's Ladder, the steep staircase that connected the town centre to the Wickham Terrace escarpment where their boarding house sat, Gia felt Taddeo's hand go to her back to guide her. She couldn't be sure if he felt the pins hidden beneath her shawl but if he did, he made no comment.

By habit, Gia buttoned her nightgown to neck and wrist but then, on her mother's advice, left herself bare beneath. She hopped into one side of the double bed to wait. The white sheets felt cold and she held her feet against each other. Above her, floral circles and diamond shapes fought to dominate in the pressed-metal ceiling. A knock shuddered the door.

'Yes.' To her own ears her voice sounded higher than usual.

Taddeo came in, returning from the communal bathroom at the end of the hall, and took off a cardigan he'd put on over his pyjamas. 'I will turn off the light?'

'Yes.'

The switch made a hollow plunk. Streetlights afforded the curtains a wraithlike glow. The bed creaked as Taddeo got in. They each lay on their backs, side by side. Gia waited for his first move. Clasping her hands under the sheet, she felt her wedding ring.

'Well …' Taddeo seemed to be grappling within himself. 'It was a busy day.'

'Yes, it was. But nice.'

'Yes.' His voice wavered, as though he knew what was expected of him and yet was paralysed by the unfamiliarity still between them. 'Well, you must be very tired. Good night then, Giacinta.'

She frowned slightly in the darkness. 'Oh, good night.'

The bed bobbed as he turned to face away from her. Gia remained as she was, gazing to the ceiling in both relief and worry. Outside, a car went past and later she heard some distant yells from over in a park, a bottle rolling. Taddeo began to snore. It took Gia a long time to fall asleep.

❧

On the train to Stanthorpe the next morning, Gia noticed Serena and Pino sat close, their smiles giddy. She and Taddeo perched side by side, only touching if the carriage lurched. The thing was, if she thought about it, she did know how love felt. When she was in school, a new boy from Basilicata had joined their class. He had compelling hazel eyes and whenever he'd looked at Gia she'd felt a little flip in her tummy. Unfortunately he'd also had terrible green teeth but she'd let him kiss her as long as he kept his lips pressed tight together, as she did too.

Then, as a teenager, after her breasts made her dress taut and her curls were no longer constrained to braids, Gia and her girlfriends were in Villa Mazzini, the park on a terrace above her street, when they saw a young man selling coconut pieces kept fresh in half-shells of water. His skin shone a hint darker than hers and his thick eyebrows almost met in the middle. One of the girls had whispered he was gypsy or an Arab. Gia didn't care. Their eyes had locked and she'd felt the same somersault in her middle. After the others went home, she'd crept back at dusk.

He was still there, the coconut gone, his pockets tinkling with coins. Behind a rough-barked tree in the lavender sea haze, his lips had felt as soft and persistent as his hands on her breasts, and when Gia had gone home, Rosaria had worried that the bright spots on her cheeks meant she was coming down with a fever. Gia never saw him again – perhaps the gypsies who camped near the beach had moved on – but she'd never forgotten that tingling feeling of attraction.

She didn't feel so much as a stir for Taddeo. Not even friendship love, or the sibling love she had for Salvatore. A sudden anger at her mother for putting her in this situation moved to anger at herself for going along with it. Perhaps she was old to have married at twenty-three, but even from that age, a lifetime with Taddeo stretched ahead in seeming grey stillness.

For a long while, Gia didn't feel like talking. She kept her face to the window. Not that Taddeo once tried talking to her, and Serena and Pino remained in their own realm. The steam train roared through a cutting, emerging to the Darling Downs countryside of farms, pale grass, pepperings of trees and sweeping low mountains. No sea. She felt a jab of homesickness. It would be weeks before they'd receive her letter in Palmi to say she'd arrived safely.

As they neared Stanthorpe a belt of enormous, rocky outcrops rose, and even with the windows shut, cooler air snuck in with the powdery engine smoke.

'Taddi's neighbour Keith is picking us up at the station,' Pino told them. 'You might need a coat. It's cooler up on the tableland.' He put his arm around Serena as he said this.

Despite her aversion to Vilma, as they came into the train platform Gia wondered if she'd yet arrived with her film-star-handsome husband. They hadn't seen her since the ship had docked.

In the weatherboard station's slip of late afternoon shade, the air felt even colder and she and Serena hastened into their coats while the men got the luggage. Drawing her curls out from beneath her collar, Gia saw a tall man striding towards them. He wore the clothes of an orchardist and only a cotton shirt despite the chilly breeze. She was struck by his eyes – she'd never seen such a vivid blue before. They fleetingly met hers and he almost smiled. He shook hands with Taddeo and Pino then turned back to her and Serena as he was introduced.

'Keith Dawson. Serena, Giacinta, hello.'

Gia heard the different way her name sounded in his mouth, each letter enunciated in his Australian accent. It was curious he didn't address her as Mrs Poletti, though his tone had been respectful. She would've thought most would do so if they were just meeting, whether Italian or Australian. By the look on Serena's face, she wasn't impressed by it but Gia didn't mind. She actually liked it.

Keith helped carry their cases out to his Bedford truck, chatting to Taddeo and Pino as they got in the back tray with the luggage so that the women could travel in the cabin.

'You first,' Serena hissed in Italian to Gia, so as not to be in the middle beside Keith.

He smiled as they settled in their seats. 'Ready?' And Gia nodded for them both.

She had to sit close but was careful not to touch him. His arm nearest to hers moved to change gears as the truck lumbered downhill to the town centre. She saw at once his skin was freckled and tanned, his arm hairs light brown, not black like her father's. She'd no clue what Taddeo's arms were like. Keith paused for cars at the main street intersection where a two-storey hotel with sprawling verandahs sat on the corner. On the ground floor, men leant on the wide windowsills as they downed beers and a man with his sleeves rolled up, perhaps the publican, was sweeping out front. Gia saw his eyes go to her, Serena and then Pino and Taddeo in the back.

'Keith.' He gave a polite nod as was expected but didn't acknowledge the Italians.

'Jack.' Keith gave the barest nod, his smile gone.

Jack shook his head and went on sweeping. 'Better get home before the day goes.'

Gia heard the drinking men's laughter as the truck went around the corner but didn't quite understand what Jack had meant. They drove on past quaint buildings, shops thinning to houses, trees in autumnal flares of ruby and yellow. Gia was happily surprised by the town that Taddeo had told her was home to more than two thousand people. It felt strange though, seeing the trees losing their leaves for the impending winter considering that while it was still 1939, in Palmi it had been coming into spring when she'd left.

'Do you speak English?' Keith glanced over to them both as the truck bounced along.

'Yes, a bit.' Gia ignored Serena's discreet poke and kept her knee from touching his.

'That's good. Learn as much as you can. An Italian couple run the fruit shop in town. It's hard for the wife as she needs her husband to talk for her in English.'

Gia glanced sideways at him, not fully understanding all the words, yet her English was good and getting better and she could grasp the gist of what he said. She digested this as they drove on. It seemed, in the same way that he'd called her Giacinta instead of Mrs Poletti, he had a remarkably modern outlook compared to most men she'd come across.

With Taddeo and Pino out of earshot, she was emboldened to ask, 'You live here a long time?'

'I was born here. So, yes.'

She saw him catch the aliveness to her eyes as she got the joke. The first joke she'd understood in English. She flicked another glance at him when he wasn't looking and estimated he was perhaps a decade older than her, in his early to mid-thirties at most.

About ten miles north-west of town they turned off the main road onto corrugated dirt, making the truck shudder and squeak. 'This is our road,' said Keith.

Both quiet, Gia and Serena held on to stop from slipping off the seat and strained to see into the farms they passed. Front gates were only a half-mile or so apart yet houses lay tucked in glens, behind wooded belts and knolls, unable to be seen from the other homes so that each property – of mostly sixty acres, Keith told them – felt secluded, even isolated.

Apple, pear and peach trees ran north to south in orderly rows, leaves russet for the winter drop. To see familiar peach trees like those in Calabria put Gia somewhat at ease but then her gaze moved beyond to their far boundaries of tangled bush and eucalypts to rest upon the hazy undulation of violet-blue ranges. In that moment, she felt far from home. A brown dog ran out, jolting her attention back. It barked at the truck wheels before tailing off. Keith drove into the next orchard and up towards a white-painted house on stumps with very steep stairs. He turned off the engine and sudden quiet then ensued, ruffled only by Pino and Taddeo jumping down from the back tray.

Serena gave a gasp, realising she was home. She didn't move to get out. It seemed a strong wind could topple that wooden house off those stumps. Gia squeezed her hand. No wonder Pino hadn't sent a photograph of it.

'It will be all right,' Gia whispered in Italian, inwardly relieved Taddeo had at least got her a brick-walled house, sturdy like their stone houses in Palmi. 'And Pino adores you.'

Serena attempted a brave smile to stifle tears. 'Thank goodness you'll be next door.'

Gia waited by the truck as the men took Serena's belongings up the precipitous stairs. She searched for her house in the distance but it was impossible to see through all the trees. Pristine air chilled her nostrils. A soft waft rustled the orchard, dropping leaves. Unfamiliar birdcalls drifted. From the top of the stairs, Pino and Serena waved as Keith drove Gia and Taddeo on.

Further along, they turned into the next orchard and up a dusty track. Gia craned for her first glimpse of the lovely brick house with portico arches and rose bushes. Instead, the Bedford lumbered up to another timber house on stumps, but this one was even more uninviting than Pino's, for it stood unpainted, the wood silvered, its corrugated-iron roof grey. And to her the steps seemed even steeper. Again, there was a sudden quiet as Keith turned off the truck engine.

Gia stared. 'Taddeo,' she said in Italian, 'this isn't the house in the photograph.'

'No, that is a different house.' His head went down.

Keith, unable to understand them, appeared to waver between getting out and staying put.

'But this is where we live? Always. Not the other house? The brick one?'

'No. I mean yes. This house, not the other one.'

Gia's eyes stayed on the house. If it had a view of the sea, it might have been bearable but without even that ... Then she heard her father's voice. *Who falls in water doesn't drown, but who falls badly will.* 'All right then.' She spoke in English this time. 'We will go inside.'

Steep steps led to the front and back doors, between which ran a shotgun hallway. Her footfalls upon the timber and linoleum floors resonated dully in the kitchen, then in the living room with its one easy chair, no wireless or radiogram. The main bedroom had only a bed and a cupboard, the other across the hall from it was empty. The one bed was a double bed. Gia's gaze snagged on it a moment, thinking of the previous night at the boarding house with their backs to each other, then moved on. She noticed most of the sash windows were bare except Taddeo had tacked old rags over those that would cop low sun from the east or west.

'I'll leave you to it,' Keith said from the front door and Taddeo rushed to thank him.

Gia, too stunned by the house to say goodbye, heard the truck turn onto the road at the gate and regretted it. Its rumble faded west, away to Keith's farm, out of sight.

Taddeo hovered, not meeting her eye. 'Giacinta, the house—'

'I think I understand,' she said, knowing how Taddeo's mother was.

He met her gaze then, relieved, though Gia felt she might revisit the matter later on.

With dusk falling, Taddeo didn't show her around outside, for the dinner hour approached and she needed to unpack her glory box. Opening it, she was met by the scent of her home in Palmi. Closing her eyes, she smelt perhaps even a hint of the sea. But she couldn't delve to such depths. In the kitchen there were eggs. She cooked a *frittata* in the only frying pan and sprinkled salt on top.

'This is good.' Taddeo spoke around a mouthful, using only a fork to cut into it to eat.

Gia eyed his clean knife left untouched. 'Tomorrow I'll make bread and pasta.'

Taddeo appeared pleased at this but didn't look up from his plate.

At bedtime, Gia changed into her nightgown in the bathroom. The mirror was hung too high and she stood on tiptoe to brush her curls into waves. She hesitated then undid the top buttons of her nightgown. Met her own eyes in the mirror, her face impassive.

In the bedroom, just like at the boarding house, Taddeo waited until she was in bed and turned off the light switch by the door. The room went pitch black at first in the dark countryside. Gia heard him walk to the bed's other side. The mattress moved as he got in. He still felt like a stranger to her despite the past two days. She could smell the foreign scent of his sweat, even though the air was cool.

Gia tensed, waiting. Just as she began to wonder if Taddeo wanted an annulment, she felt his clumsy caresses in the darkness. He pushed her nightgown up to her waist and she opened herself to his fumbling as she thought she should, trying not to flinch. She kept quiet as he scraped and urged himself into her. Something seemed to overtake him. Heavy on her, his hot breath stale, he panted above. Gia clamped her jaw tight, bearing the hurt inside her, and mercifully it ended swiftly. He rolled away. Neither of them said a word.

She felt a trickle between her legs and, in alarm, thought she was bleeding. Then she realised it must be his seed. She was a true wife now, she thought in triumph. Still, if she was honest, it was all a bit disappointing and Gia didn't understand Pino and Serena's silly grins, her mother's and Nonna's cackles or the way Taddeo sighed happily and soon began to snore.

Her eyes adjusted. Moonlight revealed grimy streaks across the bare window. Taddeo had left the door open to the hallway and she wished he hadn't. The timber house creaked as it contracted in the cooling night. The roof iron gave sharp twangs. She flinched, the noises unsettling when used to the silence of stone walls and just then this house seemed even more precarious on its stumps. Hours stretched. Sticky and sore, again Gia struggled to sleep. In those early, dark hours, aloneness wrapped around her. She was bound. Her family were now ghosts. She quietly cried to herself, careful not to wake Taddeo. Eventually her tears, hot on her cheeks, cooled. It was only as a night breeze came in from the west, stirring the trees, that she was able to be lulled as if by the sound of the sea.

Chilli and Liquorice

Beneath me, the grass felt cool yet dry, its sponginess smoothed out since Tim had mown it. I watched a cloud, backlit by the sun and belly dirty, coasting above. It merged with another and the two sailed on into a blur. A few months before, Mum had said to me, *when you look at clouds, you see in their shapes what your heart most yearns for,* and I'd rolled my eyes, impatient when she said anything bohemian or romantic, though I knew I was being a bit mean. And I didn't tell her that now I couldn't help searching the clouds because it made me cranky to only see unrelatable things, always changing, or nothing in their shapes.

The back door flung open and Nonna Gia eyed me lying on the lawn as if I was a bit mad. Actually, I'd looked up clouds in the encyclopedia after what Mum said about them and I'd read that cloud-watching was once thought a sign of psychosis. Not that Nonna could talk – when a shaft of sunlight appeared through clouds, she'd often cry, 'Look, it's God!' Perhaps we were both a bit mad. I smiled at her but she just regarded me and, without uttering a word, went off around the side to the front yard, her slip-ons flapping.

Somehow it seemed different in the noisy glare of day compared to the intimacy of night's quiet darkness when she had talked more about her earlier life. Even so, I felt closer to her after what she'd told me so far. Protective even, though Nonna remained feisty and self-reliant. She'd spoken of 'the seed' in the same no-nonsense way she sometimes spoke of 'the bleed'. It usually would've made me squirm, embarrassed, but my face had remained neutral, maybe passing some test, showing that I was grown-up enough to hear her talk of such things, her 'woman talk'. Even if privately I veered from connecting the Nonno Taddeo I'd known to the new husband she spoke of.

I looked back to the sky and focused on the blueness then, how shapes also formed in between the clouds, but instead I found myself thinking how vivid Tim's eyes were. I sat up.

Around the front, Nonna stood watering the chilli bushes, their spindly branches bent with heavy fervent-red hearts. The old man sat on his verandah facing us and Nonna kept her back to him, even though his grandson had mown the lawn for her. I frowned. Anyone else and she'd have been foisting a plate of biscuits and perhaps several silverbeet bunches and some other homegrown vegies on them.

'I thought Frank mowed the lawn.'

The hose water sank straight through the granite soil without pooling.

'Nonna?'

'Frank hurt his back a little while ago. It's okay now but Dianne at the pub heard at the time and sent Tim around to mow, seeing as he did across the road, and he's kept coming to do it ever since.' Her eyes stayed on the jet of water. 'We'll go out to Frank's for the harvest next week.'

I strove to sound casual. 'Dianne is Tim's mother?'

'Yes, yes. Don't walk on that wet grass, you might as well be asking for pneumonia.'

'But it's summer.' Though to appease her I went and perched on the cement front steps by the rosemary bush. I furtively regarded the old man. He was obviously Australian, as Tim was, and appeared a bit frail. His eyes seemed sharp though.

'Does Tim work at the pub too?' I kept my voice low, even though there was no way the old man could have heard us from across the road.

'Why you ask?' She dragged the hose over to the rosemary bush. 'If you ask about a boy, it should be a nice Italian one. Now, Serena's grandson, Mauro—'

'*Nonna.*' I stood up. 'I'm going inside to watch TV.'

'Okay, good.' She sprayed the hose towards me but it didn't get me.

'Nonna!'

'*Boh!* Go on. Inside.' She nodded and glanced to the sky. '*Nuvole a pecorelle, pioggia a catinelle.*' *Clouds look like sheep, it'll soon bucket down.*

I wasn't sure if she meant it or if I saw the hint of a cheeky smile, considering my earlier cloud-watching, but she kept on watering as I went inside, the old man observing it all.

'Sofia, there is a letter for you.' Nonna came into my room straight from the mailbox.

I took off my Walkman and sat up on the bed. She looked at the back of the envelope before handing it to me, likely to see if the sender was a boy, which gave me the shits a bit, and then passed the letter over. I saw straightaway the little daisies Mel always drew around her name. That was the other thing about spending holidays in the country – it was too expensive to talk on the phone to friends long-distance, especially the length of time we usually spoke, but at least Mel and I wrote letters, and I sometimes got postcards from others.

Miss you, Mel wrote first, which made me happy, though she didn't ask what I'd been doing, just launched into her stuff.

I got my hair streaked at Stefan. $36 dollars! Mum said I could only do it if I paid for it myself from working at the newsagents. Gavin had his party. Everyone went. So terrible you weren't there. Guess who asked after you?!! John Peters!! He must like you!! There's a barbecue at Deb's next Saturday. A pool party!! Everyone is going. Can't you come back for it? It sucks you aren't here. I thought of you the other day. Dad picked this wog movie he made us see with him. Amadeus. *It had all this opera in it!! We must see* Back to the Future *when it's out next year. Do you reckon you'll be home then?!!*

After reading Mel's letter, I felt so unsettled I almost couldn't bear it. I'd been trying not to think of all the things going on without me. I'd already missed a party! To hear about it but be left out was torture. As for John Peters, he was a bit of a spunk but I didn't know him well or really feel anything for him. Especially now I'd met Tim. Which was ridiculous, as I'd only spoken to Tim once. What could I write back? I wouldn't mention Tim this early on and nothing I wrote about could come close to all the things Mel was doing.

I put my Walkman on, loud as I could stand it. And then, after a while, I got up, closed the door and rummaged in my bag for a Mars bar. The fabric had come away inside the base of my bag, creating a false bottom where I could hide things – chocolate supplies mostly. Not that Mum or Nonna Gia looked in my bag as far as I knew but I wasn't taking any chances, especially after the cupboard eating comment. As I chewed, the gluggy caramel, nougat and chocolate somehow made me feel better, for those few minutes anyway.

Afterwards, I scrunched the wrapper inside some alfoil that I'd also brought with me to make it easier to hide in the bin – I was an old hand. Or else I'd slip in the wrapper when I took the rubbish out for Nonna. With the reassuring sweetness still in my mouth, I lay down and stayed curled like that, listening to my Walkman. The gauze curtain floated back and forth, gently tugged each way. I contemplated Mel saying, *I thought of you the other day. Dad picked this wog movie …* Again, the curtain drifted, back and forth, at the whim of the breeze. I didn't have a dad. I was Italian when none of my friends were. All I wanted was to be normal, to blend in, be the same as everyone else, yet I mostly felt on the outer.

It was hard to talk with any privacy on Nonna's telephone as it sat in the hallway, on a polished-timber stand that had a built-in seat. Despite *Perfect Match* blaring out in the living room, I was certain Nonna was listening to my every word.

'Can't I just come home for the weekend and come back here after?'

Mum sighed. 'We've been over this.'

'I know, but Mel told me Deb's having a pool party this Saturday.'

'Sofie, that's six hours of driving for me to come get you and bring you back. Each time! And besides, you're needed at Frank's for harvest then.'

'Aren't you helping out this year?' It was something we'd both done over the years.

'This School of Arts project is so important to me, you know that. It's the first time in decades the ugly brick shopfronts are gone for us to restore the building's 1860s facade.'

I stayed silent. It felt hard to miss every holiday party my friends were going to.

'When I started in council's typing pool all those years ago, I never thought I'd get to help on a project like this.'

'You're only an assistant.' Why was I so mean to her? I knew too well Mum had given up going to university all those years ago to work for the both of us.

'Is Ma there? Let me talk to her.'

'No, she's in the shower,' I lied. 'I better go before this call costs too much.'

'Sofie ...'

'I'm staying like you want.' I hung up on her, something I'd never done before.

My heart hammered in my throat as I stared at the phone. Again, instant regret, like when I'd been cold to her before she'd driven off, but at the same time still angry I was missing Deb's party. The sofa plastic crunkled as Nonna likely leant back after listening in. I dithered in the hallway, half-expecting Mum to call back and go mad at me before demanding to talk to Nonna. The phone sat silent. I was actually a bit disappointed she didn't call to tell me off.

'You hungry?' Nonna Gia eyed me as I came to join her. 'Have some liquorice. Best liquorice in the world is from Calabria. Good for cleaning your teeth too. And coughs.'

'I'm not sick.' But I took some from the proffered Amarelli tin.

'In Calabria we'd see the yellow flowers of the liquorice plants all over the hillsides.'

Saliva and blackness flooded my mouth, the liquorice like burnt charcoal, molasses and medicine all at once. I slumped down on the lounge, rustling the plastic and we both stared at the television. On the show, a pink-and-white neon wall slid back and two contestants met for the first time, ready to go on a blind date to see if they might be a perfect match.

Suddenly I looked over to Nonna. 'Don't you like Australians much?'

'Sofia! What a thing to say!'

'Well, all your friends are Italian, aren't they?'

'All your friends at school are Australian, no?'

I flushed. She had me there. I didn't risk mentioning Tim's name or even John Peters, but asked, 'What if I didn't want to go out with an Italian boy?'

'Well, at least a European then.'

'What if he was, say, Irish?'

She exhaled sharply. 'Well, would he at least eat like an Italian?'

'See what I mean?' I sat back folding my arms, and then it snuck out under my breath, 'Just because my father was Australian.'

An ad break pelted from the television set.

Nonna stared at the screen but as if not really seeing it. 'When I first came here, many Australians didn't want to be our friend. So mainly we saw Italians, even those from far-off parts of Italy who we'd not have known or mixed with there, yet here they lived close by.'

'But didn't you have Australian neighbours at the farm too? The Keith you spoke of?'

'Yes.' She looked to her hands and her voice went softer. 'Good people.'

'But you don't see them now.' I glanced over, smug, thinking I'd won the discussion. When I saw Nonna's forlorn face though, my triumph swiftly hollowed. 'I'm sorry, Nonna, I was being a—' if I was talking to Mel, I would've said *dickhead* '—I was being stupid, sorry.'

She gave a half-shrug. 'When you leave behind your family in another place, often your friends become like family too.'

'It must've been so hard not seeing your family again like that. The not knowing ...'

Nonna looked at me a moment. Did she realise I also meant about my father in a way – it was hard to be sure. But I felt perhaps she understood I was truly open to her talking to me about her own life.

Quart Pot Picnic

Taddeo pointed out the pale dirt was crumbly granite, tiny fragments of the same rock that dominated the landscape all around Stanthorpe. It crunched underfoot along with fallen leaves as Gia trailed him through their orchard. She subtly observed Taddeo as he paused to check a tree's branches, its leaders and spurs, still acquainting herself with this man who was already her husband. And yet she was becoming more used to him. His stocky body, the way his black hair showed some thinning on top though he wasn't yet thirty. How the birthmark, along with his reserve, made him appear perhaps mean, though that didn't seem his way.

'You see a tree's true shape when it loses its leaves …' he murmured, more to himself.

Becoming aware of Gia's gaze, he caught himself and walked on. However she'd glimpsed a touch of her father in him that was reassuring.

They came to the split-rail boundary fence with the Dawson property and she saw only orchards, some gum trees and a dam – no sign of the house, or Keith.

Gia asked, 'Do you see Keith and his wife often?'

'He's a widower. Lives there with his sister. I mostly visit with Italians in the area.'

Taddeo turned back and she hurried to keep up. She couldn't see Serena and Pino's house either. In Palmi she could walk out the door and chat to someone passing by or hanging washing from a window, the stone dwellings so close that noise carried – clanging pots, church bells, children, the old neighbour coughing. It was so quiet on the farm and Taddeo was too.

She snuck another glance over to him and wondered if he noticed she'd put her hair in a neat bun to look more like her portrait for him, even if a few wilful curls still fought free.

'We should take something to the Dawsons since they watched the farm while you went to Brisbane,' she suggested, as again their footfalls crunched. 'I could make *crostoli*.' She'd seen there was enough flour and sugar in the kitchen cupboard for the simple recipe.

'All right. But tomorrow we'll go. I must work outside now. You work in the house.' The way he said it struck her. 'And Giacinta ...' He stopped again, making her stop too.

'You know, Taddeo, most people usually call me Gia.'

His face hinted he liked the other better. 'I was only going to say that perhaps it's better we don't talk to people about your being a proxy bride. That we have such a marriage.'

'Why not?'

'Many people don't understand the custom and it's considered better to have a ... a love marriage.' He looked away.

She watched as he turned from her and kept walking. Then she followed behind.

With no biscuit tin, Gia put the *crostoli* in a saucepan and popped on a lid, hoping the pastry ribbons sprinkled in sugar stayed crisp. Again she wound her hair up into a tight bun, although a few stubborn curls still strayed. Taddeo wheeled his only transport from under the house. An old steel shearer's bicycle, he explained, as she looked at its straggling remnants of hessian handle-bar bags, where the rider must have stored things during journeys between sheep shearing sheds.

The autumn morning basked quietly as Taddeo pedalled to the Dawson farm, Gia perched on the bicycle bar incongruously clutching the saucepan. Beneath them, the bicycle tyres made a gentle crunching on the gravel road. The Dawsons' property was the last at the road's end and an old cowbell hung on the gate that Taddeo said was to announce arrivals.

'The sister never leaves the place,' he told Gia as they got off the bicycle outside the gate. 'I didn't want to ask why. When she hears the bell, she looks out a window, sees it's me and then she usually waves and I go find Keith, mostly somewhere outside or in the shed.'

Gia looked up the driveway to the house. It stood silent, a window either side of the front door each with blinds down like shut eyes. On the side of the house where the driveway continued past, a geranium pot sat on the sill of an open window, its flowering over, but she recognised it as the same plant people often grew in window boxes in Italy for its red blooms. There was no sign of Keith. Gia regarded the cowbell.

'Come this way.' She held down a line of the post-and-wire fence, edged the saucepan between and climbed through. 'And be quiet.' Expecting Taddeo to resist, Gia was surprised when he followed her. 'Now you go look for Keith out the back, I'll find you later.'

Gia's footsteps on the front stairs were soft, her knock on the door loud. After a wait, she knocked again. A window slid up and a woman peered out. Her hair was cropped elfin-short, more reddish-brown than Keith's brown, and her eyes held much grey in their blueness.

Gia held up the saucepan. 'I am Taddeo's wife, Gia. I made *crostoli* for you.'

'Oh, I see. I'm Edie.' She hesitated, ducked back in and closed the window.

Gia gasped, thinking that was it, but then heard her trying to open the front door. It juddered yet remained wedged, as if it hadn't been opened for years.

'I go to the back,' Gia called out.

Edie was waiting for her at the top of the back steps that led straight into the kitchen.

'I didn't hear the gate bell.' She pushed up her sleeves.

Gia evaded her gaze and lifted the saucepan lid. '*Crostoli.*'

'Right ...' Edie peered in and relented a little more. 'They look good. Thank you.'

The house was warm from the wood stove upon which a kettle steamed. Gia had expected that someone who wouldn't leave a house would be timid, yet Edie didn't seem so.

'Keith told me you'd arrived.' Edie got teacups from shelf hooks on a yellow dresser.

Only two cups, Gia noticed, for it seemed assumed Keith and Taddeo wouldn't join them. She was also aware that Edie didn't mention anything about Taddeo suddenly having a wife after years of his being alone. Perhaps she supposed they'd been married all along.

'So, what do you think of it here so far, Gia?'

'Quiet.' She spoke before thinking. 'And I miss the sea.'

Edie considered this. 'Your English is very good.'

'Thank you.' Gia beamed. She'd been keeping up bettering her English from a book they'd each been given on the ship as well as making Taddeo often speak it with her and found it came easily to her. 'I am learning more.'

Edie regarded Gia more closely, her eyes going to the slightly crooked bun and the curls Gia could feel were not quite caught in it. She smiled. 'You know what? Come with me.'

Gia followed her, sidling through a lounge room cramped by a radiogram and worn sofas with armrests wide enough to rest a plate, then out to a louvred verandah. Air sharp with turpentine and linseed oil hit her nose. Gia stared at the clutter of paints and brushes, opaque water jars, blunt knives. An easel held a half-painted canvas of a kitchen chair. She'd never met anyone who painted, let alone a woman. It seemed terribly eccentric. She wondered if Edie also did the house chores. The windowsills were layered in dust.

Edie rifled through stacked canvases. 'Here it is.' She lifted out a painting. 'The sea.'

Gia took in its roiling green hues and foam-tipped waves, the blackened depths hinting at an anger. She faltered. 'In Palmi, the sea is—' From the paintbox she picked up a tin tube that showed its shade by a small rectangle of colour on the front. 'It is like this.'

'Cobalt violet?' Edie appeared unconvinced and was handed another. 'Mauve?'

Gia nodded, smiling now. 'But it is, I don't know how to say, soft.'

'Hazy?'

'Haz-y.' Gia sounded out the new word. There were so many to remember and pronouncing them correctly was easier with help.

Especially as the Italian alphabet of twenty-one letters didn't have a J, K, W, X or Y, though she knew some dialect words that did.

In halting words, she described to Edie the pebbly shore, its mauve sea and the mountains behind. Picking up another tin paint tube, she tried to tell her how the sea began like turquoise near the shore before melding to lavender and violet as the water deepened, not meaning her eyes to become a little wet as she spoke, though Edie must have seen.

The men never came in for tea and Edie stayed inside later on when Gia went to find Taddeo. He and Keith were in the shed beside the truck with its hood open. Keith looked over as she came in. Perhaps it was the recent talk of the sea with Edie, but as Gia's eyes met his she had the feeling of coming out onto the little balcony in Palmi and seeing the sea spread out before her, glittering in the morning sun with all the promise of a splendid day ahead.

He nodded to her in greeting. 'I was telling Taddeo I heard on the news that there's much concern about the pact Hitler and Mussolini have signed between Germany and Italy.'

'*Boh*, it will be all right,' Taddeo blustered, before she could respond, and gave Keith a look for including her in such talk. 'We're in Australia now. Very far from Italy.'

Taking his cue, Keith gave her a reassuring smile and didn't say any more. Yet as he turned away to wipe his hands on a rag, Gia thought she saw him slightly wince.

❧

First thing on Sunday morning, Pino picked them up in his cart to go to church. Taddeo at once climbed into the seat up front and Serena moved to the back to sit with Gia on upturned kerosene boxes. Gia and Serena kissed cheeks and happily squeezed hands at seeing each other again. As they faced backwards moving away from Gia's place, Gia saw Serena look for the portico brick facade, see only the timber house on stumps and, puzzled, open her mouth.

'Sssh,' Gia whispered in her ear. 'Silly Taddeo sent the wrong picture.' And Serena's face showed sympathy but also perhaps some relief that Gia's house was just like hers.

The horse's gait was a soothing clop on the dirt road but the sun gave little warmth with the cold air moving over them. They passed the property where the brown dog raced out, barking and snapping at the wheels, then it was again quiet. Gia observed the landscape's ruggedness, taking in more from the slow-moving cart. Eucalypt trees stood tall and pale-trunked, leaves sparse. Granite boulders rounded shoulders from dry grass. The air was strident and cloying. It all still felt strange to her, however she found something alluring about the rawness, its freshness.

Saint Joseph's Catholic Church on High Street in town was flanked by utility trucks, horse-drawn sulkies and big farm trucks. Inside, the white plaster walls reminded Gia of the interior of Santissimo Crocifisso and, as Mass began in the usual Latin with the women all wearing chapel veils, it almost felt like being back in Palmi. Except the priest had an Irish accent and the pews held both Australians and Italians.

Afterwards, people stood out front in the winter sunshine to talk, just as they did in the piazza after church in Italy. Gia peered around but Keith wasn't there. She noticed that some Italians chatted to Australians in English but more were speaking Italian to each other. Another group of Australians stood giving pointed looks at this and grumbling. Foremost among them, and with a glower, was the publican who she recognised from the day she'd arrived. Taddeo had since told her his name was Jack Armstrong.

'You must be Serena and Giacinta.' A bosomy woman introduced herself as Josie and pointed out her husband, Alfio, holding their little boy, Vince, as he stood talking to Taddeo, Pino and some others. 'Our farm is a few miles from yours. Vilma ended up out past Amiens Road, almost in the bush.' She looked around. 'Doesn't look like she's here this morning.'

'No, I haven't seen her.' Serena twisted to look about too but Gia didn't.

'Next Sunday a group of us is having a picnic,' Josie told them, taking on the motherly manner of one having been in Australia a while. 'After Mass we'll head to a nice spot by Quart Pot Creek. Tell those husbands of yours you all must come along.'

Gia lit up at this. 'You can call me Gia,' she beamed. 'Are you a proxy bride too?'

Josie gave her a kind but somewhat pitying look. 'Oh no, ours is a love marriage.'

Gia flattened, dismayed to feel the stigma of her arranged marriage from another Italian like she had in Italy. She'd assumed that once here it would be solely the Australians who might think it curious. Only then did she fully understand why Taddeo had told her not to talk to others of being married by proxy.

'Thank you for inviting us to the picnic,' said Serena, ever dutiful and placating. 'We should get a message to Vilma and her husband to come along too.'

At that, Gia hid her sigh.

Gia looked over as a cheer went up where Taddeo and Pino played bocce among the men on some even grass alongside Quart Pot Creek. Others like Alfio sat immersed playing cards around an upturned packing box, cigarette smoke fanning from their bent concentration. A fellow lay on a blanket absently strumming a mandolin as children ran about, Josie calling Vince back from the water's edge. The dark clouds gathering in Europe seemed very distant.

Gia's gaze returned to the spread of mostly eaten cold pasta dishes, *caponata*, roast chicken, apples and *ciambella* cake as Josie draped tea towels over to deter a few winter flies.

'Still hungry, Gia?' Vilma arched a dark eyebrow, her smile goading.

Gia had no ready reply and shook her head. It didn't help that Vilma appeared thinner since they'd got to Australia. And while Gia could at least do up the buttons of her best dress once again, she still carried some plumpness from the ship's dining room.

Vilma tucked her legs at an elegant angle. 'Or are you expecting, Gia?'

Serena and Josie looked over and Gia again shook her head, giving Vilma a scowl.

'Believe me,' said Josie, 'when the time does come, the hen might be the one laying the egg but the rooster crows the loudest.' They all laughed, except Gia, still smarting.

She folded her arms loosely over her middle. 'How is your farm, Vilma? It must be more like wilds out in the bush?'

'Carmelo has everything clear,' Vilma smiled, getting up, and Gia flushed, sure she was referring to Taddeo's birthmark. But Vilma made certain. 'Oh, when you are expecting, Gia, remember to satisfy your cravings or the baby will have a birthmark in the

shape of one, maybe for you a *ciambella* cake or spaghetti in cream.'
She laughed and strutted off.

'Ignore her,' Serena murmured, seeing Gia trying to hide her
hurt beneath bravado.

'I don't know why she hates me so much. I haven't done
anything to her.'

'Perhaps you're similar in some ways yet you've something she
wishes she had.'

Gia almost guffawed. 'Somehow I doubt that very much.'

She looked over to Carmelo. He truly did look like a handsome
film star – a stylish suit, a cigarette perched between his full lips,
hair slicked back, ready with wit and smiles for everyone.

'Let's have a photograph,' he said, getting up as the card game
ended. Carmelo was the only one there who owned a camera.
'Everyone over here in the sun.'

They all lined up, some kneeling, some standing, children in
front or up on shoulders.

'Here, Vilma, take it like I showed you.' Carmelo handed her
the camera so he could be in the photograph. '*Squeeze* the button
down, don't push it.' He stood among the men and Gia heard
him quietly add, 'Let's hope she doesn't cut our heads off.' Several
chuckled.

By then, Vilma stood some way back squinting into the lens.
'Stand closer together.'

'For old times, boys.' Carmelo did a Fascist salute. 'Sons of the
She-Wolf and Balilla.'

Gia's breath caught. She thought they'd left behind their
younger days in the Fascist youth considering the current tensions
in Europe and that they were in a far different political landscape
in Australia now. But of course all of the men had been in Italy's

Fascist youth since they were four – Mussolini made it compulsory they attend every Saturday – and since everyone went along it seemed normal. It was like Scouts, except she remembered that when Salvatore attended, once he turned eight the boys did drills using scaled-down Italian army rifles.

She'd longed to join in the fun too. Instead, as a girl, Gia had had to attend Piccole Italiene, Daughters of the Wolf, that encouraged motherhood and good housekeeping. She'd fought Rosaria about going, futilely, for apart from her mother's wishes, Mussolini had made it compulsory as well.

'*Viva Italia!*' Carmelo shouted and the other men raised their arms in Fascist salutes too. '*Viva Italia!*' they all chorused, smiling, and Vilma clicked the camera.

❧

'Taddeo, I can help you.' Gia stood in the orchard, hands on hips, her house dress, cardigan and stockings more suited to the milder winters in Palmi than Stanthorpe's bracing August chill. The cold had deepened more than she'd expected it to during her first few months there and she longed for any hint of spring's warmth.

Rugged up in a coat atop the pruning ladder, still in the habit of it being only himself, Taddeo garnered the warmth of a tiny charcoal brazier hanging from a rung to keep his hands warm in the bitter airstream. He looked down to her. 'I told you, no. You look after everything inside the house and I look after everything outside.'

Her lips stuck out a bit as she deliberated, however she went back to do the washing.

But I am outside for this work, she griped to herself and lit the fire under the copper.

Waiting while the clothes water came to a boil, she tied a scarf over her curls. She'd stopped pinning them into a taut bun. It made her head sore and it wasn't as if Taddeo even seemed to notice she'd done so to look like her portrait for him. If anything, she felt the more time they spent together, the more distant he became. Even in bed they slept mostly like sister and brother, he perhaps sensing she endured rather than enjoyed his attempts to be a husband. There was certainly little chance of her expecting, she thought dryly, still riled at Vilma.

Steam drifted from the boiling copper as Gia stirred the clothes. Her gaze ventured to Taddeo. He wouldn't even let her watch to see how he pruned the orchard, let alone talk to her about the market prices like he did with Pino. Her face flushed over the searing water. Her bare hands were raw. Silence held them in stalemate, yet Gia felt their eyes spoke a great deal in the pointed looks she gave him and the way he then avoided hers.

Gia planted Nonna's *Piccante Calabrese* seeds on the first day of spring. Several more weeks had passed and it was still fairly cold but she fancied she felt that hint of warmth she'd been hoping for. Taddeo nailed holes in the bottom of an old tin for her, into which she scooped some soil, inserted the chilli seeds and sat it on a saucer on the sunny, sheltered windowsill above the sink. There she could be sure to keep it watered. Perhaps soon she'd receive a letter back from home and then she could write again to tell them the seeds had sprouted. Gia counted out the months it might take for her initial letter to reach them and then for their return reply.

The orchard was already showing the first soft downs of budding and a few nights later Gia found Taddeo sitting on the back steps smoking and gazing appreciatively at the trees. To her, the branchlets, all snowy-blossomed in promise, looked as if they reflected the stars overhead but she kept that to herself. Maybe she should have said it to him. However as he realised she'd come up behind him, Taddeo looked down, stubbing out the last of his cigarette on the step and the moment was gone.

It was Father's Day that September evening in Australia, which felt strange to Gia considering in Italy they celebrated it in March on Saint Joseph's Day. For the two of them the day hadn't been any different from usual Sunday Mass since they had no fathers to visit and no children. It was just them. Taddeo glanced up at her and Gia gave a smile.

When she didn't speak, he cleared his throat. 'I will plant the beans next week.'

'I'll help you. I can work both in and outside the house.' She remained stubborn.

Taddeo shook his head. 'Giacinta ...'

'Gia. And if together we work hard, maybe one day that nice brick house in the photograph you sent might really be ours.'

He grimaced, still self-conscious about that, though Gia thought she saw a look cross his face, as if the prospect of her idea did grasp him.

From along the road came a rumble and they both turned in surprise to see Keith's Bedford headlights flickering up towards the back of their house. They exchanged glances, thinking something must be wrong for him to come by, especially at such an hour, and Gia feared Edie might be ill. It had been a little while since Gia had seen Keith and Edie, for Taddeo indeed chose to only visit with other Italians, as he'd told her. If he needed to go next door to the Dawsons, he mostly went off alone without telling her, not seeming to realise she might want to come and perhaps see Edie.

As Keith drove the truck right up to the steps, Gia pulled her shawl around her old house dress and Taddeo stood up.

Keith got out, the metal crash of the door behind him loud in the still night. Without any greeting, he said, 'We just heard on the wireless, Britain's declared war on Germany for invading Poland. And Menzies just announced Australia is at war too.'

Caponata

Hearing Frank's truck pull up out front, I put the bag that hid my chocolates in the wardrobe amid the fog of cedar balls. Hopefully the closed house wouldn't get too hot in the few days Nonna and I were out at the farm for harvest. After meeting Tim, I didn't feel like eating much anyway but it was better to leave the chocolates behind. I had to share a room with my cousin Lena at the farm and she'd likely go digging in my bag for a tape, find a chocolate and announce it to everyone in her annoying, naive way. Though twelve, she was still so sheltered by Frank and Connie. It got on my nerves. By her age, I'd already been coming home from school to an empty flat, even if it was just for an hour or two before Mum got in from work.

Frank came up the path whistling and without knocking barrelled inside and along the hallway straight to the kitchen. 'You didn't make *caponata* again did you, Ma?' And even from my room I could hear the usual mischief in his voice.

'Oh, get away with you!' Nonna cried, sounding more hysterical than necessary.

The whole house was bathed in *agrodolce*, a sweet and sour aroma from the frying eggplant, capsicums and zucchini from her garden, as well as red onions and garlic. Since breakfast, she'd had them cooking in a saucepan of olive oil, balsamic vinegar, brown sugar, a handful of salt and her secret ingredient, lemon zest. Its richness had smelt a bit much first thing in the morning as I'd sat and eaten some toast. The stereogram had been going since that hour too, and just then 'In Napoli' coursed from the speakers, Dean Martin's smile dipping into his sung words.

'Dino helping again too, is he?' Frank teased Nonna, giving me a wink as I came to join them. 'How are you, Sof?' He kissed both my cheeks twice, his wiry moustache chafing me.

Frank's moustache, eyebrows and chest hair were akin to Tom Selleck in *Magnum, P.I.* and he embraced his Italian-ness in an easygoing way that Mum didn't so much. Though I noticed he tamed his curly hair into waves with some type of gel product. Again, to please Nonna, I hadn't straightened my hair but I had forced most of my curls into an unruly plait.

'Right!' Frank rubbed his hands together. 'Ready to roll?'

I nodded. 'I'll get my things.'

Again, he began whistling, this time along to 'In Napoli'. Frank had a way of cares resting lightly on him and not taking much too seriously. Which was mostly cheering, except when you wanted anything deeper from him.

My favourite memory of Frank was when I was about four. That year, 1972, the Stanthorpe Apple and Grape Harvest Festival was also the town centenary and we later found out nearly sixty thousand people had crammed into the main street to watch the Grand Parade. People crowded along footpaths and out windows, perched on roofs and shop awnings. Frank had whisked me up onto his shoulders from where I joyfully watched the entire procession of floats and marching bands going by, feeling like I had a dad. But Connie was already pregnant with Lena by then and after she was born, and especially once Sam followed, Frank was only ever an uncle to me.

'We got everything?' Nonna Gia locked the front door.

From the shadows of the portico, Zucchero peevishly watched on, perhaps aware our getting in the truck meant he once again faced a couple of days left alone, being fed by the neighbour next door. He could still get into the laundry to sleep but I hoped he'd be okay.

As Frank put our things in the back of the truck, I nodded towards the old man across the road. 'There he is again. Always sitting there, watching.' I stared back, my eyes a little more exaggerated.

'Eh?' Frank furrowed his brow, looking over. 'Is that right?' He gave him a wave.

The old man didn't wave back.

'*Smettila*. Stop it,' hissed Nonna. 'Sofia, get in.' She shoved the big, lidded saucepan of cooling *caponata* into Frank's hands. 'And *you*, hold this.' Nonna climbed up into the cabin after me and gave Frank another glare as he handed her back the saucepan to nurse.

Nonna needn't have worried. It was like nothing could rouse the old man.

Frank drove us out along Stanthorpe's main street, tunelessly humming Joe Dolce's 'Shaddap You Face' to himself. He still thought the song funny though the rest of us rolled our eyes at it by then. We passed the pretty buildings and shops that dwindled to houses and trees in full summer leaf. Sitting on the bench seat with the sun hot on my bare legs, I found myself thinking of Nonna being driven along this way, coming to the farm for the first time in Keith Dawson's truck. And now it was me sitting in the middle.

I turned to Frank. 'How is your back going?'

He halted mid-hum. 'Oh, right as rain.' He changed gears. 'Ma reckoned someone put the *malocchio* on me, right, Ma? Lucky for that chilli.'

She gave a grunt and shifted the saucepan slightly, making it emit the sweet and vinegary aroma of the still-warm *caponata*. I turned to her.

'How come Tim is happy to mow your lawn but the old man is unfriendly and stares?'

There was silence and, for several moments, I felt besieged by it and the smells in the close cabin of seat vinyl and *caponata*, despite Frank's window being down.

Nonna blustered, 'I paid Tim and gave him a drink.'

Frank glanced past me to her and back to the road. 'I wouldn't worry too much about him. He had a stroke a while back. Can't do much these days.'

'Oh.' At once I felt sorry for the old man and for staring back at him like I had. I glanced at Nonna, my mouth twisting. It would have helped if she'd told me that earlier.

Switching course, she said to Frank, 'We didn't see you at Mass on Sunday.'

'Oh, we went on Saturday night this week,' he smoothly replied, sliding me a look.

About fifteen kilometres from town, we reached the turnoff. The road was sealed these days but the orchards of apple, pear and peach trees standing north to south must've looked similar to when Gia had first arrived, even if I knew many of the older trees had been replaced by now. Front gates still sat almost a kilometre apart, however I guessed more clearing between them must have gone on over the decades for most houses were no longer hidden from each other.

Lena and Sam dangled on the front gate in wait, and when we drove in they closed it behind us, chasing the truck's dust up the drive. Frank and Connie lived in the same timber house where Nonna and Nonno had begun their married life. It still had steep steps and a shotgun hallway but in recent years they'd painted it white, added verandahs and closed in underneath with orange brick. All since Nonno Taddeo had died, when I came to think of it.

The lower brick didn't match the upper timber but it kept the storage area cool. It was an Italian cantina under there, musky with hanging *salume* from the annual pig slaughter (always done in midwinter's *la luna calante*, the waning moon, that Nonna told us was the optimal part of the cycle for the female pig). There were also preserved olives and vegetables in jars, homemade wine, and passata from tomato day, all of which we all had to help with – conveniently each task occurring on weekends or school holidays so Mum and I could be there, returning to Brisbane with boxes of whatever we'd helped pick or pickle. Except this year Mum had decided not to join us, and at that moment I didn't feel so bad about hanging up on her.

'Salvatore, give Nonna a kiss!' Nonna cried as ten-year-old Sam dodged away.

Connie took the *caponata* and leant over to kiss my cheeks. 'Lena had me set up beds on the verandah for you two tonight.' Her eyes were very dark, almost as black as her hair, and crinkled, for she seemed always smiling. 'Early night tonight. Big day tomorrow.'

～

'What's ready to pick tomorrow?' I asked Lena from my camp bed beside hers.

She slapped at her arm despite the acrid smoulder of a mozzie coil. 'Peaches.'

I groaned, knowing how their fuzz itched.

'When did you get a Walkman?'

I heard the wonder in her voice and knew Lena still looked up to me, being four years older and living in the city. It made me feel bad for being irritated by her naivety.

'For my birthday.'

'Can I have a go tomorrow? Mum won't let me get one. Says it'll make me go deaf.'

'You can listen for a little while but I need to save the batteries.' Springs nudged at my back through the thin mattress. 'Hey … is your mum friends with Dianne at the pub?'

'Who? Mrs Dinning? I don't know.' Lena pushed back her sheet. 'Do you like my baby-doll pyjamas? They're new. Oh, you probably can't see them in the dark.'

'I saw them before when we were brushing our teeth. They're nice.' I'd worn such pyjamas last summer and I smiled with fondness for Lena. 'We better get to sleep.'

But my eyes stayed open. If Connie and Mrs Dinning had arranged for Tim to do the mowing, they must be friendly. Unless it was just small-town helpfulness. But if they were friends, Connie might help bring round Nonna so that I could see Tim. I pondered when he might next be over. Grass grew faster in summer but I wasn't sure just how long might it take to need mowing.

The darkened timber house spoke in creaks and soughs. Crickets chirred. Far in the distance a dog howled, a forlorn, reaching arc despite the summer night's balminess.

'They might have gone to school together,' Lena said suddenly out of the dark.

'Who?'

'Mum and Mrs Dinning.'

'Oh. So, the Dinnings have run the hotel a fair while then?'

Lena pulled the sheet back up. 'No, just a few years. But they're not blow-ins.'

⌒

At midday, the table in the feathery shade from the peppercorn trees was a welcome sanctuary after many hours in the hot orchard. Whiffs of sunscreen and sweat drifted as we all sat down along bench seats to set-out plates and bowls, mismatched to cater for the extras there. Nonna Gia sprinkled pepper around on the tablecloth to deter flies and I self-consciously looked along the table to the local youths there for summer holiday work, but they chatted on between themselves.

Nonna plonked her serving bowl of *caponata* in the table centre and Connie placed platters of roast chicken in among the bread baskets, lettuce in oil and vinegar, bowls of tinned tuna mixed with onion and tomato and a reheated *truscello di Messina*, meatball and ricotta bake – Connie's family was from Sicily. Frank went straight for it, unaware of Nonna Gia's puckered lips when she saw he didn't go for her *caponata* first, but then Nonna saw Sam's plate.

'Salvatore, don't cross your cutlery over or you'll have many crosses to bear!'

'*Non … na.*' He puffed out his cheeks but moved his knife and fork apart, likely unaware what a cross to bear even was by the look on his face, I thought, watching him.

'Did you put chilli in this *caponata*?' Connie asked Nonna.

I lowered my forkful and Nonna frowned at her. 'What's wrong with you? I never put chilli in my *caponata Calabrese.*'

I gingerly tried to detect any underlying heat but the sweetness of the *agrodolce* was busy singing away any sharpness. Besides, the peach fur itched, my shoulders hurt from the picking-bag straps digging into them all morning and I could've been at Deb's pool party that afternoon. I so resented Mum not helping with the harvest when I wasn't able to get out of it.

'Must be some fancy job for Elena to miss the pick this year, eh?' It seemed Frank was thinking the same.

Nonna Gia muttered in Italian and I caught her saying, '... *egoista*.' Selfish.

'It's a very important project on an old building,' I spoke up, suddenly defensive, though I'd been begrudging Mum only moments before.

'El was always smarter than you at school, Frank.' Connie chuckled, shaking her head as he gaped and exaggerated a hurt look at her.

'Come on, everyone, eat,' said Nonna. 'Frank, some more tuna? A meatball?'

Lena said, 'If I'm good at school, maybe I can go to the city too?'

'But we'd miss you too much.' Connie fought to hide her alarm.

'And what would you eat?' Nonna cried. 'You don't need to leave when you have us.'

'Oh, Nonna!' Lena beamed.

I bent over my plate as though I wasn't really paying attention, but I was.

Frank added, 'Besides, you can help Salvatore when he runs the farm one day.'

I glanced to Sam wiping his mouth, seemingly oblivious. And I couldn't help but wonder, when Mum got pregnant did anyone say to her, *you don't need to leave when you have us.*

Lena fell asleep almost at once in her camp bed, yet despite my tiredness after that day's harvest, I lay awake breathing the mozzie coil's pungency and listening to the crickets whirr. I longed for some chocolate. Something. That bit of lunchtime conversation had played over in my head all afternoon as we'd gone on picking. I wanted something sweet. Needed it. Maybe I could go and sneak a spoonful of leftover tiramisu from in the fridge. I kicked off the sheet.

In the summery night, the hallway linoleum felt almost warm beneath my bare feet. Frank and Connie had had it laid a year or so ago and its new vinyl tang lingered. It was softer than the thin lino we'd barrelled along as young kids when it was still Nonno Taddeo's house. *Smetti di correre*, he'd yell at us, *stop running*. But Lena, Sam and I wouldn't be stilled. Nonno's eyes showed he thought me the ringleader and in his balled fists and frustration I sensed he felt I was corrupting the others just by being there. Perhaps I was.

Hushed voices and the kitchen light made me stop unseen. Nonna and Connie were still up.

'... no, Elena has that big job on now.' Nonna's murmur.

I strained to listen, wishing Frank wasn't snoring so loud behind a nearby bedroom door. Keeping to the dim hallway, I leant closer, my toes curled on the lino.

'But she does seem, a bit ... unsettled.' Connie then, very tentative. 'Maybe if you—'

'No.' Again, Nonna, '*Quando la pera è matura casca da sé.*' *When the pear is ripe, it falls by itself,* meaning what was coming would come and one just had to be patient.

I wondered what that had to do with Mum. Again Connie spoke, but softer, and I didn't catch her words. Frank's snores persisted. I took a step closer, making the floor creak.

'Sssh, is someone there?'

As swiftly and quietly as I could, I hastened back to bed and slid in, forcing my breathing to still. Luckily, Lena kept sleeping. I heard Connie or Nonna come to the end of the hall to peer out to the darkened verandah. Moments ticked. I almost sat up and asked what they'd been talking about but I knew I'd only get in trouble for eavesdropping. Instead, I feigned sleep. The footfalls returned to the kitchen and soon after I heard their bedroom doors close. I lay pondering what they'd meant about Mum. Again, crickets chanted close and far off in the distance, the dog made sad howls. The house voiced its creaks and sighs. I opened my eyes. I'd assumed they'd been talking about Mum, but maybe it was about me.

After Frank dropped Nonna Gia and me back to her house – and Zucchero's gladness – we'd barely opened the windows before she asked me to go up the street and buy a bottle of milk. I must've had a look on my face for I was tired and just wanted to lie down and watch TV.

'We need it for coffee in the morning.' Nonna pushed some coins in my hand. 'And hurry, the shop will soon shut.'

More likely she wanted to have milk mixed with Tia Maria that night, which she usually did after spending a few days at Frank and Connie's. Also, as a rule, the foot bath and Epsom salts would come out too, Nonna placing the old dishwashing tub on towels to protect the carpet in front of her lounge chair, before immersing her red-painted toes.

I didn't look to see if the old man was on his verandah. I still felt bad for staring back when I hadn't known he'd had a stroke. The main street was quiet. The setting sun assailed the shut shopfronts, their glass glinting. I got the milk as the grocery shop was closing, and also a KitKat I slipped in my pocket. When I came out, the sun had already gone and streetlights were blinking on. The hotel bar on the other side of the road showed cheery light and people within. A Mondo Rock song drifted from it, 'Come Said the Boy', but it was silly to think it was a sign or had any meaning to do with Tim.

I crossed the main road, going out of my way up the side street that led to the railway station to take a closer look at the pub on the corner. My gaze ran along the guest rooms on its top floor to the far end at the rear where Lena had told me the Dinnings lived, wrinkling her nose at the idea of living in a noisy pub. But the dwelling part that appeared to be both upstairs and down at the back was furthest from the public bar and even from the other side of the road I saw it was well-kept.

Carnations bordered a cement path to the Hills Hoist between the kitchen and the chook pen, which was closed for the night. The last sets of French doors stood open on the verandah above. I realised one was likely Tim's room and in that moment wasn't sure if I was relieved or disappointed there was no sign of him. I turned back and hurried on past. I'd only been gone about fifteen minutes but it was almost dark already – twilight never lasted long in southern Queensland. Nonna would be worrying.

From the pub behind me came a soft whistle, not a wolf-whistle, more teasing or appreciative.

Heat rushed to my face. *Was that for me?* I couldn't tell if it came from the bar or above and kept going, head down. But then, something made me chance a wary look back. Someone had come out onto the verandah and leant on the railing. *Tim*. He grinned and gave a sort of wave. I smiled and held up the milk as if to say I had to hurry home and didn't glance back again. My steps were fast and light, my body humming. I'd got what I needed. I hadn't imagined it. He'd felt the same instant connection from the moment we'd met. I almost skipped into Nonna's street.

'Sofia!' Nonna Gia was waiting just inside the front gate. 'It's almost dark!'

'Sorry, Nonna.' *Shit*. I'd only been gone about twenty minutes by then. I got out the KitKat I'd planned to hide. 'I was buying this too.'

'Come on,' was all she said, taking the milk, and I hoped my face wasn't still flushed.

At least she couldn't accuse me of being a cupboard eater this time and, besides, how was it so different to her wanting a Tia Maria after the days out at the farm. But, in truth, just thinking of Tim doing that whistle … nothing could touch me just then. As I closed the gate, I found myself looking over through the falling darkness. The old man wasn't on his verandah.

❧

I waited until Nonna was in the shower and rang Mum, wanting to talk to her about what I'd overheard at the farm. But as soon as I heard the long-distance beeps overlapping her hello, misgiving clutched me. I wasn't sure I even had anything to tell really, just a lurking disquiet.

'Mum, it's me. We're back from the harvest. How's the building going?'

I heard her surprised intake. 'Well, I recall I'm only an assistant, of course …' Her tone was wry. 'But the building's lovely verandahs are now restored.' Neither of us mentioned that I'd hung up on her last time and as she talked on I didn't want to interrupt. Yet hearing the shower taps turn off, I wished Mum would hurry and finish so I could talk more before Nonna came out.

'Frank had a go that you weren't at the pick.'

Mum laughed. 'Probably misses me.'

'How come he got the farm?' I kept my voice low – the bathroom door was right across from the hallway telephone. 'Because he was the son rather than a daughter?' *Or because of something else, like me, perhaps,* was what I really wanted to ask.

'He's always worked on the farm, since he left school. Before he even left school. Where's this come from? You know running the farm wasn't something I wanted to do.'

The bathroom door opened and Nonna Gia stepped out in her brunch coat and a fog of steam and Felce Azzurra talc. Seeing her face, I couldn't tell if she'd overheard me.

'Well, Nonna's here,' I told Mum, saying goodbye and handing over the phone.

Leaving my door ajar, I listened but all Nonna spoke about was the peach picking and that season's prices. The sheer curtain billowed. I smelt and then heard raindrops pattering. Clouds must have come in. Good. Rain would make the grass grow faster for mowing.

'*Ciao, ciao, ciao, ciao.*' Nonna said her usual four goodbyes and put down the phone. She brought in a fresh waft of Felce Azzurra. 'I didn't tell Elena you came home in the dark.'

'What? It was dusk, not dark. God, I'm sixteen, I go to movies with friends at night.' Even if to the early session and we got dropped off, but Nonna didn't need to know that.

'Don't say *God* like that. I worry about you. Let's make a time that you must be—'

'I'll do the right thing, okay. I'm not a kid.' I couldn't believe it. I'd only come back a bit later. We'd been getting on so well before we went to Frank and Connie's. I loved how she'd been confiding in me and that feeling of being treated as more grown-up. Surely grouping me in with Lena for a few days hadn't undone all that. 'Look, it's fine, I don't need a curfew.'

Her eyes darted to mine at the word. She pressed her lips. 'You know, in the war—'

'The war was *ages* ago now ...' My earlier tiredness flooded back.

'But you don't know—'

'We did it in Modern History in grade nine,' I interrupted again. 'It was so boring.'

Her eyes became stony. 'And did they teach you how in Australia all Italians, even naturalised ones, had to register as enemy aliens? Even those born in Australia if their parent or grandparent was from Italy.' She gave a sharp nod. 'The police fingerprinted us and had photographs of us and we had to check in at the police station once a week.'

'What? *You?*' I stared and sort of almost laughed. Nervous laughter. It was so strange hearing such words coming out of Nonna's mouth. Like it was another person talking.

'That is a no then? They did not teach you that? How they would spy on us, raid our houses? Take things they never returned?'

'What?'

'Not only that, for many it meant getting interned, just for having Italian blood. Taken and put in a jail camp.' She looked at me harder. 'And all of us Italians had a nightly curfew.'

Stone by Stone

Gia noticed on the newspapers Taddeo bought that the headlines got wider and blacker as fighting ramped up in Europe in 1940, ending the initial quiet period of the conflict. In those first months after Keith had come to tell them of Menzies' announcement, she felt it seemed like they were hardly at war at all. Except that being 'Italian aliens' they had to register at the police station and supply four photographs of themselves, despite Taddeo having been naturalised as a British citizen of Australia.

'This is awful, like we are outsiders, criminals even,' Gia said to Taddeo when they got back to the farm afterwards and he nodded, looking downhearted, but they accepted it as best they could.

Then in June, Italy joined the war to fight against the Allies and the mail between Italy and Australia stopped, cutting them off completely from family. All of a sudden the war felt more real. It pained Gia to think of her mother's last letter. *Your father worries but does so too much. In Palmi the sun is shining and we are all in good health. It would be nice if you'd write about how your house looks inside. (Mrs Poletti keeps asking.)* At least they should be safe in Palmi, she consoled herself, knowing that during the Great War fighting had been focused in Italy's north. And at least Salvatore was too young to fight.

Being Italian aliens in Australia, she and Taddeo also now had to report in to their local police station each week and as they emerged from the one in Stanthorpe that morning, a man passing by on the footpath sneered, 'Bloody dagos.' Another stared and gave Gia a brief kindly look but was silent, for it was a tense time to show any compassion to Italians. While it hurt, in a way she understood. Australia might have been at war for many months but they were all only then really having to adjust to the seriousness of the situation.

Edie, who despite her reclusiveness kept up with all the news and opinions from the radiogram and newspapers, had explained to Gia that many Australians still grieved the loss of a generation of bright young men in the Great War and weren't keen to send off another lot. 'But, of course, young blokes born after the last war don't remember it and are keen to sign up.' What Edie said that most stayed with Gia however was that Keith, being over thirty and in a reserved occupation, wasn't expected to enlist for the time being. And even though deep down Gia knew she shouldn't hold that close, that she had no right to, she did.

As she and Taddeo waited out front of the police station for Serena and Pino to finish reporting in too, Vilma's husband, Carmelo, emerged from inside and, seeing them, came over.

'I had to give the *bastardi* my camera.' He shook his head.

'Oh.' Worry tinged Taddeo's voice. 'Do you think they might deport us all? I've been naturalised but I know others weren't able to. It was hard for me to save up the five pounds to do so.'

Carmelo shrugged, busy lighting a cigarette, and Gia sensed he thought Taddeo soft.

Seemingly oblivious, Taddeo looked around. 'Is Vilma not with you?'

'She's sick.' Carmelo glanced towards Gia, who remained quiet.

'But she must report in.' Taddeo's voice went a bit shrill. 'She might get in trouble.'

'Yes, yes.' Carmelo waved his cigarette and again cursed about the camera. 'I need a drink.' He strode off, headed for the hotel and, just after, Serena and Pino came back out of the police station.

The four went to Café Majestic for lunch and when Pino requested glasses of orange squash for them all Gia was swift to jump in, 'A sarsaparilla for me.' She glanced to the fancy soda fountain, determined it wasn't up to him to decide what she wanted.

But Pino got his back afterwards, knowing she and Serena would then be an hour or two buying supplies. 'Taddi and I might see if Carmelo is still around and have a beer.'

'Are you sure that is a good idea?' Gia asked Taddeo as they drew up out front of the hotel. Through the open windows she could see Jack Armstrong giving them a sharp look from behind the bar.

Pino half-laughed, '*Cristo*, Gia, surely the man's entitled to a beer if his wife has a sarsaparilla!' He cuffed Taddeo's shoulder, funnelling him inside before either could reply.

'Don't worry,' Gia said, seeing Serena biting her lip. 'They should be all right.'

She frowned. 'Oh, actually, I was thinking about Vilma.'

'Whatever for?'

'She must be quite ill not to report in and Carmelo's at the hotel leaving her all alone. I feel we should check on her but Pino won't take the horse and cart all the way out there.'

Gia rolled her eyes, but then she saw Keith's truck parked further along the street and looked about, hoping he mightn't be too far away. 'They'll be at the hotel a while. If you're that worried, perhaps we can manage a quick visit.'

Again, Gia sat in the middle of the Bedford's bench seat between Serena and Keith.

'We should have told Pino and Taddeo where we'd be,' Serena hissed in Italian.

Gia switched to English. 'We will be there and back in half an hour, Keith said.'

He glanced over to them both. 'If you only stay a few minutes.'

The dirt road out to Amiens was very rough with impenetrable virgin bush that rose in a forbidding welter right up to the roadsides. It cast sharp shadows, rippling the sun, as the truck pitched and laboured. Gia couldn't help her knee bumping Keith's leg, feeling the jolt of his warmth through the thinness of her cotton dress while Serena gazed out the side window, seemingly more preoccupied by Vilma.

'Must be very different here to Italy,' he ventured. 'Edie said you lived by the sea.'

'In Palmi.' Gia nodded. 'It means palms. My father works on a fishing boat.'

'Don't mind a bit of fishing myself, Giacinta, but I don't get much of a chance.'

She looked over at him. 'You may call me Gia, that is what most do.'

Keith kept looking straight ahead but was smiling. 'Righto then, Gia. It suits you.'

'Because it is short?' Her first joke in English.

He glanced at her bright eyes then chuckled. Gia felt a rush within her. She smiled back. They drove on along the uneven road. Again, their knees bumped.

'I saw an article in the paper, not long after Taddeo said your ship would've got in. They called it a bride ship.' Keith's eyes stayed looking forward. 'It said one of the women wouldn't come ashore because she didn't know her husband. Are most Italians here married by proxy?'

That stunned Gia a bit. She hesitated, unsure how much English Serena was taking in. Her own had kept improving during that first year in Australia but Serena still spoke to the Italian shopkeeper in Italian.

'Well, the lucky ones marry for love.' Seeing him frown, she blushed, wondering if he grasped her unhappy predicament or simply thought her foolish for entering such a marriage.

Again, he looked over and she saw his eyes flick to Serena who kept peering out the passenger window, not seeming to be following their conversation closely. 'Don't worry. I've always been lucky at cards ...'

'Oh?' Gia crinkled her forehead at what she realised must be an Australian saying.

'... unlucky in love.' Keith gave her a swift wink and she felt another fluster inside.

⌣

Not much further along they came to a stump that marked the entrance to Carmelo and Vilma's farm and Keith remarked, 'This'd be one of the old soldier settler properties that were abandoned.' At Gia's questioning look, he added, 'After the last war, the government gave land to returned soldiers. Though most poor blokes weren't farmers beforehand and had their own demons to battle. When the Depression hit as well, many didn't succeed.'

Blokes. Gia had heard Edie call men that too. It was endearing in a way. She let the word silently roll on her tongue. Keith was a bloke. As they drove in, she could see at once that Carmelo was a lazy farmer, likely putting more time and money into his suits and belongings, like the camera. Saplings from long-ago axed eucalypts had sprung up among the orchard trees that bowed in neglect without having been pruned or their fruit thinned.

Keith stayed in the truck and turned it around ready to go while Serena and Gia went up to the house. It amazed Gia to see the house was more a shed with pieces of corrugated iron among the timber walls, its few windows shut despite the sunny day. Serena seemed less surprised and Gia wondered if she'd somehow heard about it and that perhaps accounted for her concern. She let Serena knock. There was silence and she knocked again, more urgently.

From somewhere inside, Vilma yelled out, 'I'm sick. I can't have visitors.'

'Vilma? It's Serena, Pino's wife. I won't come in. I just want to see you're all right.'

'I'm good. Just sick. Sorry you wasted a trip. Carmelo's not here.'

Serena dallied. 'I know. I saw him at the hotel in town. Pino's not here either. I got a lift out. Please, Vilma, let me just see you for a minute and then I'll go.'

Again, there was silence. Gia glanced back to the front gate where the truck idled, ready to leave. She couldn't see Keith. They heard the scrape of the front door and she turned back in time to glimpse Vilma immediately push the door back almost closed.

'You didn't tell me *she* was here too,' barked Vilma and Gia flushed.

'Are you all right, Vilma?' Serena spoke gently. 'Is there anything you need?'

'No. Thank you. Just go, *please*. Carmelo might come back.' Vilma kept the door only ajar a crack but they'd both seen her black eye, the cut above her lip. 'I beg you. *Go*.'

The quiet seemed almost suffocating to Gia as they returned to the truck, despite their footsteps on the crunchy dirt and the engine's rumble. If Keith noticed something was wrong, he sensed not to ask. Serena sat in the middle. The truck ride back to town passed in silence.

'Anytime you need a lift again, just ask,' said Keith, wishing them well when he dropped them off.

Gia's eyes met his as she held the door while Serena climbed out. 'Thank you.' And she caught the slight inclination of his head as if to reassure her about what he didn't know.

The people, horses, cars and general bustle of the main street seemed so jolly and almost unreal after the rigid hush out on the Amiens farm where Vilma was.

'We mustn't tell anyone,' Serena said. 'Not even Pino and Taddeo, for Vilma's sake.'

'What? Are you sure?' Still troubled, Gia's hand went to the *cornicello* at her throat.

'What could they do? There's no way Vilma can leave her marriage.'

None of them could, Gia knew. Italians had no divorce. And if they tried to leave anyway, there'd be only talk, and shame, on them and their families, any possibility of a normal life ruined. But on the way home in the cart, she found herself staring out to the far distance with its wounded bushland where she knew Amiens to be and kept thinking about Vilma.

❧

From the kitchen window, Gia saw Taddeo striding back through the orchard looking somewhat alarmed. He took the back steps two at a time. 'The peaches have dangerously deepened in colour overnight,' he told her. 'We must start picking at once.'

'On a Sunday?' Gia put down the frying pan.

'The peaches won't wait for church. Early December peaches ripen in a rush and must do their softening in the train and shop window, never the orchard.' Taddeo was suddenly all business. 'If we don't pick the lot before Wednesday, they won't reach the Brisbane market until Saturday, when the agent clears his stand at low cost. And in this heat the peaches will be no good when markets reopen Monday. We'll need Pino to come and help us.'

'Us?'

Taddeo didn't quite meet her eye. 'Yes, we have to hurry. I'll need your help too.'

The three of them picked into belted hessian bags. 'Be fast but careful,' Taddeo said from the stepladder to Gia on the ground. 'Early peaches have more syrup than late season.'

The sun strafed down on them. Cicadas screeched at full pelt in the heat. Pino looked over from picking and Gia felt self-conscious in her dress and sunhat, her curls below the brim dripping sweat, knowing she wasn't as fast as them. But from

Pino's expression she sensed he saw she was picking well amid battling the discomfort of working above her head. A truce settled between them.

'Take care not to bruise them. It won't show now, but it will later,' Pino called to her.

Even in the packing shed, her sweat streamed in the hot, humid air ripe with fragrant peach and the unpainted bush-timber walls. Pino kept picking as Taddeo showed Gia how to grade the peaches into the same sizes and pack them so they wouldn't move in transit.

'Sort by quality,' he said. 'The price of a case is set on the poorest peach it contains.'

Gia nodded, thinking how different Taddeo was in this mission, his shyness gone in his assurance, knowing well his task. Nothing mattered but getting the produce to market to receive that summer income for them to survive the winter when there was none.

'I need to help Pino keep picking. Will you be all right here?' Taddeo was already backing away. 'Call me rather than pack wrong. If we have to redo it, we'll miss the train.'

Her eyes met his. 'Don't worry, we won't miss it.'

They packed until after dark, finishing just before the eight o'clock curfew, and at dawn Pino and Taddeo loaded the peach cases onto the cart as the mare stood patiently. Gia understood the train left that morning at seven and it was ten miles to the rail siding with the horse only able to go at a heavy walking load pace. They had to leave as soon as curfew ended at five. Just before it did, she went to put on her hat.

Pino grabbed Taddeo's arm. 'You're not letting her come to the siding, are you?'

Taddeo nodded towards Gia coming over to them, knowing he'd told her in bed the night before that the siding was a rough place of men and swearing and even a bloody nose for the chance queue jumper. 'I said if she wanted to, she can come to see the peaches go. She's earnt it.'

Having overheard, Gia smiled as she drew up to them both. 'Time to head off then?'

In the cool, early, tobacco-spiced air, the siding was alive with carts and men, banter, spitting and friendly ragging. Gia saw two timber freight carriages on the rail track with their side doors slid open but no train engine, and Taddeo told her that each grower was responsible for packing their cases under the stationmaster's eye until both cars were precisely loaded, ready to hook onto the arriving fruit train.

'But you must stay on the cart, Gia,' he warned. 'Women don't usually come here.'

She didn't argue, aware this was likely the only time he'd let her come along to this male domain but grateful he had this once. From the cart, she watched Taddeo load the peach cases, his muscles working. It was about a year and a half into their marriage but she still didn't feel any romantic love between them. And she was yet to fall pregnant, for they'd continued to be distant in bed. However she recognised Taddeo was a good man, decent and gentle at heart, if a little stilted in his manner, and he had allowed her to come to the siding when she doubted Pino would have let Serena.

Thinking of Vilma stuck on that isolated farm at Carmelo's mercy made her shudder. There mightn't be any divorce in Italy but there was in Australia, though Gia doubted Italian Catholics ever did so. And apart from the shame it would still bring if Vilma did divorce, she'd struggle to survive. Like Gia's parents, it was unlikely Vilma's could afford her fare back to Italy. The woman always bore the brunt of what ensued, Gia knew, unjust as it was. And so, they each had to make the best of it. But the reality felt harsher when the marriage had been by proxy.

She regarded the various men working the siding, Italian and Australian, and knew it was perhaps for the best that she didn't happen to see Keith among them.

Time Falls

The dark car trundled along the road and stopped out front of the farm. Peeking from behind a curtain edge, Gia saw the same two police inside it staring over towards her. They didn't get out but their presence crept onto the farm and up the steps into the house. It was unsettling and sinister, especially the not knowing.

Throughout 1941 the war drummed on, the orchards continued to bud and fruit, drop leaves and bud again, and she and Taddeo kept up their usual routines of the farm, town, Sunday Mass, reporting in and sometimes visiting the others, yet always keeping to curfew. All the while the car had started to appear with the men inside it watching.

'Just ignore them,' said Taddeo, but as Gia went about her chores she couldn't help often going to check if the men were still there.

After a while, the car turned around and headed back in the direction of town. Until it would return the next time.

Into the small suitcase, Gia packed another singlet for Taddeo. 'What about pyjamas?'

'Perhaps my older set.'

She put in one more pair of socks. 'What about the farm? The pruning, the picking?'

'It has to be left until I get back.' His shoulders sagged and she sensed him thinking of all the years spent hand-clearing, planting, carefully pruning. 'I should go over to tell Keith.'

Apart from the newspaper articles, they'd had word when they last reported into the police station that all Italian men should have a bag packed ready. Internments had begun.

'I'll make some *crostoli* to take.' Gia closed the suitcase lid and at Taddeo's look said, 'Edie likes them. It's not right her never leaving that house, don't you think?'

◆

Again, the two of them got on the old shearer's bike, Gia clasping a saucepan of *crostoli*. She felt Taddeo's arms holding her steady between them as he steered. The latest newspaper he'd got had reported that influential Italians, businessmen and those with Fascist links had been interned, but in the bright sun, Gia closed her eyes. Cool air gushed past. In that moment, it seemed impossible the police might arrest everyday farmers, shopkeepers and labourers, some who'd been decades in Australia. Then she thought of the police often watching their house and opened her eyes once more.

At the Dawsons' gate she gave the cowbell an extra-long rattle. Edie stuck her head out the geranium-pot window askance, but seeing Gia her smile broadened. They could hear hammering in the shed from Keith making packing cases to replace those gone with the last apple consignments. Taddeo went to see him and Gia avoided doing so, heading straight to the house's back steps.

'I'm so glad you're here.' Edie grasped Gia's arm. 'There's something I've been wanting to show you.' She led her to the louvred verandah where a painting sat on an easel.

Gia stopped still, not speaking. She stared. It was of a lavender and violet sea, hazy, with a pebbly shore and mountains behind.

'Keith reckons the sea is meant to be blue, not my deep-green or your mauve.' Edie hovered, somewhat nervous. 'I told him it depends on the place. Or how each of us sees it.'

Gia breathed the linger of linseed oil blended into cobalt violet and mauve applied to the canvas in dense strokes. In her pause, outside, a curlew's call faded. It wasn't the Costa Viola, Edie couldn't know how that looked, but its similarity clenched Gia's heart.

'It is very, very good, Edie.' She hastily wiped a tear.

'Oh, I didn't mean to upset you.'

Gia shook her head. 'It's the war. We can't get or send letters to Italy any more.'

'I'm sure your family will be safe.' But Edie's words sounded wooden.

'Could you try at the post office to send my letter? They might let an Australian?'

'I don't think they'd let me either, the countries are at war. I'm sorry, Gia.' Edie held her gaze, both knowing she wouldn't go into town. 'Well, I could ask Keith, but I doubt—'

'I understand – please don't ask Keith.' Gia blushed and turned away.

But Edie saw, Gia knew, for she frowned a little, though she pretended not to notice.

~

In High Street, Gia and Serena came out of the Arcadia Theatre with their arms linked after watching the newsreel. Gia could hear, behind them, Pino talking animatedly to Taddeo but she still felt hushed, blunted by what they'd seen. She didn't know what was worse. The raw, unfettered images that she conjured in her own mind in silent hours over the copper and scrubbing floorboards. Or the black-and-white sharpness of newsreels that recapped the steep escalation of Japan's bombing of Pearl Harbor, Singapore's fall … and the Allied bombings in Italy.

She gripped Serena's arm. 'It doesn't mean it's close to Palmi.' And Serena nodded.

But in the discord of coming from the theatre's darkness out into the glare, Gia pictured the red of Nonna's plaited chillies framing the kitchen window that showed a grey sea of warships. And her anxiousness for Nonna, her parents, Salvatore and the little school knifed at her. She hadn't been able to write to them since Australia's winter of 1940 and now it was again almost winter, two years later.

Out on the footpath, Josie, holding Vince by the hand, waved for them to come over. Alfio stood talking to Carmelo, and Gia saw Vilma with him and again her usual self. She looked Gia up and down and hooked a brow but gave Serena a smile.

'You all coming to the Majestic to eat?' Carmelo spoke in a cloud of tobacco smoke.

'Yes, do.' Vilma feigned a cajoling look, resting on Gia. 'You must be hungry?'

For once, Gia was glad Pino shook his head for them all. 'I must collect the horse and cart from Pierpoint's before it gets dark or the old girl mightn't get us back before curfew.'

Josie picked a reluctant Vince up into her arms.

'We're going with them,' added Alfio, 'since the police confiscated my utility truck.'

'*Bastardi.*' Carmelo shook his head and waved his cigarette. '*Ciao*, then.'

The couple sauntered off. Vilma threw a look over her shoulder – as if she had it all with her good-looking husband. Though to Gia, knowing what she now did about Carmelo, it was as if Vilma was walking off to nothingness. She wondered if their having stayed quiet was better or worse for Vilma and sighed. Just then, Jack Armstrong's hotel seemed loud and jarring as they neared the corner to get to Pierpoint's a little way beyond it.

Being late Saturday afternoon, the public bar bellowed with rowdy drinkers leaning out windows while others spilled from the door onto the footpath. But then, seeing the Italians approach, voices fell and eyes deadened in loathing, tracking them as they went by. Gia felt a prickling rush over her.

'Hey, you dropped something …'

Alfio turned around to cop a punch to his face, swiftly followed by a second. Blood spattered the footpath. Pino lunged, getting in a blow, but another fellow hit him, making him stagger back. Serena let out a cry and tore from Gia to him. In Josie's arms, Vince screamed.

'Please, we mean no harm.' Taddeo held up his hands in surrender, to laughter.

'Would you look at this bloke?' The one who'd first hit Alfio turned to his mates. 'Got paint thrown on his face, poor bastard.' He turned back and punched Taddeo.

Gia went to help him and Taddeo roughly pushed her behind him, shielding her. She looked wildly about the near empty street. 'Help! Police! *Police!*'

'They won't help *you*.' More laughter.

'What's going on out here, lads?' Jack emerged from serving, his beer apron on. 'Ah, bloody dagos. Clear off! Can't you even let us have a beer in peace?' Several cheers.

Alfio held a handkerchief to his bloodied nose. 'We didn't start it, they hit us!'

Jack came up close to them all, his eyes blazing, his voice dangerously quiet. 'I've seen the photograph, you scum. That's right. You, you and you, all in it.' His jabbing finger shook with hatred. 'Some picnic by the creek. All of you giving fucking Nazi salutes.'

In shock, none of them responded. Jack sneered and spat. It landed on Taddeo's shoe.

'You're all scum. And you're all goners! We'll mark off each and every one of you.'

The drinkers started up slow, deliberate claps and, stunned, the Italians backed away.

❦

Gia found Taddeo standing in the orchard. The late autumn air chilled her. Leaves fell in dry whispers, here and there. Soon the ground would be covered in thousands of them. She drew up beside him. In the distance they heard the barking dog that ran out at any car on their road.

'I've no war with Australia.' Taddeo's words came out in a sigh. 'I didn't even want to be in that photograph, let alone do the salute. I didn't even want to be in the Fascist youth.'

Gia pressed her lips together, silent. For once he had more to say than her. She saw his eyes move to the thriving trees that he'd nurtured from plantlets, the promise that they held.

'When pruning, there is always a choice. Immediate gain. Or for a tree to have a long life and produce quality. Better to neglect them late than to overbear a tree too early.'

They both began to hear the engine of a truck rumbling along the road.

'And not just with the next year in mind, but with the next and the next after that.'

Of course the truck came closer, right to their gate, but it wasn't Keith's Bedford.

Taddeo turned around. 'Gia, please go and get the suitcase.'

Her eyes went to his, suddenly realising, as if she'd been in a daze. Gia ran to the back steps, the cold air like glass breaking against her face. They kept the suitcase by the front door. She grabbed it and rushed out to see two armed police shoving Taddeo onto the back of a truck where half a dozen other Italian men already sat, Pino and Alfio among them.

'Wait!' She ran up with the suitcase and they threw it on after Taddeo.

'Be safe, Giacinta,' he called out in Italian.

'Taddeo!' She hadn't even a chance to say goodbye.

The truck took off, lurching the men backward. Gia watched, their dark eyes on her as they moved away. Then she thought of Serena and began running. Already the truck was gone from sight, its rumble fading as she ran in its wake, kicked-up dust hitting her throat. By the half-mile or so, a stitch nipped at her side but she pushed on and up through the open gate. Out front of the house, Serena was sobbing, slumped to a crouch, her dress hem in the dirt.

'It will be all right.' Gia hurried to her. 'Pino and Taddi are together.'

Serena raised her wet face. 'They took them. They actually took them.'

Gia cursed Carmelo's photograph but had a feeling the arrests may have eventually happened anyway, the way the war was going.

'Come inside and wash your face,' she said to Serena. 'It will be getting dark soon.'

'I don't want to stay here on my own. I'm too frightened.'

Gia deliberated. 'Then stay with me tonight.' She embraced her. 'We'll be all right.'

Night wind buffeted the tableland, turning the orchard into a frantic sea and testing the house's timber walls with fiercer gusts. A slack piece of roof iron clanked with each blast but mostly there were the usual creaks as the air grew colder. Lying in bed beside Serena made Gia recall her first night there with Taddeo but she didn't feel such helplessness any more. The door was shut and cotton curtains she'd made now covered the window glass.

'Where do you think they've taken them?' Serena asked in the darkness.

'First thing tomorrow, I'll ask Keith to drive us to the police station to find out.'

'Oh no, Gia, I'm afraid to go and be asking them and you can't be alone with Keith.'

'Course I can.' Gia moved onto her side, facing her. 'Jack Armstrong knew about the photograph and the police must have too, but how? I wonder where Carmelo had it developed.'

'I don't understand how they could take the men, leaving women and children alone.'

Another gust hit the house. Gia didn't answer. Her fingertips found the *cornicello*.

'Gia ...' Serena's voice came again in the dark. 'There's something you should know. I think that I might be expecting a baby.'

Space yawned as Gia and Keith sat at either end of the bench seat while the Bedford juddered towards town. Yet she was sure they both felt that which had been growing between them from the first day they'd met. At the same time, Gia was anxious for Taddeo. Perhaps she didn't love him in the way that made her feel that little flip in her middle, but he was a good person and she'd come to care for him. She kept her gaze ahead, barely speaking, and Keith seemed more reserved too.

At the police station, the sergeant spoke to Keith, ignoring Gia. 'You've just missed them. They've been taken from the watch-house to the train station for the internee special.'

Keith roared the Bedford past the hotel up the incline of Railway Street. Gia strained forward and gasped in relief to see the train still at the station. They ran to the platform and found a crowd gathered, hissing and jeering at the internees. Behind barred train windows the Stanthorpe internees stood crammed in with other Italians picked up from neighbouring areas, some yelling back at the crowd. Steam billowed and the train began to move.

'Taddeo!' Gia couldn't see him and tried to get nearer the train windows.

Further boos and taunting erupted from the platform. The train gathered momentum.

She saw Pino. 'Pino! Where are they taking you? They won't tell us.'

'We don't know!' he cried as the train pulled away.

Steam gushed over the platform. Shouts rose. Several men roughly pushed at Gia.

'Oi!' Keith grabbed her arm. 'She's with me.'

'That'd be right.' Jack came over. 'Bit of dago on the side while the other half's off.'

Gia assumed he meant Taddeo being gone and couldn't believe his words.

Keith baulked but thought better of it. 'Come on, Gia.' He began steering her away.

'No wonder his wife left him!' Jack shouted at their backs. 'And his sister like she is!'

Gia felt Keith again teeter, but he kept hold of her arm and got her safely to the truck.

⁓

Once more, space yawned between them as the truck sped along.

She glanced over to him, uncertain if it was true he might be still married. 'Keith …'

'Just— give me a minute.' He stared ahead. She saw his hands clench on the wheel.

Town buildings melded to houses then trees and bush. They'd never driven home so fast. The engine was straining. Then suddenly he turned earlier than their road, onto an old bush track, scrubby trees scratching the truck's sides. Gia had to hold on. They came to a clearing with mammoth granite boulders appearing to almost form a dwelling that she'd later learn had been a hideout of the bushranger Thunderbolt. It seemed a lonely place and she hid her uncertainty at being there. With the engine off, the hush was immediate but for a crow's forlorn, unanswered caw.

'I should've belted him.' Keith kept gripping the steering wheel, wrestling within.

She almost asked, but didn't. A breeze moved the crowns of nearby eucalypts.

'What Jack said ...' He exhaled, almost a grim chuckle. 'If only it wasn't true.'

Gia hesitated, burying her disappointment. 'Taddeo told me you were a widower.'

'Some assume.' Slowly, he released his grip. 'But my wife left. Because of Edie.'

'Oh.' It was so unexpected to be speaking alone with Keith like this. She felt disloyal to Taddeo right then being taken away. Yet at the same time, part of her understood Serena's warning about not letting herself be alone with Keith. Slow heat pulsed between them. But any such feelings were futile, Gia knew. She clamped her hands. 'She left because Edie doesn't leave the house?'

'No, Edie hasn't always been like that.' He exhaled slowly. 'You know, I've looked out for Edie since she was sixteen. Mum and Dad had died by then and the farm was ours. Some years later, I married Jean and she accepted Edie still lived there too.'

Gia shrugged. In Italy it was usual for various family to live together by necessity.

'Jean and I went to the coast for a stay. Autumn's the only time of year we could get away from the orchard. But it rained every day so we came back early, and found Edie ...'

When he didn't go on, she looked over. 'Found her where?'

Keith kept faced to the windscreen. 'With another woman. Romantic like.'

'Oh.' Gia couldn't hide her surprise. She'd never known of such a thing.

'Jean was angry that I wouldn't kick Edie out so she left instead.'

Silent, she regarded the enormous granite boulders, not quite sure what to say.

He sighed. 'The thing is, Jean is Jack's sister.'

'Bloody hell,' Gia burst out in her Italian accent and they looked at each other.

'I won't ask where you picked that up.' He smiled, but sadly. 'Jean always wanted to go up north where her sister was. It was a good excuse to go, I think. But she didn't want the scandal of her leaving to be on her or her family. So, before she left town, she told a lot of people about Edie, including Jack, of course. Many turned on Edie. She bears the shame of it.'

'You and Edie didn't think of leaving?'

'Why should I?' He became defensive. 'We're third generation on that farm.'

They were both silent. Gia thought of the way Keith had called her Giacinta instead of Mrs Poletti when they'd first met. How he'd encouraged her to learn more English rather than rely on others to speak for her. It had seemed such an unusually modern outlook compared to most men she knew and now she saw it again in his acceptance of Edie. Perhaps that was where it all stemmed from.

She heard the lonely crow call again. 'We should go—'

'Gia, you've been kind to Edie but if you don't want to see her, us, any more ...'

'It does not matter to me about this.' She didn't fully understand Edie but she did know as a proxy bride what it was to bear some stigma. And how much worse it must be not to even want to go outside a house because of a shame. 'She's been a good person to me.'

'Thank you.' He started the truck to leave. 'I'm glad nothing has changed.'

But it had. As they drove back, a well of feeling passed in the space between them that threatened each time their eyes met. And he as married to another as she was.

⌣

That afternoon, needing to do something ordinary, practical, amid all that was shifting and uncertain, Gia transplanted the chilli into a clay pot, for it had outgrown the tin. She sat it in a sheltered, sunny spot close to the house that was warmed by reflected heat from the water tank, for soon there'd be frosts. The air was already biting. In the orchards, more leaves bronzed on the ground in swishing rivulets, branches becoming naked for pruning.

Gia looked from the trees Taddeo had planted then back to the chilli pot and thought of her father saying, *think of us, but not so often you're too sorrowful.* And it was true that between the saying and the doing lay the sea. Surely in unassuming Palmi they'd be safe. And Taddeo would be too. Wherever he was.

She turned to Serena sitting on the back steps. 'I think you should stay here with me. We can walk next door each day to tend to the horse and chickens.'

Serena slowly nodded, still a bit bewildered, and unconsciously placed her hand on her middle.

'And I'll go and see how Josie is with Vince,' said Gia. 'Maybe take the bicycle.'

'Yes, do that.' Serena grasped that they needed to be practical. 'Can you ride it?'

Gia thought of the bike. 'Actually, I might walk. Maybe I'll see if Josie might want to come back and stay here with us too.' She didn't tell her of the scene at the train station, or about Keith's wife, or Edie. 'Keith said they should be allowed to write to us from the camp.'

'What about Vilma?' asked Serena.

'I didn't see Carmelo.' But Gia knew he'd be gone too and they couldn't leave Vilma out there all alone.

Creamy Soda and Musk Sticks

It felt strange being beside Nonna in her kitchen that morning. Everything was familiar – the chilli plaits by the door, the carton of eggs and flour packet on the table, Nonna Gia in her red apron that matched her toenails. But knowing now what had happened to Nonno Taddeo as the war escalated, how vulnerable she and the Italian women left behind on the farms had been, made me see everything differently, to see them differently, and feel protective.

The thing was, while what had occurred was new to me and I felt affected by it, it had happened long ago to Nonna. And though it felt different between us, she was pretty much her usual self, always getting on with it, and so she went about making *crostoli* as she'd planned to first thing that day, to take some to visit Serena later.

I watched as she cascaded baking flour in a pile on the pastry board, and cracked several eggs into a centre well that she called a *fontana*, fountain. 'I mix them all like this, see, Sofia?' She tipped in sugar straight from a paper packet. 'Then I put in grated lemon skin.'

'Lemon zest.' I didn't intend it to be mean, more of a gentle assistance, knowing Nonna's pride in her good English.

'Zest,' she said more to herself. 'Oh, I knew that, yes, yes.'

Intense citrus wakened our nostrils. I thought again of Nonna on the farm after Nonno was taken away. Then of Frank having the farm and Mum going to Brisbane on her own. I don't know why I hadn't thought about that more closely before. I'd so long been caught up in accepting that things were just as they were. The way Nonna had sounded so broad-minded about the Dawsons diverged from how she lived the more conservative Italian life expected of her, like worrying if I wore rosary beads with pearls to church or coming home at dusk. Perhaps she felt compelled to live like that. It irked me a bit that she felt she had to hide that openness she'd shown Edie. I guess because, deep down, I quite liked that part of her. It made me wonder about Mum having to leave and how much of that was Nonno rather than Nonna.

I watched her retrieve a saucepan of melted lard from the stovetop while humming along to 'Mambo Italiano' as Dean Martin again governed the stereogram. 'Can you believe he says *Calabrese* in this song?' She smiled and splashed in salt. 'A hint of the sea, Sofia,' and I supposed it reminded her of Palmi. She kneaded in the lard, her earrings and *cornicello* on its chain all dancing. 'Now … you can roll out each of these.' Nonna Gia divided up the dough.

I stepped over Zucchero busy dozing. 'How thin?'

'Like this.' She pointed to the moon of her thumbnail. 'And wash your hands first.'

Putting aside my usual reluctance to help cook, I made sure to roll well with the rolling pin, almost in time to 'Mambo'. Nonna didn't say anything but seemed pleased as she took over, using a crimped wheel to cut the dough into ribbons before threading each *crostolo* into a knot. All the while, I could smell the olive oil in the big saucepan getting warm.

'Time for them to chatter with the oil.' She chuckled. 'You get it?'

I didn't.

'Oh, Sofia, *tsk*, in Italy *crostoli* are also *chiacchiere*. Chitter-chatters or rumours. For *carnevale*. You can make them like angel wings or tie them into knots.'

I noticed as she put each of them in the hot oil that the wings were tied, but loosely.

Nonna teased the bubbling *crostoli* with a spatula and the kitchen filled with a rich, sweet aroma that was warm and cheerful. I hovered as she fished them out in crisp golden batches, laying them onto paper towels on trays. 'Can I sprinkle on the sugar?'

'Not yet. Another step first. I make them different this time.' She began melting dark chocolate and plucked two dried chillies hanging by the back door.

I frowned as she pounded them with her pestle and mortar.

'Chilli in chocolate? Nonna, you'll ruin it.'

'Just wait and see.' The liquid chocolate swallowed the smoothly ground chilli in one swirl and Nonna set about dipping both ends of a *crostolo* knot into the hot melted darkness.

'Lovely, delicious foods are comforting, Sofia, I know that.' She placed each of the chocolate-dipped *crostoli* back on the trays to dry and I sensed she may also be referring to me with the chocolates. 'But when we cook the same things that our ancestors cooked, it connects us to them, and it also brings us back to ourselves.' Only then did she let me sprinkle the lot with icing sugar. 'Here, taste.' She handed me one, chilli and all.

I hesitated, but there was no way I wasn't going to bite into it. There was a crunch and then a sweet warmth. It tasted good, I had to admit. Perhaps because it was chocolate and the chilli was subtle, or that I'd come to know the history of my great-great-grandmother giving Nonna the *Piccante Calabrese* seeds in a paper bud all those years ago. I smiled.

'So, it's all right then?' Nonna busied herself putting another batch in the oil and I was grateful she didn't gloat.

'Okay, so chilli in chocolate is all right, but it's not like *heaps* of it in spaghetti.'

She checked the clock then glanced at the shorts and singlet I was wearing. 'You can't go to Serena's like that. You might as well be asking for pneumonia.'

'Nonna, it's *summer*. Besides, do I have to go? I'll be all right here.'

'Why don't you put on that other dress I made you? And brush your hair!'

~

With a biscuit tin of *crostoli* in her arms and corset-girdle firmly on beneath a flowery dress, Nonna Gia led the way along the main street towards the Quart Pot Creek end. I walked just a little behind, glancing at the pub across the road but not seeing Tim. We passed Pierpoint Motors and went over the creek bridge to the cream-brick motel Serena and Pino had run since selling their farm some years before. Its sign glinted three and a half stars.

I found it hard at times to see Pino now, for he was the same age Nonno Taddeo would be had his heart not given up on him. All my life I'd known Nonno's friend Pino was like a brother to him and that Mum and Frank called Pino and Serena *zio* and *zia*, uncle and aunt, in the manner of migrants and descendants in a new country with no other family. But it was the first time I'd seen him since I found out he and Nonno Taddeo had been interned.

'Did you see how well the basil is going, no?' Pino greeted us as we came in the back way to the motel's larger end unit where they lived. 'In that garden bed over there. I put the chicken manure on it this year and it's going *boom*!' He slapped his thigh and grinned.

'I'll give you some to take home.' Serena smiled, despite knowing Nonna grew it too.

'I won't have a coffee,' Pino told us. 'Too much to do.'

'I brought *crostoli*,' said Nonna. 'We might not leave you any.' She was smiling.

He gave her a pretend old sparring look. 'I got to fix the shower in room nine.'

'Pino, for heaven's sake, please call a plumber,' Serena called out after him but he'd already gone around a corner and we heard his slides flapping away on the cement path.

I'd never really considered it before but the ordinariness of Pino that morning made me realise how so many people must go about their everyday lives with decency and normalcy while carrying hard memories from their past, Nonna and Mum among them.

Serena ushered us inside and at once went about making a stovetop coffee using Nescafé instant, the way some older Italians preferred to, she and Nonna Gia speaking Italian between themselves in the kitchen.

I perched on the sofa. It didn't have a plastic cover like Nonna's, it was covered in clean sheets instead. Spotlessly clean carpet emitted the same crisp meadow deodoriser smell. Along one wall stood the 'good' cabinet of crystal glassware and *bonbonniere* figurines with netted sugar almonds. A vase of fake flowers was on the coffee table and on the dining table a bowl of fake fruit, both on doilies. Up on the bare-brick wall hung a faux-gold–framed print of Venice's main canal. As far as I knew, neither Serena nor Pino had ever been there, but it was Italy.

Serena carried over a tray set out with pretty Italian pearl lustre cups and a matching pot that steamed. Coffee aroma drifted sharp and rich around the three of us. I smiled at Serena, thinking with concern of her being pregnant and afraid when Pino was taken away and interned, but of course I didn't feel I could say anything about this.

'Have another *crostolo*, Sofia,' urged Nonna and I dutifully bit into one, raining crumbs on my lap. She turned to Serena. 'She needs feeding with good, home-cooked food.'

Did she again mean the chocolates she'd sprung me eating? Or perhaps I was still just feeling caught out and self-conscious about that. If she told Serena I'd be mortified.

'My daughter-in-law says she's too busy working to cook.' Serena reached for one too. 'She buys those frozen meals. I took around a lasagne. It's the grandchildren I feel for.'

'*Si, si.*' Nonna's gold hoops jiggled. 'Elena is the same. It's Sara Lee or McCain …'

'Sometimes we get takeaway fish and chips for tea,' I baited them. 'Or even Chinese.'

'Oh, not Chinese.' Nonna screwed up her face. 'All those funny spices.'

'You put chilli in chocolate!'

She glanced at Serena and then, not about to be outdone by a teenager, her look turned crafty. 'Tell me, Serena, how's your grandson, Mauro? Sofia has been asking.'

That kept me silent for the rest of the visit, right up until Nonna Gia went off to the bathroom as we were about to leave. I carried the tray of cups and plates to the kitchen for Serena.

She touched my arm, smiling. 'You and your nonna are so alike in many ways.'

I almost sighed.

'You don't want to hear that at your age, I know, but it's true. In a good way. Elena too. The Poletti women are very strong. I've seen just how much they've had to be.'

I wanted to ask more with her mention of Mum's name then, but we heard a flush then the tap and Nonna came out of the bathroom, breaking the moment, and gathered her things to go.

Serena gave me a hug goodbye and murmured in my ear, 'Ask her about us women on the farms during the war.'

'What was that?' asked Nonna sharply.

'I told Sofia that Mauro already has a girlfriend at school but you never know.' Serena smiled, ever peaceable, and as we left, on impulse I swiftly kissed her cheek again.

The midday sun walloped down as Nonna and I walked back across the creek bridge and up the main street, both of us quiet. It was a relief to reach the shade of the awnings over the footpath.

'I suppose you want fish and chip takeaway for lunch.'

'And potato scallops?' I asked hopefully.

'Whatever you want.' She got out her Glomesh money purse and I knew I was forgiven for talking about Mum getting Chinese takeaway in front of Serena.

I held the paper-wrapped warmth to my chest, smelling salted hot chips and battered fish as we walked back into Nonna's street. A neighbour's sprinkler gave off a brief air of cool as we passed. Two magpies cheerfully ducked and strutted beneath the water for a drink and a bathe. Unsurprisingly, the old man was sitting out on his verandah, perhaps trying to get the scant breeze. In the burning noon light, I could see the intense blueness of his eyes but just then I was really only thinking of getting the takeaway to the back-patio table.

The afternoon stretched, hot and listless. I peeked into Nonna Gia's stifling bedroom, dim with all the venetians drawn but at least the fan was on. She'd pulled back the bedspread and lay on top of the sheets with a wet washer over her eyes, her feet with their bright toenails barely reaching two-thirds of the way down the bed. At least she'd taken off the tight corset-girdle. It hung over a chair, airing.

'Nonna? Are you okay?' I put a glass of water on her bedside table.

'I've got a "head",' she complained. 'It's that old oil they fry the chips in. Not like good olive oil.' I decided against saying it was more likely the heat.

'I might go for a walk. I'll only be a little while.'

She gave a grunt, and before she might say more I hastily sidled out the front door.

It was even hotter back in the snack bar amid the fug of fried food beaten down by a greasy fan. I let the fridge air waft over me for a moment as I got out a can of creamy soda.

Sipping through a straw, I ambled along the shopfronts right down to the cool of the creek. The metal bridge railing seared my arms as I leant on it so I just bent forward to see the water. Cloud shapes reflected on the dark surface, too wispy to mimic much. Over on the grassy bank, a family who seemed to be tourists were taking photos of each other by the water. Local kids kept to tree shade on bikes. Further along, perched in the shade on the top of a picnic table with his feet on the seat, sat Tim, head down, writing in an exercise book, not having seen me.

I hesitated. I'd hardly really spoken to him but it was such a brilliant chance to talk to him without Nonna being around. Perhaps the only one I'd get. Maybe I could just say hi and keep walking. I began heading over, turned back, then made myself keep going towards him until it was too late to stop without being seen. He didn't even look over as I approached, still absorbed in what he was writing. But then he must've sensed me and glanced up.

The wattage of those eyes up close suddenly made my hands sweat. He smiled and hastily closed the exercise book, placing it to his side away from me. I saw he had on a Midnight Oil T-shirt from a Festival Hall concert in Brisbane the year before. *So, he came to Brisbane sometimes.* I wished I'd changed from the stripy T-shirt dress I usually only wore at home. In the dry heat I could feel my limp curls had gone straggly.

'How's it going, princess?' He smirked. 'Or is it *principessa*?'

'Don't call me that.' I went pink, unsure if he was sending me up or it meant he'd taken the trouble to find out the word in Italian. 'Well, I just thought I'd say hi.' I stepped back as if to go but then took another sip. The vanilla soft drink bubbled in my mouth.

He moved along the picnic tabletop. 'Sit down if you want.'

'Okay, then. I guess.' I casually climbed up beside him, putting my feet on the seat too. 'Did you want this? I'm full.' I took the straw out of the creamy soda can. 'It's still cold.'

He rummaged in a pocket. 'Swap it for a couple of musk sticks?'

'Oh, okay. Thanks.' I sort of laughed. He seemed a bit old for musk sticks and they weren't really my favourite but I didn't say so. 'You're finished school, right?'

'A year ago.'

I bit into a musk stick, its pungency filling my nose. 'Do you work?'

'At the pub, of course. Mum and Dad expect me to take it over down the track.'

'But you're doing study?' My eyes slid to the book he was sheltering.

'No, uh—' Tim hesitated, seemed about to say something, then changed his mind. 'I guess you go to one of those Catholic girls' schools in the city. Too posh for us country folk.'

'What?' I flushed, a bit affronted, then realised maybe he was self-conscious or trying to protect himself. 'I go to a state school. Mum couldn't afford a posh one, on her own.'

'Oh, sorry, I didn't mean to say— I was being a bit of a dickhead really.' He didn't ask about me not having a father.

I shrugged but I was smiling. 'Yeah, *testa di cazzo*.' What was I doing? I never usually brought anything Italian into it with a boy, especially an Australian one.

'*Testa di*— ? That sounds really bad. Or is it dickhead, is it?' He laughed. 'Oh, right.'

'Well, since you learnt *principessa*, I thought ...'

We laughed together then and his eyes held mine a moment longer.

'You know, I don't usually show anyone this ...' Shyly, he handed me the exercise book and I suddenly wondered if he wrote poetry or something.

I opened it to a drawing of a tree. 'Oh.' He hadn't been writing at all. I slowly turned page after page of intricate lead-pencil sketches, mostly trees and the creek, some of the hills – obviously anywhere that wasn't in the vicinity of the hotel. 'You draw.'

He chuckled a little nervously. 'They're terrible, I know.' He drank from the can.

'How'd you learn?' I kept turning pages.

'I've just always liked to draw. No-one else in the family does. My dad reckons only sissies draw so I don't do it around him any more.'

'They're actually not bad.' I finished flicking through the pages, not truly showing how impressed I was. 'My mum's working on a special building project in the city. At the School of Arts.' I hoped he might think she was maybe an architect rather than a council project assistant. 'The rest of the family always worked on the farm but she didn't.' I heard myself babbling. 'If you want to, you should go to art school.' I handed the exercise book to him.

'Yeah, right.' He gave a short laugh.

I shrugged and with a smile slid off the tabletop. 'I better get back.'

'No worries. Good to see you.'

'You too.' We looked at each other for a beat. That whisper of something between us swelled. I hoped my bum wouldn't look too gigantic in the T-shirt dress when I turned to walk back. His hand moved over the exercise book. I wanted to tell him not to worry what his father thought, but I didn't know Tim that well yet, so I just said, 'You should do what it is you want to do. My mum did.' I smiled again and he didn't seem to know what to say so I left.

But as I walked home my assurance waned. What I'd said wasn't entirely true. Mum had only done the best she could with the hand she'd been given. And I hadn't been thinking. I was used to the city, not a small town and its talk. If Tim's mother, Dianne, went to school with Connie, she likely knew exactly why Mum had really gone to Brisbane. There must have been talk at the time. My cheeks went hot. It wasn't fair. I wondered if Tim knew too.

❧

When I came in the back door, Nonna Gia had a big, stiff piece of dried salted cod out on the kitchen table and was at the sink filling the container she would use to soak and rinse it in water for several days. Zucchero must have been locked in the laundry. Typical that she had to get out the *baccalà* that day, as if to make a point that her Italian fish dish would be superior to getting battered fish from the takeaway.

Looking up, she didn't give her usual greeting of asking if I was hungry. 'Sofia, where have you been?'

'I told you, out walking.' In the heat, the fish smell tugged at my stomach.

'Serena rang. She said she saw you sitting in the park with a boy.'

'What? Are you serious?' I hadn't thought of the motel being on the other side of the creek. And of course, nice as Serena was to me, she'd always be on Nonna's side.

'Who is he? It's not right you being alone with a boy. What will I tell your mother?'

I headed towards my room. 'It wasn't planned or anything. I just said hello.'

'Hello? Come back here. Hello to what boy? Some stranger?'

I flushed. 'Tim Dinning.'

'*Him*. Why? You shouldn't be talking to him.'

'Why not? Would it have been okay if it was Zia Serena's grandson, Mauro?'

'You're seen alone with any boy and it affects your reputation.'

'You mean because people will say I'm like Mum? 'Cause she got pregnant with me?'

'I'm trying to protect you. You don't know what might happen.'

I met her eye. 'I'm sixteen and I haven't done anything wrong, Nonna.'

'Well, just stay away from that boy.'

'What? No. Why?'

She kept looking at me, almost as if looking through me, or seeing something else.

'Perhaps I should call your mother.'

'Call her then! *Jesus*, we were just *talking*.' Exasperated, I strode to my room.

'Don't say *Jesus* like that!' she called after me.

I flicked off my thongs. One hit the spotless bedroom wall leaving a mark. I listened. The water pipes clunked as out in the kitchen Nonna resumed rinsing the cod rather than calling Mum. I sat on the bed, still smarting that she'd actually told me to stay away from Tim. The lady next door was hosing her lawn. I felt a little of its coolness reach through my side window and heard the magpies lining up on the fence.

I went over to the mirror and brushed my limp curls into a ponytail. Tomorrow I'd straighten my hair even if Nonna protested. I kept looking in the mirror. The magpies outside warbled. There was that which was kept buried and never spoken of, and then what was in plain sight yet unseen. Nonna saw in my face what I couldn't. It made her uneasy, I realised.

The mark left on the wall caught my eye and I felt bad about it. I bent to swiftly rub it away and went back out to the kitchen.

It Lives and Falls

Again, Serena, Gia and Keith sat on the Bedford's bench seat being jolted along the rugged road out to Amiens. Cold air coursed through a crack in Keith's open window, carrying the astringent, syrupy scent of the bush that grew hard up along the road edge. Each time the truck pitched Gia let her knee touch his. He allowed his arm to press against hers often. Perhaps Serena didn't notice from the far passenger seat, or pretended not to, bent on collecting Vilma. But to Gia a silent crescendo was intensifying between her and Keith.

The makeshift dwelling of corrugated iron and timber seemed even bleaker beneath wintry cloud. Serena knocked as Gia and Keith stood just behind her. This time the door opened almost at once and Vilma stood there, dressed as if going into town, although her hair was tousled. She held a cigarette, a reek of spirits beneath the tobacco as she exhaled.

'Well, if it isn't the three musketeers …'

'Vilma, is Carmelo gone?' Serena tried peering into the house. 'Our men were taken and interned too. We thought you might stay with us rather than be out here alone.'

'I'm glad he's gone.' Vilma tripped over her words. 'And his farm can go to hell.'

'Will I help you pack a suitcase?' asked Serena.

Vilma frowned. 'What for?'

'To come stay with us.'

'I'm not going anywhere with you lot.' Vilma looked straight at Gia, who reddened in front of Keith. 'Nowhere.' She stepped back and forth, steadying herself. 'But *you* can come back later.' Vilma smiled at Keith. 'On your own.' She tugged open her blouse's top button.

Gia pursed her lips and nudged Serena. 'If she doesn't want to come—'

'I don't.' Vilma exhaled more smoke. 'Just got some peace, at last. Go on. Get.'

Serena faltered. 'We could come back another day. When you're feeling a bit better?'

'Not you two, just him …' Vilma undid another button.

～

Serena trudged straight up the back steps when Keith dropped them home to Gia's house.

'Don't worry,' he said to Gia as Serena went inside. 'With the rationing, Vilma will soon run out of whatever grog her husband left. Maybe she'll think clearer then.'

'I don't know what I did but she's never liked me.' Again, Gia blushed. 'Anyway, before you go, I wanted to ask you how to fix this.' She led him underneath the house.

He regarded the flat tyre on the shearer's bike. 'Cripes, this old girl should be a museum piece. Perhaps I should teach you how to drive instead.'

'I don't think Italians are allowed to drive at all now.'

'No-one's going to see out here.'

She looked swiftly at him. Despite the gloom under the house, the blueness of his eyes blazed. Her middle somersaulted. From upstairs drifted Serena and Josie's voices in the kitchen. Hollow thumps as Vince skipped along the hall. She could feel the warmth of Keith's breath on her forehead they were standing so close.

'You're not tempted to go back to Vilma's, are you?' she murmured.

'Gia … what do you reckon?'

They kept looking at each other. What was between them teetered on a knife's naked edge. She knew it was wrong but just then she cared about nothing except that moment. Cold breeze swept through under the house. The orchard's last dead leaves skittered across the trodden-down path and were caught by the back step. Keith kissed her. Its heat, the force behind it, made her draw back. His eyes searched hers. Their lips crashed again, mouths impatient, meeting in rhythm.

'Zia Gia, where are you?' Vince barrelled down the back steps.

They tore apart.

Gia only just found her voice. 'Under here,' she called. 'Looking at the bicycle tyre.'

'I had better go,' was all Keith said as Vince bounded up. He ruffled the little boy's dark mop of hair. 'I'll see you next time, little man.'

'Why does he have to go now?' Vince asked Gia, staring as Keith started up his truck. 'Can't he fix it?'

Gia bent down to pick him up in a piggyback. 'It's just the way it is.'

That night the countryside lay still and silent. Not a hint of wind, no barking dogs. Even the nocturnal birds seemed hushed. It got cold, very cold, and in a quiet, icy creeping, a frost began blanketing the landscape. Inside the timber house, their breaths hung in the air.

'Are you awake?' Serena whispered to Gia.

'I might have to put more socks on, my feet are frozen.'

'Here, warm them against mine.'

Gia shuffled around in the bed. The tongue-and-groove timber ceiling gave a creak.

'Gia, I'm worried for you.' Serena had waited until she thought Josie and Vince would be asleep on the mattress in the other bedroom opposite, but she kept her voice low, for sound carried through the open fretwork above the bedroom doors. 'You and Keith—'

'There's nothing to talk about,' Gia shot back.

'If I can see it, soon others will. Imagine the shame if—'

'Are you happy to be married to Pino?' she interrupted again. 'Truly happy?'

'He is my husband for life, so I have to be.'

Gia moved her feet away. 'I want to be modern. Taddeo is not modern. He's my parents' choice, not mine. Do you like Pino being bossy, making all the decisions?'

'I like that he makes me feel safe. He is decent.' Neither mentioned Carmelo. 'And I don't mind him making decisions. I don't like that responsibility.'

'Serena, I want that responsibility. If I had my time over, I would never marry by proxy. Yes, Taddeo is kind, but we aren't close. I don't feel love for him, or him me.'

'You must only accept and understand one another. Whatever else is what it is. Besides, you can't unmarry. Hoping for anything else is useless.'

Gia, about to respond, let her breath go instead. She rolled onto her side, putting her back to Serena. Her fingertips went to her lips, again feeling Keith close. It was dangerous territory, she knew, for she could live a steady life with Taddeo, each chapter unfolding with expected evenness and tedium. It felt so unjust that she craved more, that more was in reach, tantalisingly close, and yet to grasp it could mean losing both that and what she already had.

❧

Avoiding the cowbell, Gia held down a line of the post-and-wire fence and silently clambered through. She felt like a thief keeping close to the house so she wasn't seen from the windows, and would've hated Edie to think she was avoiding her. But her draw to Keith wouldn't relent. The shed loomed, open and shadowy, and, to her disappointment, empty. Perhaps Keith was in the house. Then Gia heard a dull thud, and another, and she followed the outer shed wall to where he swung an axe, splitting wood using a flared stump as a chopping block.

Perhaps sensing her, he turned and she rushed to him this time. He left the axe in a log and met her, their lips seeking and hungry for what they'd barely tasted. All that was frail and undone sank away, and like fugitives they sought each other. In guarded quiet so as not to alert Edie, together they sat down on a grassy spot hidden from the house by the shed wall.

'Do the others know you're here?' He held her close, his lips in her hair.

'No, Serena has gone to feed her chickens and horse. And I didn't see Edie.'

'What are we doing?' he said. 'It's hopeless.'

'I know.'

They gazed at each other. He lifted his hand and stroked back her curls from her forehead, ran his fingertips along her cheek. 'You have such lovely eyes, Gia.' He tilted his head and kept looking at her then kissed her again, a soft, single kiss.

'What are we going to do?' she asked.

'Nothing.' He swore in a sigh. 'We can't. I feel bad enough, Taddeo gone like he is.'

She looked down. 'I know. I don't mean not to be true to him. But, I don't— love him. Or he me. I didn't choose him.' Gia looked again to Keith. 'I never expected to feel this.'

'Me either. But I saw what scandal did to Edie. You don't want to go through that.'

They were both silent.

'Gia.' He turned slightly. 'I've been thinking for a little while now, the way the war's going, I might … well, things are getting worse. It doesn't feel right me being here, not doing my bit.'

'No … please don't …'

'And I know I'm older, but I can't stay just because I'm in a reserved occupation.'

But she also knew why else. 'I know we must stop. We will stop. You don't have to do this. Just think about it first. Properly. Think of Edie.'

He was quiet. The orchard trees stood bare in obedient rows along the boundary fence and beyond it bushland rose up entwined. To Gia's dismay, her eyes filled with tears.

'Gia …' He drew her to him as she shook her head, unable to speak, and held him tight.

She felt she could have stayed like that always. The two of them hidden, warmed by the winter sun, in the pretence of no war, or marriages, or shame. She slanted her face to his and again they kissed, more fervently, lost in all that had been withheld, and that couldn't be. His hand on her leg moved the skirt of her dress slightly. Her fingers clasped his hair, drawing his mouth deeper into hers, knowing it was unlikely they'd be alone again.

Perhaps instinct made them stop, or Gia knowing Serena would be getting back and so she should too. They both stood up and he held her, kissing her one last time. Then Keith returned to cutting the timber. Each axe blow dropped with leaden finality as Gia snuck along the shed, the house edge and back through the fence.

Keith drove them all into town to the police station to report in. Josie sat holding Vince on the bench seat in between Keith and Serena, who rode in front too since she was expecting. Gia perched alone on the tray behind. She glanced through the back windscreen and Keith's eyes met hers in the rear-vision mirror. He looked away first. She gazed over the desiccated landscape, feeling its cold.

In town, they all avoided the hotel and after reporting in went separate ways for supplies and errands. Gia ventured to the post office in case a letter from her family might be there. It was daunting going into the impressive building with its tall clocktower and the lion-and-unicorn British coat of arms over the window, let alone to ask for mail using an Italian name. But to her surprise she was handed an envelope and saw at once it was from Taddeo. It had been more than a month by then since he'd been taken away.

Out front she sat on a bench and found the envelope opened out into a form page of about twenty spaced lines on which to write, beneath instructions in German, Italian and English to keep to those lines. Taddeo said he was at the Enoggera Internment Camp in Brisbane. *I am well and so are Pino and Alfio. We have food and a place to sleep.* His letters to her in Italy had always been short and stilted yet she could tell he'd written this in a general manner, as though a censor would be reading it before she did. And like his letters to her during their engagement, there were no words of love but there was care. *I hope you are well, Giacinta. Don't worry, the farm will be all right as it is until I can come back. Keep safe.*

Gia looked to the sky with the letter still open in her hand and felt terrible. Instead of Keith's eyes, she saw Taddeo's and their dark, gentle kindness. She bit her lips. It would be so easy if Taddeo was a cruel or callous man like Carmelo, but he wasn't. He just wasn't passionate or in love with her. In her heart, she knew she mustn't hurt him, or betray him. That Serena had been right. She should never have let herself be alone with Keith.

~

When they got back to the farm and Keith helped them down from the truck, he said, 'Gia, before I go, may I speak to you for a moment?' He sounded so formal, not himself.

Josie, who didn't suspect anything, took Vince's hand and went into the house carrying parcels. Serena gave Gia a look and followed upstairs with some other supplies.

He kicked at the ground. 'I've signed up,' he said simply. 'I leave in a few days.'

The blow took Gia's breath. But in rectangles of reflecting sky the house windows watched on so she carefully kept her face impassive. Keith scraped his boot over a stone.

'I wasn't sure if I should leave Edie. But, of course, she'll be fine.'

Still stunned, she had to drag the words out. 'Do you need me to get supplies for her?'

'Gia, Edie knows. About us.' He shook his head at her questioning look. 'I didn't tell her. She'd guessed already apparently. Then she told me she saw you leaving the other day.'

Gia didn't know what to say, her cheeks afire. 'Where will you go?'

'To Enoggera Barracks. For training. I don't know if I'll get leave before I'm posted.'

'So, it is goodbye?' She'd been straining to keep back tears but suddenly didn't care.

'It will be for the best,' he said. Neither of them touched the other. 'Stay safe, Gia.'

The same words as Taddeo. And now Keith too going to the same place as Taddeo.

❧

Gia walked out deep into the bare orchard and stopped. The silence clung. There was barely the hint of a current in the frigid August air. The landscape sat quiet, the men all gone from surrounding farms. She placed her hand on the trunk of a peach tree, as Taddeo had. Usually, he'd be pruning then. Hand-ploughing the vegetable plot ready for spring sowing. Spraying nicotine to kill the woolly aphids that hung in fine wisps from branches. She would be washing the tobacco stains from his work clothes afterwards. *You do the work inside the house and I do the work outside.*

But while she, Serena and Josie had carried on with the usual tasks around the house, what money remained from each of their farms' last summer consignments was dwindling. 'I can make a little on the side by sewing,' Josie had said, yet Gia knew it wasn't enough. Already they relied heavily on the eggs and vegetable patch for food, and they had no way of knowing how long the men were interned or how long the war may go on.

More people were turning on them too. In town, Serena, shy about her imperfect English after three years in Australia, had asked the Italian shopkeeper for flour in Italian and an Australian customer had then chastised her. 'Speak English! Aren't you one of us?' *But we aren't*, thought Gia, and it was such Australians acting like that who made it so. The word was that few hired Italians any more. And no assistance was available to them. Here they were, women, one expecting, and a child, left on farms with equipment they weren't sure how to use, not allowed to drive even if they knew how. Since Keith had left almost two months ago, they faced a ten-mile walk to report in and get supplies until they worked out how to use Pino's horse and cart. With no-one to show them and the prospect of the horse bolting, Serena still insisted on the long walk, even in her condition.

If only her parents were near or she could write to them for advice. *Worries fall away as you knead the dough*, Rosaria often said, making pasta. *But I would've looked to the sea*, Gia thought. Watching it change and soothe in the light. Even that had been taken from her. She peered at the sky, its cloudless stark winter blue a great sheet of sameness. Yet, as she continued to stare up into it, it seemed to reveal its spates and folds, flurries of particles, the atmosphere always moving, ongoing. *Sempre avanti*, she remembered Nonna would say. *Keep going, ever forwards.*

Beneath her palm, she felt both the rough and smooth of the peach bark, and as Gia brought her gaze back, she saw the orchard revealed its promise and wanting in the naked trees. Their graceful boughs and leaders, the delicate tracery of spurs and branchlets readying to shoot. It wouldn't be too long, she realised, before the returning leaves began to show and all that could have been done would have been missed. Struck, Gia turned and ran back through the trees.

Nearing the house, she was tempted to yell out her idea to Serena and Josie but first went into the shed to look where Taddeo kept most things for the orchard. The secateurs hung on a nail. Gia saw a drum of Black Leaf 40, the tobacco solution she'd scrub from Taddeo's work clothes after he'd used it to spray the woolly aphids. She crouched to read another drum label that read *Paris Green* and assumed it must be a fertiliser. The granite soil certainly seemed dry and coarse, so unlike the rich, loamy volcanic soil she'd known in Italy.

Suddenly the front gate screeched, followed by pounding steps. Frowning, Gia hurried out to see an Italian boy of about twelve running up to the house. Seeing her, he stopped and tried to speak but had to bend with his hands on his knees a moment to get his breath.

Gia turned to the house and shouted, 'Serena! Josie! Come out here!'

The boy straightened as the others came onto the steps. 'Ma sent me with a message. There's a lady out at Amiens that you know. She's in a bad way. You need to collect her.'

'What do you mean, a bad way?' asked Gia as the others drew up beside her.

His gaze skidded away, embarrassed. 'I think Ma said a man got to her.'

'Your ma is Mrs Russo, no? Tell her we will collect Vilma,' Josie told him.

'Wait, let me get him a glass of water first,' said Serena. 'And Josie, you should keep Vince here. Gia and I will go.'

Josie turned to them. 'How on earth are you going to get all the way out to Amiens?'

'Is that where you've run from?' Gia asked the boy, surprised and also impressed.

'We're a bit closer in, but yes.' Then he admitted, 'I got a lift partway from a farmer.'

'You'll have to try putting the horse on the cart,' said Josie.

Gia shook her head. 'It will be quicker to take Keith's truck. Maybe Edie can drive.'

❧

At the Dawsons' gate, Gia made sure to ring the cowbell and she and Serena hastened up to the house while the boy dawdled behind. Gia felt anxious about how Edie might receive her since knowing about her and Keith. She'd avoided going over there for the past couple of months after he'd gone and felt awful about it but feared what Edie might say, especially now in front of Serena. As it was, Gia knew they were coming to Edie with a big ask and wondered just how long it had been since she'd set foot off the farm, or if she could even drive.

Edie stood at the back door in her paint smock, her face unreadable.

'We're sorry to bother you ...' Gia's voice trailed off under her gaze.

'We need your help.' Serena took over. 'There's a woman alone out at Amiens. We need to go and collect her.'

Edie frowned. 'Pardon? I'm sorry, I don't know how I can—'

'Can you drive – the truck?' Gia deliberately didn't mention Keith.

'I haven't for a very—'

'A man has done something to this woman,' Serena persisted, her English all at once coming easier to her in the urgency of the situation. 'Her name is Vilma. We don't want to call the police until we see her first but must go now – she could be hurt.'

Edie looked from her to Gia and then the boy standing back a bit. 'Where is she?'

The four of them squeezed onto the Bedford's bench seat, Edie in the driver's seat still in her paint-spattered smock. She gingerly started the ignition, barely turning the engine over, and tried again with better success. For the first time, Gia realised just how high they were up in the cabin as Edie edged the truck down the incline to the gate and out onto the road.

'I'm a bit rusty,' Edie said, grinding the gears, 'so hold on. I know a back way.'

She rode the clutch most of the time, swearing under her breath, and Gia sensed it was better Keith wasn't there to see this. And yet, as much as she dreaded what they might find out at Amiens, a part of Gia rejoiced that Edie had finally been compelled to leave the Dawson farm for a bit. When they got to Vilma's, Gia half-expected Edie to stay in the truck but she got out with the rest of them, burying her trembling hands in her smock.

Mrs Russo was waiting by the door. 'She's inside in bed,' she told them, pulling her son protectively to her side. 'No-one asks for this type of thing but she's—'

'Who was the man?' asked Gia.

'Who knows? A travelling knife-sharpener I never seen before came door-to-door just yesterday. And there are still swaggies about, most decent, but some mean. He might return in time, or there'll be others. Best take her back with you. It's not right her being alone out here.' Mrs Russo nudged her boy and they headed back along the road to their own farm.

Inside the shed their shoes crunched over glass and a kitchen chair lay broken. It was really only one large room with a curtain to separate the bedroom and that was torn open. Vilma lay curled in bed, the covers over her. For an awful moment Gia thought she was dead but when Serena gently touched her arm, Vilma rolled over, listless and rambling in a reek of alcohol, her left eye blackened and jaw swollen.

'Vilma, it's Serena. We're going to take you home with us, *cara*.'

Her eyes still closed, Vilma shook her head. 'Too tired,' she moaned. 'Just too tired.'

Seeing Serena's gentle care and feeling awkward and ineffectual herself, suddenly Gia felt like she was the one who was five years younger out of the two of them, instead of Serena.

'I'll gather some of her things.' Edie's eyes met Gia's, and she could see that all was okay between them.

'Gia, help me get Vilma out of bed.' Serena pulled back the covers and they saw the dry rust of blood on the sheets. 'Come on, Vilma. A short trip and then you can sleep.'

Wrapping a blanket around her ripped nightgown, Gia and Serena supported Vilma on either side as she limped out to the truck. Gia could feel just how thin Vilma had become.

'It's all gone,' Vilma slurred, still drunk and in shock. From the truck cabin she peered out the windscreen through half-slit eyes, seeing not the bare trees but perhaps the fruit that had grown then rotted under Carmelo's neglect. 'It lives and then it falls ...' She became conscious of Gia being there and, perhaps trying to grasp some scrap of dignity despite her pathetic situation, she hissed, 'I'm not staying with *her*.'

'Vilma, that's where we're all staying,' said Serena. 'Gia is helping you.'

'It's all right.' Edie spoke up. 'She can stay with me.'

And while Gia thought Edie appeared to be in a bit of a dilemma too, considering her own past and reclusiveness, it was as if she saw or understood in Vilma something they didn't.

They sat Vilma in a hot bath with a bottle of gin Edie found in the lounge room cabinet.

'To kill off any seed of that *bastardo* still in her,' said Josie, who'd decided to walk over to the Dawson farm with Vince when she'd heard the Bedford return.

Gia didn't know of such things and was as surprised as when young Serena had taken the lead at Vilma's. She watched Josie tilt the bottle to Vilma's lips as she sat pink, sweating and almost asleep in the steaming water. It had often annoyed her how Serena and Josie deferred to their husbands, but watching them wash Vilma as best they could, carefully dry her and edge on a clean nightgown, she realised there was more to each of them that they'd kept from the men.

Edie appeared from out in the kitchen where she'd been keeping Vince busy doing some drawing. 'We'll put Vilma to bed in Keith's room.' She avoided Gia's eyes.

Vilma, semi-conscious, gave a moan as the others half-carried, half-walked her.

It was the first time Gia had seen Keith's room and she looked around at the timber furniture and one of his hats on a wall rack, a part of her absurdly, silently fuming that Vilma lay where he usually slept, her face on the pillow where he put his face. Vilma, of all people.

'It's good that she sleeps,' Edie said to them out in the kitchen.

Gia saw Edie's hands were still trembling. 'We'll be back first thing in the morning.'

'Then Vilma can think about telling the police.' Serena gave a firm nod, her hand again on her middle as if it were a sentinel to her baby, or comfort.

'Perhaps,' said Edie. 'But I'll be betting she won't want to.'

Pizzette Fritte

Well after midnight, I still couldn't sleep. I kept thinking of Nonna and Keith. Then him gone too. The women left on the farms. Of Vilma in that bath. I turned on the lamp. Its cosy glow in Nonna Gia's cream and apricot colour scheme was at once reassuring. And even though I felt unsettled, I was glad she'd confided in me about it all. That she trusted me to speak to as a fellow woman.

Hearing Nonna's faint snores, I didn't turn on the hallway light so as not to disturb her and padded out to the kitchen. The fluorescent stammered on. Zucchero was up too, peering out to the garden from the laundry window. I went and scratched his ears.

'What is it, gorgeous boy? What can you see out there?'

The Hills Hoist gleamed under the moon. The grass was getting long again from the summer heat and rain. Zucchero baulked as a bat or a night bird flew off from the vegetable patch, rattling Nonno Taddeo's makeshift trellis. It still stood, for he'd died before he could make a replacement one and I'd seen Nonna refuse Frank's offer to take it down. The new star pickets and wire remained in the shed. I thought of Nonno taken away to the internment camp and it hurt. Especially when I recalled him quiet and gentle in the garden, carefully tending plants, even if he seemed to avoid me. It was easier to feel softer towards him since he was gone and I wasn't picking up his reticence towards me.

I wandered into the lounge room and stood next to the TV set. The wedding photo sat faintly illuminated by the thinner reach of the fluorescent. I considered Nonno's solemn expression, the way he shyly turned to try to hide his birthmark, always looking slightly away. It seemed my whole life I'd never been able to quite catch the fullness of his gaze. Perhaps it was solely because Mum had had me before marrying, but I wondered.

Conversely, Nonna Gia's eyes at times looked straight into me, seeing beyond what I even saw in myself. I again looked at the chilli amulet at her neck, her lovely, smooth skin, her cheeks plumped by smiling. Still so young and yet she'd travelled to the other side of the world to be with a man she barely knew, leaving all her family behind for good. And little did that youthful woman in the photograph know of the challenges to come in those first years.

In that moment, standing in the quiet night, I felt so proud of Nonna's braveness. Not just in those war years but in telling me how she'd fallen in love with Keith. Perhaps once I'd have judged her severely for it. However, knowing now how it was for her married by proxy, I actually felt a bit sorry she and Keith couldn't be together. And sorry for Nonno too, that he and Nonna hadn't been a better match. That they'd had no choice but to remain married.

'Sofia, are you up?' Nonna's voice reached from the front bedroom. 'You all right?'

I realised the faint snores had stopped. 'Just getting a drink of water, Nonna.' I flicked off the kitchen light and went back to my room.

However, I still couldn't fall asleep. It occurred to me that Nonna trusting in me and how it made me feel more worthy, also made me realise how bare I felt about my father. The scantness of what I knew about him and how he was rarely, if ever, spoken about made me feel incomplete, a bit lost. Eventually I put on my Walkman. Anything to quell the loud silence that I so needed to fill.

I awoke to so much brightness streaming past the curtains I realised I'd slept late. Voices were in conversation just beyond my closed bedroom door and I pushed from sleep, trying to focus. Nonna was at the front door talking to someone. I sat up with a start, recognising Tim's voice.

'I'm happy to keep on doing the mowing, Mrs Poletti. Really, it's no trouble.'

'Thank you but Frank's back is better,' said Nonna. 'He would prefer to do it. Bye now.'

I heard the door shut and leapt up. Through the gauze curtain and venetians, I saw Tim close the gate behind him and jog over the road to his grandfather's place. He perched on the verandah rail with his back towards Nonna Gia's house while he talked to the old man.

'Sofia?' Nonna opened the bedroom door.

I jumped. 'What was Tim doing here?'

'You slept late this morning.' She spied a T-shirt hanging over a chair and straightaway folded it. 'He won't be mowing the lawns any more.'

'Why not?'

'It is better that Frank does it. You hungry? Get dressed. I'll cook you breakfast.' She went out to the kitchen before I could answer.

I stifled irritation. My main chance to see Tim, gone. I again looked out and saw the old man shuffling inside with a walking stick while resisting Tim's attempts to help him.

❧

'I think we need a break from Dino, Ma.' Frank shuffled through the records.

'How about Mario Lanza?' suggested Connie.

'I reckon a bit of ol' blue eyes, since he has such a great name.' Frank winked, sliding a Sinatra record from its sleeve and 'Come Fly with Me' began flowing from the stereogram.

I looked at Nonna, knowing she preferred cooking to Dean Martin but, as if oblivious to the change in music, she kept making *pizzette fritte*. I helped her top some of the crunchy, golden pizza doughs with crushed tomatoes, basil leaves and pieces of mozzarella that she then finished off in the oven. On the rest of the little fried pizzas she spread pesto, made from Pino's basil, and added on grated *Parmigiano* and thin slices of prosciutto to crisp beneath the grill. Connie got a bottle of Kirks lemonade out of the fridge and sat down at the kitchen table with the rest of us.

'Delicious, Ma,' Frank said around a mouthful, looking over with satisfaction to Sam and Lena busy chewing. 'Elena's missing a good feed.'

I straightened. 'Do you miss her, Uncle Frank?' It felt right being on Mum's side.

Connie stifled a chuckle and turned to Nonna. 'Ma's cooking her usual *riso di Natale* for Christmas Day,' she said of her mother's rice dish. 'You'll make your *baccalà* for Christmas Eve?'

'I'll do turkey in wine again for Christmas Day,' jumped in Frank, ignoring my comment. 'Bird in a big pot covered in a couple of bottles of red – after a few hours of cooking, as tender as.'

'A man cooking …' Nonna sighed. 'Your father would never have cooked a thing for Christmas but I suppose all things happen these days.' Her attention turned to Lena and Sam. 'You two haven't eaten enough. Don't you love your nonna? I got some cannoli for dessert.'

After we finished helping Connie with the dishes, Lena tugged at my arm. 'Let's go to your room.' She turned to Sam. '*Not you.*'

'As if I care.' He flicked Zucchero's tail, making him dart off to the laundry.

Lena launched herself on my bed and straightaway asked, 'Can I listen to your Walkman?'

'Pick three songs.' I sat cross-legged on the floor filing my nails as Lena read through each song list on the back of the tapes, determined not to miss an opportunity.

At least my bag with the chocolates in it was tucked safely back in the wardrobe.

The bedroom door was ajar and Frank's voice drifted from out in the lounge room as he sat down. 'I don't see why Tim couldn't keep doing the mowing. Saved me having to.'

'It is better you do it,' Nonna said, then, 'Shush now, I want to see that singing show.'

The television was clicked on at the high volume it usually was.

I was sure I'd heard Nonna tell Tim that Frank preferred to do the mowing. Frowning, I looked over to Lena but she had the headphones on while reading another tape cover. Part of me wanted to call Nonna out on it but for the time being it seemed better not to say a word.

I got out my writing paper. That morning, when I'd gone with Nonna Gia up the street to get groceries, I'd looked across and seen that the hotel had a private letterbox near the side gate. There was no way I'd ring Tim, not yet, especially if Nonna might overhear me. I looked at my writing paper edged in tiny stars. Maybe he'd think it childish. I liked stars, Mel flowers – but it was different writing to a boy, especially one slightly older. I could hear Nonna out at the laundry tubs so I tore off a page from a spiral notebook by the telephone. Better it looked to Tim that I hadn't gone to too much trouble anyway. I put away my writing paper thinking I hadn't written a letter back to Mel. But there just wasn't enough to say to her yet.

I chewed on the end of a pen. I didn't want to sound too keen. *Dear Tim?* No. Best to keep it casual. I wrote, *Hi Tim.* I chewed the pen more. *I hang out at the old train platform sometimes and listen to music. Some good views up there. You should bring your drawing stuff. I'll be there on Friday at about three anyway.* The pen went back in my mouth. Should I add, *if you happen to be free?* Or, *if you're not working?* Just to cover myself if he didn't show, or ... Stop it, I told myself. *Il troppo stroppia. Too much is too much,* as Nonna would say. Just sign off. I put an S, rather than my whole name, just in case someone else saw it.

'Nonna, I'm just going up to the newsagents to buy some chewing gum.'

She looked over from the tubs, up to her elbows in suds. 'Why do you want to chew like that on a piece of rubber for? Like a cow? Plenty of good food here.'

'I won't be long.'

And I wasn't. I don't think I'd ever walked so fast past the pub. But I did manage to flick the envelope into the letterbox as I went by. Now it was up to Tim.

Luckily, Nonna was roasting capsicums on Friday afternoon so I could easily get away on my own for a walk just before three. 'I promise I won't go near the park,' I told her. It was true.

At the railway platform's far end where I waited on a bench, a hedge hid the road so I couldn't see if Tim was approaching. Or not. I didn't want it to appear I was looking out for him, so I sat side-on, feet on the seat, facing the hills. I'd feel silly if he didn't turn up. It was quarter past three. I put on my Walkman as if just hanging out, not waiting, but kept it low.

'I guess you must be S.' Tim gently flicked my ponytail. 'I'm T, just behind you.'

I laughed a little, though if Uncle Frank had said that as a joke, I would've rolled my eyes. 'You got my note? I mean, I realise you did get it but did your mum or dad see it first?'

'Mum saw the envelope but I said it was from a mate, about cricket.' He sat down and I shifted my legs at the same time. 'I take it your grandma isn't too keen that you see me.'

'Oh, any boy, I think. Especially if they're not Italian.' It came out automatically and I'd long believed that, but since learning about her and Keith, I wasn't sure I was being fair.

'Hey, if we're meeting secretly, maybe I need a fake black moustache?'

I gave him a look but kept smiling. I'd had two boyfriends, both Australian, neither of whom Nonna knew about, and I'd learnt sometimes the Italian difference could get in the way. I could be going along thinking all was well and then … Like when my first boyfriend said, 'Gee, you've got lots of hair, hey? I mean, on your head but your arms too, not like a bloke but more than other girls.' I was fourteen and that summer Mum worried that I kept wearing long sleeves. Though, if I thought back, Nonna was pleased that I wasn't risking pneumonia.

The following year, after I'd realised my arms were no different to Mel's or my other female friends', I had a new boyfriend who I naively thought I'd end up marrying. I couldn't come to a party the Easter weekend as I had to be with the family at Stanthorpe and he'd said 'Oh, the Greek thing'. I'd thought he was joking. 'You mean Italian.' He'd frowned. 'Same diff, isn't it?' It occurred to me that he also called people from any part of Asia Chinese. Eventually it petered out between us. He wasn't an unkind person, I guess he just didn't think much about other cultures. But right then, breathing Tim's crisp scent beside me, it was easier to let such things go. And I felt it would be different this time. Besides, inside I was singing.

'You're right, the view isn't bad from up here. I'd forgotten.' He gazed around.

'So, what do you do at the pub?'

'Oh, general dogsbody really.' He laughed. 'Bring in kegs. Restock the bottle-o. Help Mum carry meals out from the kitchen if Fred's flat out. Make beds. Clean the urinal.' Seeing my crinkled nose, he laughed again. 'Not posh enough for you, *principessa*?'

I hit his arm. But as he got out his sketchbook and a pencil, I was thinking I would convince him to go to art school, one day. He started making rough strokes on the page. I peered over and saw he wasn't drawing the hills but rather the little timber station building.

I hesitated. 'I wasn't joking about my nonna. She can't yet know I'm seeing you.'

'Relax, it's not like I'm putting you in the picture.' Tim fixed those eyes on me. 'Not on paper anyway.' And he touched the tip of my nose, the ski-jump bit, and I didn't protest.

I watched him draw, wanting to stay for ages but on edge, careful of how long I was gone. That Nonna had been trusting me with her private past made me uneasy at not being truthful back. Yet somehow those old secrets didn't feel quite as crucial as her stopping me seeing Tim if she knew, and her not wanting him to mow made me think that would happen.

'So,' Tim kept drawing, 'what do you want to do when you finish school next year?'

'Me?' I sort of laughed and blushed. 'I don't really know yet.'

If I was honest, the one burning thing I wanted to do was find out about my father, as though I couldn't think about the next part of my life as an adult until that was resolved. However, there was no way I was going to bring that up and have Tim thinking I was some type of crazy. I mean, who didn't know much about their own father? My cheeks stayed hot.

He went on sketching and we talked about music. Time rushed by. The tracking sun told me I should get back before Nonna began telephoning Italians all over Stanthorpe, who'd be looking out their windows to report to her if I passed by. Just thinking of it, I couldn't help checking our surrounds but the platform was out of direct view for the closest houses.

'I'd better be going in a minute.'

Tim glanced to his watch. 'Yep, me too. Just a sec.' He did a bit more shading and then tilted the finished picture towards me to see.

'It's good. It looks exactly like it.'

'Ha, don't look too close. Keep it if you want.' He tore out the page. 'Then you don't have to worry who might see it and the invisible couple there too.' He met my eyes, teasing.

'Yeah, right.' My smile was wry. But he'd said *couple*. 'Thank you.' I didn't have any pockets so I folded it and put it inside my Walkman, flat against the tape. 'I really better go.'

'I'll stay a bit so no-one sees us leaving together if you like.'

I smiled again, and as I got up he caught my hand and pulled me close. His lips suddenly met mine, once, twice, and then his breath warm against my cheek.

'Same time on Tuesday maybe?'

'Okay.' And then I was walking along the platform, feeling him watching me, and when I turned to go, I saw he was. I waved and he did too.

Heading back with 'Soul Kind of Feeling' in my ears, it was as if my feet barely touched the footpath. By Nonna's street I almost waved to the old man sitting out on his verandah, but of course I didn't. Inside, the house smelt of roasted capsicum and Nonna Gia was at the table putting each one, still hot, in plastic bags to sweat as that helped remove their blackened skins.

'You hungry?'

'No.' I went to the sink for some water. 'You want help getting the skins off, Nonna?'

She looked up, surprised. 'Okay. That would be good.'

'I'll just put this away.' I held up the Walkman and went to my room.

I took out the sketch inside and hid it with the chocolates in the bottom of my bag. My fingertips brushed the foil and paper wrapper of a KitKat and I realised I actually was hungry, but I didn't feel like I needed one of the chocolates. I touched my lips and smiled.

'Sofia?'

I came back out, patted Zucchero, then washed my hands before Nonna could remind me. She eyed me as I sat down. I didn't even say a word about her soppy Dean Martin record.

Within the Fray

The women all sat on the big sofas in Edie's lounge room. Vilma smoked a cigarette, ashtray perched on the sofa arm. Outwardly, her injuries had healed, and what anguish and shame she was forced to carry she stifled and tightly withheld, deflecting any attempts at sympathy. As Edie foresaw, Vilma wanted no police to know, no chance of Carmelo finding out. Holding Vince on her lap, Josie kept peering dubiously at the art materials on the verandah. Gia waited until Edie handed Serena a glass of water and then went back to broaching her plan.

'Between us, I think we can do it. First we prune my farm and make any mistakes there.' Gia could just imagine if Taddeo was hearing this. 'Then Serena's and Josie's farms, but I think that's all we can manage.' She glanced a little self-consciously at Edie then Vilma.

'Don't look at me,' said Vilma. 'I care as much about Carmelo's trees as he does.'

'I think it's a good idea, Gia.' Edie nodded. 'And with Keith gone I've been promised a couple of girls from the Women's Land Army to help here.'

'See?' Gia turned to the others. 'Other women are having to do such work too.'

'It's because of food shortages,' Edie added. 'With so many farmers away in uniform, or … well, Australia still needs food for us all and our soldiers overseas, as well as the visiting American army. I read in the paper we even send food back to Britain to help them too.'

'So, we should always have a market to sell to.' Gia gave Edie a grateful look.

'But we don't know what to do with the trees.' Josie hoisted Vince back as he squirmed. 'And how can Serena work in her condition?'

'I know a bit, and Serena can do lighter work.' Gia remained stubborn. 'Besides, do we have a choice? Once last summer's money runs out, we won't even be able to buy flour.'

It was cold up a stepladder, secateurs in hand, feeling the same southern airstream that made the naked peach branchlets stir in shivers. Feeling the chill stiffen her hands, Gia understood why Taddeo had hung the little brazier from a ladder rung to occasionally thaw his fingers. She hadn't forgotten his words to her in the orchard that last day just before he was taken away. *When pruning, there is always a choice. Immediate gain. Or for a tree to have a long life and produce quality. Better to neglect them late than to overbear a tree too early.*

The trees must be still young, she thought, for she knew Taddeo had spent time up in north Queensland cutting cane and then laboured on other farms before he could afford the deposit on his own. And after that he'd cleared his land and planted the trees himself. If there was one thing that she might get right for him in his absence, it was to honour his orchard.

Gia called over to Josie at the next tree. 'Prune back a bit harder, to the next nub.'

Josie frowned. 'Won't we get less peaches doing that?'

'We can't be greedy and overburden the trees or we'll pay for it next year.'

'Next year?' Serena looked up, not having really thought about how long Pino might be gone. She bit her lip and with Vince kept picking up cuttings for stacking and burning.

From over to the side, Vilma half-heartedly added to the pile and examined a nail.

Gia got down and awkwardly moved the stepladder to the next tree. The wooden ladder was heavier than she'd expected it to be, especially with her wrist and hand already getting sore and blistered, being unaccustomed to the secateurs. She looked to the dozens upon dozens of trees yet to prune, took a deep breath, and climbed the ladder once more.

The further she got into the orchard, the more Gia began to realise that each tree was different with its individual characteristics, history and strengths, as well as weaknesses. And she was learning herself that one needed the temperament for pruning, an instinct for it, and that Josie had a temperament more for ploughing and its straightforward satisfaction. With this, Gia hid her own fatigue, knowing that any sign of her own reticence risked Josie becoming mutinous.

Edie kept to her house, but around midmorning she came over carrying baked scones, still warm and wrapped in a small tablecloth, along with a jar of homemade peach jam. They sat amid the trees and ate, grateful for the heat of the scones and what little warmth the sun gave. Only Vince stayed on his feet, eating fast and wanting to run off as Josie beckoned him back.

'Can you just picture if the men could see us?' Serena said, but she was smiling.

Vilma left most of her scone and lit a cigarette. 'A lot can go wrong between now and harvest. Why not just leave the trees as they are and get what fruit we can off them?'

Standing up, Gia brushed crumbs from her dress. 'I want to do this right, for Taddeo.'

She didn't mean to, but her eyes met Edie's then and while neither said anything they understood each other, and, for the time being, each kept the other's secrets.

⌣

When they got to Josie's orchard, having done Serena's in between, Gia was starting to hit her stride. She had to be faster, for September's impending spring warmth, and growth, meant the time for pruning had almost passed. With less to eat and much work, her dress hung looser, except in the sleeves, as her arm muscles had grown stronger. The women first pruned the orchard behind the house then moved to the front where trees grew right up to the road.

It was quiet but for Josie and Serena softly singing. Vince napped curled in a rug and Vilma, her eyes cynical, kept silent as Gia urged them on. As they pruned, it occurred to Gia that each tree was shaped not just by the pruning then or of the year before, but of the years before that. And it affected all those after. Perhaps, in some way, it was the same for them all.

They heard a vehicle coming down the road, gunning and skidding a little on the dirt, its kicked-up dust billowing over the trees, and looked at each other. Rarely did anyone come down the lonely dead-end road without a purpose. Their eyes followed the dust. A utility came into view, two men riding in the back and a couple more inside. They pulled up, laughing and raucous among themselves as they got out. Gia and Josie came down from the ladders.

The driver slammed the door and came closer, the other men shadowing him.

'Well, we had to see it for ourselves, didn't we, lads?' Jack Armstrong folded his arms. 'Bloody dago women thinking they can do men's work.'

Serena and Josie rushed to crouch protectively near Vince, while Gia stepped forward.

She grasped the locked secateurs like a knife in her right hand. 'What do you want?'

'You bloody eyeties think you can compete with our farms?' Another man glared.

Jack laughed. 'Look at them. I don't reckon they know what they're doing.'

The women remained still and quiet. Gia stood her ground, aware of Vilma just off to the side of her doing the same.

Another bloke sneered. 'They'd never get a spot at the siding anyway.'

'At least our CWA women are helping the war effort and calling for dago women to be interned too.' Jack mockingly doffed his hat to them and moved to go. 'Nice day for it.'

'*Nasi in culo,*' Vilma suddenly called out, as if in agreement, but while the other men appeared to think she was responding *nice and cool* in her Italian accent, Jack clearly realised she was taunting, even if he couldn't know that in a way she'd told them they had their noses up their arses.

He looked to Gia and Vilma, both standing somewhat defiantly. His gaze slid to Serena who looked fearful, both her hands over her showing pregnancy, and then to Josie holding Vince.

'Must get lonely out here with your menfolk gone.' His lips curled in a smile. 'Must get pretty scary all the way out here at night … *all alone.*'

Sniggering, Jack got in the utility, the others following. The women didn't move. He revved the engine, skidding up gravel, and drove off, the men in the back howling like wolves.

Those howls stayed with Gia the entire long, desolate walk they had home, all of them subdued. The far-reaching landscape that had felt to her before so fresh and alluring in its ruggedness and its long-limbed eucalypts and granite outcrops suddenly felt bleak, the air raw. She was glad Edie hadn't been around when the men turned up, knowing what she did about her and Keith and Jack Armstrong's sister. She realised just how awful the likes of them must have been to Edie to make her retreat into her house for years afterwards. There was no way she'd let this incident set back the small steps Edie had made in venturing out and making friends again.

'We don't tell anyone this happened,' she said to the others when they were back in her kitchen. 'Not even Edie.' Her eyes went to Vilma, who frowned, though more in curiosity.

'No, I'm writing to tell Pino.' Serena's eyes remained tearful.

Gia put her hands on her hips. 'And what can he do? It's just us here now.'

'Gia's right,' said Josie. 'Alfio will only worry and be unable to do anything. I don't want him suffering further in that detention camp.'

Vilma's hands quivered, though whether with fear or anger was unclear. 'The question is, how did they know what work we were doing out here?'

'We're being watched, obviously.' Gia glanced at Vilma's hands and she shoved them in her dress pockets. 'I'd say all Italians are being watched.' Although if she thought about it, she hadn't seen the dark car parked on the road since the men had been interned. It seemed that watching them had perhaps become more furtive and by locals too, not just police. 'You know, I've wondered who told Jack about the photograph from the picnic.' She kept looking at Vilma, who shrugged.

'Who knows? You can't trust anyone. I'd better get back to Edie before it gets dark.'

'Don't take the road.' Serena wiped more tears. 'Or perhaps stay here tonight?'

Vilma smiled. 'I don't think we'll get another visit tonight. See you in the morning.'

From the back door, Gia watched Vilma head off across the farms, the tip of a lit cigarette glowing in the grey dusk. She thought of how the two of them had stood defiant to the men while the others cowered. In a way, she agreed with Vilma that it was more likely Jack's style to be comfortable back at his hotel, laughingly picturing them out at the farms on edge at every tiny noise. He was the type to wait until they relaxed again and weren't expecting it. Even so, she went around locking every door and window, just in case.

Serena said to her, '*Il diavolo fa le pentole, ma non coperchi.*' *The devil makes pots, but not lids*, meaning whatever bad was done would be exposed in the end.

But Gia didn't answer. Thinking of Edie, she was starting to consider that men like Jack usually got away with what they did because others let them.

'What's for dinner?' asked Vince, and Josie smiled and gave him a swift cuddle.

'How about *stracciatella*? Eggs in broth?' Although there was no meat for the broth.

The stove was lit, a pot put on, and they went about the evening as best they could to make Vince feel like all was well and that they weren't straining to hear out into the darkness.

⌣

Vilma relayed to them that two Women's Land Army volunteers had arrived to stay at Edie's. 'One is called Beryl. She is twenty-two and seems capable. Her husband is fighting overseas. The other is Shirley, just seventeen, and has only lived in the city. Fortunately, it is Beryl's third farm job. Not sure how much use the city girl is going to be in the orchard though.'

Probably more use than you, thought Gia, watching Vilma again light up a cigarette.

As it was, Gia had to go next door to ask Edie about the fertiliser and saw for herself Beryl making fast work of the pruning on her own while Shirley and Edie picked up the cuttings for burning. She smiled. It was wonderful to see Edie out of the house with others.

'Hello! You are doing good work!' she greeted them, impressed by Beryl's pruning.

Hearing her accent, Beryl and Shirley each swung round and stared, remaining silent.

'Oh, I meant to say Italians live on the next farm,' Edie told them. 'But just women.'

The two looked at each other, still guarded, especially Shirley, but Beryl came closer.

'Just three of us and a little boy.' Gia almost explained about their husbands being interned but then didn't, hating how it made them all sound like the criminals they weren't. Besides, Edie would no doubt explain it to them later. 'It's our first time getting ready to harvest a crop,' was all she said, and it hung unspoken but understood that she and the other Italian women hadn't been offered Women's Land Army help like Edie had been.

Beryl took off her hat as though to get a better look at Gia, revealing her own auburn hair pinned to the side. She regarded her with sharp brown eyes and Gia suspected that with her husband at war, Beryl likely wasn't too keen on Italians, Germans or Japanese people.

At their continued silence, Gia turned to Edie. 'Is Paris Green the fertiliser?'

'I only know it as a paint colour.' Edie chewed her lip, conscious of the others' quiet.

'It kills rodents and insects,' Beryl said suddenly, seeking Gia's eyes. 'Or you can use Bordeaux mixture instead. There's a fertiliser shortage because of the war. Best to use manure.'

Shirley looked at Beryl as if she wouldn't have helped Gia herself but stayed silent.

'Thank you very much.' Gia smiled to Beryl and then Shirley. 'We mean no trouble, only to get a crop done so we have enough to eat.'

Beryl hesitated and turned to Edie. 'I'll need to go to the sawmill and get some pine to make the packing cases ready for when harvest comes.'

'Of course,' Edie agreed. 'Yes, Keith did that. Do you know how to drive a truck?'

'Pretty much. Trucks, tractors, I've given them a go on other farms.' Beryl smiled and again looked at Gia as if waiting for something.

Gia realised she'd mentioned the sawmill also for her benefit. 'Perhaps I can come with you and get wood for our packing cases too? We have a horse and cart but we are still working out how to drive it.'

'Well, someone might have to learn eventually,' Beryl said, and again addressed Edie. 'With the petrol rations we may all need to use it. That truck looks like it's a guzzler.'

In misty wet splendour and spring leaf, the orchards showed apple and peach blossoms of pink and white. Beryl suggested the rainy day was best spent making the packing cases and it worked well to do so all together in Keith's shed. The timber pieces from the local sawmill were rough bush pine full of knots and splinters, and Gia was aware she wasn't the only one timid at first in hammering in nails, then growing more confident. She could hear Vince complaining he wanted to hammer too, pushing away the colour pencils and paper Edie gave him to draw.

'Here.' She thrust a Sunshine Milk tin of old nuts and bolts to him and his eyes lit up.

Pleasant rain pattered on the corrugated-iron roof and Gia looked from the boxes out the open shed door to the blossoming orchards. Amid her hope fear clutched, for there was a long way to go yet and it all could easily come to nothing. Would Taddeo be proud or cross she hadn't let the orchard be, as he'd said to. It was hard to know. Perhaps he hadn't realised he'd be gone so long. Surely he understood she had to do something to survive in his absence.

'We need a song, eh?' Josie began singing a Calabrian folk one and Serena joined in.

Edie smiled yet Gia saw Beryl and Shirley exchange sideways glances at it being an Italian song. But it did lift the ambience in the shed. She looked around, noticing nails Keith had put in the walls to hang tools, an old pair of his boots now cobwebby, some rust-flecked tins of fasteners. A part of her relished this, feeling close to him, despite her despair for what couldn't be. Yet she also felt guilty, having been thinking about Taddeo just moments before.

At least they each remained safe in Australia for now. The last newscast she'd heard on Edie's radiogram had reported Naples being bombed because of its port and Gia thought at once of her parents, Nonna and Salvatore, and all she knew. How Naples sat near the ankle of Italy's boot, Palmi further south at its toe. And she worried whether it was further south enough.

'Oh!' Serena stopped singing and clutched her middle. 'The baby must have heard us. It is moving.'

Josie leant over to place her hand to feel. Her eyes shone just as Vince's had earlier at the tin of old nuts and bolts. Vilma and the others smiled, even Shirley, and Beryl said, 'Hey, I know a song we can sing, do you know this or I can teach you ... it's called "You Are My Sunshine" ...'

Later, when they got home, Gia passed the chilli plant and saw the rain had woken its tiny white flowers. In her gladness, she crouched to peer closer, despite the drizzle that kept falling on her back. The *Piccante Calabrese* lived on. Just seeing the blooms and thinking of Serena's baby, she couldn't help but feel that maybe everything was going to be all right.

～

The rain stopped not long before daybreak. Everything dripped. Gia awoke as its lulling patter ceased and saw the faint dawn grey illuminating the window. Serena was still breathing heavily in sleep beside her. Rain drips carried quiet resonances from the gutters and downpipes.

Without warning, the front door crashed open followed by the bedroom doors. Police swarmed in yelling. Serena screamed. From across the hall Vince began shrieking in tears and fright.

'Get up! All of you out here!' the sergeant shouted. 'This is a raid!'

In their nightdresses and holding Vince in his stripy pyjamas, Josie, Gia and Serena huddled in a corner of the living room. The police yanked open cupboard doors, tipped out kitchen drawers onto the floor, upended mattresses, tore through Gia's glory box of linens.

'Where's the radio?' demanded the sergeant.

'We don't have one!' Gia cried.

The sergeant turned to a constable. 'Get a ladder and check inside the roof.'

Vince was hiccupping in fear and Josie strove to keep him quiet. The sergeant looked them up and down, Josie clutching Vince and Serena pregnant. Gia was sure he took in the meagreness of the possessions they'd strewn about, none of which were on the banned list for enemy aliens. She noticed the constables throwing him uneasy glances, wondering what to do next.

'Look downstairs,' he said gruffly. 'There must be something here that shouldn't be.'

Gia glanced at Serena and Josie. None of them dared move as they heard the police tearing through the shed and the packing cases stored beneath the house.

They took the old shearer's bike, cramming it awkwardly into the police car boot. Its lid wouldn't close so a constable had to tie it down, denying the sergeant a dignified and swift departure. Gia stood at the window watching until the car headed off up the muddy road.

Summer Storm

I sealed the envelope of my letter to Mel, drew tiny stars on the back and came out to the kitchen looking for a stamp. The salted cod still soaked in its container of fresh water. I wrinkled my nose. Outside in the vegie patch, Nonna Gia was bent over, slip showing, Zucchero circling her stockinged legs. She paused to pat him and croon something I couldn't hear, making me smile.

'Nonna!' I opened the back screen door partway. 'Do we have any stamps?'

'In the tin on the fridge.' She hesitated. 'And can you get my cardigan, the green one.'

In this heat? 'Where is it?'

'In my wardrobe, at the far end.' Bending down again, she put her backside to me.

I glanced at the kitchen clock as I went past. Half an hour before I was meant to meet Tim at the train station. It felt hot in the house and even stuffier in Nonna's bedroom. As usual, her room was imbued with the cloying citrus of her Santa Maria Novella perfume. Almost on cue leading up to her birthday each year, Nonna hinted to Mum and me that she loved that perfume so much because they put Calabrian bergamot in it. A small glass bottle of it sat on top of her duchesse next to the usual crystal trinkets, a tissue box and a ticking clock. What looked like one of Nonno Taddeo's old combs with a couple of his grey hairs still entwined held my gaze a moment.

It felt funny opening Nonna's wardrobe when she wasn't there. For many years it had stood in the old bedroom of the farmhouse, and in this brick house the wardrobe still held its same clove and old shoe scent, at once rocketing me back to childhood when I'd hid in there. Trying to find the green cardigan, my hands scrabbled among the coat hangers, for Nonna hung several items on each one. And then, down the far end where she'd told me to look, I noticed a wooden box about the size of a school case jutting from behind the shoes.

La lingua batte dove il dente duole. The tongue always goes to the sore tooth. When I was younger, I went through a stage of trying to find some item to do with my father. I had no idea what I was searching for really but the notion of coming across something like an old photograph of my mum and dad together was too tantalising. Even though Mum had told me many times that there weren't any and in all my searches of our flat I didn't find one, I just couldn't quite believe her. There had to be something. Maybe even hidden at Nonna's house.

My eyes wouldn't leave the box. Why there'd be something about my father in there I don't know, but then, there could be. Maybe being saved until I was eighteen. I'd seen that in a movie once. A letter from a guy's dead father given to him when he turned twenty-one. I strained to listen. The house was quiet, Nonna still outside. I drew out the wooden box.

It had a worn leather handle and little clasps on front. No lock. Definitely something inside by the feel of it. Barely breathing,

I opened it and exhaled in disappointment. Inside were old artist's paints. Tin tubes, half-used and hardened with time; tiny, squat glass bottles showing paint hues dried and cracked inside; brushes stiff and losing their bristles. It must have belonged to Edie Dawson. Strange that Nonna had it. I went to close the lid and felt the bottom tray shift slightly. I moved it again and realised it had been lifted away at some stage.

Levering up an edge with my nails, I saw hidden underneath were several envelopes aged to a pale flaxen. Old-fashioned looking letters, before Mum's time so before my father too. Nonna Gia's letters. Warmth brushed my arm as Zucchero pressed against me. I gasped. Nonna must have come inside. I flung back the envelopes and shut the box, fumbling with the clasps. I got it back in behind the dresses and shoes just as she came down the hallway.

'Sofia?' She regarded me. 'I thought I had some stamps in the tin but I don't.'

'I can't find that cardigan.' I tried not to sound breathless, feeling myself sweating.

She went past me and took it from underneath another cardigan on a coat hanger.

'Oh. Right. Well, I'm going to the post office now to send Mel's letter.' I edged past her and Zucchero to get my bag from my room. 'I might look at the shops too while I'm out.'

'Which ones?' She trailed me to the front door. 'You want some money?'

'I'm okay, thanks, Nonna.' I glanced to the old man watching on and hurried up the street.

I thought of the police upending drawers and going through Nonna Gia's glory box in their raid on the farmhouse. Not that I'd done anything that terrible, but Nonna showed she trusted me by telling me that stuff and there I was looking inside boxes I shouldn't and now meeting Tim again without telling her. I couldn't stop sweating. Why she'd wanted the cardigan was mad. It was muggier than usual for Stanthorpe with a storm brewing. I could feel my curls puffing out more by the way they moved on my head and cursed I hadn't had time to put up my hair.

The brick-and-render post office with its tall clocktower and lion-and-unicorn British coat of arms above the front window didn't appear to have changed much in decades, and as I went to the front counter I found myself picturing Nonna Gia there picking up Nonno Taddeo's letters. It must have been intimidating for her to come into such a British-style establishment as an Italian woman during the war, especially to collect mail from her interned husband.

While Taddeo was my nonno, I felt sad for Nonna that what was between her and Keith ended when he went to war. She'd done 'the right thing' and remained with Nonno but how hard it must've been to have stayed married by proxy when they weren't in love. I guessed she'd had to retreat into the Italian community or risk being shunned by it, and the Australian one too, as Mum had been in a way, for falling in love with an Australian. But I felt impatient with all this. It didn't stop people mixing or falling in love, just constrained and made secret what shouldn't have to be.

In my letter to Mel, I'd written, *I've met a boy who's a bit of a spunk, an older boy,* as if to show that trumped John Peters or anyone we knew from school at the parties she was going to. *And he has the most amazing blue eyes.* But I didn't tell her much else, not even Tim's name or that he worked at the pub, though I knew she'd have been impressed by that. It was just too risky if Mel wrote back about it and Nonna happened to see. I'd at least first need to tell Mum and maybe she could help me to convince Nonna about Tim.

Climbing the hill to the train station, I saw a bank of storm clouds clustering in bruised unison along the farthest mountains, still a way off yet. Tim was already waiting at the end of the train platform. As I got closer, he turned and gave me that smile and a sunniness rushed through me.

'Hello.' He held my cheeks in his hands and kissed me straightaway, for longer this time, and I could taste that he'd just eaten a raspberry ice-block, his mouth still cool.

We sat down and he flicked the ice-block stick off the bench to the ground. I didn't say anything but I would've put it in the bin.

'I was at Pop's yesterday and saw the grass at your grandma's is getting pretty long.'

'Yeah, well, I don't reckon Uncle Frank is that keen to mow it.' I kept looking at him and raised my eyebrows a bit.

He laughed and put his arm around me. 'Oh, I get it, me just being there might corrupt her granddaughter.' Tim looped one of my curls round his finger.

'Whatever. Forget my nonna, what's the deal with your grandfather?'

He looked puzzled. 'What do you mean?'

'I see him staring across at us all the time.'

'Does he? I wouldn't think anything of it. He can't get around much since his stroke.'

I halted briefly. 'Is he— is he all right in the head?'

'Yeah. He seems sharp enough. Just can't talk any more, poor bugger. Anyway ...' Tim drew me to him again and said into my hair, 'Let's not waste time talking about them ... you smell so pretty, Sofie, like peppermint and flowers ...' And again, I let his lips find mine.

~

'Sofia! Come and help me make the *baccalà alla Calabrese!*'

Great. I turned off the TV and came into the kitchen. Beyond the café curtains, lightning flickered in the looming violet-black sky. It felt very still and close, making more pungent the pieces of floured cod Nonna Gia was adding to onion and garlic already frying in olive oil. She motioned for me to pass her an old glass Bickford's cordial bottle of wine that Alfio and Josie made at home from their grapes.

'How much?' I unscrewed the cap.

'I'll do it.' She grabbed the bottle and I sighed, causing her to look over. 'All right.' Nonna gave me a poke. 'You add the chilli.'

'*Me?* How much?'

The first hint of thunder rumbled from the sky.

Her eyes narrowed. 'Well, however much you think you'd like to put in.'

'None.'

She gave me a look and handed across the ceramic chilli pot of her dried *Piccante Calabrese* flakes. It had its own small wooden ladle. I scattered a spoonful into the pan. It didn't look much. Another. She didn't say a word. I deliberated and added a larger spoonful, wanting her to be happy. A breeze began to stir out in the garden, and at the next thunder Zucchero rushed under the table. Nonna stirred in the chilli and added cherry tomatoes picked from her garden that afternoon, bay leaves and basil. And finally, stoned green olives from an old Citrato antacid jar, diced potato and some cooking water.

She looked at the clock and I saw too that *Perfect Match* was starting in a minute.

'We must first shut all the windows before that storm gets here,' she insisted. 'Hurry now,' and I knew it was useless to argue that it was still hot inside.

Perfect Match blared. My sweat trickled. I eased my legs up from the couch plastic. Only the back screen door allowed some fresh air into the stifling house swamped in the aroma of cooking salted cod. I wondered what Tim was doing at the pub just then. What would he think of my current setting? We couldn't only ever meet at the train platform.

'When is Frank coming to mow?'

The *baccalà alla Calabrese* simmered.

Nonna kept looking at the TV screen. 'He should have done it before this rain.'

The storm edged closer.

I kept my face to the screen too. 'Maybe you should get Tim back to do it.'

Lightning flashed. The TV buzzed and snowed as the transmission fell in and out.

'I better shut it off.' She got up. 'We should eat now, in case there is a blackout.'

We sat at the table, Zucchero hot at my feet but refusing to budge. I could see the storm's violent flight seething closer, flashes lighting up the café curtain lace behind Nonna. Gusts carrying rain scent shuddered the back door that she had left open since it was sheltered by the patio awning. My scalp was damp, but maybe that was just my hot head.

'Here we are.' She dished steaming *baccalà alla Calabrese* into bowls.

We each ate a spoonful. The tingle stung me at once. My mouth hummed and prickled. I made myself swallow. My throat started burning, then my chest. Through watery eyes, I looked over at Nonna Gia nonchalantly eating another spoonful. I ate some more as if all was well, knowing this chilli heat was down to me. A thunderclap made us all flinch. Zucchero took off into the laundry. Outside, a few drops plunked the awning and then came the deluge. Nonna casually reached for a drink of water, cheeks flushed, a slight shine to her forehead.

'It's burning you too!' I cried. 'I'm sorry, Nonna. I put in too much.' I thought guiltily of how she'd spent days soaking the salted cod in a container and diligently changing the water until it was ready to cook with.

Shrugging, she took some more. 'It's not so bad.' But then she smiled. '*Non tutte le ciambelle riescono col buco.*' *Not all doughnuts come out with a hole.*

'What—'

'Things don't always turn out as planned.' She put down her fork. 'You want me to make you something else?'

I shook my head. It was my misstep. I'd eat it. But I took a mouthful of bread first.

'A little at a time at first is kinder. It gradually readies for what is to come.' She clearly wasn't as affected by the heat as me so it was a fair thing to say, and sensible. Then, seeing the bite I'd taken out of my slice of bread, she pointed to it and added, 'Make sure you finish all of that piece or you'll lose one year of your life.'

And so, the seesaw teetered back again.

After the storm passed overhead, steady rain kept falling into the night. I lay in bed listening to it and wondered if Tim was still awake too, lying in his bedroom that opened to the hotel verandah as the rain poured beyond. We'd both sensed that connection between us from the first instant and Nonna must have seen it too, making her anxious. But I was determined to have my own story, not one that copied Mum's and ended in everyone being upset. And I didn't want to spend any more time staring at cloud shapes. I already knew what I wanted.

A strip of light appeared under the bedroom door – Nonna Gia going to the bathroom during the night as usual. I rolled onto my back. The gauze curtain floated at the open front window. The rain fell straight down. I dozed. But the strip of hallway light stayed on beneath the door. Perhaps Nonna wasn't well. It was my fault with the chilli. I pushed back the sheet.

At the door, I heard a soft resonance of music and followed it out. Nonna sat on the lounge, lit only by borrowed light from the hallway. The stereogram lid was up and the black shine of a record whirled as Dean Martin sang 'Everybody Loves Somebody'.

I frowned slightly. 'Are you all right, Nonna?'

'Of course. Did I wake you?'

I shook my head, perching on a couch arm. 'Why do you like Dean Martin so much?'

'Oh, he's Italian, of course.' The answer came rehearsed, as if to a familiar question.

'But isn't he American?'

'His father was Abruzzese and his mother parts Siciliani and Napoletana.'

'Why is it so important he's Italian?' I couldn't keep the weariness from my voice.

'What do you mean?'

'Because you couldn't be with— Well, it's why you don't want Tim being around, isn't it? He's not Italian.' I paused. 'And no-one talks about my father because he wasn't Italian.'

I held her stare in the shadowy light. The stereogram spun softly on. I waited, half-hoping it might prompt her to say something about him, but as usual when it was about my father, Nonna clammed up. Suddenly I burst into tears and ran to my room.

'Sofia?' She flapped in her slippers after me.

I got into bed, facing away from the door. 'Go away.'

The bed dipped as she sat on the side with my back to her. I sensed her deliberating.

She sighed. 'I understand it is hard, *cara nipotina*.' She stroked my hair. 'I do.'

'Not really, you don't.' But I let her keep caressing my hair. 'If you're so against Australians you must be against me too since I'm half-Australian.'

'How can you say that? You're my granddaughter and I love you.'

The rain poured on outside, both of us quiet.

'Sofia, never think I'm against Australians, *cara*. Never ever. Especially when—'

The catch in her voice made me turn my teary face to her. She glanced to the drifting gauze and I half-expected her to go mad at me for having the front window open.

But she only sighed and her gaze fell back sadly. 'Especially when there was a time that I loved an Australian more than any other person I'd ever known.'

And straightaway I thought of the letters concealed beneath the base of the artist's case that I'd assumed were Nonno's. How

I hid the chocolates in the bottom of my bag. Perhaps what was between her and Keith hadn't ended when he went to war, even if she'd stayed with Taddeo. Nonna surely hadn't needed her green cardigan on such a warm day. Maybe she'd hoped I might find the letters. Her way of telling me what was so difficult to say ... But I hadn't read them and so I couldn't be sure. I looked at her again.

Frost Fires

Loud banging on the back door made Gia wake with a start.

Serena clutched her arm. 'Oh no, another raid!'

'Gia! Josie! Wake up!' came Beryl's frantic voice. 'Frost! There's frost!'

Gia leapt out of bed, the chill of the timber floor invading her bare feet. She hurried to open the door and Beryl barrelled in. 'We must light fires to save the setting fruit.'

'Now?' Gia looked out into the pre-dawn darkness. 'But the curfew … We're meant to stay inside from eight at night till five in the morning.'

Beryl glanced at the kitchen clock. It was just after four. 'Well, it's up to you but you could lose your whole crop otherwise.'

In hastily grabbed washtubs, barrels and tin cans, they lit dampened straw and green wood. Striking a match, Gia thought of the risk they were taking. She pictured the smoke curling towards town, its sharp scent leading the police straight to them

181

breaking curfew. How they'd be arrested. For while mostly men got interned, at church they'd heard that some women had been taken in too, along with their children, as there'd been no place for them to stay at an orphanage. But then, Gia knew, without a crop they'd likely go hungry within the year.

Between the seven of them, they could only defend three of their four orchards and hope that Josie's, the furthest away, wasn't ruined. They worked quietly, shifting through the freezing pre-dawn darkness to fan the smouldering fires with pieces of packing case as Vince slept on in the house. It was a later than usual spring frost but they'd come to learn that Stanthorpe could get frosts anytime between April and October, being Queensland's coldest place where it sat high on the tableland. And the air dipped colder just before sunrise.

Gradually, the smoke wisped and drifted over the orchards in a dense layer, protecting the young fruit. Gia watched it in tangled relief and fear. Sunrise wasn't until after the five o'clock curfew lifted, closer to half past five, but it usually became light before the sun appeared.

'Do you think the smoke will reach into town?' she called to Edie over the boundary.

Edie looked to the distance. 'I'd reckon other orchardists will have frost fires going too that should mask it.' But she didn't sound entirely confident.

In the smoky hush, Gia tensely willed the sun to rise, for curfew to lift. Her arms ached but she kept fanning, her gaze revisiting the hint of paling to the east. In the distance, the brown dog barked. Gia heard Serena gasp. She froze, straining to listen. They all did. Yet no sound of an approaching vehicle followed. Above, the smoke sat, trapped by the cold, still air. Clutching the piece of packing case, Gia went back to fanning, alert to any sound.

Curfew passed and finally the sky began to lighten. The first kookaburra call rang out. Over beyond the boundary stand of eucalypts, sun peeked weakly through leaves and crooked dead branches. Gia sighed. The fruit was safe, and they were too. They could douse the fires.

'Well done, all of you!' Even she heard the shake of relief in her own voice and tried to cover it with a bit of a laugh, self-conscious as Vilma curved her a look.

'This calls for a good breakfast!' announced Beryl.

On her way inside, Gia noticed the smoke had also protected the chilli pot by the house, its green, heart-shaped cherries just starting to blush. She smiled.

With eyes red-rimmed and clothes acrid from smoke, they gathered in her kitchen. Sunlight streamed through the dissipating haze and Josie cooked eggs. They squeaked in the pan while Vilma readied some old bread to fry. All of them sagged with exhaustion but cheered in relief, despite not knowing what damage there may be to the setting fruit at Josie's orchard.

Beryl eyed Serena pouring boiled chicory from the coffee pot. 'I might wait and have a cup of tea back at Edie's, love.'

'I'll try it.' Shirley held out a cup, enticed by the rich aroma in the cold morning.

Gia glanced at Edie sitting on the back step, a plate on her lap as she ate a fried egg. The others were busy and talking. Vince stood on his chair singing an Italian nursery rhyme. '*Il codino, d'un topino, fuor da un buco, un dì spuntò, venne il gatto ...*' *The pigtail of a mouse, poking out a hole, one day it dawned, the cat came ...* Gia was glad in a way that Beryl and Shirley didn't understand it. She went over to Edie. 'Are you still doing your paintings?'

'Sometimes. At night.' Edie smiled. 'But these days I'm mostly too tired by then.'

Gia hesitated. 'It's been a little while … have you heard from Keith?'

Edie cut another piece of egg and kept eating. For a moment, Gia feared she wasn't going to answer, but then she nodded. 'He sent a letter. He's going well. Still at Enoggera.' She looked at her and spoke more softly. 'Let him go, Gia – there's no point to it, you know that.'

She bit her lip. 'Yes.' But it felt as impossible as fighting the moon's pull on the sea.

'Here.' Vilma nudged Gia's arm with a plate rim. 'Your egg. You must be hungry.'

Vilma's eyes danced, unreadable. Gia swiftly took the plate and looked away, unsure if Vilma was having the same old go at her or if she'd overheard her and Edie talking of Keith.

~

It played on Gia's mind and she needed to see if Vilma might say something about Keith without anyone else around. Glancing at Serena's burgeoning middle, she said to her, 'I'll walk over to feed the horse and chickens for you today.' Serena smiled in thanks. 'Vilma can come with me.'

'Whatever for?' Vilma was tying on her headscarf to help the others plant beans but Gia saw her notice Josie struggling to push the hand-plough. 'Oh, if it's what Gia wants.' She blew her a sardonic kiss as Gia glowered.

They walked along the road, Gia up ahead while Vilma dawdled, smoking a cigarette again. Gia pondered if at some stage Edie had taken her back for more of Carmelo's supply.

'You're going slow on purpose.' She turned accusingly. 'Do you want to be like Carmelo and let the others do all the work?'

Vilma shot her a look of venom but said nothing. Gia smugly sensed her walk faster, if deliberately not quite catching up to her, and at least Vilma hadn't said a word about Keith.

Serena and Pino's farm seemed very quiet, more quiet than usual. Gia stood for a moment looking around. A faint breeze flustered the trees. Then she realised she couldn't hear the usual tutting and bustle of the chickens and hastened over to their hutch.

'Bloody hell.' Gia put her hand to her mouth.

Vilma drew up to her. 'What is it?' Then she saw. Every chicken was dead. 'Foxes?'

'No, look, their throats are cut clean, like by a knife. And not long ago either.'

'Jack Armstrong's lot?'

'Could be anyone.' Gia looked all around. As lonely as the farm felt, who knew what eyes were lurking behind trees and brush. She prickled. 'Oh no ...' She spun towards the shed.

'What?'

'The horse!'

The shed was empty. The mare's rope had been cut.

'You think they've stolen her?' asked Gia.

'I don't think they'd keep something that obvious. More likely like the chickens.'

Gia's eyes met Vilma's. She shook her head. 'Not a horse. We have to find her. We'll need her come time to get the cart to the siding.' Already Beryl had been mixing kero and Shellite in with the rationed petrol to make it go further.

They searched around outside and under the house and Gia ran on into the orchards with Vilma tailing her. In her urgency, Gia almost twisted an ankle on the uneven dirt. She paused to catch her breath and caught a glimpse of movement near the back boundary. Vilma came up beside her and they both saw the mare tearing at tufts of grass through the split-rail fence.

'She's still got some rope on, thank God,' whispered Gia. 'You go left, I'll go right.'

It took a while to catch the horse and Gia led her back. 'We have to take her with us.'

'The chickens too,' said Vilma. 'Think about it. It'll be hard without their eggs but it's been ages since we've had some meat. The carcasses will make good broth as well.'

Gia made a face. 'Will they be safe to eat?'

'We'll decide once we get back but they seem pretty fresh still.' Vilma climbed into the hutch and again Gia looked around, wondering if the culprits were still nearby watching.

She thought of hearing the dog barking at dawn when they'd been out fanning the smoke, how there'd been no rumble of a vehicle that followed, and was glad she hadn't let Serena come on her own to feed the animals that morning, especially in her condition.

It occurred to Gia they must be an unexpected picture as they returned along the road, she leading the mare and Vilma carrying the chooks by their feet, throats still dripping blood on her dress. She glanced over at her, both perturbed and with some respect. Often she felt Vilma was a cold person, that stoniness perhaps born from awful experience. And yet she couldn't help but feel from that same experience came a force that, in this instance, gave Vilma a certain practical strength.

'*Gobba a ponente, luna crescente. Gobba a levante, luna calante,*' Vilma suddenly chanted in a sing-song voice and Gia looked up to see the faint moon setting in the midmorning sky.

Hump to the west, crescent moon. Hump to the east, waning moon — the little nursery rhyme they had been taught as children in

Italy to learn the lunar phases, except the moon shapes were the opposite way around now they were on the other side of the world. Their eyes met. Gia began to smile but Vilma snickered as if laughing at her. And that was the thing with Vilma, Gia never felt she could quite trust her. And she hadn't forgotten about the picnic photograph.

The young peaches they'd protected from that late frost thrived over the next few months and the time to harvest came on fast. Together, they picked in a flurry, Gia crying out, 'Be gentle! Taddeo said December peaches have more syrup than late season, so pick *careful*!'

They all worked on one farm, then moved to the next, Vince running about playing between trees and the shed. Gia and Beryl picked from up ladders, Shirley and Vilma from down below. Gia's hessian picking bag hung heavy from straps chafing her neck and waist. She and the others sweated and burnt in the sun, the Italians in their scarves and dresses, the Australians in their Land Army shirts-and-shorts uniforms and brimmed hats.

'Watch not to bruise any,' she called to them again, echoing both Taddeo and Pino. 'It won't show up until later and the price of each case is set on the poorest peach inside.'

In the packing shed, no breeze stirred the peach-perfumed mugginess attracting bees and flies, and the corrugated-iron roof created an oven. Sweat coursing, Serena and Josie graded and packed peaches into the timber cases they'd all made. Edie nailed on the lids, her hands flecked with bloody splinters from the rough bush pine, and with a stencil inked the farmer's surname on one side, the agent's name on the other. Maybe ten cases to one agent, twenty cases to the next, the consignments expected by sellers in Brisbane's fruit market at Roma Street where the train line ended.

'I don't reckon there's enough petrol to get to the siding and back,' Beryl called to Gia. 'Safer to take the horse and cart in case the truck breaks down and we miss the train.'

'I'll need to take the horse back to collect the cart – do you know how to hook it on?'

'I might,' said Shirley, surprising them. 'My dad drives a baker's cart in Brisbane.'

Gia smiled, relieved. Already she felt exhausted and they had much yet to pick, even with the stunted crop left after the frost at Josie's. She hoped Serena and Josie were grading the peaches to size and packing them so they wouldn't move in transit as she'd shown them, for she didn't have time to check. Gia worried too about the siding, recalling the rough manner of the men, the cut-throat joggling for carriage placement. Especially if among them were the men who'd come by with Jack or those who may have killed the chickens. But just as she'd seen Taddeo put aside his shyness in the necessity to get the produce to market, Gia knew she too would need to push on in order to get those summer earnings for them to survive through winter.

All of them, except Serena, loaded the cart in the dark before dawn. Even with the strength she'd gained working in the orchards, Gia found the timber boxes of peaches heavy – as the others must have, for together they took longer hoisting them aboard than Taddeo and Pino would have. With an anxious eye on the lightening sky, Gia recalled departing at first light for the ten miles to the siding that the horse could only walk while hauling such a heavy load. The train left at seven. Already they were late and would need longer to stack the boxes onto the carriages.

'Good luck!' Serena waved.

From up on the cart's seat with Beryl and Shirley, Gia hid her worry and smiled to Edie and Josie waving too as Vilma only nodded, though she appeared pleased. 'Back soon!'

But she felt nervous and tried to steel herself on the way, keeping her eyes to the orchards and waking bushland they passed. Gia wondered what her parents would make of her sitting with two Australians atop a cart loaded with peaches that a group of all women had grown, picked and packed for themselves. As much as she tried to fit in and be like all the rest as Rosaria so wanted, it seemed without meaning to she always ended up being the one needing her best dress pinned, or falling in love with an Australian, or suggesting that the women keep the orchards going.

Tobacco smoke drifting sharp told Gia they were nearing the siding and her hands dampened as it came into view. The coarse scene was as she remembered – men swearing, strident laughter and ribbing as well as harsh words or the odd rough shove if the queue was breached. The two freight carriages stood in wait on the rail track, side doors slid open, each grower taking a turn packing in their cases and the same stationmaster watching with clipboard in hand. Worriedly, she thought the carriages already appeared quite full.

'Well, here we go, girls,' murmured Beryl.

Shirley had the reins and directed their cart in at the back of the queue.

'Oi!' shouted a fellow driving his cart up behind. 'Get out of the way!'

'Ignore him,' Beryl said under her breath.

The night before, they'd decided it best if Beryl and Shirley went to the siding in their Land Army uniforms rather than the Italian women on their own, but Gia understood they were still all women and they were broaching a male domain.

'Oi!' The fellow jumped from his cart and came over. 'What you think you're doing?'

'Waiting our turn,' said Beryl, mildly.

'Well, you can get to the back. Proper farmers first.'

The three of them silently stayed put. Several watching gave whistles and laughed.

'Oi!' He grabbed the mare's bridle, tugging it to steer their cart to the side.

'Get out of it!' Beryl jumped down. 'We're from the Australian Women's Land Army, can't you see?' She pointed to the badge on her hat.

'Means nothing. Not real army. Now clear off!' He gave her shoulder a push.

Gia jumped down. 'Leave her alone. We're not doing anything wrong.'

He heard her accent, took in her dark eyes, her olive skin darker from the sun, curls barely contained under her scarf. 'That right?' he sneered. 'Then why is your lot with Hitler?'

'We only want to put in this consignment and we'll be out of your way,' said Beryl.

The queue edged forward leaving an opening for Shirley to move the cart up. Gia looked around for the stationmaster but he appeared either immersed, or pretending to be, in checking that both rail carriages were being precisely loaded. It wouldn't be much longer until the fruit train arrived, hooking them on and continuing towards Brisbane.

'Let 'em go,' another male voice suddenly called out. 'We all got to get this lot gone.'

Gia felt many eyes on them. Her breath clutched. The fellow swore and let go of the bridle but remained there a moment, his eyes still on Gia. It was as if his loathing reached out and curled around her. He spat on her chest and stalked back to his cart.

'Hey!' cried Beryl, but Gia grabbed her arm.

'No, if that makes him quiet … let him.' Gia saw some others laughing, though there were a few Australians shaking their heads, not going along with it. 'We need to get these peaches on this train and come back with more yet.' But she pointedly left the spit there.

At their turn, the stationmaster indicated a spot inside the carriage. 'Keep it neat.'

Gia, Beryl and Shirley worked as fast as they could with the heavy, splintery cases.

'Stack them higher,' barked the stationmaster. 'And you need to go faster.'

They heard the train horn leaving the siding before theirs, about twelve miles away.

'Bloody hurry up!' shouted the fellow in the cart behind them.

'You!' The stationmaster pointed at him. 'Next carriage is now free.'

Gia felt her back straining as she stacked the crates. She pushed on, ignoring the sting as her sweaty curls hit her eyes, her soaked scarf dripping, her legs getting shaky. Numerous men who'd already loaded their produce hung around to watch and wager between themselves whether the women would make it. Most stood, arms folded or hands on hips. In the distance they all heard the gentle but relentless shushing of the approaching train. Gia ran to the cart.

'We won't make it!' Shirley almost slipped over in haste and fatigue.

Billowing steam appeared above the far tree line. A dozen boxes to go.

'Almost there, girls,' cried Beryl. '*Come on!*'

The train came into view, letting out a resounding blare.

'Last one!' Gia cried, lifting in the final crate.

And despite themselves, some of the men gave a brief cheer.

❧

Though muddy, the dam at the Dawson farm felt delicious in its coolness. Only Beryl and Edie could swim and the others paddled near the edge in their underclothes. Gia smiled to herself. The peach crops were all in and to market, the apple harvest not ready until January and Christmas just a few days away. She splashed Serena and Josie, all of them laughing. Vilma sat on the bank with her feet in the water. Vince splashed her and to fend him off she jokingly gestured a *mano cornuta*, 'horned hand', her index and little fingers extended, her other fingers curled into her palm, a signal often used back in Calabria to ward off evil.

Gia gazed at the afternoon sky, amber in the sultry heat. She wasn't sure what hurt more – her back and shoulders from all the picking and lifting, the stinging nicks and insect bites or the undersides of her feet from the ladder rungs. But any pain dulled when she thought of their peaches selling at Brisbane's market. And after next month's apple harvest, they'd have enough money to get through the winter. She looked over the unlikely group of women and beamed.

❧

Edie turned up the radiogram in her lounge room and Glenn Miller's 'In the Mood' surged through the house. She grabbed Vince to dance, letting him trampoline on the sofa to be near her height. With no pasta racks, Serena hung fresh-made spaghetti from a straw broom, its handle wiped clean, balanced on kitchen chairs. More spaghetti hung drying over spoked chair backs. Gia cut into her first-picked chilli and its tangy, strident scent took her straight home.

'I've been saving this!' Josie produced two bottles of grappa from the big straw bag she'd brought over with her. 'I don't think Alfio will mind after all the work we've done.'

'I should think not.' Vilma stopped dancing to open a bottle.

'There's some beer of Keith's too,' called Edie from the lounge.

Beryl went into the front sleepout where she and Shirley lodged and came back with two bottles of Stone's Green Ginger Wine. 'I was keeping these until Christmas but ...'

Dusk was falling, crickets in shrill force as the sinking sun barely took the heat. The radiogram played. Forks twirled spaghetti, the Italians showing the Australians how. Then in the lounge room they twirled, the Australians showing the Italians dances to American hits, Beryl's red hair as wild as Gia's dark curls. Glasses clinked in cheers and *salute*. And amid the singing and revelry no-one heard a truck pause down at the road nor the gate's cowbell.

Gia had just jumped off a sofa, glass of ginger wine in hand, and whirled past Josie when Keith came in the back door in army uniform carrying a khaki bag. She lost her breath.

'Keith!' Edie ran to him, as Gia wanted to, and gave him a big hug.

'What in blazes ...?' He looked around at them all, bewildered but half-amused.

'We got our harvests in.' Gia came over, smiling, her curls damp from dancing.

'That's right,' grinned Josie. 'Every last peach on our farms.'

His eyebrows went up. 'By yourselves?'

'Us all together.' Edie was beaming and Gia could tell he saw at once that she'd blossomed in their company.

Beryl introduced herself then Shirley, and formally added, somewhat incongruously considering her wild hair from dancing just then, 'Australian Women's Land Army.' She stood almost as tall as Keith. 'My husband is posted overseas.'

'I think I might be in your bedroom.' Vilma gave Keith a look that agitated Gia.

'Remember I wrote to you about that,' Edie hurriedly told him.

'Why don't I get you some spaghetti?' Serena offered. 'I'll just need to put it back on the stove.'

'I got a few days leave for Christmas.' He put down his bag. 'What about curfew?'

'Everyone's staying here tonight.' Edie rushed her words. 'We're celebrating.'

Slow smoke curled as Vilma smiled. 'But you may have my bed. Your bed, I mean.'

Still bemused, Keith looked to the others and shook his head. 'I've a swag in the shed.'

❥

The night deepened. Serena had gone to bed, as had Vince, his hands and arms still speckled with Edie's paints. Shirley too had retired, after retching from too much grappa, her first foray into drinking. With Billie Holiday playing low on the radiogram, Edie and Vilma lay on opposite sofas. Gia watched Beryl and

Josie persevere in a long game of canasta at the kitchen table, and in the same arc of light Keith sat at the top of the back steps finishing a tallie of beer.

'*Scusa.*' She edged past him on the pretence of going to the toilet out the back, not knowing why she'd reverted to Italian but suddenly a little nervous.

In shadows near the shed, she waited, wondering if he'd follow. Much had changed since he'd left. That she'd been part of the reason he'd gone remained. But the heat of the chilli and green ginger wine warmed her mouth, and her belly. The summer night pulsed, alive. It might be the last time she could see him. Her bare feet hesitated in the dirt. Much longer and she'd need to go back. He had to know she was waiting, hoping. Perhaps he didn't want to risk seeing her alone, the knowing of that hum between them. She pressed her lips together, again tasting the heat.

But then Keith rose from the back step. 'I might turn in.' He left the bottle behind with a chorus of good nights.

Gia took a sharp breath. He must have been watching her in the shadows, for he came straight for her, pushing her against the shed wall. Their lips rushed to meet, the heat of ginger, chilli and malt fusing and fading, and then only the taste of each other as they thirsted on, unable to pull back. His hand smoothed up under her cotton dress to bare skin. She pressed closer to him, wanting to feel all of him, her fingers ploughing into his back.

The swag scarcely veiled the hardness of rammed dirt in the shed's gloom. Caught between earth and heat, Gia let herself fall away, feeling his chest bare, his lips moving down to her breast, his hand on her. He murmured what they couldn't risk and Gia knew he was right, though just then didn't want him to stop, couldn't bear them to, and in honeyed fullness and drenching dark, they each found bliss and oblivion.

Gia felt someone nudge her shoulder and she opened her eyes, initially confused where she was. Her temples thudded from the ginger wine. It was first light. She realised and gave a start, making Keith stir too. Neither of them had meant to fall asleep.

'Get up, Gia,' Edie hissed. 'Back in the house before anyone else wakes.'

Gia scrabbled to her feet, red-faced and hastily buttoning her dress.

Seeing Edie, Keith groaned. 'What time is it?'

'I warned you.' Edie shook her head at him. 'How could you? For Gia's sake.'

'I wanted to.' Gia futilely raked at her unruly curls. 'It is love.'

'It doesn't matter.' Edie kept her voice quiet. 'It can never be.' She looked at each of them and relented slightly. 'I'm not trying to hurt either of you.' She sighed. 'I just know how it is to live with blasted hopelessness.'

Always Ever

It was in about grade six, I think, after we'd learnt cursive writing in pencil, that it was a matter of how neat your writing was before the teacher then let you proceed to using a pen. Each day, more students earnt their blue Bic pen, the rest of us looking up in envy from our pencils. More and more blue appeared, until I was one of the last with dark scrawls filling my page, spots here and there smudged by an eraser. It soon became the dwindling pencils that the others' eyes went to rather than the pens – to see the few who weren't quite together with all the rest.

I tried hard to make my writing neat and restrained, fingers clamped around my chewed pencil. But it seemed no matter how hard I tried, the words kept wanting to break free of the lines, to loop and meander into eddies. The same determined running hand, I realised, as Mum's and Nonna's handwriting, as though it was something already in us, handed down.

Nonna told me she'd struggled to learn handwriting and remembered her teacher's hand resting on her shoulder. *'Ask the angel of writing, Gabriel, to help you.'* But she hadn't asked. Stubborn. Wanting to do it herself. Her cursive script untangled little but it was never flawless. 'Yet I learnt to write, when my father hadn't had the chance to. And you have too.'

'What does it matter how perfect it is anyway?' I'd wanted to know.

'It just has to be clear enough so that it can be read. And that is the important bit.'

But to me, letters were still just shapes, the words yet to fill with true meaning. And just as I'd inherited Nonna's writing, I was also stubborn. Wanting to do things myself. As if it would somehow make me less like Mum and Nonna, my heritage … everything that marked me out as different, not realising that just by doing so it was actually making me the same.

By the creek, a protective curve of a granite outcrop and dense brush almost enclosed us, though I still felt myself baulking at any shadow and the slightest rustle. But the whispers were merely the breeze stirring. Tim tossed back his hair with a flick of his head. Dry grass needled my back but my legs looked perfectly brown in the shade. Above me trailed the languid shifting of a cloud, though removed, distant. I wasn't really looking closely enough to see anything in its shape.

'Are you ticklish?' Tim ran his fingertips along the outside of my leg to my shorts.

I flinched slightly. 'A little.' But I didn't want him to stop. Not yet.

'I bet you are here …' He continued up my bare arm. 'You're only just bearing it—'

'Okay, stop.' I smiled and turned my mouth to his.

The air was hot with that sweet, dry, grassy smell. I could feel grass in my hair and knew I'd have to get every last blade out before I faced Nonna Gia back at home. But then, maybe she'd understand. For she'd loved someone she shouldn't have – and being with Tim wasn't anywhere near like that, and neither of us were married. Perhaps that's why she didn't disown Mum when she'd got pregnant while unmarried. Other parents certainly did, and it didn't matter if they were Italian or Australian.

Tim looked at his watch. 'Shit. I have to go.'

'Yeah, me too.' I sat up into the sun and started skimming grass out of my hair.

He helped me. 'I love your curls.'

'Really? So does my nonna. I usually straighten them when I'm at home.'

'Don't. They're sexy.' He lifted them and kissed the back of my neck. 'Lucky for you I had better get back to the pub.'

I smiled and picked another piece of grass from my hair. Did he really mean what I thought? Being almost two years older, he'd likely slept with girls before but must suspect I'd never been with a guy, like truly, in that way. In that moment, what had happened with Mum getting pregnant loomed large. I just knew I couldn't, wouldn't, let that history repeat with me.

'You okay?' In the hot sunlight, his eyes shone a brighter blue.

'Course.' I stood up and brushed down my clothes.

'Sof ...' He caught my hand and gave me a look as if to say he wouldn't ever hurt me. However, just because I was inexperienced in some ways didn't mean I hadn't had any experience with boys at all and so I wasn't silly enough to fall for that one.

'Have you ... been with many other girls?' I even hated the sound of myself asking.

He gave a self-conscious groan and smirked. 'What? Where did that come from?'

Of course, he must have, with his looks, especially those eyes. 'Any Italian ones?'

Not that I considered myself just Italian, I was Australian too. But I needed to know.

'Well, there were a few Italian girls at my high school since there're lots of Italian families around Stanthorpe, and yes, don't worry, I know they can have stricter dads.'

I froze. That wasn't where I'd expected or wanted the conversation to be going. We'd hardly spoken about our parents yet and I dreaded the question about my father coming up, as it inevitably would. Especially since people mostly reacted by becoming awkward, or fleeing.

'You'd better go if you're expected back at the pub. I've been gone too long too.'

'See? Your nonna is strict, she's Italian, but that's not a bad thing.'

Right. And I also noticed it was 'nonna' now, not 'grandma' like he'd said before. I stood on tiptoe to kiss him goodbye and he held me there.

'You don't have to answer this, but you only mention your mum, where's your dad?'

I sank back down. 'Um, he died. Before I was born. The family doesn't talk about it.'

'Oh, right, I'm sorry.' Tim seemed to digest this. 'Well, I'd better get back.' Perhaps he was ill at ease, but he gave another smile. 'You staying with your nonna for a while yet?'

'Until mid-January.' I rolled my eyes a bit but smiled too. It was only mid-December.

Tim left first and I waited so we wouldn't be seen together, especially as I walked back along Quart Pot Creek past where Serena and Pino's motel sat opposite. I put on my Walkman and fast forwarded the tape to The Cars' 'Just What I Needed'. It came on as I got to the shops and I walked home suppressing a stupid smile, my steps light. When I got to Nonna's street, I even jumped up and hit the leaves of an overhanging kurrajong tree. Was the verandah shade playing tricks or did the old man turn his head, I couldn't be sure – the sun was in my eyes.

The smell of two-stroke and fresh cut grass rushed into my nostrils and I came around the side driveway to see Frank mowing the backyard wearing a tatty pork-pie hat. I waved from the patio, he waved back. Nonna Gia came out while I was still winding the headphone cord around my Walkman, as if she'd been watching out for me.

'Elena phoned,' she called almost accusingly over the mower. 'You missed her.'

'I thought she was ringing tonight?'

'She is going out, she said.'

'Oh. Will I call back now?'

Nonna shrugged. 'If you want.'

Frank came close to turn around at the patio edge and flicked the mower engine down a couple of notches. 'Oi, you got grass all on your shirt.' He roughly brushed at my back.

I twisted, hiding my blush, hoping Nonna hadn't heard. Of course she had.

She said to Frank, 'This one likes lying on the ground looking at clouds.'

'Head in the clouds.' He shook his head and winked. 'Just like Elena.'

'No, I'm not!' It came out more forceful than I meant though Frank only laughed, turned the mower back up and kept going.

I didn't look at Nonna but I could feel her eyes stayed on me.

Ready for church in her best floral dress over the corset-girdle, cream handbag on her arm, Nonna Gia regarded me lying on the lounge. 'Is that hot water bottle helping?'

I adjusted it over my middle. 'A bit.' We heard the car horn beep out front.

'Pino and Serena ...' Nonna hurried over and pecked me on the head. 'I'll be back in an hour.' And, even though it was a hot day, she added, 'I'll make you some soup for lunch.'

As she shut the front door, I looked over at a Madonna and Child holy card sticky-taped to the kitchen wall. Perhaps I was wrong but the way I saw it, Nonna mainly went to Mass because there'd be gossip if she didn't. And also for the conversation and weekly catch-ups out front afterwards. It seemed to me her most devout commitments were family, food, wearing the *cornicello* around her neck and to tend to her *Piccante Calabrese* bushes so they never died.

From my spot on the lounge, I spied a butter-biscuit tin sitting on the kitchen bench below the Madonna and Child. I got up. Of course, inside it was sewing thread and pins, not biscuits. Annoying. I tried the tea-towel drawer. Hidden in the middle was a half-eaten Cadbury Dairy Milk, its wrapper concealed by a layer of baking foil. I smiled and broke off a row of chocolate, folding the foil back just as Nonna had disguised it. I really

needed some and at least it conserved the supplies in my bag for
the time being.

With the hot water bottle back on me, I watched music videos
as I did at home on a Sunday morning and wondered if Mum was
in bed with a coffee and the paper as she usually was. I thought
of calling her but didn't. Long-distance calls were so expensive
and anyway I was old enough that talking once a week was fine.
Besides, she'd be down in a fortnight for Christmas. It crossed my
mind that since she'd been out the night before maybe she wasn't
alone, but I doubted it. Mum wasn't usually like that.

When I was growing up, sometimes men asked Mum out and
I'd be babysat by one of her friends or the lady next door. But it
wasn't all the time or anything. Once I heard a friend say to her,
'It must be hard, El, when you have such baggage,' and it wasn't
until later on I learnt that was partly to do with me. It was as if
Mum loved my father and that was it for her. Although when
I was about ten there was a fellow, Mike, she went out with. He
was nice too, with red hair, freckled arms and a big handle-bar
moustache. It was the seventies after all.

One time, the three of us had been to a movie and were
walking back past a toyshop when he suddenly said to me, 'Sofie,
pick anything you want, anything at all, and I'll buy it for you.'
I'd looked at Mum to see if it was for real and she'd nodded,
bead earrings jiggling. I was so overwhelmed, I walked up and
down the toyshop's aisles struggling to choose, not wanting to
get anything too expensive that might put off Mike. In the end,
I picked a little animal collapsing toy. It was a standing zebra, and
when you pushed in the base it stood on the zebra would nod or
bend down. It was one of the cheapest things I could find.

'Are you sure?' Mike fussed. 'Is that all? You can have
something else too.'

But I assured him I was very happy with that. And I was. I treasured it.

He and Mum saw each other for almost a year and it was nice to go out, the three of us, like we were a real family. I'd secretly think of strangers assuming he was my dad even though we didn't look alike, but I liked that feeling. Mike never came to Stanthorpe or met Nonna and Nonno. I once heard him and Mum arguing about it when I'd gone to bed. Not long after, she didn't see Mike any more. Mum said he'd wanted to get married and she didn't. I was angry with her for some while. We could have finally been a 'normal' family. But she told me it wasn't right to marry one person if you still loved another.

I looked from the television screen to the wedding photos on top, the last piece of chocolate going gluggy in my mouth. Did Taddeo ever know that Gia had loved another? My grandparents were married for more than forty years. I felt for him, and also Nonna, for them both. For each being in the whole unreasonable situation that had led them to being married by proxy.

The hot water bottle was cooling. I took it to the bathroom and poured it out.

From the hallway, outside Nonna's bedroom, I glanced at her wardrobe door. Just looking at it made me feel guilty. But in truth I really wanted to see the hidden letters now I suspected they were more likely from Keith Dawson. The crystal clock on the duchesse told me there was time. I shouldn't. They were Nonna's private letters. She'd told me so much already. But. Her version. And it was curious how she'd sent me in there for the green cardigan that hot day. Another beat. It was likely my only chance to really know.

I went over to the wardrobe. When I raised the lid of the artist's box, it again gave up its faded scents from the dried-out tin tubes of oil paint, murky linseed oil and its own timber. The glass bottles of caked watercolours tinkled as I levered out the bottom tray. There were at least a dozen envelopes addressed to Edie Dawson but I soon saw that all the letters began *Darling G* and ended *always ever, K*. Only an initial. Just as I had signed off to Tim.

It seemed, apart from Gia and Keith, only Edie knew. For there was some written discussion about Gia being careful that none of the other Italian women found out, not even Serena, for Taddeo's sake. It struck me both Gia and Keith seemed very conscious of how Taddeo might be hurt, or shamed. Each of them sounded protective. Yet it was clear that by then their love overwhelmed all else. And I could tell it was a deep love, not just a crush. Perhaps the uncertainty and precariousness of life during the war played a hand in them taking the opportunity to be together that would be forever lost once Taddeo returned. But they *really* loved each other.

I know it is hopeless, Keith wrote, *that the time we have might be so short and the aloneness afterwards will be so long, yet I still love you. In moonlight, in hot sun and cold falling rain, it is you. Always you. In sunshine and shadow, it is ever you. Always ever, K.*

It felt so strange reading that. I expected to feel some resentment towards Nonna for betraying Nonno so greatly. However, I found myself thinking of the life in Nonna Gia, her fervency in all she had to give, the love she doled out to us grandchildren in kisses, hugs and food and even the odd thrown slipper, well-aimed. Perhaps the way Nonno Taddeo had been benign but always remote and quiet towards me was how he'd been to Nonna Gia too. Had he eventually found out about Keith Dawson? I couldn't be sure, but I knew it must've felt a bit lonely, a bit sad for Gia to be married to someone and not feeling fully loved and wanted by them. Mum turning Mike down was really the kindest thing she could have done for him.

The crystal clock ticked stridently. There wasn't time to read all the letters. I carefully placed them back under the paint tray and returned the box to the wardrobe, checking all was as it should be. Even if it felt like not everything was, that I was still missing something. I was a bit stirred up. On edge. Something kicked over in me. It was like the anticipation of tossing a coin, just before you find out it's heads or tails. That moment of not quite knowing.

On the back patio, Zucchero was again spread out in deep sleep underneath the banana lounge. He barely flicked an ear as I lightly sat down overhead and stretched out my legs. I stared at the vegetable garden, picturing Nonno Taddeo silently bent over the plants, out the back. I thought of Nonna Gia hosing her chillies and the enormous rosemary plant out front. All these years I'd assumed Nonno wouldn't talk of my father because he'd disapproved of Mum being with an Australian but what if it had as much to do with Nonna and the past.

And there it was again. *La lingua batte dove il dente duole. The tongue always goes to the sore tooth.* My thoughts thrummed. Yet I sensed I couldn't press Nonna on it. It seemed tactless to try. I wasn't sure I even wanted to. I thought of Mike in the toyshop. *Sofie, pick anything you want, anything at all, and I'll buy it for you.* That feeling of being overwhelmed and torn. Sometimes it was easier to hope for what was out of reach than to actually get it.

Out front, a car door closed followed by a parting beep. I heard the gate click and the familiar footfalls of sensible, low-heeled shoes on the cement side driveway.

Nonna came around the corner and her eyes met mine. 'You hungry?'

Fire and Brimstone

'Are you almost finished, Gia?' Josie tapped on the bathroom door. 'I need to bath Vince.'

'I'll just be a minute.' Gia hastily refolded the letter from Keith, the bathroom the only place she could read or write the letters Edie had promised to help hide from the others.

In the darkness of not knowing what was happening to her family in Italy, how Taddeo was faring in the camp and where Keith might be posted, her only hints of light for the time being lay in awaiting letters and the January apple harvest. It was harder since Keith had left the second time. She'd stood alongside the others to watch him leave in his army uniform, unable to clasp him, or to cry, or to call out that she loved him. Instead, she'd kept her arms folded tight across her chest as her heart ached. His eyes met hers last. And so, another year began in war and uncertainty, 1943 seeming tentative in going ahead, all of them in limbo.

Serena looked up from the stove as Gia came out. 'Looks like a storm is coming.'

Gia went to the back door. The air felt close but the late afternoon sky was clear. Her gaze lowered to roam the orchards, the peaches gone but the apple trees heavy with fruit.

'No, from the south-west,' said Serena, and Gia strode to the front windows.

An enormous thunderhead banked in sinister, rumbling approach. Great curls of amassing cloud already darkened the landscape, though closer flaxen summer grass retained a stoic brightness before the onslaught. It was so still, as if the landscape held its breath. Gia ran again to the back door and stared at the apples, knowing what the green-tinged cloud meant.

'I have to cover the vegetable garden.' She hurried into her shoes.

Serena frowned. 'It needs rain—'

'But not hail.' Gia rushed out as Serena moved the pot from the stove to follow.

Together they did their best to spread old sheets over the tomatoes, cabbages and beans but there was nothing they could do for so many apple trees, except hope. In the eerie stillness Gia ran about finding heavy stones to place on the sheet edges knowing what was to come. All the while, in her mind she was swearing every word she'd picked up from the men at the siding.

It felt so cruel. The apples hung perfect, ready for harvest in a week or a fortnight at most. Gia was tempted to go and start picking as many as she could but it was futile. The storm was coming in fast. She felt the air cool as the front reached them. A faint stir and then the sudden whoosh as a gust swept in. Arrowing lightning crackled white down the dark sky. Thunder detonated almost right over them. Serena squealed and covered her head.

'Quickly.' Gia grasped her arm and helped her hurry to the back steps, for Serena was heavy in her middle, being in her last month or so before the baby was expected to be born.

Then, remembering the chilli plant in its pot, Gia ran and hauled it in under the house. Rain spattered down just as she followed Serena inside. Josie appeared with Vince wrapped in a bath towel, her face showing worry. At her questioning look, Gia shook her head.

'It's green,' was all she said, and Josie understood.

Wind whipped. Suddenly the rain went from a patter to torrents. It was wild, the gusts and downpour hurling the orchard branches one way then another. Fruit fell. The sheets over the vegetables sagged under the water's weight. Gia watched them dragging at the trellised beans and tomatoes. *Just don't hail*, she said over and again in her mind. With the rain bucketing down so loudly on the corrugated iron roof, inside they couldn't speak to each other without almost shouting.

The first hailstone sounded like a rock being thrown, then there was another. Josie let out a cry. She clutched Vince. His eyes were huge. Hail roared onto the roof. As big as eggs, it pummelled everything – flaying the apple trees, sagging the sheets onto the vegetables. Serena slumped and put her head in her hands while Gia stood at the back door, staring out to the torrent, her mouth dry.

❦

'Beryl is leaving,' Edie murmured when Gia came straight over the next morning.

'Because we lost the apples?'

'She got a telegram.' Edie dropped her voice lower. 'Her husband has been killed.'

'Oh no ...'

Birds still cried out, breeze fissled tree leaves, yet all else seemed muted. Shirley and Gia took Beryl into town on the horse and cart. Used to seeing Beryl sweaty and dirt-smeared in her Land Army uniform, Gia regarded her in her smart travelling suit, jacket buttoned, skirt below the knee, her red hair, usually wild like Gia's, neat in a hairnet. She seemed so different. Stifled. Returning to her normal life, though her life could never be the same again. Beryl held her port on her lap and kept her face brave but she remained distracted, in shock.

At the train station, they followed her onto the platform, Gia carrying Beryl's case for her. Shirley gave Beryl a swift embrace and Gia kissed her cheek, tears in her own eyes.

Still dazed, Beryl got into a carriage, saying, 'I'll just be gone for a bit to see the folks,' and forgot to say goodbye.

They watched the train go, not sure if she'd be returning, though they doubted it.

Shirley turned to Gia. 'Well, we should get some supplies then since we're in town.'

Still watching the train getting smaller in the distance, Gia recalled the first day she'd met Beryl and Shirley at Edie's. How initially the two had baulked at Italians being on the neighbouring farm. Then how Beryl put aside any prejudice to help them, causing Shirley to follow her lead. Beryl had helped them when her own government wouldn't, when her own husband was off fighting overseas, and she had their loyalty in return. Gia felt sad, knowing in her heart Beryl wouldn't come back. With a sigh, she glanced at Shirley and nodded.

'I'll meet you at Pierpoint's. I'm going to see the latest newsreel first.'

She sat in the dark of the Arcadia Theatre, the staccato, posh voice of the newsreader jabbing at her. One report expressed great satisfaction at Italy suffering heavier bombings and Gia came out feeling winded, miserable and more worried for her parents, Nonna and Salvatore, the neighbours, all the children she'd known at the little school, their families.

Preoccupied, she walked from the Arcadia towards Pierpoint's and suddenly realised she was outside Jack's hotel. It was the first time since Taddeo and the others were punched on the footpath out front that she hadn't crossed the road to avoid walking there. Being late morning, only a few drinkers were perched inside in the quiet dimness but Jack saw her and couldn't resist coming to the door.

'Big hailstorm.' He folded his arms and chuckled. 'The bloke upstairs mustn't be happy with you lot.' His eyes moved to the heavens. 'Might be fire and brimstone next.'

Gia ignored him and kept walking, her nails biting into her palms.

After Josie put Vince to bed, she, Gia and Serena sat at the kitchen table vainly trying to work out how they might make the peach harvest monies stretch through to the following year.

'I will start catching rabbits,' said Gia. 'Perhaps there's a trap in the shed. Or I could make one. And if we sacrifice buying some flour and other things for a bit—'

Serena glanced at Josie. 'It will take more than that, Gia. What are we to do – have no bread, milk or eggs, only vegetables, fruit? No soap or matches. Think of Vince. The baby.'

They all fell silent.

'Mrs Valetta, the seamstress in town, once offered for Vince and me to come stay with her,' said Josie, finally. 'I'm sure she'd take Serena as well, with the baby coming and all.' She looked to Gia. 'If you're okay to stay with Edie?'

'Why wouldn't I stay here?' Gia gave a toss of her head, suddenly angry with them both, for she sensed at some stage they'd already discussed going to Mrs Valetta's without her.

Serena's eyes widened. 'Oh, Gia, you couldn't. Not on your own. Not after those men came around.' Her voice dipped. 'And not after what happened to Vilma.'

'One harvest lost.' Gia slapped the table. 'We can come back from this.'

'Of course we can,' Josie hurriedly agreed, 'but Serena will be better off in town nearer the hospital with her time so close. And Vince needs to start at school.'

Gia placed her other palm softly on the table and looked down at her worn hands splayed on the timber. 'I understand, I do, it's just—'

They heard a bang out near the shed. Then running footsteps. Gia jumped up. Josie followed just behind her. Together they peered out the window into the night.

'What is it?' Serena's voice trembled.

'I can't see anyone—' Then Josie clutched her throat. 'Oh, *Dio* ...'

Gia flung open the back door and charged down the steps.

Josie ran after her. 'Gia! It's already too late! *Gia!*'

Fire roared up in the darkness, the shed wall well alight. Gia at once felt the heat driving her back. She ran under the house and grabbed a hessian sack, dunking it in the mare's water drum. Already flames were licking up over the shed roof and she beat futilely at the blaze.

'Josie, help me.' She tried to grab some of Taddeo's wood-handled tools closer to the shed doorway but hot gusts and smoke forced her out. Above, the corrugated-iron popped loudly.

Josie grabbed her arm, pulling her back further. 'He won't care as long as you're safe.'

But watching the shed burn with almost everything needed for the orchard inside, Gia wasn't sure. Especially when she felt this mightn't have happened had some people not taken umbrage at the Italian women keeping their harvests going. And it had been her idea to do so.

Serena stayed on the back steps, glancing behind to be sure Vince hadn't woken up. 'Thank goodness you kept the mare under the house, Gia,' she called out, then gasped. 'Oh no, *look*.' She pointed towards her and Pino's farm and the orange glow of their shed alight.

'No doubt mine will burn too.' Josie's face was grim, she and Serena resigned.

Gia looked from her burning shed to the blaze in the distance and smoke beyond that, her eyes prickling as all that they had unravelled in the harsh light. Most of all, she felt for Taddeo.

✦

'*Fire and brimstone next*, that's what Jack said,' Gia told them when they were all around Edie's kitchen table the next morning. 'I know it was him.'

'Or he likely got a couple of youths to do his dirty work for him.' Edie gave them all a sympathetic look but shook her head. 'There'll be no way you can pin it on him.'

'And not a chance the police will believe dago women over him,' added Vilma.

'We should press Jack on it though, don't you think, Vilma?' Gia shot her a penetrating look, thinking again how he had somehow been given Carmelo's picnic photograph showing the men posed with arms outstretched in the Fascist salute. 'Don't know what he might say.'

'Leave it alone!' Edie's raised voice surprised them all. 'All that hatred he holds, you don't know what he might do.' She caught herself and looked down. 'Please, just leave it be.'

Uneasy without Beryl, Shirley said, 'I'm going home for a bit. And I want to see how Beryl is too. The Land Army should send out others to replace us. I'm sorry, but I'm going.'

'Us too.' Josie nodded. 'Serena, Vince and me will stay at Mrs Valetta's in town.'

Gia didn't say a word, just kept her gaze on the tabletop.

'I'll drive you to the train station in the truck,' Edie offered Shirley. 'Dear Beryl got the latest petrol ration tickets last month. And on the way, I'll take you two and Vince to Mrs Valetta's. But I won't get out and Gia isn't to come.' As Gia's head came up, she added, 'I know you'll only want to go and confront Jack. But I'll drop you home first.'

They all looked at her and Gia shrugged, stifling her anger. 'I will walk back home.'

Within the hour, Edie had backed the truck from the shed ready to drive the others into town.

Serena gave Gia a hug goodbye and felt her rigid stubbornness. 'Make sure you stay with Edie,' she whispered, not mentioning Vilma. 'Just think, when I next see you, I'll be a mamma. Who knows if this little one might be a boy or a girl ready to see you?' She patted her middle.

Gia relented and hugged her back. '*Buona fortuna*, Serena. I hope it all goes well.'

As they drove off, from the truck passenger window Josie called out, '*In bocca al lupo!*' *Into the mouth of a wolf*, wishing Gia and Vilma luck.

'*Crepi*,' responded Vilma, in kind. *May it die.*

Gia pursed her lips. The gate with the cowbell hung open. She could have gone with them as far as her own house where Serena and Josie still needed to get their belongings, but she didn't want to pass up the opportunity to be alone with Vilma. The two of them stood silent as the truck turned onto the road. Both waved, as the tension between them swelled. Gia tried to be calm but seethed knowing the fires had to be Jack, hating that he seemed to have finally succeeded in breaking up the group of women on the farms.

The truck had barely gone when she rounded on Vilma. 'That photograph from the picnic, it was you, wasn't it, who gave it to Jack?'

'I think you need a lie-down after all the excitement, Gia.' Vilma got out a cigarette.

Gia lunged and knocked it out of her hand. There was a taut, silent moment. They each glared at the other. Vilma slapped her arm. Gia slapped hers back. To Gia's horror, her own eyes filled with tears. Vilma scoffed and bent to retrieve her cigarette.

'It was you. I *know* it.' Gia scowled between a sob and clenched teeth, and strode off.

❦

When Edie got back, she came and found Gia sitting down by the dam and saw she was crying. Wordlessly, she crouched down beside her. Moments crept by. Currawongs shrilled.

Gia spoke first. 'I don't know what's wrong with me, I can't stop.'

'Let yourself cry. It's all right.' Edie gazed over the water.

And in that quiet, drowsy light, Gia bent and wept into her knees. She cried for the harshness of being cut off from her family, for Taddeo and the others being taken away, Keith leaving, Serena and Josie going, Beryl, Shirley, even Beryl's husband. For all their toil in the orchards undone, the malice. For Edie and her fear. And for a girl from Palmi who'd wanted to work in the little schoolhouse yet had married by proxy and come all the way to Australia.

Edie hugged her. 'Dad used to say to Mum something like, all that crying you women do, but you're as tough as nails.' She sighed. 'Let's fetch your things. You can stay here.'

Gia wiped her face. 'Thank you, but no. Not with Vilma.'

Edie frowned. 'I can't ask her to leave, Gia. Particularly after what happened to her.'

Gia glanced at her, tempted to mention the talk that might come about if it got out that Edie was living alone with a woman now Beryl and Shirley had gone. But it wasn't Edie she was really angry with, it was Jack most of all, and Vilma. It did hurt though, that Edie could seemingly put Vilma before her, especially considering her and Keith. It helped Gia settle on what she'd been thinking of doing next. For Taddeo. She owed him that much.

'I'll wait until March when the beans are ready to sell, I can manage doing those on my own, and then I might go to Brisbane.'

'What? By yourself?' Edie looked dubious.

'I've been before.' In her bravado, Gia didn't admit it had only been for a matter of days. 'I want to go to the Red Cross headquarters and see if I can find out any news of my family or at least Palmi. And I will try to see Taddeo and somehow explain what I can't in a letter.' She didn't say if she meant about the fires or Keith.

Edie glanced sideways at her. 'I don't think they let internees have visitors, do they?'

Neither of them voiced what they were thinking, that Keith was at Enoggera too.

'But I must at least try, for Taddeo.' Gia looked at her with reddened eyes. 'Edie, I'm not going to tell Keith I will be in Brisbane. And, please, don't you either. Promise me.'

'Yes, I think that's for the best. I promise I won't tell him.' Edie nodded. 'And I can watch your place while you're gone and feed the horse. I'll even water that prized chilli plant of yours.'

That almost brought Gia back to tears again. 'Thank you.' She went to the dam edge and splashed her face. Ripples agitated and then gradually the broken water again stilled.

Gia got the beans off to the Roma Street markets that first week of March and a day later headed east following the same route. The train left behind the granite outcrops, orchards and low-sweeping mountains that she was coming to be so familiar with, the trees already showing autumn coppers and yellows in their leaves. It hurtled through the cutting, leaving the Darling Downs and steaming on towards Brisbane. She sat with her hands clasped, a suitcase on the rack above.

In her dress pocket was a piece of paper with the particulars of a boarding house near the train station. Edie had said her parents used to stay at it when they'd gone to Brisbane. Gia hoped the place was still there. Her first trip alone. She gazed out the window, watching the trees growing denser, feeling the air becoming warmer, moister, and all the while getting closer again to the sea.

Mixed Grill and Egg Flip

The woman Gia spoke to at the Red Cross headquarters was kindly but no-nonsense. 'I'm sorry, dear, we don't have any word to give you about your family or their town. Only what the latest newsreels say, that heavy bombing continues in Italy's south.'

Gia walked back down Brisbane's city streets feeling somewhat adrift and jostled along the crowded footpaths. A car horn made her jump, a tram racketed by. Fumes bombarded her after the quiet, clear air of the farm. American GIs seemed to be everywhere, as well as women with primped hair and Australian soldiers keeping to their own amid bursts of laughter and hijinks. Passing a harried café, she breathed in aromas of frying meat and perfumed sweat that overflowed with the clamour of conversations and wartime tunes. The air pressed close, still humid and syrupy with summer not long over and carrying on it a briny hint of the sea's unseen presence.

Following a map drawn by the boarding house owner, Gia found Central Station and scanned the timetables for a train to Enoggera. She found it confusing that the Enoggera Army Base seemed at the same place as the internment camp and was also referred to as

Gaythorne, and there were stations for each. Somewhat nervous but still resolved, Gia boarded a train, telling herself, *I'll go to the first one, Enoggera, and I can just come back if I get lost.*

Beyond the train's windows, city buildings thinned out to houses then countryside dotted with homes and farms in Brisbane's northern suburbs. She thought of Taddeo. Of Keith. Her fingers laced, unlaced and laced again. At Enoggera Station, she disembarked to find several shops and houses, a hall, scrubby bushland and a creek. The stationmaster pointed her in the direction of the army base and she set off up the road, army jeeps and trucks trundling past, a few soldiers wolf-whistling at her.

As the busy army base came into view, Gia faltered. Her gaze roamed over its daunting guard towers and barbed-wire fences. It was so big. Incredible to think of Keith and Taddeo each somewhere inside. She suddenly realised the true difficulty of her aim to see Taddeo.

Across the road was a general store. Inside, there was only one customer, a woman with a basket in the crook of her arm, and Gia waited until she left. 'Excuse me.' Her accent gave her away at once. 'Could you please tell me where the internment camp is?'

The man behind the counter looked her up and down. She expected perhaps some animosity but he surprised her by pointing out the window to the far end of the compound.

'You got someone in there, love?'

Gia hesitated. 'My husband. He is a farmer from Stanthorpe.'

'They've got close to a couple of thousand locked up in there. Seems a waste with all the manpower shortages. I doubt you'll see him but good luck.'

'Thank you very much.' Gia smiled, comforted by both his and the Red Cross lady's shows of decency in the hostile climate towards Italians. At least not all Australians were driven by fear like Jack, she thought. Perhaps it was different when you lived each day dealing directly with people affected by the war or gazing across to where the internees were.

With renewed nerve, she headed to the camp and as she drew closer, Gia saw there were actually two tall rows of barbed-wire fence around the internment perimeter, one inside the other, and several guard towers manned by soldiers with guns. With more than one entry gate, she couldn't tell which was the main one. The closest to her sat where a road named Newman ironically met with one called Bliss and it amazed her to see ordinary houses right across from the base.

Steeling herself, Gia went to the camp gate and enquired about seeing her husband.

The guard shook his head. 'You can only write a letter. You understand?'

'I have come a long way ...' She tried to persist and explain but he just wouldn't budge and, in the end, Gia could only acquiesce and back away.

She'd expected it though it was still disappointing. That they could only communicate by a limited quota of censored letters was hard enough but Taddeo's were always so stilted, brief and rare anyway. Sometimes it made her wonder if he even remotely missed or worried about her at all. Although, to be fair, she had kept her own letters short and not told Taddeo about the farm. Gia imagined writing the things she really needed to say and he just not replying.

Back at the road, she turned to look again at the camp. Behind the barbed wire, the prisoners milled about, clustering in what shade was cast by buildings in the treeless yard. The various huts, long, low structures, tent rows and latrines looked forlorn under the beating sun. It was hard to discern any faces. The internees appeared all the same from afar though Gia knew different nationalities were mixed in together, whether Italian, German, Japanese, Albanian, Austrian or from elsewhere. Enemy aliens, naturalised or Australian-born, or soldier prisoners captured by the Australian army in battles overseas – a potent mix considering there'd no doubt be pro-fascists and anti-fascists among them. None she saw resembled Taddeo.

She stood, feeling conspicuous. Nearby eucalypts hissed in the breeze. Perhaps Taddeo could see her. She didn't dare wave with the guards watching. Gia only hoped if he did see her that he understood she cared, even if he was cross at her for coming to Brisbane. She headed back to the train station. Among the cicadas and birdcalls came a far-off crackle of rifle training somewhere on the army base. In that moment, she felt very small in the world.

It was cooler by the water at the city botanic gardens. The wide river rippled olive-grey, its tide running out and baring the mangroves. Gia could smell its salt, though the Brisbane's underlying muddiness couldn't match the clean potency of the sea that she so craved. The trip had always been futile, she knew, but the prospect of it had kept her going in the aftermath of the hailstorm, the fires and the others leaving, in the constant *not knowing* of the war.

And now she sat feeling at a loss as she never had before. There was nothing more to do but get a train back to Stanthorpe in the morning and wait for Taddeo to return one day. As he would. And have children, as they would. And life would go on at the farm. Except hers would be in the house, not the orchard. And she could never see Keith alone again.

Gia gazed down the river. Somewhere in the distance, out of view, it met the sea. So near and yet a stretch too far. She realised she was looking towards where the *Viminale* had docked at the next riverbend. Where she and the other proxy brides had met their husbands in the shadow of the half-built Story Bridge. Her eyes moved to the steel girders that now met in the middle; complete, resolute, vehicles moving across it as if the bridge had always been there.

Life marched on. *Sempre avanti*, as Nonna would say. *Keep looking ahead*. Dear Nonna. Yes, life kept on, ever-changing. There was a comfort in that. It was almost midday. She had half a day left in Brisbane and Gia realised, for possibly the first time in her life, she alone could choose what to do. The city bustled with cafés, theatres and a general suspension of reality. She had some of the peach money. Suddenly, she felt hungry. Starving in fact.

～

'I'd like the mixed grill, please.' Gia smiled at the Astoria Café waiter and refolded the menu.

He appeared to assess her small stature. 'It is a steak, a lamb chop, liver, sausages, a fried egg, bacon and tomato.'

'Yes.' She reopened the menu to the drinks. 'I'll also have an egg flip. With malt.'

He put his pencil behind his ear and took the menu, eyebrows raising as he went.

Gia surveyed the crowded café. Its lantern lights accentuated the warm patina of the timber chairs and tables that she by then recognised as silky oak, often used in Queensland-made furniture. Edie had told her so when she'd admired her dining table one time. An air of fresh waffles cooking rose over meats and fish frying. She clutched at her middle. It was as if all the time they'd been eating very little and labouring on the farm, she'd been so driven that she'd put the hunger from her mind but now it engulfed her in a gnawing rush.

Before the peach money had come through in December, it had got to the point they'd had no meat, milk or eggs and little flour for bread or pasta, mainly only vegetables and fruit. She and Josie had each fainted. The two of them had laughed at their baggy dresses. But it hadn't been funny. And just when the peach money gave them a reprieve, without the apple harvest they suddenly needed to stretch it much further, even with the bean money, for its market price had been low. Gia knew she could only savour this one café meal as a treat.

The waiter put the egg flip down and Gia slid the tall glass in close. The first sip made her close her eyes. Creamy, cold, delicious; the raw egg and malt enriching the vanilla flavour. With a thud, the ceramic plate of mixed grill landed on the tabletop, meat burnished, fat glistening, the tomato just charred. She grabbed the knife and fork, again back in the ship's dining room, and all that worried her and failed in promise couldn't reach her for a little while.

Walking along Edward Street afterwards however the food sat in her like a cannon ball. She ambled aimlessly in clinging silence as the city clamoured all around. A woman with claret lips, her arm linked with an Australian soldier's, went by and Gia thought of Keith. At once she felt despair that she could never divorce. She remembered her mother saying, *think of the dishonour, for us and you, if the marriage failed*. Reluctantly, Gia strove to push him from her mind.

The afternoon matinee at the Regent Theatre was *Rudyard Kipling's Jungle Book*. Gia recalled Pino laughing when she'd suggested the picture theatre that first time in Brisbane. And in Stanthorpe, they'd only ever gone to watch the newsreels at the Arcadia, not a proper movie. In fact, Gia had never seen a movie in a picture theatre. They couldn't afford to in Palmi. She decided to go, one last treat knowing the lean months ahead that she'd face on the farm alone. Trailing others, she gaped in amazement at the theatre foyer's red-velvet drapes and gilt mirrors, the murals and grand marble staircase to a mezzanine promenade.

Afterwards it was already dark outside and, still too full for dinner, Gia returned to the boarding house. With the window pushed up to catch the slightest current in the warm night, she went to bed early, her suitcase mostly packed to catch the train in the morning. Dance music wafted from City Hall, and below on the road a ding and sigh as a tram sailed off.

She thought of the farm. The collapsed burnt shed. The orchard again starting to drop its leaves and, come winter, the pruning to be done. After the fire, they'd picked through the ashes beneath the heat-bent corrugated iron but found little they could salvage. Gia had been so down about its loss along with the apple harvest and the others leaving that she'd left the ruins be. However, now having some distance from it all, it occurred to her the secateurs were metal. Perhaps they'd survived the fire and lay hidden under the ash.

Gia's breath came out in a rush. Right then, she knew she wasn't going to be chased off by men like Jack or a hailstorm. Even if the others didn't want to, she was going to go back and work the farm, the same way Taddeo had on his own, and be sure it prospered. The timber ladder might be gone but if she found the secateurs, she could at least prune by standing on a kitchen chair or climbing the trees perhaps. She smiled to herself. Even if she got in a smaller crop, it would be something.

A knock at the door made her jump. Frowning, Gia hurried a dress on over her nightie. She opened the door and gasped to see Keith in his army uniform, a bag over his shoulder.

He shook his head, exasperated. 'I've spent the day going out to Stanthorpe and back trying to see you.' Then he sighed. 'I've got two days leave before I'm posted overseas.'

'What?' At once, she knew it was useless to have tried to push him from her mind.

He clasped her to him. 'Before I go, I hoped to take you to see the sea.'

The bus trundled along the Pacific Highway to the South Coast, heading towards the beachside towns from Southport to Coolangatta. Gia loved that the highway shared the ocean's name and that some of the beaches Keith had told her the bus would stop at along the way had names like Mermaid and even Palm, like Palmi. The bus was overfull with servicemen on R and R, the soldiers filling the aisle as well as the seats. Tobacco smoke drifted. Up the back someone played a guitar, and others sang and larked about in anticipation. Keith put his arm around Gia and she smiled and rested her head on his shoulder, putting everything but the present from her mind just then.

It was too big to think about him leaving soon so she kept to the smaller. The touch of his hand often caressing her arm. Their closeness and warmth. His fresh lemon soap scent. For this short time, it was only the two of them, all else waning to the background. Bushland blurred past the window, sugarcane fields, farms, a service station, a timber sign painted *Half-way Creek*. And all the while, the air getting denser, saltier. Then the bus turned east.

'Gia, look.' Keith pointed towards the windscreen.

She saw her first glimpse of the sea in years, its water sparkling in the morning sunlight. Her breath seized. The bus turned south again, the highway running parallel and a block back from the Pacific Ocean. Gia twisted, seeking snatches of lively blue in between low buildings and houses.

At Coolangatta, they carried their bags up a steep path, to where Greenmount Guesthouse sat atop its lush bluff of fernery and Norfolk Pines, commanding magnificent views of ocean in front, beaches either side and mountains behind. Gia regarded the rambling two-storey timber building that had long verandahs and a rooftop gazebo. Red-roofed and painted white, it made a pretty picture among the pines, palms and frangipani trees.

'It's been a popular place for years,' Keith told her, '… especially for honeymooners.' And then when he had to explain to her what that word meant, he actually seemed to blush a little, making her smile.

Leaving their bags in the room, they went out again straightaway and walked over the road to the bluff's edge. The ocean spread out before them. Turquoise deepened to dark blue, glittering in motion. Gia took a deep breath of the sea air amid the nearby pines. It wasn't the mauve sea of Palmi but it was almost like being back on the little balcony of home.

She clutched Keith's arm and held him close. 'Thank you. This means the world.'

＊

Gia interlaced her fingers with his as they lay in bed, their bare skin salty in the clement air. 'I made Edie promise not to tell you I'd gone to Brisbane.'

'And she bloody kept her promise too. We had a right row over it, I have to say.'

'What? But then, how did you—'

'I'd headed off up the road and Vilma came running after me. She told me where you were. I don't know if Edie knows she did. I kept on going to get back to Brisbane quick as I could.'

'Vilma …?' Gia frowned in surprise, but put it out of her mind, feeling him hold her closer.

Keith sighed. 'I wish we had more time.'

'I wish we had forever, but let's not think about that now.'

At the open window a curtain wafted, and beyond it dusk stretched lavender to the distant mountains. All the while they were lulled by the nearer hush of the sea – a swish, a sigh, like the curtain's drifting. The walls were white, the timber furniture dark, its flecked grain warm in the lamp glow. From the storey beneath floated up a hint of jazz music from the games room.

Gia lay her head on his chest. 'I love you.'

'I've loved you since that first day,' he told her, fingertips trailing through her curls.

Her tear trickled onto his chest and he sighed her name. Gia's mouth found his. And with unhurried grace the sky faded from mauve to violet into night.

Coolangatta's beach teemed with people in the baking sun and to Gia it felt like summer, not autumn. At the Greenmount end, a beauty contest was in shrill progress as part of a daily stage show, and out front of the surf lifesaving pavilion a large circle of people danced the hokey-pokey. She and Keith walked along the water's edge. Colourful umbrellas and towels dotted the bright sand.

Swimmers sauntered to the water. And, higher up the beach, they could see an intense athletics carnival raging between American GIs and Australian soldiers.

'If you weren't on the farm, what do you think you'd most like to do?' he asked her.

She grasped her skirt as a wave surged too high, at the same time the breeze ballooning her hair. 'Oh, some more learning maybe. Then I could be a teacher at a little school. What about you?'

'I can't see myself leaving the farm. My grandfather cleared that land by hand.' Keith skimmed a stone into the waves. 'But living here with you, well, that would be something.'

'Yes.' Gia saw his eyes were more striking near the blueness of the water's glare.

They walked on, quiet. She could tell Edie hadn't told him about the shed fires and didn't mention it or Jack. An occasional wave boomed louder. People shrieked, frolicking in the water. At the athletics carnival, a cap gun cracked the air and there was cheering as a race began.

'That fellow, Tom, from my unit, who we saw at breakfast … he said we could borrow his motorcycle for a ride later,' Keith told her. Her face must have shown she'd never been on one. 'But if you don't want to—'

'That will be good,' she agreed, happy whatever they did.

Late afternoon, they rode down from the bluff, Gia with her arms wrapped around Keith from behind as he sped them towards Point Danger. Her curls streamed in the wind. She rested her cheek against his back, her head tucked in the curve of his neck, face to the ocean's expanse, feeling the surge of the motorbike and his chest beneath her hands.

At the point, the road petered to sand and ended. They left the bike under a pandanus tree and clambered out over jagged black rocks getting showered in sea spray. Each time a mammoth wave rolled in and exploded against the rocks it was terrifying and exhilarating. Keith drew her to him. Their lips met, tasting of the savage waves. And Gia never wanted to forget.

❧

When Keith brought the motorcycle back, the fellow soldier from his unit, Tom, was sitting on the verandah with another bloke and two women. A cane table before them balanced jugs of beer as well as cocktails with slit pineapple pieces wedged onto the glass rims.

Seeing Keith, Tom grinned. 'She rides smooth, doesn't she?'

Keith tossed him back the keys. 'Not bad. Thanks, mate.'

'Yes, thank you very much.' Gia grinned at them all, her face flushed, still on a high.

The other bloke frowned at her accent. 'Hold on, are you Eye-talian or something?'

Gia's smile quivered. The women glanced at each other and back to her stony-faced.

'What's that matter?' Keith stepped forward. 'She's an Australian now.'

The bloke stood up. 'Only that they're the bastards who we're supposed to be fighting.'

'Steady on, lads.' Tom attempted a chuckle. 'All's fair in love and war, don't they reckon? We're just having a quiet drink here.'

'Thanks for the ride, Tom. Appreciate it.' Keith ushered Gia in front of him.

'Talk about sleeping with the enemy,' the bloke muttered, sitting back down.

Keith spun round. 'What did you say?'

'Keith.' Gia grabbed his arm. 'Please … let's go.'

Tom nodded to them both. 'I'd listen to her, mate. Not worth it.'

Keith glared at the other bloke, shook his head and reluctantly walked away.

The warm day had been a ruse, Gia decided, for by nightfall, the sand, cool and damp, spoke more of the autumn that it was. Together, she and Keith sat on the beach in darkness, away from the bonfires and other couples.

'I'm sorry about what happened before.' His hand sought hers.

Gia only shrugged. But she understood why Edie hadn't told him of the shed fires and Jack, seeing how Keith had readied to fight in her defence. He'd argued she was Australian. Officially she was, she thought, but she was Italian too. And as much as she held her new country in her heart alongside her birthplace, Gia knew people like that fellow at the guesthouse or Jack didn't see her as a 'true' Australian and were unlikely to any time soon.

Music drifted from a packed dance at the pavilion where they were playing the Vera Lynn song 'We'll Meet Again'. Hearing its pathos, Gia thought of Keith soon leaving and began to cry. 'I don't want you to go.'

His arms went around her. 'It'll be right,' he murmured into her hair.

The night waves gently rushed and retreated in a rhythmic barcarolle, endlessly breathing, forward and back, a refrain that would go on, long after they'd gone.

Back in the room, they lay entwined, still hearing the ocean. Eventually, Keith dozed but Gia didn't close her eyes once, not wanting the night to end, to lose a moment holding him in the nothingness of sleep. Through the salty glass she watched the sky gradually lighten to dawn's rose-grey and grieved that their last night together was over. She saw Keith awake too, staring at the ceiling, and put her lips to his. There was nothing more they could say.

~

It was a muted trip in the bus back to Brisbane compared to Gia's excitement on their way to the coast. Again, many soldiers and GIs were on board but this time a lot of them slept, seemingly exhausted from their days of R and R. She and Keith held each other, aware that every mile brought them closer to being apart, all that could be staying just out of reach.

'Keith …'

He heard her voice catch. 'It'll be right,' he soothed as before, but his face was strained.

In Brisbane, Keith took her to the train station and they kissed a final, long time, not caring who saw or whistled. That he was in uniform said it all. A little shakily, Gia stepped up into the carriage that would take her back to Stanthorpe. She could barely mouth goodbye as the train heaved forth. Keith waved, his eyes staying on her. She kept waving, drawing inside as the train gained momentum, then leapt up to glean one last sight of him. He'd just turned, rummaging in his pocket for a handkerchief and walking off in the wrong direction.

Fragments of Shadow

Frank plunked the crate of peaches down on Nonna Gia's kitchen table.

'Not there! How are we supposed to eat later? Put them in the laundry, for God sake.'

'All right, all right.' Frank hoisted up the crate again. '*Jesus*, Ma.'

'Don't say *Jesus* like that!'

'For God's sake, all right, I won't,' he muttered, going into the laundry.

Nonna pretended not to hear. 'And bring back the bucket and broom to take with us!'

Watching them, it occurred to me how it seemed different between sons and mothers compared to daughters and mothers. Some sons anyway, like Frank. It was almost as if sons didn't delve too much into what their mother's lives might have held before they came along. They were simply busy getting on with it and it was mostly about them. Daughters, possibly, saw, or looked, more, maybe seeing into themselves at the same time. Judging, distancing, aligning.

Or perhaps it was that I'd started seeing beyond Nonna to Gia and in turn, past Mum to Elena. Since Nonna started telling me of her past, I was thinking about things I hadn't before and seeing them in different ways. Maybe Frank might too if he had the chance to know and Nonna didn't just consider it 'women's talk'. Or possibly he wouldn't really want to know. I came out of my thoughts and looked over to realise Connie had been watching me.

She smiled. 'Come on, kids, back in the truck. Off to the cemetery.'

Nonna got in the truck cabin beside Frank and from where the rest of us were perched in the back tray we could hear them gently bickering through the wound-down windows.

'Sam, hold on properly,' said Connie, as we took off.

I saw her cast a discreet but intentional look over the road to where the old man sat watching us go. Neither she nor he flickered any reaction. I almost queried her but then Lena started speaking to me about some TV show she'd been watching and the moment was gone.

It was a short drive to the cemetery and the truck felt big and high as we rattled along a tidy, narrow lane among the headstones and statues. We bundled out at Nonno Taddeo's grave – a bed of black granite with gold lettering and a ceramic photograph of him taken back when he'd been about fifty. As usual, his face was turned away ever so slightly to almost hide the birthmark. *Poor Nonno. Had he loved anyone else like Gia had loved Keith?* And then I felt sadder. *Had Taddeo ever had the opportunity to love anyone like that at all?*

Dust muddied by rain and a few bird droppings marred the granite. Nonna got out a bottle of detergent and ordered Frank to follow her with the bucket as she bustled off to the nearest tap. In the cemetery's quiet we could hear her telling him, 'You just carry it. I'll put the detergent in – you put too much last time.' I looked away from them to Lena and Sam ambling off, seemingly tight-roping between the graves so as not to step on any. I moved closer to Connie.

'Do you remember who used to have the farm next door to you?' Like Frank, Connie had always lived in Stanthorpe and pretty much knew its comings and goings.

'Zia Serena and Zio Pino, of course.'

'I mean the other side. Before the Mitchells were there.'

She shrugged. 'Mitchells had it far as I know. Since I was born anyway. Why?'

'Oh, just wondered who'd had a farm there longest, that's all,' I said, covering.

Connie was younger than Mum but hadn't been born later than about 1950, meaning Keith and Edie Dawson must have left their farm by then. I gazed over the cemetery at all the headstones. All together, they almost appeared like a crowd of people standing in a field, short and tall, shoulders squared or rounded, somehow reminiscent of those they stood for, the past townsfolk. Keith Dawson might be among them, I realised, unless he'd been killed overseas in the war. My eyes went to Nonna coming back towards us and I considered if she might also come here alone, perhaps to visit Keith too.

Under her strict instruction, Frank swept Nonno's grave, scrubbed it with the soapy water and then rinsed it clean with another bucket of fresh water. Respectfully, we all stood around as the granite swiftly dried to a shine in the afternoon breeze. Nonna Gia had brought along a new fake flower wreath encased in a clear plastic dome and placed it on his grave next to a couple of other faded ones. Pale, flowery stars on unrelenting black granite. No-one said *Buon Natale*, but tending his grave for the upcoming Christmas was that gesture for him.

Frank made a swift sign of the cross and kissed his fingers. 'Right then.' Feet restless, he smoothed his moustache. 'Don't worry, Dad, I'm keeping an eye on them all, especially Ma, you know what a troublemaker she is.' He gave me a wink.

'Oh, get away with you.' Nonna shook her head, though she was smiling.

Frank laughed. 'Until next time, Dad. Come on, you lot.' And he moved away to get Sam and Lena back up in the truck.

Connie gathered the bucket and broom and I picked up the detergent bottle, getting some on my hand. I glanced back to see Nonna reach into her dress pocket and place a few stems of her rosemary on the grave as well. *Rosemary, the herb for remembrance*, she'd once told me. No-one else seemed to notice her do it, so I pretended not to either, but the private gesture made my throat tighten. I'd always thought couple-love was either deep passion, like that between Gia and Keith, or unrequited, nothing in between, but I was beginning to see there could be varying natures to love. Even the kind that was unsought, yet crept in, quiet and enduring, like that Gia and Taddeo seemed to have had eventually in their proxy marriage.

From the truck rear as we drove off, I observed the gravestones catching late sun on their backs and suddenly wondered if Keith Dawson was actually still around. Just because the farm had sold didn't mean the Dawsons were gone, though the old paintbox in Nonna's wardrobe made me think Edie wasn't in Stanthorpe any more. But it was possible Keith could have moved into town, as Nonna and Nonno had. And he might've had another wife and a family of his own, as Nonna Gia did. All the while keeping their secret through the decades, perhaps passing each other in the street with not so much as a flicker of recognition.

⌣

'Come on, I'll dink you,' said Tim. 'Only way I can show you this spot and get us back in time. It'll be worth it, you'll see.'

I looked at the metal bar between the seat and handlebars of his bicycle that he expected me to sit on. I'd always ridden my own bike. A girl's bike at that. 'What if someone sees us?'

He rolled his eyes. 'Come on. I'll ride fast.' He reached out and playfully tugged the front of my cap down lower. 'Hurry up, the chips are getting cold.'

I climbed on while he held the bike steady. The bar immediately dug into the back of my thighs.

'Can you hold these too?'

I really wanted to hold on with both hands but wanting to impress him, I took the hot chips wrapped in paper in one hand, held on with the other and prayed he didn't have a stack. Coming home with grazes or a broken arm would be impossible to explain away to Nonna. Especially when she thought I was by myself at the shops. I was finding it harder not telling her what I was up to, but if she still didn't want Tim to even be around to mow, I doubted she'd let me see him. And already I didn't feel I could give that up.

Tim pedalled fast out of town with the ease of a confident rider. The bitumen rushed beneath us. I felt my cap shift a little and ducked my head into the wind. A truck ploughed past, its roar and draft shaking me. 'It's okay,' Tim said near my ear and we sped on, past where the houses petered out and the summer landscape yellowed to paddocks and eucalypts interspersed with peach, apple and plum orchards and the occasional low-lying crop. A few vehicles overtook us and I prayed none were Frank or Connie.

The metal bar bit into the backs of my legs. I could feel every slight dip and rise in the seemingly flat bitumen, each twig or loose stone. My hand holding onto the bike began to sweat and slip a little and I clutched harder, until my knuckles were bone-white. The chip paper dampened beneath my other hand. It felt like we were riding for ages, even after Tim turned off the main thoroughfare and down a lonely road where there were at least no other cars.

I could see the bitumen was ending and braced as we bumped down onto gravel, the bike sliding a little and regaining traction. Tim barely slowed, and as we juddered along I found myself trying to recall the last time I'd had gravel rash – was I nine perhaps? It had stung terribly in the shower. I think it even got pus in it afterwards. And then scabbed. I just knew I didn't want that now. Still, it was exhilarating riding so fast out into somewhere I didn't know, sitting with Tim's arms either side of me, his chest against my back.

Past the edge of the last farm, the brush and eucalypts rose up around great outcrops of granite and the road dwindled to a track. Tim brought the bike to a halt and I hopped off, resisting the urge to rub the backs of my legs and bum. And we had to get back into town yet.

He kissed my nose. 'See? You survived.'

'Just.' I surreptitiously dried the hand I'd held on with.

Pushing the bike, Tim led me uphill along a track where the trees and bush became so dense they blocked out the sun, but then it opened to a rocky outcrop. Granite loomed metres high in walls and deep crannies that formed a kind of cave.

'This was one of Captain Thunderbolt's hideouts,' Tim grinned. 'The bushranger ...'

'I know who he was.' I gravitated towards what looked to be the cave opening.

He leant the bike against a tree and overtook me. 'You have to kind of go in like this.'

Just beyond the opening, the granite narrowed to a tunnel that made us edge in sideways. After several metres it opened out into a sort of room almost surrounded by the massive granite slabs. There was no ceiling, only a slight overhang, so light poured in. I looked up to fleecy clouds drifting across blue. Slits in the rock at different intervals showed views out over the landscape and down the highway, making it the perfect lookout.

'Do many people come here?'

Tim shrugged. 'Mates and I used to come here at night to hang out drinking when we were underage. We'd light a fire. Tourists come sometimes but mostly this place can be deserted.' His eyes met mine.

'Better have these chips before they get cold.'

We sat side by side, leaning against a granite wall that curled up smoothly, like a breaking wave. Tim took out some rolled paper and a pencil he'd had in his back pocket and sat them on the dirt. I let him eat most of the chips and wished we'd brought drinks as well.

'How come you couldn't meet up yesterday?' he asked around a mouthful.

'Oh, I had to go with the family to the cemetery, to, um, for my nonno for Christmas.'

'Italians are big on cemeteries, hey? Especially around Halloween.'

'All Souls' Day.'

'Right. Your nonno must have died a bit younger. Your nonna doesn't seem too old.'

I brushed salt from my shorts. 'I feel sorry for him, he ... well, didn't have it easy.'

Tim kept looking at me but there was no way I could tell him what I really meant. Instead I said, 'Did you know Italians all around here were interned during the war?'

'Interned? What do you mean?'

'Taken away and put in detention camps, like jail.'

He almost smiled, incredulous. 'Are you having me on? I've never heard anyone say anything about that and I've been here my whole life.'

'That's just it. I didn't know either until Nonna told me just recently and it happened to my own grandfather. I think after the war people must've just wanted to get on with it.'

'My granddad was in the war. Fought in it, I mean.' He shrugged, seemingly indifferent to talking of the past and I guessed perhaps you could be that way if you didn't feel it might directly affect your present. He smiled. 'Come here, we don't have much time.'

I tasted the salt on his lips. There was only the hush of the breeze and far-off trills of currawongs. As I nestled into his shoulder, the granite curve held us both.

'That day I first saw you in the backyard, I felt something between us straightaway.'

He kept tracing up and down my arm with his fingertips. 'I felt something then too.'

'Funny, hey? As in amazing, not ha-ha.'

'Yeah, amazing.' He mimicked me as if I was a kid, but his eyes were teasing. His hand cast about for the paper and pencil. 'I don't usually draw people, but is it okay if I draw you?'

I watched him trying to smooth out the rolled and crumpled paper. 'I don't know ...'

'You can keep it. Unless it's bad, then we can rip it up. I know you don't want anyone to see it.' There was a slight edge to his voice at that and while uneasy, I felt unable to say no.

I looked at my watch. 'Well, it will need to be quick ...'

'Okay.' He again fought to flatten the paper against his thigh.

'Don't make me look like—' I grimaced. 'Well, I realise I've got chubby cheeks.'

'Don't be stupid, but I know I'm not good enough to get you as true and pretty as you really are.' He was already pencilling swoops and crosslines on the paper and I let that go, even if I knew he was just being a flatterer. I wrapped my arms around my knees.

The afternoon sun turned the light red-gold and together we sat, me mostly still, Tim peering and sketching. Caught between the languid summer day and the short time we had.

'Almost there.' His forehead crinkled and I worriedly saw his slight frown. 'Okay ...'

He handed me the sketch. I looked at it, a bit askance. The face he'd captured was looking slightly away into the distance. It appeared to be mine, and yet I felt it wasn't truly me.

'I usually draw, like, landscapes, or, um, trees and things.' He hovered anxiously.

'It's good,' I said at once, although I wasn't quite sure yet what I thought.

Tim took it from my hands and rolled it back up, giving it to me to put in my pocket.

'You can draw really well,' I told him. 'Seriously, you should go to art school.'

He waved that off with a laugh. 'The next time I can meet is probably Sunday.'

'Oh, I can't then.' I rolled my eyes. 'Nonna makes me go to church with her.'

'I'll be there too. Good Catholic boy.' He grinned, pushing my arm. 'You should see your face. I only go to keep Mum company. How 'bout Sunday arvo? We'll come back here.'

I made a face. 'Sorry. We've been invited to go to lunch straight after Mass with her Italian friends. It will go on all day. There's no way I can get out of it.'

'Right … You know, if people knew about us, I could come along too.'

I guffawed. 'You don't understand. Me bringing you to a get-together of Italians, my grandparents' oldest friends, would be a big statement, like *major* … like we were about to get engaged or something.'

'Whatever.' He shrugged. 'Come on, we better get back. Don't want to be *found out*.'

I didn't respond. Obviously, my needing to be secretive was wearing thin. We were both quiet on the ride back and I held on with both hands. I considered how, like me, he didn't have other siblings and that was perhaps why he went to church with his mum when he didn't appear to want to. It seemed that although he was eighteen and an adult Tim remained careful to please his parents, whether going to Mass, hiding his drawings or working in the pub. In a way, that was a bit like me being in an Italian family, so maybe he'd come to appreciate my situation. All of it.

'Where have you been?' Nonna Gia demanded when I got home. 'I was about to ring Frank to drive around and find you.'

'I was just out walking. I'm sixteen. It's not like it's dark or anything.' But I felt bad.

Closing my bedroom door, I waited, expecting her to barge in after me but she didn't. I unrolled the drawing. Perhaps it was the eyes that I was undecided about, the way Tim had portrayed me looking to the distance. I folded the piece of paper and hid it in my bag beneath the lining along with the other sketch and the chocolates. It occurred to me he'd drawn my face almost to the side, looking away, just as Nonno Taddeo's usually was in photographs.

~

'We're on track for the School of Arts to reopen in February.' The drive and gladness in Mum's voice flooded down the phone line as she immediately dominated our call. 'It still has the original fireplaces. And copper-plated staircase. Incredible to think of all who've climbed it in a hundred and twenty or so years.'

'That's good.' I strove to hide my irritation that she seemed to always assume she had the more worthy news to relay first. I'd been thinking of telling her about Tim.

'Know what I love most about this building, Sof? That it was first an idea by women for women. A place for young women arriving alone in Brisbane in the 1860s and needing a safe place to stay while they trained and worked as domestic servants.' She ignored my deliberate silence. 'Diamantina Bowen was among those women behind it, and setting up Brisbane's first maternity hospital—'

I interrupted. 'That's good. It's fine, Mum, I don't need a history lesson. I get it.' And I did get it, knowing Mum had arrived alone in Brisbane a century later in the 1960s with not much help.

Only recently she'd told me that when I was little, we'd lived in the room of a share house because back then landlords didn't like renting flats to unmarried women on their own. I only really recall a fringed light shade and the smell of curries cooking from that time. I think she mentioned the others in the share house were hippies. But I do remember when we could rent our own flat, because my first day of grade one photo was taken out front by the letterboxes, and when we drove past there again not long ago, Mum had told me we could only move there thanks to the first benefit for single mothers being introduced that year, in 1973.

'If there's no news, I'll go then. I'll bring your green-and-white dress for Christmas.'

She sounded a bit miffed and I suddenly worried I'd been a bit too indifferent about her work. 'Yep. Thanks. And sorry, Mum. It's good what you're doing. Really.'

'That's okay. I know I'm a little preoccupied by this project. I'm exhausted actually.'

I tugged at a thread sticking out from the cuff of my shorts. It just didn't seem the right time then to mention Tim, or to ask Mum about the Dawson farm as I'd intended.

After we said goodbye, I glanced to where Nonna was out of view with the television loud as usual. The Stanthorpe directory sat on a shelf in the phone table and I hurriedly turned to the surnames starting with D. There were no Dawsons listed at all. But perhaps they had a private number. I put back the phone book and went out to Nonna and Zucchero in the lounge room.

It was *Perfect Match* time again and Nonna Gia sat eating *lupini*, her bare feet up on a leather pouffe and showing her toenails she'd freshly painted, red as usual.

'You hungry?' She offered the snack bowl of butter-coloured beans.

I shook my head and sat down. Zucchero's head came up at the noise of the sofa plastic then he lay back on the carpet. Perfume from the crate of peaches in the laundry permeated the house.

Another two *Perfect Match* contestants about to meet for the first time stood nervously as the neon-lit wall slid back. They made a tentative embrace, each trying to take in the other without being obvious as the slick host worked to smooth over the awkwardness.

'It's a bit like the proxy marriages,' I suddenly said. 'The couples on this show.'

Nonna stopped eating. 'How do you mean?'

'Meeting for the first time and having to be together whether they like it or not.'

She stared at the screen and I wondered whether it had occurred to her before. If she was even aware that might draw her to watch it. 'It's not quite the same,' she said, finally.

❧

Of course, Nonna made us make peach jam on the hottest day. The kitchen trapped the stifling sweet fog of the peaches on the stovetop while Dean Martin decreed 'Memories are Made of This'. Zucchero retreated outside to the banana lounge and I wished I could join him as I carried hot sterilised jars back and forth from the laundry to the kitchen.

I wiped my sweaty face. 'Nonna, if I get pimples for Christmas, I won't be happy.'

'What?' Head-scarfed and aproned, she barely glowed.

'It has to be the hottest day!'

'Never complain of the weather. If it's hot, it helps things to grow, if it rains, it gives them a drink and if it's cold, it gives them a break.' She stirred the pots, intensifying the air heady with peach, lemon zest, mulled cinnamon sticks and a little ground *Piccante Calabrese*.

'Nonna, I was wondering, when we went to the cemetery the other day ... Well, I just wondered, is Keith—' I suddenly wished I hadn't tried to ask, especially when she was so busy, but then, it would be harder sitting face-to-face. 'Um ... is Keith Dawson's resting place there too?'

The spoon faltered and she gave a final stir. 'No.' Nonna banged it on the pot edge several times. 'Now, come on, we have to jar this batch for the church stall.'

I kept quiet then, but the sureness of her answer wasn't lost.

In Hurrying Days

Alone, Gia hurled another piece of the shed's heat-warped corrugated iron onto a stack. Its hollow clang echoed across the quiet farm. With the toe of her shoe, she flicked over an item the fire had incinerated beyond recognition, but she'd salvaged the secateurs as hoped and a few other blackened metal tools. She regarded the chilli bush, still growing, tucked in its spot near the sheltered warmth of the water tank. Autumn's chill had set in and there were more leaves on the ground than left on the peach and apple trees, the cold air tinged with chimney smoke and the closer sharp scent of old ash.

In the distance she heard the barking of the dog further up the road, and, soon after, an engine hum from the direction of town. It had a fuller sound than Jack's utility but Gia still tensed, being there as she was on her own. Straining to hear, she fancied it had a resonance like the old Bedford and at once felt that wonted kick to her heart. But Keith was off fighting somewhere like New Guinea, or one of the other islands in the south-west Pacific, by then.

The truck got closer. She heard it pause out front and wiped her face. As the truck lumbered up to the house, Gia saw at once it was the Bedford with Edie driving and, beside her, Serena holding her baby and Josie with Vince on her lap, waving from the passenger window. No sign of Vilma thankfully – Gia had avoided her since returning, unsure of her motive in telling Keith she was in Brisbane. Especially as hostility remained between them since they'd slapped each other.

Gia ran over as they all got out. 'What are you doing here?'

'Well, we couldn't let you have *all* the fun on your own.' Josie gave a wink.

Vince ran to hug Gia's legs and she bent to squeeze him. 'You've come back to stay?'

'You've got dirt on your face!' he pointed, and Gia wiped at it, realising as he giggled that she'd only put on more soot.

'I think Mrs Valetta has had enough of us under her feet.' Serena smiled.

Unable to stop grinning, Gia came over to kiss the baby. 'How's Ignazio doing?'

'Always hungry and getting bigger.' Serena adjusted him in her arms.

'He's a fat baby,' agreed Gia.

'Pino said in his last letter it'll be easier for Australians if we call him Ian but he'll still be Ignazio for at home. Isn't it good they're being released from the camp?'

'What?' Gia frowned, and they realised she mustn't have heard from Taddeo yet.

'Not home here,' said Josie quickly. 'They've been sent to Bundaberg to cut sugar cane because of all the manpower shortages. Alfio said at least the three of them have been able to stay together. Carmelo was sent west for road building.'

'A couple of internees have been sent to my farm too,' Edie put in, and shook her head, smiling. 'Vilma's pretty pleased they're there so she doesn't have to work as much.'

'Well, I guess that's good …' Gia trailed off, unsure how she felt, for it seemed pitiless the interned men were being sent to other farms, many of them likely owned by Anglo-Australians like Edie, while she, Serena, Josie, and who knew how many other Italian women had to keep coping by themselves.

Josie put her arm around her. 'All that matters for now is us women are together again and we're going to keep these farms going.'

'Too right,' smiled Gia, borrowing a phrase of Keith's and kissing Josie's cheek.

'Me too!' chirruped Vince. 'I'm not a woman!'

'Yes, you too.' She laughed and went to the back of the truck to get their bags.

Edie followed and out of earshot from the others asked, 'How are you? All right?'

Gia looked at her, though neither mentioned Keith. She wondered if Vilma had told Edie that she'd broken the promise and sent Keith to her, but she only nodded. 'And you?'

'I miss him.' Edie shrugged and chuckled. 'Silly really. I didn't realise how much I'd come to rely on him when I shouldn't have. Some days … I don't know.' She didn't finish.

'You'll be all right.' Gia patted her arm. 'We have to be.' She hoisted out the bags.

~

With the shed fires having burnt the barrels of winter sprays, Gia convinced Edie to drive her and Josie into town for them to go to the hardware shop. 'You don't need to get out of the truck or even park in the main street,' she assured her. 'We can roll the barrels around to the lane behind.' Though Gia hoped Edie leaving the farm again might steadily free her more.

'Only if we don't go near the hotel,' said Edie. 'Gia, promise me you won't.'

Gia sighed, knowing Edie sensed she still itched to confront Jack about the fires. 'All right.' It was easier to agree, especially since the hardware shop sat further down in the main street from the hotel anyway.

She'd never been in a hardware shop before, but at once Gia liked its distinct smell of timber floor and the paints and oils, seeing the shelved boxes of nails, screws, bolts and nuts and all manner of contrivances able to be bought piecemeal, the number needed put in a paper bag. Lanterns and straw brooms stood by a giftware counter, wheelbarrows near the door. She and Josie observed warily the traps, shovels and pitchforks dangling from rafters above them.

An assistant came over and Gia asked, 'Do you have a spray for pests for peach and apple trees?'

He gave her and Josie each a long look. 'Lime sulphur is probably best. We keep it out the back,' he said, 'and I should warn you, be careful of your eyes when using the stuff. It's ruinous to clothing too.'

'Thank you,' said Gia, exchanging a glance with Josie as they followed him.

'Do you have a power pump?' he asked, pointing to a vat on wheels with a petrol engine above. 'Or one of these?' He indicated a barrel spray on a sleigh with a hand pump.

'That one.' Gia pointed to the second. Being under the house it had avoided the fire.

His expression was sympathetic. 'Well, after using it you'll sleep well that night.'

Gia nodded and shrugged, just hoping the spray would work to protect their orchards. She felt all too conscious they were spending what little money they still had that might have been better going to towards food. Yet they couldn't risk losing any of the next crops.

She and Josie each trundled a barrel out along the footpath, aware from passing looks how incongruous they must seem in their hats and dresses. Gia smiled to herself, liking that they were doing something others didn't expect them to. The Bedford was parked around in the back lane and Edie got out to help them lift the barrels onto the tray.

Josie brushed her hands. 'Did you see Jack Armstrong sitting across the road?'

'No, where?' Gia started off, hearing Edie call out behind her, '*Gia* …' and then her yelling to Josie, 'Why did you have to say anything!' But nothing could've stopped Gia just then, white-hot fury rising in her. At the corner, she scanned the other side of the road. Jack sat on a bench outside a shop holding a baby wrapped in a light blue shawl, a pram alongside him. Gia waited for some cars to pass and marched across the road, right up to him.

'I know it was you,' she fairly spat. '*Fire and brimstone next*. You burnt our sheds!'

He glared at her, pale eyes cold. 'I'd be very careful going around accusing innocent people, missy. Problem with you eyeties is that Latin hot blood makes you unstable.' He kept his voice low so as not to upset the baby, but it was strained with hard menace. 'And as the war shows, your lot are good at backing the wrong horse when it comes to your neighbours.'

Gia knew at once he was also talking about Edie. She leant in, her tone as icy. 'I hope your son grows up to be a better man than you are.' She glanced at the baby in his arms.

'Get out of here,' he said, glowering.

Gia stepped back, satisfied, knowing he was hamstrung by holding the baby. A shop door tinkled and Jack's wife, Myrtle, came out with a parcel, oblivious to Gia. Jack got up and hastened to give her the baby. By the time Myrtle realised something had happened, Gia was already jogging back over the road to Josie watching from the corner.

She grabbed Gia's arm. 'I think he's coming over! Quick, Edie has the truck started.'

In the cabin, Gia saw Edie's hands shaking on the wheel. 'It's all right. Let's go.'

Jack had just got across the road to the corner when he saw the Bedford with Edie in it. 'Go on! Get!' he shouted with contempt, slapping the side. 'Go on back to your *women*.'

❧

Gia loathed the rotten-egg stink of the lime sulphur spray. It made their eyes smart, ruined their clothes and left a metallic lustre over the bare winter trees, robbing the bark of its warm hues. But then the first spring rains washed the trees clean and bright and by then the film had done its work to prevent pests. It had been several months and she'd had no repercussions from Jack, but as Gia walked over to see Edie, she knew he wouldn't forget, that he'd just be biding his time.

Rattling the cowbell on the gate, Gia saw one of the Italian internees who'd been allocated to replace Beryl and Shirley emerge from the shed.

She waved and called out, 'Is Edie there?' And he pointed to the house.

Gia climbed the steps to the back door. Cigarette smoke met her before she saw Vilma sitting in the lounge room, her back to her as she listened to the radiogram.

Gia hovered at the door, not quite inside. 'Is Edie about?'

'Edie!' Vilma called, without turning around.

Edie appeared, took in the stand-off, and went outside to sit with Gia on the back steps.

'Oh, Gia, I haven't had a letter from Keith for months. I can't bear it. It feels like ages.'

'Well, it must be hard to write where he is.' Gia frowned a bit. She missed him and worried for him, but she'd endured years cut off from receiving letters while feeling anxious about her family. It made her realise that Edie hadn't quite understood just how relentless and severe that was. 'I wanted to talk to you about the packing wood ...'

'But surely he must write soon—' Edie stopped as Vilma came to the back door.

Her eyes sought Edie's. 'I just heard it on the news now. Italy has surrendered.'

'What?' Gia stood up, clutching Edie's shoulder. 'What does this mean?'

'Giuseppe! Mario!' Vilma called to the men in the shed. 'Italy has surrendered!'

They both ran out. 'We can go home!' one of them shouted.

'Then Taddeo and Carmelo will be able to come home too,' said Edie.

For the first time in a long while Gia and Vilma's eyes met.

❧

Despite such momentous news, any change to their situation seemed agonisingly slow in coming. Gia went about edgy and restless with no word of Taddeo's return and no mail yet from Italy. Even the curfew for aliens remained throughout most of Queensland, and Gia had a feeling that while Italy now fought on the side of the Allies, few Australians seemed willing to let go of the fact that Italians had originally fought under Mussolini and Hitler. Especially those like Jack.

But as usual, the orchards began to flower and so she, Josie and Serena continued on. With Vince at school and Ignazio dozing in a crate, just the three of them sat under the house hammering the bush pine into packing cases. Edie and Vilma did theirs separately next door since they still had Giuseppe and Mario there to help. And for Gia it just wasn't the same as the year before, when all the women had worked together in Keith's shed.

'I wonder what Beryl and Shirley are doing these days,' she said to Josie and Serena.

Before either could answer, she looked up to see, out of the blue, Taddeo, Pino and Alfio walking from the road to the house, following the direction of the hammering. Serena saw too and let out a cry. Throwing down her hammer first, she ran straight to Pino, Josie hastening to Alfio's outspread arms. Gia, emerging last, met Taddeo's impassive gaze. They embraced, their awkwardness unnoticed by the others immersed in their own reunions.

Josie was crying. 'Oh, this is so wonderful! We can all go home again.'

'Pino, look! Isn't he big and handsome?' Serena thrust a half-asleep, startled Ignazio into his arms and Pino cooed and kissed at him.

'*Che putto,*' he proudly marvelled at his robust cherub. 'He's as big as a calf!'

They all laughed, except for Taddeo. Gia felt him keep looking at her and noticed his face went beyond its usual seriousness. He took out an envelope. Gia could see he'd already opened it and her mouth went dry, knowing of her betrayal.

'Before in town, I went to the post office,' he said, 'and this was waiting.'

Her heart thudded in her throat. The others hushed.

'It's from the Red Cross.' Taddeo put his hand on her shoulder. 'It is wretched news, Gia. Your whole family were killed in the bombings.'

It must have been close to dinner, for beyond the lamplight and the window the sky had darkened. The house was quiet but for Taddeo moving about gently in the kitchen, the others gone. Gia still lay on her side in bed. Staring towards the bare wall, her eyes raw. The room grew cold. She couldn't move. Reaching for the blanket on the end of the bed even felt too much.

On cooler nights in Palmi, the kitchen fire had beckoned. Nonna sometimes fried balls of dough and trickled on a little warm honey she'd kept in its comb from summer. Angelo told his stories, but often Rosaria's voice was louder, and Gia's too when Salvatore took more of the honey balls. It was like she'd stumbled through those years in a way, not truly understanding what she had. Always looking out to the sea and what else might be.

Again, Gia wept. She could almost smell the rosemary-scented olive oil Nonna put in her hair. See her leathery hands deftly plaiting the strings of chilli that hung about the kitchen and framed the arched window to the sea. But even the kitchen was gone. Just rubble left. That place of such light and comfort where she and Salvatore would run to in childhood, straight to Nonna's skirts. Gia could still feel the heavy cotton in her small fists.

But then Salvatore was gone too. That seemed especially cruel when she thought of his boyish body swamped in their father's old wedding suit suffused in wormwood. He'd only ever exchanged vows in proxy, never his own, it seemed, considering he'd still been at home and the Red Cross letter made no mention of anyone else other than her parents and Nonna being in the house. Gia hoped that in the three years since they'd been cut off, he'd at least had a chance to find love. She was glad he'd pinched those extra honey balls.

Her mother had been such a dominant presence – pushy, strong, yet downtrodden by tradition and a fear of stigma. Gia still wondered if Rosaria's part in arranging the proxy marriage had been her way of perhaps trying to free her daughter. All those times she'd chastised Gia for looking to the sea rather than doing her chores. The clunking trundle of the two-foot rolling pin as Mamma thinned dough on the tabletop. Rosaria's sure scrape as she cut the pasta into ribbons of linguine. Her rough smoothing down of Gia's curls. Kisses from hard lips.

Somehow, it hurt too much to even picture her father, perhaps because of Angelo's gentleness, his simple want to write stories that was denied by illiteracy and obligation. She recalled his chapped boatman's hand covering hers the day he'd taken her to the port at Naples. He, Mamma, Nonna and Salvatore had been all together in the house when it was bombed. She wondered if it had been night, if they'd been asleep and unaware, or sheltering beneath the kitchen table. If they'd been frightened. More tears leaked onto her pillow.

Gia tried to gather herself. In a way, she'd already been grieving the loss of her family for years, knowing it was unlikely she'd ever see them again. But it had been easier to think of them back in Palmi going about their everyday lives. Not simply gone. Her fingers went to the *cornicello* at her neck that had indeed kept her safe. She remembered then too her father saying that Australia would keep her safe. More tears came. Again, the pain cleaved and she tried to push them all from her thoughts. But between the saying and doing lay the sea.

Edie placed the painting on the floor against the bare bedroom wall that Gia still faced. 'I should have given it to you ages back when I first painted it,' she said. 'I didn't think.'

With swollen eyes, Gia stared at the brushstrokes of a mauve sea, the pebbly shore and mountains behind. The lamp had been turned off, the light beyond the window brighter by then, though she didn't know if it was the day after, or the one after that.

'Thank you,' she rasped.

Edie came closer and Gia saw the concern in her eyes, so like Keith's, yet their slate-blue was without the vividness of his. 'Tomorrow, no matter how you feel, you need to get up.' She smoothed back Gia's hair and the gesture reminded Gia of her mother and made her cry.

Edie went out to the kitchen and Gia heard her say, 'Look after her, Taddeo.'

'Are the fellows gone from your place now?'

'Yes, and Vilma too. Carmelo came back.'

'I'll help with your orchards,' he offered. 'And come stay here, rather than be alone.'

Edie must have shaken her head for she said, 'I'm letting the farm go until Keith comes back. I just want to paint. But thank you.' She paused. 'You're a good man.'

Sempre avanti. Nonna's voice came like a whisper, a thought in the back of the mind. *Keep looking ahead*. Gia poured some water on the chilli bush. It had always been precious but now more than ever before – her only link left. She'd kept some seeds in the paper bud Nonna had given her and, in time, she'd put another little tin on a saucer on the windowsill and grow more, but not yet, not yet. Gia slumped to her knees, though she wasn't crying. It was more of a numbness now.

From the orchard, Taddeo was watching and he tentatively came over, his shadow falling across her. 'The priest said he'll say a Mass in your family's honour.'

She nodded, still looking at the chilli plant. Her hands rested open. Her palms empty.

'I was wondering ...' he shifted his feet, 'who pruned the orchard?'

Gia's voice sounded weary, far away, anticipating his displeasure. 'I did.'

'Oh.' Taddeo paused. He put his hand on her shoulder. 'You did good work, Gia.'

She looked up. Again, Nonna's voice. *In Australia, Taddeo will be your husband, but also your mamma, father, brother, nonna, all of us.* And he was. She had to accept it.

～

Serena brought around some eggs from her new chickens and Josie a lasagne she'd made, though she had no meat and only a little cheese to put in it. Nibbling at a small slice and hearing the two of them chatter between themselves, Gia felt a part of herself starting to come back into the present again. She watched Josie pick up Ignazio.

'Did you knit this outfit too small for him, Serena? He's like an overstuffed salami!'

Gia almost smiled as Serena chastised Josie. 'Poor Ignazio, he's just big for his age.'

'Between us, I might have another on the way.' Josie gave a grin and lowered her voice, even though Taddeo was outside.

'I think Alfio was too long in that camp … since he's been back, he won't leave me alone!'

Gia smiled along with them as the others chuckled but it made her think of Taddeo and how he hadn't tried to be with her since he'd returned. Perhaps he didn't want to be with her in the way Alfio did Josie, but she considered he might be denying himself. As if he'd been respecting her grief. Moved, she felt a stir of fondness for him and his quiet compassion.

In the bathroom, Gia brushed her curls into waves. The mirror now hung lower for her height and Taddeo had quietly accepted that she'd shifted it in his absence, even though she'd seen him having to stoop a little when he shaved in the morning. She went down the hall, saw him already in bed and flicked off the light switch. In the dark she got in under the covers beside him. They both lay on their backs, her eyes open looking to the ceiling. The timber house gave its familiar creaks in the cooling air.

Gia moved onto her side. She kissed Taddeo's cheek. He flinched in surprise and self-consciousness, even though it wasn't his cheek with the grape-juice birthmark. She kissed his cheek again, and then his mouth. He went to touch her hair or perhaps push her away but her lips again sought his, her kiss more penetrating, and he began to respond. Gia slid her hand to him and he gave a slight groan. She kissed harder, felt his hands seek her breasts. So much lately had been about death, but in that moment she just wanted to feel alive again, to feel life.

She tugged at the drawstring of his pyjamas, felt him wanting her. Bare beneath her nightgown, Gia slid herself onto him. Again, he seemed to try to push her away yet she kept moving, moving in deeper, quickening rhythm. And Taddeo was overcome by pleasure and couldn't stop her. Together they panted in the dark. For the first time, she let herself begin to take wing with him, calling out into the night. But he hastily clasped at her arms, shifting so she was brought back down and he moved to be above her, his breath hot against her cheek.

'Only the man should be on top,' he murmured. 'It's not decent otherwise.'

Doused in surprise, Gia went still and quiet as he panted on alone above, not seeming to notice the change in her. It didn't hurt her, nor give any bliss, and was swiftly over. Taddeo kissed her forehead and rolled away, giving a little moan of contentment as she lay unmoved.

'It's good to be back,' he sighed, closing his eyes. 'Pino said he'd come with the horse and cart on Sunday so we can all go to church, just as it used to be, will be.'

Gia never said a word. Before long, Taddeo began to snore and she shifted onto her side, putting her back to him. She gazed at the wall, moonlight illuminating the curtains enough for her to make out the sea in Edie's painting, though in the darkness the hues held no life. She'd tried to do the right thing as a wife but only felt she'd betrayed Keith. Gia realised in a way she'd revealed to Taddeo that her lovemaking had changed after being with another. Yet she suspected that as long as she submitted to him beneath thereafter, he'd remain oblivious.

She tried to sleep but could only think of Keith, simply wanting to be able to talk to him, to tell him what had happened to her family and to feel his arms around her in comfort.

Unravelling Light

Even from the church pew that Nonna Gia made us always sit in, about midway but closer to the back than the front, I could see the priest perspiring as he delivered his sermon. The side doors were hooked open but that Sunday offered no breeze and the cicadas were at full throttle. They chorused in cascading waves as the sermon droned on, and I sat as if lulled, sedated, still feeling a stunned sadness for Nonna's family dying as they did, and also for Nonna, for how alone she must have felt, even with a husband and others around her.

I'd known she hadn't any family left in Italy. It was a line spoken, not really thought about, just accepted like many other things you're told when young. I slipped a sideways look at Nonna Gia, her eyes to the priest. Again, she had on the corset-girdle beneath her dress. It couldn't be comfortable in the heat. Had she ever been able to be truly happy in her life after her family died in such a traumatic way, I wondered. I wanted her to be happy. Such a thing hadn't even occurred to me before but I realised I cared very much. She deserved that at least.

That morning, I didn't peer among the pews considering if anyone might be related to my father. Instead, I looked for a man about a decade older than Nonna, with vivid blue eyes. I looked even though she'd told me Keith Dawson wasn't the church-going type. I didn't really know why I looked except I'd come to have a strange feeling after the sureness of Nonna's response that he wasn't in the cemetery.

However, edging a glance behind, it was Tim I saw sitting several pews back. He gazed out a side door unaware but Mrs Dinning was staring right at me. We both swiftly looked away. Surely I'd imagined it. I snuck another look. Mrs Dinning's gaze rocketed away from me once more. Thrown, I wondered if Tim had told her about us, annoyed as he was with the secrecy and that I didn't feel able to bring him to the lunch at Josie and Alfio's that day. My cheeks flamed. I didn't look again.

Out front afterwards, I warily looked for Mrs Dinning and Tim among those hanging around to talk. If Mrs Dinning knew about Tim and me, she might say something to Connie who'd tell Nonna before I had a chance to get Mum on side. Lena had said Dianne Dinning and Connie had gone to school together. It had to have been the two of them who'd organised for Tim to mow Nonna's lawns when Frank did his back. But I saw no sign of the Dinnings, nor of Frank and Connie, luckily.

'Hurry up, Sofia.' Nonna hustled me back to Serena and Pino's car, which was by then permeated with the smell of her usual *caponata* that we were taking to the lunch, its pot wrapped in tea towels on the backseat.

As we drove off, I still didn't see Tim or his mum. My gaze circled back over the dwindling figures out front of the church and while all looked as it usually did, I had a sense there was something I wasn't quite seeing.

Josie and Alfio's place sat on a road everyone called 'the fruit run' on the outskirts of town, an area where locals and tourists bought produce direct from orchards and farms. I liked how Josie and Alfio's house sat behind their fruit shop. Some maybe cringed at the Italianate columns, curly balustrade and arches over the original weatherboard but to me their place had warmth. Height marks on a wall, old sofas on the patio, a makeshift *bocce* court – a real family house.

Nonna made me carry the *caponata* out the back to where Alfio already had the brick barbecue well alight, wood smoke billowing over the tables set under the grapevine-covered pergola. Vince, once that little boy left with the women on the farms and now with as much grey hair as black, carried over swordfish steaks and fennel sausages from the extra fridge that sat outside under the patio.

'You trying to smoke us out, Dad?' he joked and Alfio pelted him with a look.

Frank laughed, handing Vince back his beer. 'That's going a step too fire, isn't it?'

Vince took a sip. 'He flames to please.' Both unwittingly smoothed their moustaches.

Nonna jabbed Frank as she went by to go inside. 'You weren't at Mass this morning.'

'Ow! *Ma!*' He rubbed his arm. 'We went last night.'

At least Mrs Dinning definitely couldn't have spoken to Connie at church then. Lena came up and saw I hadn't brought my Walkman so went off to the trampoline where Sam and the kids bounded about. Through the open kitchen window, I could hear Nonna Gia, Josie and Serena speaking rapid Italian and it occurred to me I'd never seen Vilma in their circle.

Someone nudged my arm and I baulked as Serena's grandson, Mauro, a big bull of a boy who took after his father, Ignazio, loomed next to me. He offered a can of lemonade.

'Your nonna said you might want this.'

'Oh, thanks, you didn't have to.' I took it and swiftly went to stand beside Connie, feeling a bit mean, but Mauro appeared just as relieved to retreat back to the *bocce* game.

I glanced again at Nonna in the kitchen, wishing she wouldn't meddle even if she was just being protective. If only Tim could know that I didn't feel uneasy bringing an Australian boy among all the Italians, it was more about the past, before I was even born. I wanted to be open, but I also had to tread carefully, knowing I wanted to be able to have what both Nonna and Mum couldn't. In a way, I was glad Nonno Taddeo wouldn't see it this time.

'I saw Mrs Dinning in Mass,' I ventured to Connie.

'Who?'

The smoke of charred swordfish and fennel sausages assailed us, and Vince cried, '*Dad!*'

'Dianne Dinning. From the pub.' I took a sip of lemonade.

'Oh, right.' Connie kept watching Alfio cooking. 'We don't really know them well.'

The lemonade can in my hand stung cold. 'I thought you went to school together.'

'Who told you that?'

'Lena.'

She swivelled. 'Oh. Well, that was years back and Dianne was a bit older than me.'

'I thought you must know her since Tim did the mowing for Nonna. Maybe the old man across the road—'

'How's your mum's work project going? I was thinking, it's been a really good year for Elena. Your mum deserves a lovely Christmas, don't you think?' She patted my shoulder.

Somewhat baffled, I watched her head inside to the kitchen.

Josie and Alfio sent us home with a case of overripe Roma tomatoes so the next morning Nonna had me help her slice the whole lot in halves. We then had to place them face up on old flyscreens in their frames that Nonno Taddeo had kept for drying tomatoes in the sun.

'Now the salt.' Nonna sprinkled liberal handfuls and threw one over her left shoulder, nearly hitting me in the face as she warded off any bad luck.

Through the back windows pushed open wide I could hear 'You're Nobody till Somebody Loves You' drifting out from the stereogram in the depths of the house. Like Frank, I was starting to feel I perhaps needed a bit of a break from Dino.

I carried a flyscreen over to the clothesline to balance it across the wires.

'Don't let them slide!' Nonna's voice was almost hysterical.

'All right. *Geez.*' Several tomatoes slid a bit but neither of us mentioned it.

In all, four flyscreens, one in each quadrant of the Hills Hoist, lay in full sun for the tomatoes to dry. Nonna Gia stepped back with a look of satisfaction, especially at the cloudless sky.

I looked at my watch. 'Nonna, can I walk up to town? I've been helping for ages.'

'Well, okay. But be careful.' She dug around in her dress pocket and pulled out ten dollars. 'Here, in case you want to buy something.'

I felt guilty knowing I was going to meet Tim. 'Thanks, Nonna.' I kissed her cheek, inhaling a faint scent of sweat and Felce Azzurra. 'I'll make sure I'm not too long this time.'

As I came out front, I slung on my bag and gazed back at the old man across the road. Nothing changed in his face, his eyes staying on me as I clicked closed the front gate. Despite his stroke or what anyone said, it seemed to me Mr Dinning knew exactly what he was seeing and doing. Already late, I hurried on up the street and past the hotel to the train station.

Tim was sitting on the farthest bench along the empty platform. 'Shit, Sofie, I've been waiting for ages. I'm meant to be helping Dad, you know.'

'Sorry, I'm sorry, I couldn't get away, I was helping Nonna with the tomatoes.'

'Yeah, well, it's not paid work like mine.'

I bit my lip. We didn't kiss as usual upon meeting. 'Did you tell your mum about us?'

'What? Course not. You'd go stupid.'

'I saw her staring at me in church.'

'What are you talking about?'

'Twice. I didn't imagine it.'

'Well, I don't know why then because she doesn't know.' Tim shook his head. 'Even though I *should* tell her.' We both went quiet, but after a beat he sighed and smiled, his eyes vibrant in the hot light.

'Oh, I'm sorry.' I threw my arms around him and got on his lap. 'It's a crap situation, I know.' I kissed him. 'As soon as Mum gets here in a few days, I'll try to tell her about us.'

'*Try?* For shit's sake. Why's it such a big deal to have me as your boyfriend? 'Cause I'm not a wog?'

I cringed at him using that word. 'It's just, I don't …' It was so hard to explain without going into Mum's past or the situation regarding my parents. How I didn't know my father. I'd look like an idiot, pathetic. And I couldn't talk about Nonna's past, that was private.

'Seriously? That's all you can say?' Tim pushed me onto the seat beside him.

I faltered. 'You don't understand …'

'You got that right.' He stood up. 'I better go.'

'What?' I stayed seated, hoping it would make him sit back down. 'I just got here.'

'I've been waiting ages. I don't need Dad to crack the shits on top of everything else.' He deliberated a moment and raked his fingers through his hair. 'You have to … just decide what you really want.' He walked off along the platform without even a goodbye.

'I'm going to tell them,' I called out after him. 'I will!'

He didn't turn around. Tears filled my eyes. Sometimes the leg rope of family and culture and the past pulled too tight. But I also felt impatient that it should even matter. I put on my Walkman, not really listening. It was hot sitting in the sun, the breeze just enough to make it bearable and to dry my face. The song distorted. I opened the Walkman, winding the chewed tape back on the reel with my finger. I wished Nonna had never told me of an Australian with blue, blue eyes, and that I hadn't fallen for one too. My hand stopped. I stared out over the town. I'd assumed the old man across the road was Mr Dinning. But if he was Dianne's father, he'd have a different name to her and Tim. It could be Dawson. I sucked in a breath.

I thought of Nonna telling Tim not to come and mow the lawns any more. How she'd said Frank wanted to go back to doing it when he didn't really. In that moment, everything shifted. It couldn't be true, surely. But Nonna had said often enough, *never count up your money before the game ends or you'll lose it and more.*

I strode back down the hill past the hotel without so much as a glance in. Along the main street, people moved out of my way on the footpath. Noon sun stippled in between shade as awnings reached and ended overhead. I was trying to think, to get my thoughts right before I got home. But I was walking too fast. I couldn't help it. I tried to decide if it really mattered that Nonna Gia had secretly loved Keith Dawson and then I had secretly loved his grandson. Maybe it was serendipity. A funny story I'd tell my own granddaughter in years to come.

But something didn't sit quite right. It was like being in Mass trying to recognise someone related to my father who I'd never seen a photo of, thinking I'd just *know.* How that was quite wretched really. *For me.* I saw that now. And I had an awful sense I was again letting myself be naive and romantic rather than really looking, really seeing. I was sixteen, almost seventeen, I couldn't keep slipping back into the comfort of thinking like a kid any more, always with my head slightly turned. I had to look at what was, face on.

Rounding the corner into our street, my sleeve caught as I passed some roses reaching over a fence. I released the hooky tendrils, my hands impatient, but it gave me just a moment to collect myself, to realise I had to think more about all this before I said anything to Nonna. Especially as it might not even be true. And, just like I'd come to realise the futility in searching for my father's relatives in strangers' faces, I also knew the danger in imagining what *might* be and how that made you start to think in all sorts of ways you usually wouldn't.

The verandah on the opposite side of the road was empty but it was lunchtime. I banged the back screen door as I came into the kitchen and let my bag fall to the floor.

At the sink, Nonna turned around and blinked in surprise. 'You hungry?'

I went to speak, then wavered, suddenly not knowing what to do.

She gave me a funny look. 'I make us some pasta.' I stood fixed to the spot as she put two pots on the stove, one for the water, the other for the sauce. 'Sofia, set the table, please.'

I went over to the cutlery drawer, stood looking at the handle, and yanked it out.

Nonna frowned. 'What is wrong with you?'

'Nothing, it's just hot today.'

She eyed me sideways but didn't say anything else. I set the table and went out to the back patio while she cooked. Zucchero was in his spot on the cool cement beneath the shade of the banana lounge. Stroking his tummy, I felt my breathing become a little slower.

'Sofia! *Vieni a mangiare.*'

I came in to see Nonna dishing up bowls of pasta in red sauce and thought it perhaps fitting we had angry spaghetti that day. I didn't even protest. She poured us each some mineral water. I could feel her regarding me but kept my eyes to the yellow tablecloth.

'*Tutti i nodi vengono al pettine*, Sofia.'

'What?'

'All knots are caught by the comb.'

I didn't ask what she meant. Instead, I twirled spaghetti on my fork, just as she'd taught me when I was little. She didn't try to say more and ate gazing out the screen door.

I put down my fork. 'Is there salt in this?'

'*Certo!* What do you think, I wouldn't put salt in a tomato passata? *Santa Maria.*'

Frowning, I began eating again. The kitchen clock ticked.

'No.' I put down my fork again. 'Something's not right. It tastes … bland.'

Nonna's dark eyes fixed on me. '*Scusa?*'

No-one dared say a bad word about her food. I gave an uneasy shrug. 'I don't know.'

But she began smiling. 'The only thing different with my sauce today is I didn't add any *Piccante Calabrese.*'

Surprised, I took another mouthful, realising it was true. And not only did I miss the hum of the chillies, I could admit to myself that, for me, it now lacked something without it.

Nonna Gia patted my arm, still smiling but with what strangely seemed to be a trace of sadness in her eyes as well. 'You are ready, my *carissima.*'

Of the Divided Night

Taddeo picked the peach harvest from up the stepladder, Pino taking the fruit from the lower branches. Gia looked out to them from under the house where they'd set up the packing area until they could rebuild the shed. It was still hot, even with the flow through, and her curls dripped sweat, much to Serena's concern considering Gia's heavy pregnancy.

'Gia, you must be having twins, or be further along in expecting than you thought.'

'What?' Gia's hand absently went to her middle. 'I can't worry about that now.'

'Well, I'm going to get you a drink of water. Watch Ignazio for me.'

'Don't be long.' Gia glanced from Ignazio in his makeshift playpen on the dirt floor to Serena disappearing up the open slats of the back stairs. She kept on sorting and packing.

Harvest day pushed on, everyone jaded, for it was near the end of the season and weariness subdued their rhythm of picking, packing and nailing amid the barraging heat, peach fuzz and pungent stencil paint. Gia felt uncomfortable, the baby often

270

making her adjust position, but she was determined to show Taddeo that the harvests completed in his absence had been done well and she could go on being involved in future rather than be relegated to the house again.

By late afternoon, the crates sat stacked beneath the house up to the floorboards and Pino and Serena had just left for home with Ignazio crying and crochety by then. Taddeo and Gia were heading up the back steps when Edie came running over from the boundary fence.

'Edie …?' Gia saw the tears coursing down her cheeks and hurried back down.

'Oh, Gia.' Edie was still holding the telegram. 'Keith's been listed as missing.'

'What?' Gia's heart plunged to a dead gallop. 'Are you sure?' She stifled her breath, stilling her face to be impassive in front of Taddeo. 'Let me see.'

The telegram said so little, seemed so flimsy considering all it held. Gia went to speak but couldn't and looked to Edie still crying and then to Taddeo, who took it from her hands.

'It mightn't mean the worst,' he told Edie. 'He could have to hide out somewhere.'

'Yes, yes, it might be that.' She wiped at her cheeks though tears kept coming and took back the telegram. 'I'm sorry. I shouldn't have rushed over like this.' Edie's eyes met Gia's and darted away. 'I'll come and tell you if I hear anything more.'

Gia grappled and found her voice. 'Please, stay here, at least have dinner with us.'

'Yes.' Taddeo nodded. 'You don't want to be alone just now.'

Edie forced a smile. 'Really, I'd rather be. I'm all right. I shouldn't have come running over here like a chook with its head cut off.' She stuffed the telegram in her pocket, her gaze going to Gia's middle and getting teary again. 'I'll come back and see you tomorrow.'

Edie scampered off towards the boundary fence before Gia could easily come far after her. She stood watching Edie go, a slim figure with elfin hair she cut herself, and couldn't help feeling ill at ease. But concern for Keith overrode all else just then and she felt her hands shaking. *Not Keith too*, she thought, *not as well as my family*. Gia wanted to shout and weep, her anguish gushing in flood across the landscape. But she could give nothing away, and so balled her hands in her pockets and with roused fortitude she followed Taddeo upstairs.

'I wonder if Vilma ever goes to visit Edie,' Gia said, as the two of them sat in the living room before bed. 'She stayed with her for quite some time while Carmelo was interned.' The baby blanket she was knitting felt hot on her legs. Again, she wrestled not to think of Keith then.

Taddeo folded the newspaper to its next page. 'I saw her and Carmelo at the siding.'

'You never told me that.'

He shrugged and kept reading.

Gia chose her words carefully. 'So, Vilma looked well? She seemed happy with him?'

'I suppose so. They'd got in an apple crop.'

In the distance on their road came the barking of the dog. Gia stopped knitting and strained to listen. The expected drone of an engine followed, carrying in the still night. Coming closer, they heard it roar. Its tyres fishtailed, skidding on the gravel road. They looked at each other and Taddeo put down the paper.

'Gia, turn the lights off. Quickly now.' He went to the front window.

Again, the car thundered, getting nearer. Tyres spun. The engine gunned. Gia came up beside Taddeo in the darkness so she could see out too. In the half-moonlight they could make out the pale road beyond the front fence. More skidding and the utility roared into view. Jack's utility, Gia thought, though it was hard to be completely certain in the gloom. It rumbled past and they heard glass smash near their front gate, perhaps a bottle thrown from the car window.

'It's going on to the Dawsons'.' She clasped the windowsill.

'Probably just young fellows letting off steam.'

Gia pressed her lips. In a similar way, he'd chosen to explain away the shed fires, insisting there was no solid proof Jack was behind them. She'd let it go, sensing Taddeo's fear, especially after his being belted outside the hotel and then interned, but this was Edie, alone, and there was more to it than he knew.

'Taddeo … Jack Armstrong and some men came in a utility once before. When we women were alone pruning.' Gia saw him frown in the darkness. 'They only said things,' she added swiftly. In that moment, she was tempted to also tell him about Edie being with a woman and Keith's wife, Jack's sister of all people, leaving because of it. But, deep down, she had an awful feeling Taddeo wouldn't understand and that perhaps he wouldn't let her see Edie any more either.

Far off, from near the Dawson farm, they heard the engine heighten. There was a screech of tyres and then a loud bang followed by more squealing rubber and fishtailing.

'They must have gone through the gate.' Taddeo reeled one way, then another as though working out what to do. 'I wish we had a telephone.'

Gia grabbed his arm. 'You must go over there. Edie is alone.'

'I'm not leaving you, not in your condition.' They heard more screeching and roaring of the engine, as though the utility was doing laps around the Dawson house, terrorising Edie. Taddeo wavered, looking torn – he could only go over on foot since the police had taken the bicycle. 'What if I'm halfway over there and they come here next and you're all alone, Gia?'

'But you don't understand. Jack really has it in for the Dawsons, some old feud.'

'He has it in for us Italians too. Hopefully Edie sits tight inside and they go soon.'

Taddeo went to the back steps with Gia right behind him. From their farm, they couldn't see anything, only listen. It was awful hearing the engine circling and bellowing around and around the Dawson house, sullying the gentle night with the trees, the stars, all else so calm and beautiful. There was another roar, then a lull and Gia clutched Taddeo's arm, frightened they might be going inside to Edie, but then the utility's engine gunned again and it took off up the road, making both of them rush back to the front windows. They reached them in time to see the utility hurtle past, gravel skittering, and heard it heading back towards town.

'No matter what, I want you to stay inside and keep everything locked.' Taddeo lit the kerosene lantern. 'I mean it, Gia.'

'Yes, yes.' She was crying by then. 'Please, just go and make sure Edie is all right.'

She stood on the back steps watching him leave, the lantern bobbing in the darkness.

Taddeo turned around. 'Lock the door, for Christ's sake!'

She heard the fright in his voice that he was trying to veil and hurriedly did so.

The kitchen clock ticked loud in the hush. They'd usually be going to bed then. The ensuing quiet made the thunder and scream of the utility now seem otherworldly, like it couldn't have happened. Gia tried to sit and stood again, on edge and wringing her hands. She felt utterly exhausted from packing the harvest all day yet wide awake and on alert. Looking again at the clock, she realised Taddeo might be some time.

It would be a little while before he'd even reach Edie at the farmhouse and if he couldn't convince her to come to them, he might stay and have a cup of tea with her to help calm her. On top of the upset of the telegram about Keith missing, no doubt it would take time for Edie to settle. Gia didn't want to go to bed so she went and sat in the easy chair. She picked up her knitting again, the methodical click, click of the needles gradually soothing her nerves as the house kept her company with its creaks.

'Gia ...' A hand gently shook her shoulder. She opened her eyes, disconcerted. Taddeo stood leaning over her. He looked haggard, like he'd aged since he'd been gone, and she glanced to the windows to see it was still night and her knitting had slipped to the floor.

'Don't mind that.' Taddeo crouched to her height in the chair. 'Gia, Edie is dead.'

'What?' She gave a start. 'What did they—'

He shook his head. 'By her own hand.' Taddeo bowed his head. 'I must have been too late only by minutes.' He began sobbing.

Stilled by shock, Gia stared into nowhere. Fragments, pieces, falling in those moments. She lifted her hand, leaden, to Taddeo's shoulder, feeling him weeping. Her eyes were dry.

'I'm sorry.' Taddeo got out his handkerchief and wiped at his eyes. 'Men shouldn't do this.' He stood up again. 'I'll have to wake Pino to take the cart into town and get the doctor.'

'What time is it?'

'After ten.'

Neither spoke of the crates of peaches waiting to be taken to the siding at dawn, that there was no getting around it having to be done for them to get through the next year.

'Wash your face.' Gia was numbed, trancelike. 'And have some water before you go.'

He nodded and did so, coming back to her side as he readied himself to leave. 'Don't go over there while I'm gone. I warn you, Gia, please don't.'

She saw his distress and promised she wouldn't. As it was, she could barely move.

In the bright sunshine, the gate with the cowbell lay flung some way from the posts where it had hung. Recalling its gentle way of telling Edie that visitors were arriving, it hurt Gia to see it, to think how the intruders had smashed their way in. Just then, she hated herself too. For stealthily climbing through the fence without ringing the bell on her first visit, thinking she was so clever, believing she could draw Edie out from her hermit existence, that she even should.

At Taddeo's insistence she'd waited until Edie had been taken away before coming to the house. In the dulling shock, tears threatened so close that she barely held them back and only then from anger. Gia hesitated at the bottom of the familiar back steps, aware of Taddeo watching her from behind. So much felt different. Tentative. As if she was about to climb the steps for the first time. She thought of herself holding a saucepan of *crostoli*, Edie waiting on the top step in her paint smock. The kettle steaming away on the wood stove. But the doorway was empty.

'I'm going to check the shed and lock it all up,' Taddeo told her.

Turning around, Gia saw his face and sensed he wasn't keen to go back into the house again. 'I won't be long,' she said. 'I'll just make sure the windows are all shut.'

There was mainly tinned food and the usual staples in the kitchen. Edie must have been drinking her tea black since there was no milk. Gia threw the bread out onto the grass for the birds rather than allow it to go mouldy, wanting to leave the kitchen in some semblance of cleanness for when Keith got back. Just then she couldn't think of it being *if* he got back.

Gia avoided the bathroom where Taddeo said Edie had died, even though it had been cleaned up by then. And coming to Edie's closed bedroom door, she couldn't bring herself to turn the knob, knowing just her lingering scent would be her own undoing. How fragile Edie must have been at Keith being missing, possibly dead, when the men had circled the house in the utility, terrorising her. How alone she must have felt that it pushed her over some precipice she may have been nearing and trying to avoid for some time.

Thinking again of seeing the utility truck careering past, Gia felt a sick grimness clutch her. It had been impossible from a distance to read any number plate in the half-moonlight or see the occupants inside. Of course, there were many utility trucks in town, on surrounding properties and passing through on the highway. And with no apparent forced entry to the house and Edie's death by her own hand, the police had said there was little they could do.

Opposite Edie's closed bedroom, Keith's door stood open. The room again looked how he must have left it, though the air smelt stale from Vilma's cigarette smoke. Gia ran her hand along the chest of drawers with its warm silky oak patina. A clock sat on top. Unwound. She picked up a hat from the wall rack. Putting her face to its hollow, she breathed a faint hint of perspiration and hair oil.

'Please come back and I'll help you through this,' she whispered, and placed it back.

Before she left, Gia crossed the lounge room, manoeuvring her bulky figure around the sofas and radiogram to follow the sharp tug of oil paints, turpentine and linseed oil in the louvred verandah. The dusty window ledges and strewn water jars and blunt knives seemed the same but the easel was bare and the wooden paintbox shut. Coming closer, she saw a note left on the paintbox lid and in Edie's hand only two words, *For Gia*.

Tears filled her eyes. Her hand went to the timber box, feeling its grain, the worn leather handle and the little clasps on its front. She opened it and leant in, tears dripping on the half-used tin tubes and tiny glass bottles still rich with flowy paint. 'Oh, Edie …' Her fingers traced along the row of glass bottles making them faintly tinkle against each other.

She remembered that first day she'd come to visit, when Edie had shown her the painting of the sea with its roiling green hues and foam-tipped waves, the blackened depths alluding to anger. It made her want to see it again, to perhaps see how Edie saw. The canvases remained stacked against a wall. Gia bent to flick through them. But for her movement, the silence of the house closed in. She felt like an intruder and hoped Edie might understand. No doubt Taddeo was waiting outside wondering what she was doing and Gia hoped he didn't come in to get her.

A canvas, smaller than the others, slipped forward hiding its face, and without thinking she flicked it back to see. Her breath drew in as she drew out the painting. It was of Vilma, languid on one of the sofas, completely nude. A cigarette trailed smoke from her long fingers and she lay with her head back, her dark hair cascading around her shoulders down to her breasts with her nipples painted dark plum and taut.

'Gia?' Taddeo's call came from the back steps, not quite inside.

'Stay there! I'll only be a minute.'

The sea painting forgotten, Gia clutched the small canvas, knowing she couldn't leave it there for anyone to find. She tried prising it from the timber frame and looked around for a knife, anything to get it off. It came away with ragged edges and she went to the paintbox, using the same knife to lever up the bottom tray and conceal the painted canvas beneath.

'Gia?' Taddeo was coming inside. 'Where are you?'

'Out on the verandah.' She closed the paintbox lid and, slightly breathless, pointed to the note on it as he appeared. 'Edie left me this, I need you to carry it home for me.'

❧

Edie's funeral was small and at a far, lonely spot in the cemetery, for they'd been told by the sexton that those who died by their own hand were not permitted to be buried near any of the sections denoted for religions. Even in death, thought Gia, Edie was separated from others. Only she, Serena, Josie and Vilma stood by in attendance, Taddeo just behind, the children left at home with Pino and Alfio. Gia wished Beryl and Shirley could have been there too. And Keith, of course. It seemed impossible he may return one day to this.

Vilma wore a hat with black netting veiling her face and though she appeared stoic and unmoved, Gia thought her knuckles looked white as she clenched her handbag in front of her. Gia looked up into the sky – clear, blue, silent, an expanse seemingly close and embracing yet remote, impervious. She looked down again as the coffin went below and they threw flowers.

Afterwards, as they were leaving, Gia glanced back to the far, wretched pile of dirt and saw the sexton already heading across the cemetery with spade in hand to fill it in. Ahead, Serena and Josie murmured between themselves. Thinking of Edie's painting, Gia went over to Vilma, who walked stiffly a little way apart from them.

'It's just awful, isn't it? How are you with it?'

Vilma let out a short breath. 'I know you mean well, but please, just leave me be.'

She strode off without a word more to any of them.

'She's a funny one,' said Josie, linking her arm through Gia's. 'Like a prickle.'

Gia watched Vilma go, a black figure rummaging in her handbag for a cigarette, walking alone all the way back to Amiens, where she didn't want to be, to a husband she didn't like.

~

At home, back in her house clothes, Gia fried up some eggs and bread and sat unable to eat as Taddeo tucked in. Her pregnancy hung heavy on her then and she reached to rub her back.

With his fork, Taddeo cut his egg into pieces, the metal on china grating at her. 'The doctor said he'd let the army know about Edie,' he said around a mouthful. 'To tell Keith.'

'Did you hear if the police went and saw Jack?'

'They say there's nothing to go on. It was probably just youths letting off steam.'

'No, I don't believe that.' She couldn't let him use that same avoidance this time. 'Maybe Jack heard from someone at the post office about the telegram?' she ventured, thinking he might have terrorised Edie on the chance there'd now be no reprisal from Keith. 'We could ask to—'

Taddeo flung down the fork with a clatter. 'You have to let it go, Gia. The likes of Jack Armstrong will always win here. He's got the right name, the right birthplace.' He pushed back his chair. 'The rest of us just have to get by, keep our heads down and hope we're left be.' His hand shook as he reached for his hat by the door. 'I must get back to work.'

Gia stared at the plates of congealing egg. Taddeo hadn't spoken once about being taken and put in the internment camp but she realised it remained with him, an unseen scar.

She carried the plates to the sink. Her new chilli plant sat in a small pot by the open window, its tender foliage bright in the sunlight. Looking beyond it, she saw Taddeo heading out into the orchard and could hear the leaves rustling, the day shifting.

Pesche con Crema

With the streetlight slanting through the venetians, as I lay in the dark I could just make out the curve of beach and mountains that Edie Dawson had painted. I wondered if Nonna had hung it in my bedroom rather than hers to have it close, but not to see it all the time and be reminded of Edie and of Palmi and her lost family. It struck me that perhaps, as much as you loved and remembered amid the pain, some days you just needed to live your own life.

Poor Edie. I saw that it still hurt Nonna to speak of what happened, despite it being decades ago. I'd almost put my arm around her. I should have. It just felt a bit funny to, even if we'd become closer. I'd always been the kid, her arm around me, not vice versa. Unsure, I didn't want to come across as condescending. One minute, Nonna Gia could be so tender in confiding and the next revert to being pragmatic, perhaps a long-practised way of protecting herself.

I thought of Edie's paintbox in the wardrobe and the letters inside. But I didn't recall any nude paintings in there. I don't think I'd have missed that. I was burning to know whether Keith had returned from the war and also if Jack Armstrong ever got what he deserved, though it seemed likely he probably didn't. After talking about Edie, Nonna had understandably wanted to stop there for the time being and so we did.

I looked at the bedside clock, counting down until the hotel's closing time. Fifteen minutes to go. I steeled myself in readiness to walk up there, then, in the night. Nonna was asleep, the house in darkness for almost two hours. If she found me sneaking out, Nonna would be so hysterical I'd never be allowed out on my own again. But I had to see Tim.

It gnawed at me the way he'd left when we'd last met at the train station. And we hadn't got to arrange to meet next as we usually did. I had to talk to him. I sensed I could lose him otherwise. It was time to explain about my family, my father, and to ask if his grandfather was Keith Dawson. Time for the secrecy and shame to start to end. And it felt impossible to ring the hotel with Nonna maybe hearing or to go there in the day with Tim's parents about.

The clock ticked over to midnight. I got dressed and put on my running shoes without socks. Easing the bedroom door shut behind me, I heard soft snores from Nonna's room. No sign of Zucchero. I moved through the dark house to the back screen door. Its opening click was like a rifle shot. I froze, barely breathing, then slipped out. The breezy night felt restless. Low clouds sailed overhead, strangely fast. Maybe that's how they were at night – I'd never looked before. Black shadows. I kept to them, heart thudding, hoping no weirdos were about. The old man's house observed me with blinded windows. A dog barked a few houses away.

At the main street, a semi-trailer roared through, its lights blazing and I pulled back. Everything was shut except for the hotel. At that late hour, even the motel vacancy sign had been switched off at Serena and Pino's. Most of the street looked deserted except for several cars and utes parked out front of the pub where people stood around talking, getting ready to leave. One of the blokes gave a low wolf-whistle as I walked past. I kept my head down not looking at any of them and walked with purpose as though I was returning to the hotel.

Thankfully the side gate was well-oiled and silent as I let myself in the backyard, the chook house all shut up for the night. I peeked in the kitchen window where a light was on but no-one was in there. The next window abutted the bar and I saw the front door was now shut. Tim's father put barstools up on tables while behind the counter Tim loaded glasses into a washer. I tapped the window ever so lightly. Tim looked straight over. His eyes widened. He swiftly looked to his dad who hadn't noticed and pointed for me to meet him out the back.

'What are you doing here?' he hissed. 'Are you all right?'

'I had to see you,' I whispered.

Light fell from the hallway through the open back door and he pushed me around the side of the verandah into the darkness. Our lips met, hungry for one another, even though we'd fought last time, the dark and the late hour conniving against us holding out on each other.

'Shit, Sof, what if one of those drunk deadshits out front had had a go at you?'

'I'm okay. It was the only way I could see you.'

'I'm sorry. I shouldn't have left like that. I was being a dickhead.'

Mr Dinning called out, 'Tim?'

I shied further into the shadows as he came to the back door.

'Dad, I'm just going to walk home a mate from school, she only lives a couple of streets away.' He didn't wait for an answer, hurrying me off the verandah without being seen.

We walked the long way around so we didn't have to pass the people that still stood talking out front of the pub. Tim felt for my hand and in the darkness its warmth reassured me.

'You don't have to walk me back.'

'Sweetie, there's no way I'm letting you walk home alone.'

I smiled at him calling me sweetie for the first time. Coming to him had been the right thing. 'I can't be long in case Nonna wakes up. But I had to tell you why it's been hard for me to tell my family about us.' I took a breath feeling his gaze. 'It has to do with my parents.'

And as we walked past houses and shopfronts shut up for the night, the lonely backstreets to ourselves, I told him how Mum had fallen pregnant to an Australian fellow she'd loved very much. How it was a big deal that they hadn't been married. And that he'd died before I was even born. Tim kept looking at the road as we walked but he was listening intently, taking it all in with a slight frown. I didn't tell him Nonna's story as well. I couldn't.

'But there are other things too,' I explained, 'that go way back, that make it hard too.'

Tim stopped, letting go of my hand. 'So, your dad was from here? Stanthorpe?' His questions thudded into me. 'And he died before you were born. About seventeen years ago?' He saw me nod. 'But you don't know who he was?'

'Not really. Mum always called him Arro.' I had to finally say it. 'No, I don't know.'

'Arro? But— Shit. How could your family think that was all right? Even your mum?'

I opened my mouth, instantly going to defend them. That curious long-held instinct of trust in those older people who were around you when growing up. But thinking about it, I knew it wasn't okay what they'd done. No matter how heartbroken

Mum was or upset Nonna Gia and Nonno Taddeo were, they should have told me more. Not conditioned me to accept the not knowing. Especially Mum. Tim was the first person to really be on my side about it.

'You must think I'm an idiot,' I said.

He shook his head and hugged me. 'None of it's your fault.' But he looked unsettled.

I wanted to kiss him then, like I've never kissed anyone. Not caring who knew, what it meant or who'd be upset about it. It seemed so often, especially in times past, people had to deny who they were and who they wanted to be with – Nonna and Keith, Edie Dawson, Mum, the brides and grooms married by proxy, even Vilma. It had to stop. But as I moved to kiss him, Tim let me go, turned and kept walking. A bit taken aback, I kept walking too, unsure if he'd realised my intention or not.

We came to the corner where the hooky roses shone white in the dark.

'Mum will be here day after tomorrow,' I told him, as if that said it all.

He only said, 'We'd both better get home,' but gave me a kind smile as he moved to go.

Again, no kiss. I frowned a little, confused. But as I walked back along the footpath, I felt him watching me and turned to see him wave from the end of the street and then walk off.

At Nonna's fence, I saw a lamp on in her bedroom and panicked. Noiselessly, I ran around the side and could see the bathroom light was on. She must be in the toilet. In that split moment, I deliberated if I should get back to my room or hide outside. I couldn't risk her checking in on me as she sometimes did. Zucchero watched me ease the back door closed without clicking the lock. The toilet flushed. I stole back to my room and got into bed, shoes and all, just as the bathroom door opened. Beneath the covers I kept as still as I could, sweating and stifling my hard breathing. I heard the doorknob's soft turn, a pause as Nonna Gia must have looked in on me and then the door closing again. Slowly I released my breath.

It was ages before my heart slowed and I felt able to get up, take off my shoes and change back into my nightie. I brushed the grit from the end of the sheets. Nonna didn't even like shoes on the carpet, let alone on a bed, or *in* it. But thankfully, I'd seemed to have gotten away with slipping out. I just hoped Tim was okay with what I'd told him. It wasn't until I closed my eyes that it occurred to me that I'd been so involved in my story, I'd forgotten to ask him if his grandfather was Keith Dawson.

In her largest ceramic bowl, Nonna mixed cake batter with a fork. 'Remember, it's *pesche* not *pesce con crema*,' she told me, as though she'd never said it to me before. 'We're making peaches with cream, not fish.'

Though it wasn't actual peaches at all – the Calabrian sweet was essentially a piece of trickery that was two hemispheres of sponge cake held together by pastry cream, shaped and coloured to fool the eye that they were, in fact, little peaches. Nonna Gia even put fresh mint leaves on top that looked just like peach leaves, but it was all a masquerade.

'Don't just stand there, Sofia. You can take the skin off that lemon.'

'Zest, you mean.' I strove to keep the edge out of my voice.

She kept mixing the batter, apparently unaware, her gold hoop earrings wiggling. I felt torn. It meant so much that she'd

been confiding in me but Tim's reaction to how my family had
kept my father from me pressed at that seeping resentment. If
I wasn't careful, it could all suddenly gush out. At the same time,
I grasped that it wasn't something they'd done to hurt me. And
so it felt hard to voice it to Nonna, as if I was the one breaking
the unspoken agreement that we all had to not mention it. As if
it was me causing the trouble.

I snuck her a look as I zested the lemon. I decided to take
another tack.

'Does Keith Dawson live in Stanthorpe?'

Her hand faltered. 'What?'

'You said he wasn't in the cemetery, when I asked.' I went to
tap the zest into a bowl.

'Put it *here*,' she cried. 'Into the batter. No talking now. I need
to think what I'm doing. Your mother's here tomorrow. I got to
get these peaches done ready for Christmas and there is so much
else …' She hunted about, then cursed. 'I thought I had red food
colouring.'

'I'll go get some.' Uneasy and eager to flee, I hastily pushed my
feet into my thongs.

'Well, go to Gianni, not the supermarket.' She got out her
Glomesh purse. 'And be quick!'

I came around the side driveway into the line of sight of the
old man on the verandah. I could just go right up to him and ask
if he was Keith Dawson. The stroke meant he couldn't speak but
surely he'd understand. At least, nod. But I walked on, bearing
my own ache.

⌒

With the tiny bottle of food colouring in my hand, I headed
straight back home knowing Nonna was frantic to get the peaches

done. I did glance over to the hotel as I went past, wondering if Tim might see me and come to a window. He didn't. And then, as I was turning into Nonna's street, I saw him about to go in his grandfather's gate. He hesitated as I ran up.

'Hi, Sofie, I can't really talk now. I'm just quickly bringing this from the pub.'

I saw he held a plate wrapped in alfoil. 'Is that for your granddad—' and suddenly I realised how to ask if the old man was Keith without really asking, 'I mean, for Mr Dinning?'

'*Sofia!*'

We both flinched and wheeled round. Nonna Gia was on the front steps, barefoot, in her apron and headscarf, hands on hips, watching out for me to return. My mouth fell open.

'*Vieni qua*, Sofia!' Her shout ricocheted down the street.

'Sorry, Tim. I have to go.' I rapidly backed away.

He nodded, somewhat bemused, then added, 'My granddad's name isn't Dinning.'

'What?'

'Sofia! *Vieni qua!* Come here. *Now!*' Nonna bordered on distraught.

The old man leant forward, watching the whole thing. I hurried across the road and Nonna pushed me inside, slamming the screen and then the front door behind it.

'I've told you to keep away from that boy,' she cried. '*Santa Maria!* What has got into you that you don't mind your nonna any more?'

But I was almost immune, jolted to think that maybe, just maybe, Dianne Dinning could have once been Dianne Dawson. And perhaps she'd learnt about her father and Nonna Gia and that's why she was staring at us in church. Suddenly I felt restless and on edge. I don't know why, it was just a feeling about Dianne after all, I had no actual evidence for it. And not that it should really matter. If Tim was linked to Nonna's past, that was how it was. But again, there was that sense like when a coin was tossing in the air, yet to fall on heads or tails.

'I think I want to ring Mum.'

'What for? She'll be at work now. And she'll be here tomorrow anyway!' Nonna gave an exasperated puff but then she saw my face and at once became gentle. 'What is it, *cara*?'

I shook my head, holding back, still grasping. The cakey smell of the peach halves cooking reached us and she glanced worriedly at the oven but put her hand on my shoulder.

I took a breath. 'I think I know why you won't say what happened to Keith Dawson.'

In time, I'd come to the other things I needed to voice. But it was a beginning. I wasn't falling back to being a kid any more.

Nonna gave me a long look, torn as the baking aroma got stronger. 'All right. We talk tonight.' Hurrying to the oven, she said, 'And ring up your mother if you want to.'

I kept standing there a moment as she bustled around. I thought about it and decided not to call. She was arriving the next day. And it was better to talk in person. I backed away.

The mail sat on the telephone table in the hall. Nonna must have brought it in when she was waiting for me to return from the shop. I saw Mel's usual little flowers on one of the envelopes. It seemed a while since I had written to her last. Almost like I was another person then. Although it must've been only a fortnight or so. I went into my room and unfolded her letter.

My hair streaks went green in the pool at Deb's barbecue. It was so embarrassing!! So glad I brought a hat! Can you believe it?!! You should have been there!! Who is this spunk you met? Amazing blue eyes, hey? And older. Bet your Grandma doesn't know! Ha! What

is his name? Does he work? You hardly said a thing. What's the big
secret? Come on, spill!

For the first time in a while, I scrabbled in the bottom of the bag
for a chocolate, my fingertips brushing past the sketches Tim had
done. And as I could hear Nonna still out in the kitchen, I ate
one, then another, and carefully hid the Crunchie and Cherry
Ripe wrappers in some alfoil as usual. I held that ragged tin ball,
letting it bite into my hand, for a long while after.

In Gathered Quiet

'Vilma's here to see the baby,' Taddeo said from the bedroom door as Gia finished changing Elena's nappy. 'Will I tell her to come in?'

'I thought you said she and Carmelo couldn't come today?'

From out the back drifted the hum of Serena and Pino, Josie, Alfio and the children already sitting talking before lunch at a table set up beneath the orchard trees. Gia had been privately glad Vilma and Carmelo had declined the invitation Taddeo insisted it polite to offer.

He shrugged. 'Well, she must've decided to come alone.'

'Send her in.' Gia put her lips to Elena's downy head, inhaling her baby scent, and lay her in the cot. She'd sewn the inside hems of Elena's clothes with red thread in the Calabrian way to protect from the evil eye but felt wary of why Vilma really wanted to see the baby.

Vilma came in carrying a bulging straw bag instead of her usual handbag and in surprise Gia wondered if it held a large baby present. 'Hello, Gia.' Vilma put it down and peered in at Elena, who was gradually falling asleep. '*Che bella*, but what a pale baby she is.'

'All babies are,' said Gia a little defensively, glad Taddeo had gone back downstairs to the others. 'Her olive skin will darken in time.'

'I'm sorry that Carmelo and I couldn't make it to lunch today.'

'You're not staying then?' Gia politely tried to keep the hope from her voice.

Vilma knew better. 'You'll be relieved I'm just passing by. Elena. It's a good name.'

At that unexpected compliment, Gia admitted, 'Taddeo's a bit upset I didn't follow tradition and use his mother's name, but I wanted it to start with an E. For Edie.'

They both went quiet. From outside wafted more table chatter, Vince kicking a ball, Josie's laughter. Vilma said, 'The war goes on and yet it seems so different … without it being just us women on the farms.' She didn't say it was also different with Edie gone, though Gia sensed she meant that too. 'Here …' Vilma took a little sack from her pocket. 'For Elena.'

'Thank you.' Gia felt the salt inside before she saw the crystals. All the others had given eggs as the traditional gift for a newborn so that Elena would grow to be a person of substance. But only Vilma had given her the other customary gift of salt, for intelligence.

Vilma moved to go. 'Wait.' Gia faltered. 'Why did you tell Keith I was in Brisbane?'

Vilma's lips began to curve, but seeing Gia's open face she shrugged, less guarded too. 'It was only fair. Things how they were. He was so desperate to see you before he left. When Edie refused to tell him where you'd gone, it felt too harsh, even if she thought she was doing the right thing. Edie didn't know how it was to be a proxy bride.'

Neither of them mentioned that Keith was still missing.

She looked Gia in the eye. 'I'd been hard on you too, I know. I'm sorry for that.'

'Oh.' Gia strove to veil her surprise.

'Perhaps we're alike in wanting more to life. I first saw it with you wanting to learn extra English on the ship while others like Serena seemed happy to let their husbands take the lead.' Vilma looked away. 'And here, I saw your husband treated you well when mine didn't. That you weren't as trapped as me. I resented you for that and for you making a go of the farm.'

Again from outside came some laughter amid the talking at the table and Gia hoped Serena or Josie didn't come looking for them. 'Sometimes I wonder,' she offered, 'if I had the chance again, whether I'd marry by proxy. Although Serena seems happy and in love.'

'I know I wouldn't.' Vilma shrugged. 'Even if Carmelo wasn't a *bastardo*.'

'Taddeo doesn't want me involved in the farm now Elena is born. He says I have enough to do in the house.' Gia looked helplessly at her, surprising herself by voicing what she hadn't to the others, yet she felt Vilma might understand more than Josie and Serena. 'I'm stuck. What was the point of it all? Doing that work ourselves? We're back where we started.' She hushed as Elena stirred. 'Worse even, now we know what we can't have.'

'No, what we did, what you convinced us to do, Gia, was a step towards starting change. For other women, in time. So maybe it's not so different for us but it will be more so for Elena, and then Elena's daughter, and so it goes on.'

Gia's eyes went to the bulging straw bag on the floor. 'You're leaving, aren't you?'

Vilma's face gave her away, though she said nothing. And Gia realised that while she'd likely told Carmelo she was going to Gia and Taddeo's baby celebration to be able to get away from him, she could have gone directly to the train station rather than come by here first as she left. Gia went across the hall to her bedroom where she hid her housekeeping tin.

Vilma followed her to the doorway. 'Oh, Gia, no ...'

She put the money in Vilma's hands. 'Do you need anything else? Any extra clothes?'

Vilma smiled with damp eyes. 'In your size?'

They both chuckled but Gia could've given her a shove considering she remained plump from carrying Elena. 'I better get back before the others come looking for us.'

'There's one other thing ...' Vilma hesitated. 'I don't know how Jack Armstrong knew about that photograph from the picnic but he must have friends in the police, for that's who I took it to.' She sighed. 'It was the only way to have Carmelo gone a while. I'm sorry about the rest.'

Gia looked at her a long moment, part of her angry, knowing how Taddeo silently suffered from his internment. Even if, with the way the war was going, their husbands likely would've been interned anyway, the photograph had given the police a reason to do so earlier. Then she shook her head, all she once might have said suddenly pointless. 'Jack and those men hate Italians. They probably would have done those awful things to us anyhow.' But Gia knew she could never tell the others what Vilma had done, knowing the betrayal they'd feel.

'I just wish I'd left before Carmelo had come back.' Vilma shook her head. 'Stupid.'

Gia kept looking at her. 'Close the door.' She pulled the paintbox from under the bed and heard Vilma exhale. 'Edie left me this. I don't know why. I can't paint.' Gia lifted the bottom where she'd hidden Keith's letters and the folded canvas. 'But you should have this.'

Vilma unfolded the canvas of herself nude and blanched, caught out. And Gia saw in her face something she'd never seen before, despite everything Vilma had been through – fear.

'Only I know of it apart from you and Edie,' she told her.

'Oh … thank you.' Vilma's voice ebbed. She refolded the canvas and placed it in her shirt against her chest before hoisting the straw bag onto her shoulder.

Gia understood then how she still loved Edie. That they could have left together but Edie maybe felt unable to go, trapping them both until Carmelo returned. 'Good luck, Vilma.'

'And you as well. And your Elena.' They embraced awkwardly.

'Come the front way,' said Gia. 'So you don't have to go out past the others.'

'Goodbye, Gia. Perhaps I might be back. One day.'

From the door, Gia watched Vilma walk to the gate and head up the road towards town. By the time Carmelo expected her home she'd be long gone on a train headed south, or maybe north. Gia knew she wouldn't see her again. Vilma was finally on her way.

～

Not long after dark, when the others had all gone home, Carmelo stumbled up to the front of the house, bellowing, 'Vilma! Get home now!'

Taddeo looked at Gia who hastily placed Elena in the cot and they went to the door.

'Carmelo, Vilma left here hours ago,' Taddeo called. 'Have you not seen her?'

That halted him a moment. He looked up at them, glassy-eyed and somewhat thrown, though Gia sensed a current running through him, a malice heightened by the drink.

'She must be in there!' He reeled towards the steps. 'I want to check.'

'Of course,' Taddeo began, 'but she's not—'

'No.' Gia barred the doorway. 'You're not coming in, especially in your state.'

'Gia—' Taddeo looked quickly at Carmelo, somewhat scandalised.

'You let your wife tell you what's what, do you?' Carmelo grasped the rail at the bottom step, swaying slightly. 'I heard all about you.' He shot her a razor-sharp glare. 'You were the ringleader, making our women think they didn't need us any more once we were away.'

'Go home, Carmelo.' Gia's voice was steel. 'And don't come here again.'

'*Vacca grassa*,' he muttered at her. *Fat cow.*

'I think you should go home.' Taddeo went down a few steps to block his way up. 'Vilma is probably there now.'

Carmelo looked from him to Gia and back to Taddeo again. He sneered, his eyes going to the house as he yelled, 'If you're still in there, Vilma, you get home. I'll be waiting.'

They watched him stagger off into the dark. Taddeo went to the road to ensure he was able to make his way home but Gia could only think of what Vilma must have gone through on that isolated farm with no witness to Carmelo's cruelty, the hopelessness of having to remain married to him. And then, once she managed to be rid of him a while, how another man harmed her. She hoped for Vilma's sake she never needed to return.

Gia was holding Elena when Taddeo came back inside. He looked at them both and shook his head. 'Do you think something has happened to Vilma? Should I tell the police?'

'No, Taddeo. Sit down.'

'But she might be hurt somewhere.'

'I think, at last, she might not be hurt any more, now that she's left. For good.'

Taddeo stared at her, stunned by the scandal, the shame this would bring for Carmelo and Vilma and their families, but as Gia kept looking at him, his brow furrowed and he sat down.

'Well … I doubt he'll stay in Stanthorpe once this gets out.' Again, he shook his head. 'But then, I never really liked him.'

Gia rocked Elena gently. She'd never really liked Vilma either, but in a small way she had come to understand her better, and could feel compassion for her.

∿

The day the war ended Gia and Taddeo embraced, and across the farms and from the main roadway carried joyous cheering and singing, banged metal lids and vehicles honking horns. Yet the usual quiet soon returned and Gia felt as if little had changed at all. Except, perhaps, there was an unseen lifting, a faint hope for what now might be. Even if, while that promise tried to bloom, she was still consumed by the heavy sadness of what the war had taken. And she kept her grief tightly furled.

Gia looked at Edie's painting and thought of her mother and father, of Nonna and Salvatore. It was hard to hear of Serena writing to her family again. She was very happy for her, but it was hard. Gia could never hear her own family's voices again, even on paper, or tell them about Elena, as she longed to. And it wasn't quite the same when Taddeo wrote to his mother with the news. Gia tried to picture Rosaria holding Elena, Nonna keeping her safe from the evil eye with a *cornicello*, Salvatore laughing, Angelo offering one of his sayings.

Incredibly, the *Viminale*, the 'bride ship' she and so many other proxy brides had sailed on out to Australia, had been sunk off the Calabrian coast right near Palmi. 'The Italian army commandeered it to carry troops,' Taddeo relayed to her when he spotted the article among the war stories that newspapers kept printing. 'In the middle of 1943, a US boat torpedoed it when the Allies attacked Palmi from both air and sea ...' He'd looked at her then, uneasily, realising it was around when her family were killed. Gia said nothing, but it felt odd to think at that time she had been in the country of one of those Allies and people like Jack.

Keith hadn't returned. There'd been no word. But Taddeo had also read it was taking troops some time to get back and so Gia carried hope. Even if some days it felt like it weighed a ton. She recalled Edie saying, *tomorrow, no matter how you feel, you need to get up*, and Gia did, for Elena. Yet she couldn't help thinking of one of her father's tales, told on a winter's night when salty winds blew hard and they gathered around the kitchen fire. It had been about a lost love between a sailor and his sweetheart, and when he never returned from the stormy sea, his love had wept ... *if the tides of the sea run full, it is the river of my tears that fills them.*

Elena ran through the pretty orchard, tripping and getting up again, still finding her feet. The peach flowers hummed with bees and Elena's dark hair shone in the morning sunlight. From the boiling copper, stirring washing with the stick, Gia looked up to keep an eye on her. She was well into expecting her next baby, and it wasn't easy for her to run and bring Elena back.

'Not too far, Elena.' Gia swivelled around. 'Taddeo? Taddeo …' But he must have been off further to the front of the property so she put down the stick and went to bring Elena closer. 'I've got a job for you. You pass Mamma the pegs.'

They were still both at the line strung between two old posts when Taddeo emerged, coming towards them in long strides. 'Keith is back! I just saw him on the road.'

Gia's knees gave a little. 'He is all right?' She could barely give her voice sound.

'He looks very thin, like he's had a hard time of it.'

'You told him about Edie?'

Taddeo looked down. 'He knew, from the army. But I told him the rest.'

The wooden peg bit into her hand but she stayed impassive. 'How was he?'

'He seems different. Very serious. Quiet. I'll go over later, once he's settled in a bit.'

'Yes, best you go alone.' Her voice was faint. She couldn't yet trust herself to go too.

～

It took weeks before Gia could go to the Dawson farm. She pushed Elena in the pram along the dirt road, even though she was getting a bit big for it. The wheels abrading on gravel reminded Gia of the first time she'd gone next door, she and Taddeo riding along on the old shearer's bicycle, she holding a saucepan of *crostoli*. The police never did return the bike to them, and when Taddeo went to ask about it they'd told him it had accidentally been lost.

Nearing the Dawson farm, she saw the *For Sale* sign on the fence, as Taddeo said she would. Keith had hung a new gate. The cowbell was gone. Gia pushed the pram up the driveway, gazing at the hushed house, its windows shut though shiny clean, the geranium pot no longer on its windowsill. She paused. It felt very hard to see Keith after all that had passed, and especially being heavily pregnant as she was. Then Elena complained at the pram being stopped and Gia pushed on up towards the shed, knowing she had to, for both their sakes.

'Gia ...'

She turned to see Keith at the back door of the house. He sailed down the steps to her and she saw he was still thin, though not as gaunt as Taddeo had said he'd been at first.

'I'm sorry,' she said. 'I should have come sooner.'

He shook his head and embraced her, held her close, despite her fuller middle, and she clung to him, her nose in his shirt, against his neck, his breath deep in her curls. They let go.

'This is Elena,' smiled Gia, as the two-year-old wriggled to climb from the pram.

Keith lifted her out and Elena went quiet in surprise. She rushed to Gia's side and stood burying herself into her mother's skirt but peeking out at him with dark, solemn eyes.

'She's a sweetheart.' He glanced from her to Gia's middle but didn't say anything.

She put her hand to it. 'I'm sorry, Keith—'

'Don't keep saying that. Things are what they are.'

But she sensed him being brave. It made her want to weep. 'Where will you go?'

Elena emerged and tentatively headed for the shed to explore as they watched her.

'I don't know yet. But I can't stay here.'

'I know.' And she knew it wasn't only because of Edie.

They stood side by side, keeping their eyes on Elena a little way off.

'I love you,' she said simply.

'I love you, Gia.'

She quickly wiped a tear. 'I'll think of us at Coolangatta. It was lovely there.'

'It was …'

But he didn't attempt to embrace her or even brush near her again.

'There's a buyer interested in the place,' he told her. 'I expect I'll be gone soon.'

And like that, what could have been ran out like water through the meshes.

∼

The Sunday after Keith moved out of his house, Gia peered around the church crammed with its usual throng for Mass. Of course, she didn't expect to see him there, he'd never attended in the past, but a part of her would be always looking out for him now that he'd left the farm. As the congregation dispersed and out front the priest circulated and parishioners spoke in their usual cliques, Josie came bustling up between Gia and Serena and clutched their arms.

'Have you seen what's happened to Jack Armstrong?' she whispered.

'No, what?' Gia turned at once and scanned the people standing about talking.

She saw, over by a tree, Myrtle Armstrong speaking to the priest while she held the hand of her little boy. Behind her, Jack stood somewhat sulkily with a black eye and cut lip, one side of his face mottled and swollen, hands on hips showing split knuckles.

Josie hissed, 'People are saying Keith did it.'

Gia looked Jack straight in the eye. 'Well, if he did, Jack deserved it.'

'Gia!' admonished Serena. 'We're still at church.'

Jack stared back at her, battered but still defiant and Gia knew that even if his hostile deeds had seemed to have ceased, a cold, silent war of hatred between them would remain.

From Sharper Dark

'*La prima acqua é quella che bagna.*' Nonna Gia sighed, the past still before her.

I couldn't keep the hollowness from my voice. 'That doesn't make sense.'

'The first water is what wets you. And that is the hardest. After that you get used to it.'

'I mean Keith Dawson leaving. I don't believe he went.'

Nonna focused on me, her eyes the words.

I shook my head, floundering. 'The water, it may be cold at first, and you get used to it, but then you can get cold again, and, and—'

'What are you saying, Sofia?'

I felt jaded by the superstitions and proverbs and speaking in riddles. It was finally dawning on me it was a way Nonna could deflect without saying what was really beneath.

'Well, if Keith did go, he must've come back. That old man across … well, I know you loved Nonno too but he's not here any more and you should be able to—'

'Stop, please stop. It's late. Time to go to bed.'

'No, I don't care how late it is. You should get to be happy
after—'

'*Carissima* …' The tenderness in the endearment reached me
and I settled down.

'All I mean, Nonna, is that can't be the end of it.'

'No, we will talk more about this, but tomorrow,' she said.
'When Elena gets here.'

I stood to go to bed. 'Tomorrow,' I said, as though it were a
pact, and she just looked down at her hands.

⌣

The moment I heard Nonna turn on the shower the next morning,
I whipped out the telephone directory and shuffled the pages to
find the hotel's number. I dialled, hoping it wasn't too early to
call. Mr Dinning, Tim's father, answered.

'Oh, hello, could I please speak to Tim please?' My palms
dampened.

'Who's speaking?'

A beat. 'Sofie.' I heard the phone being placed down and he
called out to Tim.

Then the sound of a door being closed. 'Hello? Sofie?'

'Hi, I'm sorry about Nonna yelling yesterday, she's—'

'Don't worry about it. I didn't expect you to call.'

'Oh. Well—' My face felt hot.

'Look, I can't talk now, I'm sorry.' He sounded like he was
going to hang up.

I blurted. 'You haven't been the same to me since I told you
about my father.'

'Rubbish. I feel sorry for you. You should talk to your mum
about it.'

'You feel sorry for me?'

He swore under his breath. 'I mean, feel for you. Look, I can't talk right now. Really.'

I pictured his parents trying to listen in. 'Okay, fine. Sorry.' I hung up feeling foolish and cross.

The shower was still going. I found Zucchero and carried him to the lounge to cuddle. He squirmed at the scrunch as I sat on the plastic and I let him jump down to the carpet. I thought of Mum driving out to us, smiling and happy about the School of Arts project, her little car carrying wrapped presents, the chocolates she bought each year from a department store carousel and my dress hanging in the back. I thought of Connie saying Mum deserved a lovely Christmas.

'Why don't we put up the Christmas tree?' I suggested about midmorning in the tense quiet.

'What? Now?' Nonna Gia glanced at the clock, though we weren't sure exactly when Mum might arrive. She'd only said sometime before lunch.

'May as well. It's so quiet around here.' I gave her a pointed look, since after all her talking it now seemed she wouldn't engage further about Keith Dawson until Mum got there.

I went to Nonna's sewing room that had a bed in it where Mum slept when she stayed. The room didn't get morning sun and was cool and shadowy, the venetians shut. I stood for a moment gazing at Nonna's sewing machine, the buttons and thread in jars and Quality Street tins. I breathed the persistent scent of carpet freshener and fabric rolls. My heart drummed. *What was I doing?*

It was like the tossed coin had landed but its face remained covered, waiting to be revealed. I got the Christmas tree box from the cupboard and carried it to the lounge room.

'The usual spot in the corner, Nonna?'

She looked at me for a long beat and then nodded.

The lid of the stereogram stayed down. No Dean Martin that morning. Not even the old Christmas album featuring Bing Crosby and Frank Sinatra that Nonna usually played during the tree decorating. Together we draped the plastic 'snow-covered' fir in tinsel and I hung baubles, angels on ice skates and leering Santas that seemed even more incongruous in the taut silence. I didn't realise that Nonna stood back rather than directing as she usually did until Zucchero became enthralled by a swaying bauble and she shooed him out.

'What about the nativity too?' I wanted everything just like it had been in my childhood.

Nonna shrugged, amenable. 'Of course.'

She set up her prized nativity scene over on the sideboard, the *presepio* not just of Mary, Joseph, shepherds and wise men but a whole Italian village of stone houses with a stream, working water wheel and town characters like the baker, a blacksmith and women sitting together shelling peas, all those who added to village life. Each figure was carefully positioned, except for the baby Jesus who wouldn't appear until Christmas Eve. When I was little, I used to sit before it and imagine stories about the people in the tiny buildings, all of them in lovely, perfect, cheerful families of mother and father and siblings.

I heard Mum's car pull into the driveway and glanced at Nonna. The car door closed, then the boot. Neither of us moved from the lounge room. The back screen door banged.

Mum came in juggling a bag, my dress on a coat hanger and a box of presents she put on the table. 'I could do with a hand,' she said, seeing us.

I rushed to take her bag. 'Sorry.'

'Not this, there's more in the backseat.' She gave me a kiss, looking over at Nonna.

I went out the back, felt the sun hot on my hair and tilted my face. There wasn't a single cloud in the entire sky, not one. I came around the side and glanced over to the old man watching from his verandah. Perhaps he mightn't be able to make it known in his own voice what was true, but I was close now to being able to do so for him, and Nonna. She ought to be happy. There didn't have to be covering up and shame from the past any more, enough time had gone by. I leant into the car, trapped heat mugging my face. Mum's crystal hanging from the rear-vision mirror cast rainbows over the vinyl seats. Gathering up the packages, I shut the door with my hip, again squinting across the street before I headed back inside.

Mum stood at the sink drinking a glass of water, the sleeves of her peasant blouse pushed up, bangles clinking as they slid. At the table, Nonna sat quiet, her hands fidgeting on the tablecloth. I put down the other packages. The kitchen clock ticked loudly. The hum of cars from the main road sounded closer than usual. A neighbour began sweeping a concrete path. Mum placed the glass in the sink and I sensed she and Nonna had just had one of their arguments, always kept to a whispered hiss so the neighbours wouldn't overhear, that worry of shame always close.

I looked to each of them. 'What? What is it?'

The neighbour's broom went on, a gentle, rhythmic *swish, swish* on cement. Poor Nonna looked strained. Mum turned around.

'It doesn't have to be a big thing,' I said into the silence, sitting at the table across from Nonna and thinking of Keith Dawson just over the road. 'I'm sorry for Nonno but if—' I took a jagged breath. Mum was born during the war. I'd long known that. But only recently had I learnt Nonno had been taken away and interned. Just when, exactly, did he return? I fought to catch up. Because if Keith Dawson was— then Tim … My heart thudded in my throat.

Mum pulled out a chair next to me. 'I'm sorry, darling. I didn't realise just how much it must be hurting you not to have had your father in your life.' She squeezed my hand. 'I thought not talking about him would protect you but you're still hurt, in another way.'

'What? What's this got—'

'Sofie, the thing is, about your father, well, I know I've always called him Arro, but, well, you should know that your father's name is Ross.'

'What?' My eyes began prickling. I looked over at Nonna and saw she was teary too. 'Ross?' The word wavered in my mouth. Again, everything shifted. 'Is he … still alive?'

'No,' Mum said quickly, 'sadly, that he died is true.' She hesitated. 'But his father, your grandfather, is still alive. His name is Jack Armstrong and he lives just across the road.'

❧

From my room, where I lay in bed with my back to the partly open door, I could hear Nonna going about tidying tinsel from the lounge carpet and putting away the Christmas tree box. Cross-legged on the floor beside me, Mum looked worried. Silent tears kept leaking down my cheeks. I felt shivery with goosebumps.

The shock, I suppose. I didn't say a word about Tim. Couldn't think about him right then. I just wanted to know more about my father. In a way, I actually felt relief as much as being stunned. Mum was finally talking about him.

'Ross was a year ahead of me at school. He was a good cross-country runner. Bit of a larrikin.' A smile ghosted over her face. 'I didn't have much to do with him then but we knew each other, as people do in a small town. And we knew our parents didn't like each other. But being young and caught up in our own lives, I guess at first we didn't think much about what was behind that.'

I didn't say anything, wanting her to talk on and on until I knew it all.

'It wasn't easy being a girl growing up with Italian migrant parents at that time. Dad didn't see the point of girls getting too much education. He expected I would work on the farm and marry young. And only to a good Italian boy, of course. *Keep away from Skippys*, he'd say of Australian boys. My Italian girlfriends copped the same from their dads, and the Australian ones were told to keep clear of the wogs.' She sighed. 'It didn't help that Frank happily left school early to work at the farm. But being a boy he had more freedom. For me, being stuck out there felt hard when I thought of all that was happening elsewhere in the world.'

I stared at the window with its coverings of curtains and venetian blinds, as Mum told me how she'd lie awake at night, hearing the creaks and sighs of the house, the quiet of the countryside all around closing in on her. Wishing for another life. How Gia seemed to understand her restlessness but Taddeo couldn't or wouldn't comprehend it.

'They set me up with sons of their Italian friends but I resisted getting married, for years. Dad couldn't understand why. There were so many fights between us in those days. I wasn't allowed to wear make-up, or short skirts or knee-high boots, even though it was the sixties and I was over twenty-one then. I held on to a hope of going to university but Dad said he wouldn't have me *hanging around hippies. You should be married now.* But I didn't want to marry like my girlfriend Marina did – to escape. I couldn't marry without being in love.'

My eyes went to her and I wondered if she knew any of what Nonna Gia had told me, even though Nonna had said I was the first she'd told that she had been a proxy bride. It was hard to know who really knew what any more, so I stayed silent.

'In a way it was lucky for me Marina did get married and move to a house in town with her husband,' Mum went on. 'Ma and I convinced Dad to let me stay over at Marina's sometimes and I could go out without him knowing. He pretended he didn't anyway. The only places to go in town were a party, if one was on, or the pubs. And Ma and Dad made it clear all our lives that Frank and I were never to set foot in the Armstrongs' hotel. Up until then, I hadn't.'

I looked back to the closed venetians, no longer crying, listening carefully.

'Dianne's husband and Ross mostly worked behind the bar at night – by then Myrtle and Jack were only there during the day. That's how Ross and I first got talking. He teased me for ordering crème de menthe and lemonade.' She smiled a little, but her face was also sad. 'We'd joke with each other. Then one night after closing, he asked if I wanted to go for a drive. He was pretty proud of his Falcon. I teased him about that. It went on from there.'

Her head went down and she wiped a tear. 'It's hard to truly convey to you the love that was between us, that glimmer each time our eyes met. It was like we shared a constant hum that no-one knew but us. Some nights, even now, I dream of him. I can still hear the warmth in his voice. Smell his aftershave ...' And she petered out then, keeping what was most private to herself. 'But when I wake up the horror that he is gone feels fresh once again, years on, and it hurts.' Just then, Mum crumpled a little, forlorn, and she only said, 'For me, there could never be another.'

Both of us were silent then for a bit. She sighed.

'We knew our parents would stop us seeing each other, so we were pretty secretive. Dad used to say to me, *if you marry an Australian, the second of November is All Souls' Day*, meaning there'd be flowers on my grave if I did. And while perhaps it was an empty threat meant to keep me in line, knowing how my parents felt about the Armstrongs I was even more scared what may happen to us both if they found out. If only we could have ended it ...'

It had gone quiet out in the lounge room and I pictured Nonna listening in from the hallway. But then I heard her moving about in the kitchen and Mum began talking again.

'Ross made people laugh. He had a sharp wit. Blue eyes. I wish I had a photo for you but we never took any. Didn't want to risk the film being developed at the chemist. Ross outwardly acted tough around his mates but he was kind. Not hard like his father. Maybe Myrtle's hand was in that.' She shook her head. 'You laugh just like him, you know. I love hearing that bit of him in you. I should've told you sooner, I realise now. I'm sorry I didn't.'

I still said nothing, at once feeling cheated and elated to find this out about him and me.

'Ross said if I wanted to go to uni, he'd come with me to Brisbane and find work at a hotel there or as a labourer, anything really. We talked of getting married even if our parents were against it. We were in love, young and thought we could overcome it all.'

'So why didn't you just run off and get married?' My words came out hoarsely.

'So many times, I wish we'd eloped. We were still making plans, working out what to do, deciding how to tell our parents, when Ross died. I didn't even know yet I was pregnant.'

I glanced down, feeling miserable for us all. My voice croaked fainter. 'How did he—'

Her chin trembled. 'He was driving out along a lonely part of Eukey Road towards the national park. He and his mates used to race along a straight stretch out there sometimes. It was such a shock when I heard the news … but I couldn't show it too much. That was awful.'

Again, both of us went silent. I heard Nonna clank a pot out in the kitchen.

'Marina came with me to the funeral. Neither Ma or Dad went, Ross being an Armstrong. Dad seemed surprised I went but didn't stop me since most people in Stanthorpe who knew Ross from school went. He was pretty popular. I remember Myrtle and Jack there that day. Both devastated. And poor Dianne, with her husband and little Tim so young.'

I thought of the times we'd gone to the cemetery for Nonno Taddeo in the past couple of years. Oddly, not once did it occur to me that my dad was there too. I cried again.

'Mum, why didn't you tell me?'

'I'm so sorry.' She clasped my arm and I pulled back. 'I was always going to. At first you were too little. And then as each year went by, it got harder. When Ma and Dad left the farm and bought this house, they didn't realise that Myrtle and Jack Armstrong had left the pub. It felt more impossible to tell you then with them just across the bloody road! Then Myrtle died not long after Dad and a year or so on, Jack had the stroke—'

'You should have told me from the start.'

Mum appeared to consider this but didn't quite acquiesce. 'When I found out I was pregnant, I was a mess. Ma put two and two together and so I told her everything. She was so upset. Especially that I'd loved an Armstrong. Dad was furious. Petrified the local talk would destroy us all. Not many Italians thought much of Jack Armstrong, something to do with the war. Before I knew it, I was on a train to Brisbane keeping to a story that I was having a baby and the father was from the city and he'd died. In a way it was for Ma and Dad's sake, but also yours.'

She gave a long sigh. 'Me having a baby on my own was enough to set Dad against me, let alone what the truth may have brought about considering the long ongoing animosity between our families. In the fallout of Ross dying, Jack was wild with grief and hate and looking for someone to blame. And he remained very much against migrants. I didn't want to risk you being shunned or hurt by your grandfather. To me that was worse than not knowing.'

'So, my … grandfather doesn't know about me still?'

'Not that I know of. But I wonder if Dianne suspects. Perhaps that's why she sent Tim around. I just don't know.' Mum reached for the tissue box on the bedside table.

I gazed at the carpet, numbed. As much as it was a relief to know more, everything felt distorted, still shifting. The emptiness I'd so wanted to fill had been replaced by a dark crowding in. I felt betrayed and unsettled. The difference and hate from the time of the war had gone on unchecked to reach through decades. To me. All the while as I'd listened to Nonna Gia, I had assumed my own story was different, distant to all that. Yet from the moment she'd told me that she was a proxy bride, the truth had been unfolding to this.

All That Is After

I deliberately kept my head down and didn't look across the road as Mum and I left the house. In Mum's little car, the two of us drove out to the stretch of Eukey Road that headed towards Girraween National Park. I wanted to see the place my father had died. Needed to, in a way, even if I didn't want to think too closely about that night, seventeen years ago, when it would have been very nearly pitch dark but for the moon and the car lights.

While we had passed an occasional house that sat a way off in the distance, the area felt deserted, the car doors seeming loud as we got out. Insects buzzed in dry grasses that quivered, silvery in the late afternoon light. Eucalypts and scrubby acacias whispered a sharp, cloying scent. I saw at once a weathered cross in the granite soil next to a big gum. My throat felt thick. The tree's smooth, lead-grey trunk still bore old scars from that night. Jagged tears smoothed by rain and time. Faded upon the cross I could just make out *Rosco, 1943–1967*.

'His mates put that there,' was all Mum said.

I stared back along the empty road. In me, a darkness blanketed. I shut my eyes but I couldn't shut out what that darkness evoked.

An engine gunning, tyres fishtailing, the car thundering along, sullying the gentle night. The trees, the stars, all else so serene and beautiful. And amid the tyres spinning and skidding along gravel, a roar, and then quiet. Suddenly I felt a wash of anger. My fingertips sank into my palms. I tried to stifle it, tried to hold back the tears that kept wanting to come, the scream building inside me.

'I hate you,' I whispered.

'Oh, Sof, no, please ...'

I rounded on her, shouting, 'I hate you,' and turned, running off along the road.

'*Sofie.*' Mum sprinted after me.

She easily caught me up, for I was already stumbling and crying. We sank as one to the ground, my back against her chest, Mum's arms around me. And together we cried and cried in the late radiance of the setting sun.

~

'I want to go home,' I said, as we were driving back. 'I don't want Christmas here.'

Mum glanced across. 'Well ... okay. If that's what you really want.'

We sped back towards Stanthorpe and I glared out at the passing bush scrub.

'I hate her,' I murmured.

'What?'

'I don't want to speak to Nonna.' I turned my anguish onto Gia, even though I knew how Jack had treated her. To think that both of them were a part of me, and Tim was as well, felt overwhelming right then. 'She's a hypocrite. I thought she'd cared.' But even as I was saying that, in my heart I knew it was me who was twisting things.

Mum pulled the car over. The sun was going, the landscape turning mauve in the dusk.

'Sofie, before I left for Brisbane, Ma, Nonna—' I stubbornly turned away. 'Just listen to me, Sof. When I was leaving for Brisbane, Dad wouldn't see me off or let Ma and Frank do so either. It was part of the shame, I suppose, making me go by myself.' She sighed. 'I was waiting on the train platform with my suitcase, feeling so alone, when Ma appeared. She must've walked all the way from the farm by herself, maybe even run part of the way. When she got there, she looked so relieved she hadn't missed me. She gave me as much money as she could and was crying as she told me, *do what you want to do, live your life, study, work, be a mother, do all you can and I will always be here to help you. Don't end up like ...'*

Me. Again, my tears coursed, just when it seemed there could be none left to cry.

⌣

The sun had gone by the time we reached the cemetery. Its last hint of pale yellow along the horizon lit the gravestones from behind. And above, where the sky darkened in bands of lavender to violet to dark blue, the first stars showed faint light. Mum quietly led me to Ross Armstrong's grave and I felt conscious of Nonno Taddeo buried over in the Italian section. My father rested some way away, closer to the area I guessed Edie Dawson might be.

His headstone didn't have a photograph like the Italian ones did. I mouthed his name. Ross Michael Armstrong. Not Arro.

Not even like Arro. Nor any other names I'd conjured up in all the years I'd been imagining about him. I might have been Sofie Armstrong, instead of Sofia Poletti. It was a strange feeling. In that moment, I wasn't sure who I was any more. The importance of a name, or its unimportance. It would always be too late to ever know my dad, to hear his voice, or his laugh, to sit in his lap as a child. But my middle name was Michela.

❧

It was after nightfall when we returned. Mum parked in the driveway and we sat in the darkness with the engine off for a moment before getting out.

'I understand you must be feeling angry and upset.' She kept looking through the windscreen. 'From now on, if there's anything you want to know about this that I haven't told you, anything at all, please ask me and I'll do my best to answer.'

She looked over. I was still gazing ahead but I nodded.

Mum went to reach for my hand, hesitated and placed it near my leg instead. 'I want you to know I never felt any shame like my father expected me to. That day I left, the train was barely out of the station when I realised I wasn't alone, I had you with me and, in a way, a part of Ross too, the three of us always together.'

I bit my lips and looked down, unable to speak, unsure what to say if I could. But I edged my hand closer and Mum clasped it and squeezed like she didn't want to ever let go.

Nonna Gia was sitting at the table under the kitchen light waiting for us. She sprang up as we came in and rushed to hug me tight. I stood, my arms crushed to my sides, but I softened in her embrace, smelling her faded scent of Felce Azzurra, Oil of Ulan and garlic. The television wasn't on, even though it was time for *Perfect Match*.

'It's okay, Nonna,' I said, when she wouldn't let go.

She held me tighter. 'No more shame. It has caused too much pain for too long.'

'It'll be all right, Nonna.' Gently, I extricated my arms to put them around her. And a little part of me clung onto the words, even though so much felt topsy-turvy just then.

The kitchen smelt comfortingly of garlic, passata, fried eggplant and melted cheese.

Nonna let go and gave my cheek a soft pinch. 'I made lasagne.' She gave a shrug as if she hadn't known what else to do. 'You haven't eaten all day. It'll be ready in half an hour.'

'That sounds good, Ma.' Mum got out the corkscrew to open a bottle of wine.

I almost said I wasn't hungry but instead I went to the bathroom. The mirror showed my puffy red eyes, my curls in chaos. I splashed my face and looked harder at myself. With such dark eyes and olive skin I looked Italian, though, of course, I'd always been Australian too, even if that seemed hidden. Just as the part of my name hidden between my first and last was entwined with my father's middle name. Hidden but always there, waiting to be sought.

Maybe Tim had come to see something in my face I hadn't. But then, he'd withdrawn since the night I'd told him when my father had died and that he'd been from Stanthorpe. Tim must have started to suspect then, knowing of his uncle's death. My father. How that made us cousins. My mouth went dry. I drenched my face in water again, gulping down mouthfuls.

Shutting the door to my room, I dragged out the bag with Tim's drawings hidden in the base. The one he'd done of the modest timber train station and the other that was of me. I studied my face as he'd drawn it. The way I was turned a bit away, so much like Nonno Taddeo. My face felt hot. It wasn't our fault. How could we have known? Again, I felt foolish, angry, skewed. That girl in the picture wasn't even truly me. She didn't know anything. I ripped the drawings into tiny pieces. So tiny they could never be put back together again, so no-one could see and know what they'd once been. The paper tears fluttered to the floor. And then I drew out the rest of the chocolates hidden in the bag and ate one after another.

'Sofie …' Mum knocked on the door and came in. 'Dinner's almost—' She saw the strewn paper, the chocolate wrappers I hadn't bothered to hide, my fresh tears. 'Oh, darling.' She came over and crouched beside me, her knees cracking beneath her long skirt. 'Don't be in here by yourself. Come out and be with us.'

I let her hold me as I cried some more, even though part of me still felt angry with her for not telling me more about my father sooner. But she was still my mum and I knew she'd always loved me and tried her best when there was so little help about at the time I was born. I could have been a problem that she made go away back then. Still, she should've talked to me about my father – I didn't even feel comfortable referring to him as 'Dad'. That felt too familiar. Like I'd known him. And 'Ross' didn't feel right either.

'Why Arro?' I asked. 'Why tell me he was called that?'

'Oh. Silly really. Ross's favourite chewing gum was Arrowmint. Always had some.'

It struck me that I'd been so young when she first used this term for him that in my child's mind I'd come up with 'Arro', not thinking she might've meant 'Arrow'. I'd grasped onto what was nothing but a chewing gum name. It was so flimsy. So absurd. I realised just how young and trusting I'd been in all this. Again, anger surged in me but then more tears took over.

'I'm sorry.' Mum held me tighter. 'Nonna kept saying you needed to know the truth and I kept burying myself in work to avoid what I knew I had to do. It's been tough on you.'

And it had. Yet I'd never known any different. I had gone on with the situation and everyday life because, when it came down to it, keeping on with a usual routine kind of worked best, I realised. Just as I saw Nonna, Mum, Pino, Serena and others continue to get on with it despite everything that lay behind them. Well, mostly.

My eyes went to the mess of ripped drawings and chocolate wrappers on the floor around us. 'Mum—' In that moment I knew I wouldn't mention Tim. Maybe not ever. But I had to somehow explain all the wrappers on the floor and it felt easier while she still held me and we weren't looking straight at each other. 'Sometimes I eat these chocolates. Too many. I just can't help it. I don't know why I—'

She held me tighter, rocking me as she did when I was little. 'It's okay. I understand.'

'There must be something wrong with me.'

'No, you're just doing the best you can with the situation you've been given.'

I breathed in her patchouli scent, her words sinking in. I hadn't thought of it like that.

'Really, Sof, it's a soothing thing. I was a bit the same. Years ago.' I looked up at her in surprise and she nodded. 'It's like, when you feel upset, you go to a time you felt safe and sometimes a food might've done that for you. For me, it was Nonna's *zippuli*.'

'For real?' I thought of Nonna's doughnut twists fried in oil and rolled in sugar.

'After you were born and we were in the share house in Brisbane, I made so many *zippuli* I looked like I was still pregnant. Apart from the ingredients being cheap, I guess they reminded me of a time when I was a girl and felt safe and protected, that all was well.'

I frowned. 'So how did you get past that?'

'It took time. I sought out more support. Found other more useful things that made me feel better. Gradually, I didn't need the *zippuli* any more. But let's not worry about this just now.' She kissed my forehead. 'It's been quite a day and for the time being you need to settle and let this all catch up with you. In the meantime, a few chocolates won't matter much.'

I nodded, still taking in what she'd told me.

Mum got up. 'Come on, come out in the kitchen with us. Tea is about ready.' She didn't comment on all the other bits of torn paper though I saw her eyes dart over them again.

'I'll be there in a minute.'

After she shut the door, I scraped up all the paper and chocolate wrappers and put them in the bin. Perhaps in some way she was right. If I thought about it, chocolate was something Nonna had usually bought me as a child, her hand in mine as we went to the shop. But I remembered the comfort of Nonna holding my hand the most. That reassuring warmth, the flat, firmness of a hand that had seen much hard work yet was also tender against mine. And in a way she'd taken my hand in hers when she'd begun telling me her stories. I just didn't realise until that moment, as I sat on the floor, how much I'd needed her to do so.

I heard Nonna getting the lasagne out of the oven. Its aroma curled through the house and reached under my door. 'Elena! Sofia! You hungry?'

⌣

When I went to bed, I left the bedside lamp on, its glow making the cream walls appear buttery and cosy. I lay looking up at the ceiling rose. I could hear the reassuring rise and fall of the television on out in the lounge room where Nonna and Mum were still up, murmuring between themselves. But I couldn't stay up any longer, much as I tried to. I felt worn out from all the crying and still a bit shivery now and then, and my eyes were sore.

Rolling on my side to face Edie Dawson's painting, I thought of Jack Armstrong's hatred. How awful Nonna had said he'd been. Was some of that in me? It must've been such a shock to her and Nonno that their first grandchild would also be his grandchild. As much of a shock to them as Mum being unmarried and expecting. In a way, I understood why they didn't talk about it. I felt strange being related to someone who'd done such horrible things, who'd hated Italians, perhaps still did.

My whole life had been my Italian family, our lives pivoting around tomato day, sausage-making day, celebrating our *onomastici*, our name days. Perhaps it was the Armstrong part of me who'd resisted Nonna Gia's *Piccante Calabrese* chillies. I recognised she'd been gradually putting some in my food, a little more each time, the same way she'd been drip feeding me her stories to prepare me for what I was to find out.

I rolled to my other side. The way Jack sat out front so much, looking down over us, his rigid posture, never a smile nor wave. Perhaps he really hated Nonna Gia still. Mum said Ross, my father, wasn't hard like Jack. I wondered if he was more like Tim. But just occasionally I'd seen a hint of Jack in Tim. The way the word *wog* sat in his mouth so easily when it made my insides clutch. And yet, Mel used *wog* at times too and I never said anything and she was my best friend. Jack looked unbending though. It didn't seem to me like he'd ever want to know the truth about me.

But I was so exhausted, I had to stop thinking about him, my father or Tim just then.

I awoke with a start and blinked in the darkness. Someone had turned off my lamp and the television too. The dark house sat silent. I peered at the clock. It was only a couple of hours later. My eyes still felt swollen. I willed sleep to return but the more I remembered, the more awake I became. I got up. The shag pile whispered soft beneath my bare feet. I tilted the blind to see the house across the road in darkness. It appeared empty, but he was in there. And tomorrow he'd be back out front. Maybe with all his staring he hoped to goad Nonna to leave.

I thought of her and Nonno Taddeo, retired but still living with Frank and Connie on the farm when this house in town had come up for sale – the attractive brick house with the portico arches that Taddeo had sent his proxy bride a photograph of instead of his farmhouse on stumps. How it was always going to be this particular house that they'd buy. Even without knowing who had bought the house across from it – and only a short time before, Mum had said.

The sharpness of coffee met my nostrils. Someone else was awake. In the hallway I saw Mum's bedroom door was closed and Nonna's open, and followed the light to the kitchen. Nonna Gia sat in her nightgown and brunch coat. On the table was the bottle of Tia Maria and her stovetop *moka* pot issuing coffee steam. Seeing me, she gave a start.

'Oh, did I wake you? You want a cup?' She went to get up.

'I can get it.' I got out another espresso cup without its matching saucer but she didn't comment as she usually would, only poured in measures of coffee and Tia Maria and let me add my own sugar from the fluted-glass canister on the table.

As always, the kitchen clock ticked loudly. The night outside seemed especially quiet – no breeze, barely any crickets. I wished Zucchero was around but couldn't see him. Nonna kept her eyes on her cup and seemed almost as if she was holding her breath.

'I thought it was Keith Dawson across the road,' I admitted softly. 'In a way, I wish he was my grandfather. Instead of Jack Armstrong.'

Nonna's gaze stayed low. Her fingertips rotating her espresso cup.

'I understand, Nonna, if you don't like me as much because I'm related to Jack. Especially after Edie …'

Her eyes came up. 'Don't be silly. I've always loved you, *carissima*. My strong girl.' She put her hand on my arm and I felt its warmth. 'It's almost forty years since the war ended. I know we all need to get on for the sake of next generations, but I don't think we should forget.'

La lingua batte dove il dente duole. The tongue always goes to the sore tooth.

I took a sip. 'After Keith Dawson sold the farm … did you ever see him again?'

'No. I never did.' She again turned her empty espresso cup gently around and around, creating a slight friction on its little saucer. 'But I did get one last letter from him. In 1952.'

I swiftly worked out on my fingers that was about seven years after he left.

'Taddeo had suggested we have a beach holiday. Elena and Frank were old enough to enjoy the sea. It was our very first family holiday. We didn't have many. It's hard to get away when you have a farm.' Nonna shook her head thinking of that time. 'I hinted that we go to Coolangatta, perhaps being sentimental, foolish. And when Taddeo got the brochures from the travel agent, he wanted to stay at the Greenmount Guesthouse, famous as it was then.'

And I could imagine the wrangle she must have felt. To return to the place she'd been so happy with one person, yet only able to be there with another, to have loved each of them in such different ways.

'They bulldozed Greenmount about five or so years ago,' she said. 'I felt sad when I read about it in the newspaper. Seventy years it had stood there, making people happy, giving them lovely memories of the South Coast. But some thought it too old. Funny. In Italy, they seem to hold onto the past more, let buildings stand for centuries, along with their history.'

I only nodded. What was now called the Gold Coast was known for wreckers moving in on a lot of much-loved landmarks, in order to build more and more high-rises.

'After Keith left Stanthorpe – when was that? Late 1945 – I didn't expect to hear from him again. It was better that way, we both knew. I did sometimes wonder about him though, where he was, what he might be doing. When I visited Edie's grave I always looked to see if there was some sign that he'd been too, but as far as I knew he never returned to Stanthorpe.'

'But then you did receive a letter from him?' I gently prompted her.

Nonna pushed the cup away and rubbed at her eyes, though she wasn't crying. 'I should have known how much Coolangatta had meant to him too …' she murmured. 'It was a shock to hear from him so unexpectedly like that.' She gave a sigh. 'Wonderful, and terrible.'

Coolangatta, 1952

It appeared Greenmount Guesthouse was as popular as ever, there were so many people about. The sprawling two-storey timber building still stood proud on its bluff fringed by Norfolk Pines, palms and frangipanis, just like Gia remembered. But to her amazement, someone had decided to close in all the verandahs that had seemed so sought-after by guests relaxing on easy chairs in the breeze overlooking the views, and to hang their towels on the railings of them. At least the gazebo lookout, if closed in too, remained, along with the grand views of the ocean, the beaches each side and mountains behind, even if she could only peer at them from behind salted glass.

They weren't given the same room that she and Keith had shared, though the furniture was similar. As they all traipsed back out down the hallway, Gia couldn't help glancing at the door number of that room as she passed. It felt bittersweet to return but a delight to see both Elena's and Frank's eyes light up when they first saw the ocean spread out resplendent before them, its mint hue becoming deeper blue in widening bands to the horizon. They all inhaled its fresh, lively saltiness, and with melancholy sentiment Gia thought it perhaps the closest she could bring her children to Palmi and the grandparents they could never know.

'Well, it is certainly different to Palmi,' declared Taddeo, breaking her moment.

Gia felt it was a steeper walk down the bluff to the beach with two children in tow as well as buckets, spades and a beach umbrella hired from the guesthouse. The sand was soft and clean but hot beneath the summer sun and they scampered to a spot among the throng of people.

'Not like the smooth pebbles at Palmi.' Sunk to his ankles, Taddeo fought to put up the umbrella against a brisk breeze off the water as Gia, Elena and Frank waited impatiently.

All the while, from the stage that still stood at the Greenmount end of the beach drifted snatches of a hailer announcing the daily show, while in front of the surf lifesaving pavilion people milled about awaiting the next hokey-pokey. Gia knew Taddeo would never join in.

'Let's have a paddle.' She put out her hands and Elena and Frank each grabbed one.

'I think I'll stay in the shade.' Taddeo finally had the umbrella up and steady.

The sea bubbled in on frothy waves and Elena and Frank splashed up to their knees, giggling and squealing. Gia felt its welcome coolness gush over her bare feet. The sun, the water, the air was all glorious and she snatched off her straw hat to feel it in her hair. If only Taddeo would come to the water's edge ... Glancing over her shoulder, she saw him battling to turn the page of his newspaper in the brisk, warm gusts without once looking over to them.

~

'Ma, what's this?' Frank poked at the piece of crispy battered fish on his plate.

'Not swordfish,' complained Taddeo around a mouthful and Gia gave him a look.

'It's delicious fish.' She handed Frank a chip. 'And I know you like these.'

'Can we go to the beach again tomorrow?' asked Elena.

'Of course.' Gia smiled to see both the children's sunburnt faces pleased at the prospect as they tucked into their fish and chips.

'I might stay here in the reading room,' said Taddeo. 'That sand gets into everything. The guesthouse offers several newspapers each day. And they're all *free*. Can you believe it?'

~

At the end of the third day, it began to rain. And rain. They were only there a week and from the window of their room Gia worriedly looked out at the leaden sky stretching grey to the distant mountains. Being confined inside, Elena and Frank were already starting to fight.

'Let's go downstairs to the games room,' Gia suggested, and they all tramped out, she glancing wistfully at the door number of that room as she passed by it.

She'd assumed Taddeo would stay with them but he peeled off into the reading room and his newspapers, leaving Gia to interest

Elena and Frank in a game of quoits on the closed-in verandah. It sat just off the games room, which was crowded with people playing board games and cards, an old Smoky Dawson song playing on a record player. From the nearby guesthouse kitchen drifted a yeasty scent of baking that was particularly alluring on such a wet, grey day.

As Frank and Elena whooped and bickered in their own world, Gia gazed out at the wet road that she knew snaked from the bluff down to Point Danger. It was like she'd been another person with her arms wrapped around Keith as they'd sped along on the motorbike.

'Ma, Frank keeps hogging having a turn,' Elena complained.

Gia sighed and turned to them. 'Frank, you give Elena a go now.'

'But I haven't finished yet!'

'Yes, you did. He did! *Ma!*'

A plump, blonde woman with a scarf over her head emerged from the guesthouse kitchen carrying a tray. 'Would anyone like a warm doughnut?'

Just then, Gia could have kissed her.

~

On their second-last day, the sun came back out and Elena and Frank rushed for their beach towels, buckets and spades. Gia looked over at Taddeo perched mulishly on the bed edge.

'Go to your newspapers.' Her voice sounded weary. 'We'll be back in time for lunch.'

The damp sand was perfect for making sandcastles and Frank and Elena got busy crafting a city of them with a moat. Frank ran to the water's edge and filled his bucket then ran back and poured it into the moat.

'It all disappeared!' he cried, thwarted.

Gia was about to answer when Elena said, 'Of course, silly,' and explained why.

The thump and whoosh of the waves soothed Gia with their vague monotony. People shrieked happily in the water. She thought of Keith once sitting beside her on that same arc of sand. Of Taddeo in the guesthouse reading room with his newspapers and proxy marriage. Her heart flew low, skimming what she ached for. But that wasn't Taddeo's fault. And she realised that he kept comparing everything unfavourably to Palmi only because he missed it and his family there. In the end, it all wasn't even about fault.

More rainclouds banked in but, like many people on the beach, Gia and the children stayed, the clouds giving reprieve from the sun while the beach remained warm. She watched as the water changed from lively blue to slate-grey. Tomorrow they'd head back inland to rolling downs and mountains, to the farm, and who knew if she would see the sea again.

Perhaps that's why she lingered, even as others began to pack up when the clouds darkened. The children didn't want to go either. Frank was determined that the waves reach his and Elena's hard-worked-for moat. But Gia could see by the time the tide would flood into it, likely swamping the sandcastles too, they'd need to be long gone. She made them gather their things, just as a cool wind swept up stinging sand and brought the smell of coming rain.

'Hurry up, you two!' Gia regarded the sky and the steep bluff they had yet to climb, wondering if Taddeo might leave his reading room to come and meet them with an umbrella.

Rain began to patter down as the three of them scurried back across the empty beach.

'Hold your towels over your heads.' Gia kept her voice bright. 'It's just rain. Not a storm. We're having a bit of an adventure.'

They began up the bluff, the rain pelting harder, and Gia realised then that everyone else had actually left well before they did. Guilt jabbed as she watched Elena and Frank trudge up the incline in the downpour. The guesthouse lights shone welcoming into the mist. Taddeo was watching for them from the entrance and the children broke away in a run towards him.

For a moment, Gia stayed in the rain, gazing down the road that wound towards Point Danger. The part of her still holding on for something that could never be slipped a little. Her time with Keith, she knew, was so far vanished it hid beyond reach, far beneath where the sun set each day and disappeared. Over and over gone. The rain was torrential. She let it run down her face as she slowly, dazedly turned and walked over to the guesthouse.

Taddeo stood just inside the foyer with Elena and Frank either side of him, the two wrapped in their towels and looking like drowned rats. He couldn't resist reaching out into the rain to pull her in the final few steps. 'Gia! Hurry up, do you want to catch pneumonia?'

By the time winter settled over Stanthorpe with air like icy shards that held no hint of the sea, Coolangatta already felt distant. The second-hand utility Taddeo had bought chugged fumes in the still morning as he dropped Elena and Frank off at the Applethorpe school and with Gia continued into town for supplies. He parked the utility near the bank, as he always did, to go there first before the hardware store. It was expected that meanwhile Gia would go to the post office, the drapery and get groceries, as she usually did. She watched him walk off without a word. Perhaps none was necessary in the sameness of their routine. But for a brief moment she thought of the sea, always moving, its colour constantly changing.

In the post office, an old kerosene heater gave some warmth from a far corner but Gia kept on her coat as she collected the mail. Walking back towards the door, among the envelopes she noticed a letter addressed just to her in writing she didn't recognise. No return address on the back. She turned it over again to the postmark. Southport. The South Coast. Gia frowned slightly. She went to a bench seat near the heater and took off her gloves.

Inside was a short note and another, smaller envelope. On that envelope was written only *Gia* in Keith's handwriting. Her breath drew in sharply. She looked back to the initial note, in which the writer introduced himself as the chaplain from a hospice at Southport where Keith was a patient. *He asked me if I could send the enclosed letter to you ...* Gia hastily refolded the note and crumpled it back inside with the other unopened envelope. She tucked it deep into a pocket at the back of her handbag and put the other mail in the main section.

Walking back along High Street with the cold air hitting her face, Gia could feel her heart pounding away mercilessly but when she went into the drapery with its familiar tinkle of the bell over the door her face showed only polite calm as she approached the counter.

After the two of them got home, Taddeo switched on the Bakelite radio that sat atop the kitchen counter and listened to the news broadcast and rural report while Gia went about putting away groceries, her mind running.

'Well, I better get back to it.' Taddeo reached for his hat on the nail by the back door.

He went out, leaving the radio on, though she barely noticed. From the sink window she watched him go into the shed, retrieve the secateurs and ladder, and head off into the orchard to continue pruning. It would be another hour before Elena and Frank walked home from school and Taddeo didn't usually come in again before that. Gia went over to her handbag, slid Keith's letter from the back inside pocket and sat down on a kitchen chair.

It was best not to see each other again, I know that, but I couldn't leave this earth without writing to you one last time. It is cancer, I'm told, and I don't have long. I've asked the chaplain here to send this to you after I'm gone. He's a decent fellow and kind, even though he knows I've never much been one for religion.
I still miss you, G.
   I moved around quite a bit after I left. Couldn't seem to settle. Eventually I ended up at the South Coast. Remember how we loved it here? I guess I knew after our time together the aloneness would be bloody crook, yet I don't regret a single moment we had. I hope you are happy. I hope you are well. It feels too hard to say goodbye, so instead I will say goodnight. Ti amo per sempre, K.

Gia held the page to her chest. Like a beautiful tree that had been cut at its base she slowly, stiffly, fell forward in the chair and stayed there, bent over and gasping into her knees. The surprise of his last words in Italian, that he'd taken the trouble to find them out – for she hadn't taught him any – and the heartache at them.

Her own reply came in a winded whisper. 'I will love you forever too.'

And then tears came, silent, racking, keeping her bent double. The radio kept playing, Dean Martin gently crooning. The clock hands ticked on. Her pain flowed and ebbed and flowed again. And afterwards there was nothing to do but tuck the page into the bottom of the paintbox and wash her face ready for the children to return home.

Shifting Dawn

I heard a mild wind as it began to stir the trees outside, coursing over the tableland in a falling coolness. In the lounge room, a record sleekly turned in the stereogram, the volume down low, and Dean Martin sang 'You Belong to Me' with heartfelt melancholy. It was then, sitting beside Nonna on the plastic-covered lounge, that I finally understood why she played Dean Martin so much – all except this song, the one that happened to play on the radio that last time she heard from Keith.

'It was a hit then and played often,' she said softly. 'Quite early in his career.'

I regarded her being so stoic and Nonna saw in my eyes what I thought but didn't say.

She gave a little shrug. 'How could we have been together? People didn't divorce in those days, not in the country especially, and certainly not Italian Catholics. And I couldn't hurt Taddeo in that way. He didn't deserve the shame of it.'

'Still, to have to hide what you felt like that …'

But what was I saying? So much had been hidden. That she was a proxy bride, Keith, my father. And Tim. Sifting down from generation to generation, leaving its mark.

'Perhaps I deserved it,' she said, and I shook my head but she wouldn't be swayed.

We both sat there, quiet. Leaves skittered over the back patio. The song seeped out in a soft sigh to its final verses. Hearing the words, I could have howled but instead I put my arm around Nonna, hoping to comfort her in the same way she'd been putting her arm around me since I was a child. She let her head rest on my shoulder and all that was rushed on with the night wind. The song faded away. The stereogram gently clicked and wound down.

Nonna took a handkerchief from her brunch coat pocket and sat up properly again. 'Silly really,' she said more to herself, dabbing her eyes. 'All so long ago.'

She stuffed the hankie back in her pocket and touched the *cornicello* just below her throat. Suddenly all business she undid the clasp of the chain and handed it to me with the chilli amulet hanging from it.

'My nonna gave me this the day I left Palmi and I've worn it every day since,' she said, just as she'd often told me, like a mantra, time and again. 'And now it is yours.'

I stared at it. 'You always said it would be mine once you're … dead?'

'Well …' Nonna went back to being no-nonsense. 'I changed my mind.'

Perhaps she thought I needed its protection. Especially in the coming days.

'Do you think Jack Armstrong would want to know about me?'

Nonna exhaled a bit, as if *who knows*, and I felt she didn't want to say what she might have really thought. She kissed my head and got up, rumpling the lounge plastic.

I stayed sitting, holding the *cornicello* in my hand, its chain still warm. Out in the kitchen, Nonna cleared away the coffee cups as was her habit in order to have a clean kitchen in the morning to start the day. I put on the *cornicello*. I felt the small chilli-shaped amulet beneath my fingertips and lying against my skin, Nonna Gia's warmth, and lifeforce, becoming mine.

By the time I awoke late, strong sun was heating the venetians and making the bedroom stuffy and warm. I could hear several voices overlapping in the kitchen and looked out the window to see Frank and Connie's truck parked in front of the house. Beyond it, the verandah of Jack's house was empty. I put on shorts and a T-shirt I'd left draped over the chair and gave a swift rake through my curls. I needed to go to the toilet, but edging open the door I first listened.

'... and then Dianne suggested that,' Mum was saying.

Connie asked, 'Do you want me to go with you?'

I felt myself getting hot. How could they be talking about this without me? To have spoken to Dianne Dinning already. Tim knowing. Jack. It actually made me a bit queasy.

'Perhaps it's best if just Sof and I go.'

Nonna Gia suddenly shouted out the back screen door, 'Salvatore, don't chase that poor animal! Lena, stop him!' Sam must have been in the backyard with Zucchero, Lena too.

'I dread the talk that's going to do the rounds once more people find out about all this.' Mum's voice again. 'I'm sorry, everyone.'

Frank scoffed. 'Forget about it.'

First no-one talked to me about this and then everyone in the family was talking of it while I wasn't there. And they all *knew* already. Wild fury charged through me. I mightn't have been an adult but I wasn't a child either. My hands clenched. This was about my life.

I strode out to the kitchen and they all looked over as I came in. More hotness rushed through me. Part of me wanted to yell but I could also feel the prickling of tears too close.

'Hello, kiddo.' Frank had both sympathy and protectiveness in his eyes.

'Mum—' I couldn't keep the edge from my voice. They all heard it.

'We'd better be getting back.' Frank got up. 'Plenty of work on.'

Connie came and kissed my cheeks, pretending not to notice I didn't respond as I waited for Mum to answer. She looked to her too. 'Shall I stay, El?'

Mum shook her head and turned to me. 'I've spoken with Dianne and she's asked for you and me to come up to the pub. She's not sure yet if Jack will be there too.'

'*What?*' I shot a look to the others and back. 'Why didn't you ask me about it first?'

Frank appeared as if he'd been arguing the same thing. 'Come on, Con, we'll see you all later.' He gave me a wink and went out the back. 'Sam, Lena, in the truck. Don't argue.'

'It'll be all right.' Connie gave me a squeeze and kissed the others before following.

I kept staring accusingly at Mum. 'It should be up to me what to do next.'

'This affects us both.' She noticed the *cornicello* around my neck and eyed Nonna Gia who sat at the table, arms folded.

By Nonna's look, I grasped that along with Frank she must've been arguing that I should have some say in what to do next, while Connie agreed what Mum had already done was for the best. And none of them knew about Tim and me. Since I'd learnt about Ross, I hadn't even got to talk to Tim yet. In private. Surely, he wouldn't tell anyone about us. I couldn't stand it if the first time I saw him next was us sitting across a table in the pub, all suddenly one family together. That would be unbearable. Especially with Jack watching sharply on.

I stood unmoving, not speaking I was that mad. My fists were so tight they hurt.

Mum finally said, 'I'm sorry. I thought I was helping. What would you like to do?'

'Well, I don't get to decide now, do I?' Abrupt anger grappled against tears again and I felt foreign in my own person, self-conscious and seen differently.

'I can tell them we won't come today, that you need some time—'

'Oh, so they'll think it's me that's got a problem, thanks a lot,' I said hotly. 'Of course we have to go now. But don't you dare wear something hippie – you have to dress like a *normal* person if we're going to meet them.'

For so long I'd felt hollow but all this anger was suddenly burbling up out of me.

Nonna pushed back her chair. 'I'll make some eggs. None of us can think properly when we are empty inside.' She got out the frying pan and kissed my cheek.

Jack's verandah was still empty when Mum and I left Nonna's and walked towards the main street. My hands tingled with sweat already. Nonna had suggested I change into a dress she'd made me on my last stay, a white one with tiny red dots. I didn't really want to, but did, knowing I couldn't meet my father's family

in old house clothes. Mum had put on a long denim skirt and a
white T-shirt, probably the plainest two things she owned. And
she didn't wear her feather earrings or beads and bangles. It made
her seem a bit bare. Exposed. For me. I felt a pang at what I'd
said before. Especially now I knew that when she'd hoped to
go to university, Nonno Taddeo had said he wouldn't have her
hanging around hippies. As if expressing herself in any way but his
traditionalist one wasn't allowed.

'Mum?' I stopped. 'I'm sorry I said that about your clothes.'

'Oh, sweetheart ...' She put her arms around me. In front of
everyone. We were almost at the main street and people passing
by looked over at us. But then I realised I didn't care. Maybe this
was what growing up really was. Hugging Mum meant more
than being embarrassed at who might see. 'Sofie, I'm sorrier.' She
smoothed down my hair. 'I hate to think I've forced you into
this. I guess I just thought it would only get harder otherwise and
I'd already made the terrible mistake of putting off talking to you
about all this for so long.'

I buried my mouth in the cup of her shoulder. 'Do they know
already?'

'No. Just that we want to talk about something important.
But I think Dianne suspects.' She stepped back from me. 'Don't
worry. I'll explain everything. Come on.'

I almost told her about Tim and me then, but I sensed Mum
didn't want to be late and she'd already started around the corner
onto the footpath where lots of people were about doing their
shopping or whatever. Inside I felt all churned up. It was as if
I could be calm and almost myself, like last night when talking
with Nonna in the quiet and dim light, and then absolutely fierce
with anger like in the brightness of the kitchen that morning.
Someone bumped past me and I kept my head down, not meeting

anyone's eye, as if the whole world suddenly knew and everyone must be looking at me, though of course that wasn't true.

The liver-coloured brick hotel loomed on the corner, its upper verandahs shading the footpath. With some defiance I considered perhaps rejecting Jack, my grandfather, for the way he'd treated Italians and especially Nonna Gia and Edie Dawson. Yet I knew that wasn't really my fight. This was about me, and my dad, who had loved an Italian–Australian girl.

As we neared the open pub windows, I felt the cool waft of air tinged with beer and cigarette smoke and heard the staccato calling of horseracing on a radio inside. Mum led us around to the side gate where the chickens were, for she must have been told to come to the Dinnings' residence at the back of the hotel. The same spot where I'd sought out Tim that night. I suddenly pulled back.

'What is it?' Mum turned around.

I shook my head. 'I can't.' I just knew then I really couldn't sit at some kitchen table while Mum recounted it all to them. Their reaction. Tim there. The looks I knew would come my way. At that moment, it all felt too much.

'I do want to meet them, but not yet.' I could only get it out in a whisper. 'I don't want to sit there while you explain it all, I just— I can't.'

'Well.' Mum looked unsure. 'If that's what you want. Why don't you wait out here? I'll come and get you later in case you want to come in then.'

'I think I might go down to the park by the creek.' I was already moving away.

'Sofie—' Mum looked a bit deserted. 'No matter what happens, I love you very much.'

In the late morning sun the creek glistened dark bronze, water riffling over shallows and creeping in deeper quiet up to the grassy edges. I perched on the same picnic table I'd sat with Tim that day when we'd shared creamy soda and musk sticks. When that initial connection we'd felt had snuck in a bit further. And now, he'd be with his parents and Jack hearing Mum's side of the story. I tensed just to think what he'd make of it all.

On the opposite creek bank, cockatoos foraged in the grass, toddling and chattering. A way behind stood Serena and Pino's motel and I pondered if they'd see me differently once they knew I was related to Jack Armstrong. Maybe they wouldn't want to see us any more. And while I refused to feel shame for something so beyond my control as being born, in that moment I could appreciate Nonno Taddeo's constant worry about stigma. It felt hard to know people might talk about you, judge you, perhaps choose not to be around you due to some forced circumstance like marrying by proxy or being born out of wedlock. As though being different to the majority marked you out for isolation rather than kindness or understanding.

A shuffling approached across the grass and I turned to see not Mum but Tim coming towards me. My throat tightened. I couldn't move. His face was unreadable. But as he came nearer he smiled a bit, sort of sadly, and I just barely managed one back. He sat up on the table beside me, a bit apart, without touching. Neither of us said anything. We both just sat there, looking at the creek rather than each other. Breeze washed past. I could smell the tangy sharpness of his deodorant for he was wearing a singlet.

After a time he swayed his knee, nudging mine. 'Funny how things turn out, hey?'

I snuck a glance sideways. 'I guess so.'

'Your mum told us ... about everything.'

'Yep.'

Again, the breeze swept past.

'It's sad, hey? I mean, I feel sorry for your mum. And Uncle Ross.' Tim didn't risk saying he felt sorry for me again but I supposed he did. 'I don't really remember Ross much but I still have this toy monkey Mum said he gave me when I was a little kid. Always kept it.'

'Oh. That's nice.' But it also made me think. He'd got a toy from my dad and I hadn't. Then I thought of Mike, with Mum and me in the toy shop, saying, *Sofie, pick anything you want, anything at all, and I will buy it for you.* 'Tim, about us, did you—'

'I haven't said a word to anyone,' he replied quickly. 'And I promise I won't. Ever.'

'Right.' I knew I wouldn't tell anyone for the time being but I wasn't sure I could promise the same. To be honest, I don't think I wanted any other secrets and hiding even if it meant I might one day privately tell just Mum about Tim and me, or maybe Nonna Gia. For she'd trusted me about Keith. I glanced again at Tim. 'We couldn't have known.'

'Course not. At least we didn't—' He went red.

'At least we only kissed,' I said for him, feeling older than him in that moment.

'Yeah. And, like, in Australia, it's actually legal for first cousins to marry, you know.'

I must've looked a bit surprised because he swiftly added, 'Not that I expect— I don't—'

'No. I don't think so.' And I didn't ask how he knew about it being lawful or if he'd endeavoured to find out for his own peace of mind just recently, maybe after he'd started to suspect Ross was my father.

The sad thing was I really liked Tim, loved him even, and as much as I knew that had to be over now, it was more of a door slowly closing shut rather than a sudden slam.

He looked worried. 'Are we ... okay?'

'Of course. It's just—'

'We haven't done anything wrong, Sof.'

'I know.'

He scratched at a mosquito bite on his leg. 'But, shit, of all the people we could've ...'

'Yeah. Of all the people.' And then I started to laugh. The whole situation just seemed so incongruous and messy and yet okay that I couldn't help laughing. Well, it was better than crying anyway. There'd been so much of that in the past day or so.

Tim's eyes widened as if I'd lost it, though he sort of smiled. 'They'll be down here shortly. My mum and yours. Dad has to mind the pub but Mum really wants to meet you.'

'Oh, okay.' I stopped laughing.

My hands tingled again and I wiped them down my dress. He didn't mention Jack but I guess it wasn't easy for an old man who'd had a stroke to get to the park.

The cockatoos moved further on, still showing bright white on the grass. Once more I gazed beyond them and the creek to Serena and Pino's motel. I wondered what Nonna would do if Serena rang her again to report that I was back sitting in the park with Tim.

He twisted round. 'I think Mum's coming over now. With your mum.'

I don't know why but I hurried down from the table and adjusted my dress. Tim gave me a funny look. The cockatoos flew off in a flurry of screeches. Mum came closer with Dianne beside her and I could see them both searching my face, likely for different reasons.

'Hello, Sofie.' Dianne didn't try to shake hands or hug me, just gave a smile.

I saw her eyes were blue like Tim's, and probably my father's, I realised. 'Hello.'

'I guess I did wonder,' said Dianne to Mum, like she was continuing a conversation from back at the pub. 'It's good to meet you, Sofie.' She hesitated. 'Welcome to the family.'

'Oh, um, thank you.' I returned her cautious embrace.

'Why don't we sit down for a bit?' Mum suggested, and Tim scrambled from the tabletop to sit on one of the bench seats like the rest of us.

Dianne kept looking at me, just like she had that morning in church. There was a sense the situation could go either way and after this initial coming together we could drift back into our established lives apart, even if Dianne had said I was welcome.

'I don't mean to stare.' Dianne blinked several times as if tears were close, although none came. 'I know you have the Italian colouring but I can see Ross in your face.'

'I've seen it too,' Mum agreed, and I looked down again, uncertain.

From her handbag, Dianne got out a small photograph that seemed like it had been in its wooden frame a long while. 'Here, you might like to see this. There are more to show you, I have albums at home, but for now, well, this is one of my favourites.'

Clutching the frame, I saw my father for the first time. Tears rushed to my eyes, blurring what I so wanted to see. I blinked furiously. This was my dad. He grinned, his eyes light, a sense of mischief about his expression. The photograph was old and not in colour, so I couldn't see how he truly looked, but it was him.

It was as if something surged up through me. Visceral, unleashed. I saw I had his ski-jump nose and that his dark hair was quite wavy. I felt a sense of returning, of coming home. And yet what could be still remained out of reach, for I could only ever know Ross in black and white.

'What about Mr Armstrong?' My voice came out soft. It didn't feel comfortable to refer to him as my grandfather in front of Dianne and Tim. 'Will I meet him too?'

'Oh. Well ...' Dianne looked to Mum. 'This is all probably still sinking in for him, I think. He hasn't been well, and, he's ... stubborn.'

I kept looking at my father's photo. Jack didn't want to see me. Perhaps he didn't even accept that Ross had a daughter. Or he did but, as Mum feared all along, he'd shunned me. The hurt gripped harder than I expected. I'd never know my father and my grandfather didn't want to know me. I thought of the times I'd sat in church searching the faces. Fantasising that my father had a brother who looked like him so I could see a man that was almost him. Naively, I'd assumed that once he'd learnt about me, I would be welcomed with open arms. But Jack didn't even want to meet me. The frame pressed hard into my palms. Outwardly, I mustered a nod and handed back the photograph.

❧

'I kill him,' hissed Nonna Gia in the kitchen.

'Ma, for God's sake, calm down ...'

I drifted along the hallway to my bedroom hearing their murmured arguing go on.

Through a crack in the venetian blind, I saw Jack Armstrong back on the verandah as usual, gazing out. It seemed to me he was showing a certain defiance in that he wouldn't be changed. Not to accept what was true, not even to alter his daytime routine of sitting there looking down over the street. I thought I'd feel anger at the sight of him but just then I felt exhausted. I changed into my comfortable old T-shirt and shorts and lay on the bed, curling towards Edie Dawson's painting. I gazed at the soft mauve sea. Closing my eyes, I listened to Mum and Nonna out in the kitchen arguing, their hisses like waves, back and forth, in lulling sameness ...

When I opened my eyes, the light outside had dimmed, though it was only mid-afternoon. The house, the air, seemed hushed. I went out to the kitchen and saw beyond the café curtains another summer storm loomed. Zucchero brushed against my legs and I bent to pat him, catching sight of Nonna Gia in the backyard re-staking her tomato plants in readiness for the storm. Mum wasn't about, her room empty, handbag gone. She'd probably driven out to the farm to talk to Connie and Frank without having Nonna there.

Back in my room, I again looked through the venetian to see Jack still sitting on the verandah across the road. He sat straight-backed, unmoving. How could he sit so for hours? *Why* did he? It was almost as if he was waiting, as if determined to sit something out. The air was very still. Distant lightning flickered but no thunder yet. It got darker. I sensed Jack's face turn towards me. Surely he couldn't see me behind the venetian and gauze curtains with the room shadowy. Yet he seemed to look straight at me.

I went out the front door and stood under the portico arches, facing him. His gaze met mine. From the far distance came the first hint of thunder. A cooler current stirred. Mum's car was gone. Nonna was still out the back staking the tomatoes. Without any particular notion, I found myself propelled forward. Beneath my bare feet I felt the warmth of the smooth cement path still heated from the earlier sun. The footpath's cool grass, the coarse heat of the bitumen road. Suddenly I was on the other side at Jack's gate. His eyes remained on me. Perhaps if he could speak, he'd yell to ward me off but there was only the coming thunder and breeze. I kept on.

The front steps were glossy painted timber. My footfalls were almost silent. I saw for the first time, since they were usually hidden by the close railings, the verandah floorboards swept clean and that Jack sat in a cane chair with cushions beneath him and behind. A walking stick leant against it. He was dressed well for being convalescent at home, right down to laced shoes instead of slippers. His pride still there. Though he must have submitted to help with the lacing.

My curls, wild and unbrushed, moved in the breeze. My clothes were crumpled from sleep. Feet bare. That hard gaze turned on me and feeling it up close made me inwardly falter as I came nearer. But I didn't show any hesitation. I stopped just before him, my eyes holding his.

'My name is Sofie,' I said, and added, 'Sofia,' to emphasise that I was also Italian.

Jack looked away. But then I saw him give a slight nod.

The storm thundered closer, the breeze picking up and growing damper.

'And I am Ross and Elena's daughter.'

He didn't look back at me. Refused to. I took in the firm set of his jaw, his mouth rigid, unyielding. I was standing so close I could have reached out and slapped him, yet I remained motionless, suddenly knowing I was the stronger one, for I felt no hate.

From the corner of my eye, I saw Nonna Gia emerge from under a portico arch. She stood clutching her apron, flanked by her rosemary and chilli bushes, as she watched on, a silent, protective sentinel. My hand went to the *cornicello* at my throat. I could see now that Jack's view from the verandah went out over the top of Nonna's lowset brick house with its venetian blinds covering the front windows. It reached far past the familiar rooftops and antennas and all the way to the distant ranges undulating in mauve and blue on the horizon.

The wind picked up. Dianne or Tim would likely be there soon to check on Jack and help him with his nightly routine, especially with the storm close. There was nothing else I could say. I turned to go. Jack grabbed my hand. His grip startled me, surprisingly firm for someone frail-looking. I thought I saw a tear in his eye, just one, as if it escaped before the usual control won. Or maybe he just had a watery eye. His lips fought to move but couldn't form the words. Perhaps the expression on his face said he was sorry, maybe not, but for a moment he held my hand in his, strong and warm. It was the closest I'd come to my father.

La Luna

Nonna twisted *zippuli* dough around either a sun-dried tomato or an anchovy, hiding them inside and frying the pieces until crispy. I hated anchovies so picking a *zippulo* from the Christmas Eve platter that night would be a lucky, or unlucky, dip. At least they weren't the sugared ones that Mum had once made to comfort herself. Had she told Nonna about that, I wondered. My eyes slid to Nonna's profile. Hoop earring drooping in its stretched lobe. Strong nose. Age spots along her hairline. She hadn't put on a Dean Martin record since she'd played me the song linked to Keith. I didn't know why. But no matter how close we were or what we'd shared, I couldn't know all her intricacies, nor her mine. There were always those little parts of us kept hidden.

My gaze moved around the kitchen. 'There's a lot of food here, Nonna.'

'*Boh*, it's Christmas Eve!'

She always cooked thirteen dishes for it. Something to do with Jesus and the apostles, or Calabria, I'd forgotten. The number thirteen lucky as long as you didn't set the table for thirteen, like the Last Supper. Always that loophole. But there seemed even

351

more food that year, as if Nonna was appeasing the gods with an extra saucepan of *baccalà alla Calabrese*, its fish smell competing with an oven dish of *lasagne con melanzane*, eggplant only as, like on Good Friday, no meat was allowed. Chillies waited on the board too, tender throats lined up for Nonna's angry spaghetti, the dough of which was resting. And all this for only seven of us.

Just like every other Christmas Eve, Nonna expected Frank, Connie and the kids to join us for dinner and afterwards we would all go to midnight Mass together. But since it had all come out about Mum and Ross – and me – midnight Mass would be the first time we'd come face-to-face with Nonna's Italian friends who'd endured the same hostility from Jack Armstrong. And who knew how they'd act towards us. My eyes went to the dried chillies Nonna kept hanging by the back door to repel the *malocchio*.

There was a clunk from the hallway as Mum hung up the telephone after talking to Connie again. She wandered out to us in the kitchen. 'Well, what talk the Stanthorpe bush telegraph didn't take care of, the Italian grapevine has. Only took two days.'

Neither Nonna nor I said anything but it felt odd that people I didn't even know were talking about us. I guess those who'd lived in the town long enough knew of Ross Armstrong's death and the long-held animosity between our two families, and likely mulled over the unexpected turn entwining us all. Mum hadn't left the house since the talk started spreading.

She too took in all the food on the table and benchtops and folded her arms. 'I don't think I'm going to Mass this year.'

'Elena, we got to go to Mass. It's Christmas Eve.' Nonna kept shaping more dough into *zippuli*. 'You don't have to hide in the house. And we'll hold up our heads.'

'Ma, I'm almost forty, I can decide to stay home if I don't want to see anyone.'

I guessed Nonna might be thinking of Edie. Her lips went thin and I sensed another impending argument in the same way the air stills before a storm.

'I think I might go for a walk.'

'Oh, Sof, you don't have to.'

I smiled at Mum. 'It's okay. Really.'

They were already at it again in a rush of hisses when I'd grabbed my bag and was slipping out the front door. In a way, I could understand how they each wanted to be just then. Nonna Gia would insist on going up to the shops as usual, clenched by the corset-girdle, handbag over her arm, a look on her face that dared anyone to say a stray word to her, while Mum pretty much wanted to hide out in the house and talk on the phone to Connie. I mostly felt a bit adrift and caught in between, still getting used to knowing who my father was.

From the portico, I saw Jack wasn't on his verandah. Maybe the Dinnings had taken him to be with them at the pub for Christmas. There'd been no more interaction between our families since Jack had grasped my hand a couple of days before and I guess the Dinnings didn't even know about that. It simmered strange and raw and unsettled between us all. Nonna kept telling me that letting it rest for a time would help. She was likely right, but it was hard.

I noticed the *Piccante Calabrese* bushes blooming in promise of a new crop. So often I walked by without really seeing them. Among the tiny flowers remained one of the chillies that had ripened early that summer. I felt the smooth curve of its heart shape. To think, it held seeds like Great-great-nonna had wrapped in a paper bud for her granddaughter, my nonna, to open on the other side of the world. I touched the *cornicello* at my neck, realising she'd touched it too. Did it protect me or just give the belief it did so that I'd feel braver? It and the seeds were so small they could easily be lost.

❦

Up on the main street, a couple of older women chatting outside the butchery turned to stare at me but most people went about their business. In the newsagent I bought a chocolate, but a smaller one, the gold foil circle of a coconut rough that fit in my palm. That wasn't to say I wouldn't buy two chocolates next time, but it was a start. Among the chewing gums I saw Arrowmint and almost picked one up, but couldn't. Not yet. Mum might have been perceptive about the chocolates but she'd let me down by not telling me about my father for so long. It was hard to forgive her that. Even if I was coming to see that we all had our limitations and that not talking about Ross was hers.

The shortest way to the train station was past the hotel. I was almost about to walk an extra block to avoid it but then I didn't want to be like Mum and hide, or to assert Nonna's boldness, so I went the usual way but over on the other side of the road so it didn't seem like I was deliberately trying to see the Dinnings. I put the chocolate in my bag with my Walkman and writing paper. Mel was overdue a letter and I needed to write it without Mum seeing. I had to tell Mel the boy I'd told her about was no more, especially in case she mentioned something about it around Mum once I was back in Brisbane.

'Sofie? Hey, Sof!' Tim was out the back near the chooks.

I wavered for just a moment before I crossed the road to him. He sat in the yard on an old keg, his sketchbook in hand, which surprised me. Perhaps he wasn't going to worry as much about his dad belittling his drawing any more. I leant on the gate but didn't come in.

'How you been going?' he asked.

I shrugged. 'Oh, you know.'

'Yeah.' He regarded me a bit longer, some of that old look in his eyes like when we'd fallen for each other, but then he glanced away and it was gone.

'Are you drawing?' I didn't know what else to say.

He held up the sketchbook to show me the chooks he'd drawn. 'Wish they'd keep still.'

We both sort of laughed and I nodded. 'They look good. Especially the speckled one.'

I felt bad for ripping up his other drawings, even if I hadn't meant it against him, and I would never tell him, not wanting to hurt him. Each of us went quiet. It was actually soothing watching the chooks as they scuffed and dust-bathed. Their gentle tuts and murmurs. Most were toffee brown or white, a few speckled black and white with bright red combs.

'Tim, when you told me your granddad was in the war, I guess you meant your dad's father, did you?' I had to ask though I knew the answer, but it was what had helped make me think the old man was Keith. I knew Jack hadn't been in the war.

'Yeah, my other pop lives up at Allora.' Tim looked uncomfortable and kept drawing.

Again we were silent and I wondered how much he knew about Jack. I shifted a little.

'You heading to the station?' He saw me nod. 'Want some company?'

'Oh. Probably better not.' I deliberated telling him about Jack grabbing my hand.

'Sofie …' Again, our eyes met. 'It will be better. In time. I reckon.'

Who'd have thought he'd sound the same as Nonna in some respects. But just then it all felt so up in the air as to what might happen. It was like the initial fluster of finding out had worn off and everyone was treading water while they worked out how they truly felt.

'See you later then,' I said, and he smiled, but who knew if we really would.

❧

So, in the end, it was just a holiday fling with the spunk, I wrote to Mel, keeping it breezy and never using Tim's name. *He's gone back home to Sydney so that's that. I don't expect to see him again.* I didn't tell her about my father or his family, not fully sure how I felt about it yet. Tentative about what Mel might say, considering the way she often said *wog* to me, like it meant nothing, a little joke. When really it made me feel I was somehow lesser than her and others at school, and in a way the word hurt more because already I was different in not having a dad around. Of course, Mel didn't know what it was like to have an Italian migrant background and be called a wog, or how it felt not having a father, but still.

There was space left on the page for just a line or two. I hesitated, looking from the platform to the tracks. Then I wrote, *when you said you thought of me cause your Dad picked some wog movie, I'm sure you didn't mean anything by it, but like, what's the deal with that? I mean, it's kind of a crappy thing to say. Or didn't you realise how that might sound to me?* Mel would probably put it back on me by saying she was just joking and that I needed to lighten up. Maybe I was too sensitive regarding what was different about me, but if I didn't say anything it was as if it was okay and for me it wasn't.

I folded the letter and got out my Walkman, rewinding the tape to 'Sweet and Sour', my favourite song from the TV show I'd watched a few months before. Sitting backwards on the bench, I leant with my hands on the backrest, coconut chocolate sweet in my mouth. Stanthorpe's red and grey rooftops peeked among trees. My gaze drifted to the post office clocktower, the brick chimneys of the hotel, far off to where the farm was and beyond to the hazy mountain line that gently rose and fell. A dry breeze riffled my curls. The song ended. I thought of my father. Soft quiet stretched out.

'*Buon Natale!*' Frank carried in a mammoth tuna casserole. 'Where do you want the *tonno?*'

'On the table,' cried Nonna Gia, kissing Lena and then Sam, who squirmed as usual.

'Here's your panettone.' Connie handed Nonna a box that had a picture of the sweet, buttery Italian Christmas bread, tall like a top hat and studded with dried fruit and citrus peel that was inside.

Frank winked and tousled my hair. 'Hey, *patatina.*' He hadn't called me *little potato* since I was about ten and hated it. I couldn't help laughing a little and gave him a hug back.

The seven of us crowded around the kitchen table set with the best china and cutlery.

Then the front doorbell rang.

'Who could that be?' Nonna glanced at the clock.

Frank looked at Mum. 'We're not expecting anyone else, are we?'

She shook her head, looking slightly uneasy as Nonna Gia went to see.

'Serena! Pino!' came Nonna's cry. 'Come in!'

Serena emerged from the hallway carrying a *tortiera di carciofi*, a savoury artichoke cake. 'We decided we couldn't let you have Christmas Eve without us this year,' she smiled, putting the dish on the table so she could give Mum and then me special kisses and hugs before all the others.

'*Il mondo è bello perché vario*,' she murmured in my ear. *The world is beautiful because it's varied.*

My breath drew in hard. Hugging her back, I smelt on her the 4711 perfume she gave me in a tiny bottle each birthday and guessed I'd still be getting another bottle next year. Maybe Zia Serena had said the same words to Mum too for I saw her wiping grateful tears.

'Here's your panettone.' Pino handed the box to Mum while he also juggled bottles of wine and lemonade that Frank leapt forward to help him with.

'Sofia, get out more plates,' commanded Nonna, scurrying off as the doorbell rang again and then crying out, 'Josie! Alfio! And all the family too. My goodness. Come in!'

They all traipsed down the hallway carrying dishes smelling of swordfish and a *melanzane parmigiana* as well as a *torta reggina*, fruit cake and Alfio's homemade wines.

'We thought this year we'd come and see you lot for Christmas Eve …' Josie was saying and gave a happy shout as she saw Serena and Pino had had the same idea.

Josie too sought out Mum and me first to give us tight hugs and extra kisses.

'A panettone for you all.' Vince passed me the box and I put it over on the kitchen bench beside the other two.

Everyone crammed inside tramping over the shag pile carpet and Lena whispered to me, 'I can't believe Nonna hasn't yelled at everyone to take their shoes off.'

'I know,' I said, almost laughing, and in my relief and gladness gave her a swift hug that made her look surprised but happy.

'Ma, are those trestle tables and old bench seats still out in the garage?' bellowed Frank. 'I think we'd better set up outside.'

'Yes, and, Elena, there are some lanterns out there too. We need more plates!'

'Anybody here?' came a call from outside the back door before Frank even opened it.

'Mamma!' Connie cried. Her family had also turned up unexpectedly, her mother under the weight of her Sicilian Christmas rice dish, her brother with a slab of beer on his shoulder.

'We decided we'd share Christmas Eve with you lot this year. Gia, here's a panettone!'

~

Close to forty of us squashed along bench seats at the trestle tables once the rest of Serena and Pino's clan, including Mauro, turned up as well. In the balmy evening, paper lanterns Nonna had kept from past parties swung from the Hills Hoist and fruit trees. Their soft light added to hastily set up kero lamps and candles in empty wine bottles crowded amid dishes, glasses, plates and bottles. People ate and talked and broke into song. From a large cut-off drum a *focara* was burning, a Calabrian Christmas Eve tradition Nonna's generation carried on, of keeping a bonfire going to gather around in celebration and to burn away all that is bad from the past.

'*Salute a tutti!*' cried Frank, not for the first time, and everyone again clinked glasses.

'*Cent' anni*,' Josie toasted in reply. *To a hundred years of health.*
And among all the clinking I saw she and Serena made sure not
to miss Nonna Gia's wine glass.

I couldn't take my eyes from the three women as shared looks
passed between them. And I saw them young and alone on the farms
after their husbands were interned. How they'd banded together
to do the best they could during those daunting years, despite
many like Jack being against them. Looking at them now, there
was something impressive in how the women held themselves, all
in older age, hair greying, creased faces and plumper round their
middles, at ease in who they were, how they'd lived, the griefs
and missteps, as well as the joys, and what they'd changed. For
each time they'd supported one another and pushed back, even
a little, in time change grew. So now I might go to university,
travel without a wedding ring or chaperone, marry by choice.
And it didn't matter if I had my father's surname or not.

'*Pasta arrabbiata!*' Nonna carried a colossal bowl of her angry
spaghetti from the kitchen despite more than thirteen dishes
already crowding the table. And this spaghetti was especially hot
for I knew Nonna, caught up in all the excitement, had added
extra *Piccante Calabrese*, maybe because she knew I could handle it
now, judging by the pointed look she gave me.

Just as Nonna plunked the bowl on the table, several figures
emerged from the dark of the side driveway. Everyone turned. It
was Jack, shuffling with a walking stick towards us all, Dianne
and Tim either side of him and Dianne's husband just behind.
I heard someone gasp. A hush fell over the tables as they came
closer and then an uneasy murmuring. Even the children quieted
in the atmosphere. Mum stood up at her seat. Frank did too.

'I hope you don't mind ...' Dianne smiled and also appeared a
bit unnerved, perhaps not expecting quite so many faces to turn

to them. 'We were bringing Dad home and thought we'd pop over and wish you all a merry Christmas.'

For a moment, it was so quiet there was only the crackling and pop of the bonfire. Many eyes went to Jack. He remained impassive yet his blue eyes blazed, alive and alert in the firelight. Gradually, the gazes turned to Nonna Gia. More murmurings. She took a short breath, got up and came over to stand before them, putting her hands on her hips. Jack looked at her. Gia looked back. She gave a slight nod. Her eyes shifted to Dianne and the others.

'Well, happy Christmas.' She glanced over to the table and everyone watching, and turned back to them with a smile. 'Welcome. Come and join us. There's plenty to eat.'

Dianne looked to her husband and Tim. Both appeared keen yet unsure about Jack. But as if in answer, Jack directed his walking stick towards the table and shuffled forward.

'Frank, bring over those chairs from the patio!' Nonna ordered.

I felt a rush of uncertainty, relief and also love for Nonna all at once. And I thought of her saying, *we all need to get on for the sake of next generations but I don't think we should forget*. I hadn't really thought about the word *we* in what she'd said. That I wasn't just watching on. It was up to me to remember too. The Dinnings sat down somewhat carefully among all the Italians but the ambience remained magnanimous. I sought out Mum's face and, catching my eye, she smiled, even if it appeared a little shaky.

If only Jack could've spoken. Possibly time or his debility had changed him and he was sorry. Or perhaps he'd never have said the words we wished to hear. But I sensed he still carried a toughness within him and remained a type who would've refused to sit with us all if that's how he truly felt. And he *had* grasped my hand. He looked at me. I looked at him. Was he seeing Ross or me? All around us, conversation and the clatter of cutlery on plates carried on. Frank put drinks in their hands and Josie began dishing out her *melanzane parmigiana*.

'Oh, I don't think Dad will eat eggplant,' said Dianne for Jack. 'He's a plain eater.'

'That's okay.' Nonna reached for the serving bowl of angry spaghetti that looked innocently as if the sauce was plain tomato. 'Jack might like my spaghetti.'

❧

A few went off to midnight Mass but that Christmas Eve most of us instead stayed around the bonfire and tables strewn with espresso cups and platters of half-eaten cake and panettone. Frank poured Sambuca into liqueur glasses, plopped coffee beans in each and lit them all to create blue flames. Again he cried, '*Salute a tutti!*' Many raised glasses. Dianne too, leaning across to clink hers against others, face flushed and beaming.

I noticed Jack didn't have one but then I hadn't seen him drink anything other than the glass of milk he'd nursed after a mouthful of Nonna Gia's angry spaghetti. The look he'd given her! And hers, steady, inscrutable, in return. I barely breathed. Yet he stayed, walking stick in reach, content to linger despite the late hour. And it seemed, despite the pain and damage that had happened in the past, what might be, in time, held promise.

'Who would've thought?' Mum murmured to me, and while she smiled, she seemed subdued, as though the turn of events was bittersweet. It would always be too late for Ross.

I hesitated, then said, 'By the way, that's a pretty top, Mum,' and I was truly pleased to see her again in what I'd long disparaged as her 'hippie' clothes. Relieved that neither me, nor Nonno, nor losing Ross had taken away that free aspect of her person.

She glanced down at her embroidered blouse, somewhat bemused, then gave me a hug. And while it would take more time for things to settle, it would be okay between us.

Wood smoke hung over the backyard as the bonfire blazed on and Mauro ran about with Sam and the other kids. Zucchero was nowhere to be seen, probably hiding in the safe harbour of the laundry. Nonna Gia bellowed, 'Salvatore, kick that ball into my tomatoes again, and I kick you!' And then, barely a minute later, Sam yelling, 'Nonna, it was an accident!' Being young and like Frank, it seemed he went on as if oblivious to the change in our family.

I heard a wheeze of music as Ignazio picked up his piano accordion and sat by the fire where Vince already had a *zufulo*, flute, and Alfio a *triccheballacche*, the wood contraption of three mallets nailed with tambourine cymbals to create percussion. Fuelled by Sambuca, they launched into a Christmas folk song, the older Italians singing in dialect. I felt if the fire smoke didn't have the forbearing neighbours complaining soon, surely this would.

Tim beckoned for me to come and sit beside him near the fire and I wondered what he was making of all this. Of course, Nonna wouldn't worry now about two cousins sitting together and thankfully she was too distracted to be matchmaker and encourage Mauro to sit with me instead.

'I'm glad we came over tonight,' Tim said.

'Yeah, me too.'

Jack was watching us, his face not giving anything away. Mum too. She sat between Connie and Dianne, nodding at times but not talking like the other two were, her eyes on us.

'I've never had a cousin.' Tim saw me quickly look at him. He smirked. 'Too soon?'

Thankfully the music was loud. I gave a slight laugh and almost shoved him but it seemed better not to touch, especially while being watched by Mum and Jack. Lena lay on the banana lounge listening to my Walkman, almost asleep, but I could see her also watching us through slitted eyes, maybe a little wary of Tim usurping her position. Although I couldn't help but wonder if Tim and I slightly gave ourselves away by how easily we interacted.

He threw a balled paper serviette into the fire. 'So, will you be staying at your nonna's again during the holidays next year?'

'I don't know …' It felt like ages rather than a few weeks ago that I'd been fighting Mum so I could stay in Brisbane to be with my friends. She'd probably even let me now. I looked over to Nonna joyfully clapping along to the music with Serena and Josie, her hoop earrings glinting in the firelight. 'Actually, I reckon I'll still be coming here.'

Tim smiled, facing the fire. 'Maybe we can hang out sometimes.'

'Maybe. Unless you go to art school.'

'Oh, I don't know about that.' Unconsciously he glanced towards his father and grandfather. 'Thing is, I think for now the pub suits me. And I'll draw when I want to.'

'Fair enough.' Although I planned to bring it up again one day.

His eyes went back to the flames. 'So, what's with the bonfire? It's not a cold night.'

'Well, according to Nonna in Calabria they light bonfires on Christmas Eve and dance and sing around them until dawn. But obviously, it's winter over there now.'

I didn't mention the *focara* was also meant as a burning away of the bad in the past. Looking around me at all who'd unexpectedly come to show their care out of simple decency and acceptance, it seemed we didn't need the flames, we were doing it ourselves. And in that moment I wished Nonno Taddeo could've been there to see it and no longer turn away.

The song being played came to an end, and in the lull Pino called out, 'Ah, look at *la bella luna*.' He pointed to where the moon was beginning to appear over the rooftop.

We all looked up. It wasn't perfectly full but still bright. Often, I'd forget about the moon being overhead. A bearing in the darkness. Its draw on the sea and tides within us all.

Frank suddenly leapt up to speak to Alfio and Vince and then whistled to get everybody's attention. 'How about a song that we all know the words to?' He smiled over at the Dinnings, all the Italians and finally to Nonna Gia. 'This one's for you, Ma.'

She swivelled in surprise and as they began playing a Dean Martin song, my breath caught. Nonna glanced at me. I smiled, almost teary, and it didn't matter if it felt corny and sentimental when together all the Italians and the Dinnings sang the line about the moon in 'That's Amore'. Even Mauro sang without embarrassment. Tim too, though he laughed and shook his head. It seemed they all knew and didn't mind a bit of Dino.

I looked from the moon to the fire. Perhaps there'd still be talk about for a while. And maybe we wouldn't often get together with Jack or the Dinnings. It was hard to tell yet what may come of it all. Just as it was impossible to bring back those lost to the past or to change what had happened. But for that evening, both moon and fire gave light, Jack held me in his gaze, Nonna Gia was singing and there was a fresh sense of hope. Maybe, just maybe, it was possible to keep coming together, little by little, the shifts subtle, but always changing shape.

And it was then I knew there was just one person to whom I wanted to tell the secret that I still carried. I hoped Tim might understand, and that Nonna would too.

Returning

'I put in a handful of salt then a bit more,' Nonna Gia said, tossing it into the pot of water.

I leant down to pat Zucchero nudging my leg. 'So that it's like the sea ...'

She volleyed me a no-nonsense look, having no time for sentimental romanticism with the water already on the boil. 'Sofia, the water must have salt as the pasta has none.'

'I know, you told me.' Since Mum had gone back to Brisbane after New Year's Day for work and it was again just Nonna and me, we'd been in the kitchen a fair bit.

I watched her reach for one of her heart-shaped chillies and put a knife to its neck. There was a craft to cookery I'd never quite realised. The gathering of each element, piece by piece. Touching, assessing, inhaling, considering the best way to put them together. The fire got lit, then it was you, the pan and the alchemy. Perhaps the pan was slow to heat, the change almost imperceptible at first but as it gathered momentum you had to sharpen your senses for

366

what was happening so that what you'd put in there would turn out in the end.

Nonna Gia hadn't said any more about the past. Perhaps she didn't feel the need. The *Piccante Calabrese* lay with open hearts on the wooden board. When she wasn't looking, I put my fingertip in one of their bled pools and brought it to my lips. The devil's kiss blazed. There was still a question I needed her to answer from the past. It was like a niggle that kept at me. And of course I had something I wanted to tell her about the present.

'Nonna … what was Nonno Taddeo like when Mum was born? Was he … happy?'

'What a thing to ask, Sofia. Of course.'

Maybe he hadn't ever suspected, I reasoned to myself, and to cover I swiftly added, 'I mean, most men wanted a boy in those days, didn't they?'

'Just in those days?' She gave a snort. 'Anyway, he got Frank next, didn't he?'

From the stereogram in the living room Dean Martin again played his part.

'But did you ever tell him about—' Keith's name hovered between us.

I saw the knife falter in Nonna's hand. My lips kept on stinging from the chilli.

'What would that do except cause hurt? Taddeo didn't deserve that.'

'Isn't it always better for the truth to be told though?' But I was thinking of Tim then.

'Almost always.' And when she saw my expression. 'Each situation is different.'

I pondered this as she lit the other stove hotplate and Zucchero padded to the back screen door to sit gazing out. The heat on my lips rounded to a warmth but remained alive.

'Nonna, I don't really want to go out with Mauro. He doesn't interest me.'

'*Boh.*' She shrugged. 'Then don't.' Knife in hand, she reached for another chilli.

I kept my eyes on its vehement redness. 'But from when I first met Tim, I—'

Nonna looked up, eyes like rifles. In that moment, we teetered at the edge of the shadow and I understood at once why certain things were left unspoken. But she knew. The heat spread from my lips up into my scalp. *She knew.* I was sure of that much. *Tutti i nodi vengono al pettine. All knots are caught by the comb.* It couldn't be hidden. I tensed, almost holding my breath. Neither of us wanted me to say more, I think. In the quiet between us, she went back to chopping the chillies, harried thuds flecking the board. The boiling water wafted steam.

'But you don't feel that now.' She kept her eyes down.

'No.' It was mostly the truth and in time would come to be so.

Nonna didn't answer. And so that was the end of it as far as I could tell. Just as she didn't again speak of Keith, I didn't again broach the subject of Mum and him and the past. It was back to cooking. She still wouldn't let me cut the chillies, or choose how many. But for the moment, that was okay.

'*Il troppo stroppia*, Sofia.' *Too much is too much.* And with her petite blade, Nonna finished preparing knolls of red and white, just enough chilli and garlic to scatter across the pan, making the olive oil hiss as they began to dance together. 'Now, what can you smell?'

'What do you mean?'

'Go on. Close your eyes. Breathe in.'

The sharp tang hit my nostrils first, then a little bit of acridity, followed by sweetness and last of all a current of mellow earthy oil. I opened my eyes to Nonna Gia beaming.

'It's the same scent your ancestors breathed when they cooked this dish.'

And just then it was almost as if the aroma released a trigger of deep memories that let things rise up and take shape in ourselves. Or perhaps I was just getting all romantic again.

'Nonna ...' I hesitated, leant in and gave her cheek a kiss.

'Oh, Sofia, get the spaghetti.' But I saw her damp eyes and both of us were smiling.

Jack was sitting out on his verandah when I closed Nonna's front gate behind me. I waved to him and he raised his hand in return. Maybe when I got back, I'd go and sit with him for a bit. I did that sometimes by then. Just sitting. Looking out towards the mountains together. At times watching Nonna watering her chillies and giant rosemary shrub. I don't know if she did it on purpose but often she'd put her backside to us as she bent to get the hose in underneath. Always that bit of fire in her. And I'd see Jack's lips itch with what he'd say if he could.

I walked up to the train station past the hotel, not seeing any of the Dinnings, though it wasn't long after the lunch rush and they were likely still busy. As usual, no-one was at the old train station. I sat on the bench. I'm not sure why it was the place I'd often sought out on my own. I'd started coming there before I knew it was where Nonna had first set foot in Stanthorpe and met Keith Dawson. And where Mum had sat as she'd waited to leave, carrying me within her. But I did like how Nonna had rushed there to her, to us, when all had seemed so adrift and bleak.

Yet she'd still expected Mum to mostly make her own way. Just as Nonna Gia now left it up to me how matters evolved with Jack and the Dinnings. Or she seemed to, at least. I couldn't underestimate her. I did wonder though, if I hadn't noticed the difference in her wedding photographs whether Nonna would still have told me that she was a proxy bride, or about Keith, Edie, or even Jack. But I had a feeling she might have.

Her stories had crept up on me in a way. I didn't quite realise she'd taken my hand in hers until I later felt a warmth, the kind you need when you've become so numbly cold that the heat initially hurts your fingertips. Perhaps she'd picked up on the pain I'd kept hidden too. And in preparing me for what I had to find out, by sharing her past, she was showing me that people did all sorts of things, intended or not, and that hurt was caused but there was also love too, and possibility, even if it was hard-earnt.

When I was little and learning to play Scopa, Nonna would sweep up the cards, triumph gleaming in her eyes. She always played to win, and if I cried or kicked the chair leg then she'd played to win more. It took years for me to see she'd done it because she wanted the best for me rather than me believing life would give me that win undeserved. 'If you win, it's because you worked out how to and earnt it yourself,' she'd eventually admitted. 'The way the real world is.' Perhaps that was right, or wrong. Looking back on growing up, I felt some things had been hard on me, but then, coming through it, I wasn't sure I'd change it.

I lay back on the bench. No Walkman, no chocolate, just me. The sky seemed to expand overhead, mostly blue with vivid white clouds not hiding the sun. I held my hand up against the glare, the shape of my hand so like Mum's, though perhaps like Ross's too. I'd pored over every detail of him in photos Dianne had given me, in between searching my face in the mirror. Maybe I'd ask if she had one showing his hands. Maybe. I still felt shy about the situation. It would never be 'normal' but I was realising it didn't have to be for it to be okay.

I lowered my hand. The clouds drifted on in varying shapes, some large, some small, breaking away, melding. None perfect, or imperfect. Like rocks or trees, or each of us, they just were. Different, yet with a sameness to them. And most of us accepted it was how they were. I heard Nonna's voice back when I was younger, telling me, '*The sun warms whoever it sees.* That's Mother Calabria saying to us that nature sees us all the same.' Those words in Calabrian dialect came from further back too, *u sule a chinne vidari, scafari* ... in the voices of my *bisnonni* and of those beyond, carried over on whispers and seas that surround us all.

For the brides wed by proxy,
and those who loved them.

Notes

Proxy marriages between Italy and Australia

Thousands of young Italian women came to Australia on 'bride ships' during the twentieth century, married by proxy in Italy to Italian migrant men already in Australia. Usually the unions were arranged by the man and her parents or another relative. Most women appeared agreeable.

Despite letters and photographs, many 'proxy brides' knew little of their husbands before they met. There were men who sent outdated photographs, their wives arriving to find their husbands were much older. Some women were stranded miserably on isolated farms while others had happy or at least content marriages, if only after much adjustment, often on both sides. Not all Italian marriages were by proxy though, and so due to past stigma and judgement by others, those marriages that were by proxy are rarely spoken or written about to this day.

Proxy marriage was a way of dealing with a particular situation – single Italian men greatly outnumbered single Italian women in Australia. With concerns about too many 'white aliens' or non-British

European migrants, the Australian government's immigration act issued entry permits only to Italians who were sponsored by relatives already in Australia who had employment waiting – mostly men. Or who had £50 landing money, again men in general.

Women were mainly accepted to reunite with kin. And most Italian families wouldn't let daughters travel out alone if unmarried, so often the only solution was to first marry by proxy so the young women could travel unchaperoned. This situation was also enabled by intense poverty in Italy at the time – young women were willing to take the risk to 'proxy marry' for a better life, Italian migrant men were unable to afford a return trip to Italy to find a wife and cross-cultural marriages between Australians and Italians were largely not accepted by either culture.

It is unlikely the phenomenon of proxy marriages between Italy and Australia will ever occur again in history.

Internees in Australia during World War II

At least 8000 people were interned in Australia during World War II (although the official total numbers of resident 'enemy aliens' interned at this time vary between government documents). It is also unlikely such recorded numbers include all those people interned considering that after the official camps were full, additional 'temporary' camps were established. They were often hidden out in rural bush locations and didn't always keep proper records, or those that were kept were later destroyed.

But these camps did exist and included internees like my grandfather, Annibale Boccabella, and my great-grandfather, Vitale Boccabella.

In Australia, under the *Aliens Registration Act* and the *National Security (Aliens Control) Regulations* of 1939, Italian migrants or those born in Australia with Italian ancestry were interned in the largest numbers, in Queensland especially, where pre-war animosity towards Italians existed particularly in the sugarcane industry. Most of these people of Italian background who were interned had been in Australia for years, decades, even born there, and were loyal to their new country, hardworking and had never been in trouble with the law.

And while national security was deemed the issue, Hansard records and news articles of the time confirm some in power used internment and curfews as part of a long-standing hostility against migrants for their perceived taking of local jobs and bringing new cultural ways. Government records also show that among those interned from many different migrant backgrounds, some were from or had ancestry from countries on the same side as the Allies in the war and even included Indigenous Australians for living on German missions.

To date, Australian governments remain largely silent on this. And no apology has been given.

~

Australian Women's Land Army

With male labour reduced during the war, the Australian Women's Land Army (AWLA) was formed in 1942 to ensure ongoing food production for both military and civilian requirements in the face of shortages. Recruiting age ranged from eighteen years old up to fifty, but many women as young as fifteen and sixteen were able to join by obtaining their parents' consent. Most were recruited from urban areas, had little or no agricultural experience and learnt on the job.

Members of the Women's Land Army were given a badge, a uniform and some equipment but no proper conditions or recognition. Much of the work was hard manual labour, with the women working a forty-eight hour week for a payment of thirty shillings – when the average basic weekly wage for a male employee in Australia was more than four pounds.

At its peak, the Australian Women's Land Army had more than 3000 women in duty.

After the war ended, the Land Army members were not allowed to march in Anzac Day parades nor given recognition for their contribution to the war effort. For decades, the women lobbied hard to have the Land Army recognised and were eventually allowed to march on Anzac Day from 1985. In 1994, almost fifty years after the end of the war, their work was finally recognised by the Australian government with a Civilian Service Medal.

Single parenthood

It wasn't until 1973 that the Supporting Mother's Benefit was introduced in Australia. Before then, single mothers only got financial help in the form of a pension if they'd been married at some point and could prove their husbands had deserted or divorced them, or if their husband was in prison or a psychiatric hospital. And before 1942 there was no government help at all, even if a woman's husband had died leaving her with children and little money.

To the present day there remains stress and stigma surrounding single parenthood, particularly for those on welfare, with these parents three times more likely to live below the poverty line. According to the 2021 Australian census, 82% of single parents are mothers.

School of Arts Building, 166 Ann Street, Brisbane

In Brisbane's early years, young women arriving from England to seek new lives in Australia as servants were billeted at the colony barracks, causing concerns for their safety. Passionate about looking after women, Lady Diamantina Bowen and several society ladies organised donations for a residence to house and train the new arrivals. Designed by H Edwin Bridges, the building was constructed in 1865 as the Brisbane Servants' Home for women.

Contessa Diamantina Roma, an Italian aristocrat born in the Venetian Ionian Islands, which later became part of Greece, was married to Lord George Bowen, Queensland's first governor. She spoke English in public but Italian at home with her husband. A beloved female leader of charitable works, many places bear the name Roma, Diamantina or Bowen in her honour. She also led the establishment of Brisbane's first maternity hospital, now the Royal Brisbane and Women's Hospital.

In 1873, as demand waned, the Brisbane Servants' Home became the School of Arts and later a public library. By 1983–84, under Brisbane City Council's trusteeship, much-needed repairs and restoration included the removal of the building's

1937 shopfronts and a 1955 brick upper storey to reveal the original facade. It was then utilised for the next two decades until the 150-year-old building again needed refurbishment and was closed in the early 2000s. At present, still under Brisbane City Council trusteeship, for many years it has stood empty, the elegant sandstone building with its wide verandahs dwarfed by towering high-rises alongside. Yet, there is talk that once again it might be restored.

❧

Acknowledgement to Australia's First Nations People

With acknowledgement and respect to the Kambuwal peoples of Stanthorpe, the Turrbal and Jagera peoples of Brisbane/Meanjin and the Yugambeh peoples of the Coolangatta area and to their Elders past, present and future.

❧

Thank you and tante belle cose

Thank you to those proxy brides who quietly spoke of stories long unspoken. To Hector Dinning for writing about his Stanthorpe orchard a hundred years ago, and to my own family and their Applethorpe orchards. To Megan, for being a kind listener.

Grazie eterni to my Italian grandparents, Francesca, born in Palmi, later raised in Applethorpe, and Annibale, who told me of a group of women banding together to keep their farms going after he and other men were interned during World War II.

Thank you and *auguri gentili* to Rachael Donovan, Annabel Blay, Jo Mackay, Mary Rennie and to Selwa Anthony and also Jackie French with deep gratitude. To all those at HarperCollins and HQ Fiction for their expertise and care in many ways, all significant and very much appreciated.

And deepest thanks to my husband, Roger, always supportive amid the ebbs and flows and willing to come along to wherever the latest research travels end up. *Con profondo amore e grazie. xxx*

Recipes

Note: *Measurements are as accurate as possible.*
Many of these recipes are passed down through
generations with instructions such as 'a pinch,
a handful, a sprinkling, throw in a bit of, taste to see ...'

꧂

Dino Crocetti (Dean Martin)
Song List
(to cook by)

'Volare'
'In Napoli'
'Mambo Italiano'
'Everybody Loves Somebody'
'You're Nobody till Somebody Loves You'
'Memories are Made of This'
'Come Back to Sorrento'
'You Belong to Me'
'That's Amore'

꧂

Angry Spaghetti

Spaghetti all'Arrabbiata Calabrese

Calabria and Abruzzo are the two regions in Italy that most use chilli in dishes. Angry spaghetti or *spaghetti all'arrabbiata* is typically made with garlic, tomatoes and chillies, but some in Calabria also use *'nduja*, a spreadable preserve made from pork and hot chillies (*Piccante Calabrese* and others). The idea of 'angry spaghetti' is said to go back to the sixteenth century. While *arrabbiata* means 'angry', an even hotter sauce is *incazzate*, 'very angry'!

Ingredients

extra virgin olive oil
2 chillies (or more depending on how angry!), finely diced
3 garlic cloves, peeled and finely sliced
optional: 60g *'nduja* to taste, balsamic vinegar, *colatura di alici*
400g tin crushed tomatoes or fresh ripe cherry tomatoes, chopped
400g dried spaghetti
salt and pepper, to taste
optional: *Parmigiano, pecorino* or *caciocavallo* cheese, freshly grated, or fried
   breadcrumbs and parsley to sprinkle on top, brown sugar

Method

- Heat a generous pour of the oil in a large pan and fry the chillies until they start to caramelise, then add the garlic until golden (and *'nduja* if using).
- *Secret tip: add a small dash each of balsamic vinegar and colatura di alici or Worcestershire sauce for a deeper savoury, umami background flavour.*

- Add the tomatoes, salt to taste and cook until reduced (at least 30 minutes or more – the longer, the better the flavour).
- *Secret tip: add a teaspoon of brown sugar when adding the tomatoes.*
- Cook the pasta in plenty of boiling salted water until *al dente*.
- Drain, add to the sauce in the pan along with some pepper and mix well.

Traditionally this is served without cheese but if desired add some, freshly grated, or instead sprinkle fried breadcrumbs and parsley on top.

Moonstruck Eggs

Eggs cooked in bread in the pan

There are more than five dozen names for this humble dish – Egg in a Nest, *Uova nel Cestino*, Pirate's Eye, *Gallina in un Nido* … Moonstruck takes its name from the 1980s film where it featured.

Ingredients

2 free-range eggs
2 pieces bread
optional: butter (not margarine)
extra virgin olive oil
salt and pepper to taste

Method

- Cut one egg-sized hole in the middle of each slice of bread.
- *Secret tip: for extra flavour and decadence, butter each side of bread.*
- Gently heat a frying pan and add olive oil.
- Add the bread.
- Crack the eggs into the holes in the bread. (At this point, Nonna Gia secretly dusted a smidgin of ground chilli onto the yolks.)
- Turn once the egg whites have become bright white.
- As soon as the other side has lightly browned, they are ready to serve.
- Sprinkle with salt flakes and cracked black pepper.

Best served with a runny yolk to dip the crusts into.
May also be served with fried red capsicum strips
and/or a sprinkling of chopped parsley.

Melanzane Fritte

Eggplant slices crumbed and fried

Traditionally served as an antipasto, *melanzane fritte* are also a great side dish or even a light meal – golden brown and crispy outside while meltingly soft inside.

Ingredients

1–2 medium to large eggplants
flour (optional but helps the egg stick to the eggplant slices)
2 free-range eggs
salt and pepper
breadcrumbs
extra virgin olive oil
optional: lemon wedges, chopped parsley to serve

Method

- Cut the eggplants into slices about a centimetre thick. Take care not to cut the slices too thin or during frying they'll become overly soft and oily and not hold their shape. Also, if they're cut too thick, the outside will brown quickly leaving the inside raw.
- There is no need to first salt or soak the eggplant slices as these days they're mostly grown without the bitterness they may have had. Skipping this also makes for a quicker, easier prep.
- Prepare three bowls: the first with flour (if using); the second with the eggs, beaten and seasoned with salt; the third with breadcrumbs. (Like Nonna Gia you may secretly add a hint of ground chilli to the breadcrumbs if so desired, but just a pinch.)

- Pat each eggplant slice dry, then dredge in flour, followed by the egg and finally the breadcrumbs. Do so gently for the crumbs to stick, especially around the smooth skin.
- Shallow fry the crumbed slices in olive oil. Adjust the heat or add more oil as needed. *Secret tip: Not too hot, or the outsides brown before the insides cook, but not too low or the slices will be soggy and oily. Make sure they have lots of room in the pan.*
- Put the slices on a platter lined with paper towels or keep warm in the oven on a tray.
- Arrange the *Melanzane Fritte* on a serving platter, season lightly and serve warm.

Accompany with lemon wedges to squeeze over the eggplant slices (or a salad and other sides if a meal).

Caponata

Vegetables cooked agrodolce, sweet and sour

There are as many versions of *caponata* as there are cooks ... so it's said. The first written recipes date to the early eighteenth century and while it's famously Sicilian, other regions like Calabria also have versions of this *agrodolce* (sweet and sour) dish handed down through generations over many centuries in the tradition of cooking and passing on family history, no two recipes quite alike.

Ingredients

2–3 eggplants depending on size
2 capsicums (red or yellow are best for sweetness)
2 red onions
1–2 zucchini
3 celery sticks
garlic
extra virgin olive oil
balsamic (or red or white wine) vinegar
2 tbs brown sugar
salt and pepper to season
secret ingredients: lemon or orange zest, smoked paprika, chilli, colatura di
   alici
optional: olives, chopped fresh parsley, anchovies, pine nuts,
   tomatoes ...

Method

- Chop the eggplants into cubes about the size of dice and the other vegetables as desired (they will cook down so a little thicker works best).
- To a large pan on a medium to high heat, add a generous glug of olive oil for shallow frying.
- Add the capsicum and red onion, then once caramelised add the zucchini, celery, eggplant and garlic. Fry until browned and soft, stirring occasionally, adjusting the heat and adding more olive oil as necessary.
- Add a good splash of vinegar, let it reduce then add salt, pepper and brown sugar, stirring for it to dissolve. Have a taste. It should be *agrodolce*, sweet and sour, so adjust vinegar and sugar if necessary.
- *Secret tip: 1 tsp smoked paprika adds depth, as does a small dash of colatura di alici or Worcestershire sauce for that savoury, umami flavour.* (This is perhaps when Nonna Gia would have sprinkled in some of her ground chilli.)
- Turn down heat, stir in lemon/orange zest and simmer for at least 10–15 minutes.

This is a dish served hot, cold or at room temperature, as an antipasto, salad, relish or side dish. Best served the next day as flavours develop. Will keep in the fridge for several days.

Crostoli in Cioccolato

Pastry ribbons dipped in chocolate

For centuries these have been popular throughout Italy and across Europe and Asia. In Italy, they're traditionally eaten at *Carnevale*, when towns celebrate their history, and of course different regions call them different names – *chiacchiere, cenci, sfogliatelle, nodi, bugie, ali d'angelo, frappe, cioffe, galani, sfrappole* … Beware, for *chiacchiere*, or 'rumours', can be addictive. They are best if light and flaky but still crunchy with some substance.

Ingredients

450g plain flour (plus extra for kneading)
3 free-range eggs
50g butter
100g caster sugar (raw, unbleached is best)
50ml Marsala (grappa or brandy may be substituted)
1 tsp vanilla bean extract
grape seed oil or oil of choice for frying (a generous amount)
dark couverture chocolate for melting
optional: a little powdered chilli
icing or caster sugar to sprinkle

Method

- Sift the flour into a mixing bowl. Make a well in the middle and add the eggs, butter, sugar, Marsala and vanilla, mixing thoroughly to create a dough.

- Turn the dough out onto a floured surface and knead until smooth, dusting extra flour across surface to prevent sticking as needed. (Dough should be soft, not sticky.)
- Use a rolling pin or a pasta machine to roll the dough to lasagne sheet thinness.
- Cut into strips roughly 4–5 cm wide, or to your liking. (A fluted pastry/pasta wheel cutter gives a crinkled edge.) Don't let the dough dry out before frying – if possible, cover it with a tea towel.
- Heat the oil in a deep frying pan or saucepan (a wok also works well!). The oil must be hot so the pastries cook quickly and don't absorb too much oil. Fry several strips at a time until golden without overcrowding or the temperature will drop.
- Remove with a slotted spoon and drain on absorbent kitchen paper.
- Sprinkle with caster sugar while still hot, or allow to cool completely then cover with sifted icing sugar.

Optional extra: Dipping the *crostoli* ends in chocolate

- Place a saucepan about a quarter filled with water on the stove.
- Break or chop the couverture chocolate into pieces. Place it in a heatproof bowl on top of the saucepan.
- Bring the water to a simmer, then turn off the heat and let the chocolate sit until melted before stirring it gently. (A microwave risks burning the chocolate.)
- *Optional: stir a little powdered chilli into the chocolate like Nonna Gia did.*
- Remove the bowl of melted chocolate from the water with care.
- Dip ends of *crostoli* in chocolate and place to dry on greaseproof paper.
- When dry, sprinkle with icing sugar and serve.

Best served at once or kept in an airtight container (rather than Nonna Gia's saucepan!). That's if any are left after coffee and chatter ...

Pizzette Fritte

Little fried pizzas

With their origins in Naples, *pizzette fritte* are said to be the way pizzas were first made. Likely served plain straight from the frypan, they were a street food for the poorest residents. The saying from the time, *il mangio oggi e la pago tra otto giorni* (I'll eat it today and pay for it in eight days), meant while the hunger was resolved for the time being, they had to find a way to pay later. (Although some of today's decadent versions might give rise to a different interpretation!)

Ingredients

2 tsp yeast (7g)
2 tsp sugar
100ml warm water
500g flour
300ml (1–1¼ cups) tepid water, or as much as needed to form the dough
a generous pinch of salt
olive oil for frying
toppings: basil pesto, prosciutto and *Parmigiano*; or tomatoes, basil leaves and torn fresh mozzarella, olive oil …

Method

- To make the dough, mix yeast in 100ml tepid water with sugar and leave for several minutes until it begins to bubble and foam a little (showing the yeast is alive).

- Pile the flour on a clean surface and make a well in the middle.
- Add the yeast-and-water mixture and oil into the middle, and begin to incorporate flour by drawing some from the sides into the well and mixing.
- Start adding the tepid water, a bit at a time, and incorporate more flour, until a dough is formed. (It should be elastic and soft, even moist, but firm enough to work with.)
- Knead the dough by hand for a good 10–15 minutes to form a ball with a springy consistency (poke the dough and it should spring back, leaving no trace).
- Rest the dough ball in a deep bowl covered with a tea towel for about 2 hours. Lightly flouring or greasing the dough helps it to rise and prevents it sticking to the bowl.
- The dough should double or even treble in volume.
- *Secret tip: punch it down and let it rise a number of times. The longer it is allowed to rise, the tastier it will be.*
- Once ready, form the dough into balls about the size of hen eggs.
- Flatten each out into a small round, leaving a slight lip around the edges, and fry in hot oil until lightly browned on both sides, flipping as required. (It will brown further in the oven later on.)
- Place them on a rack (or paper towels) to drain then transfer to a baking tray.
- Add favourite pizza toppings and season with salt and pepper.
- Put in a hot oven (200°C) for about 5 minutes just to melt the cheese (don't leave in too long or the *pizzette fritte* will harden).

Must be served fresh and hot straightaway.

Baccalà alla Calabrese

Salted cod Calabrese-style

Baccalà is cod that has been preserved in salt, giving the fish a flaky texture with an intense but never fishy flavour. In Italy, it's a much-celebrated dish especially at Easter and Christmas Eve, although according to southern Italian legend there is a different way to prepare it for all 365 days of the year. (Just as there are as many varying *Baccalà alla Calabrese* recipes!)

Ingredients

extra virgin olive oil (enough to coat the pan)

1 onion, chopped

1–2 cloves garlic, chopped

1kg baccalà, rehydrated – soak for 1–3 days or at least the day before, changing the water every two hours to remove the salt.

a dash of white wine

a pinch of crushed hot chilli (fresh or dried), or more if desired!

a handful of ripe cherry tomatoes, roughly chopped

a dozen or so Calabrese olives (usually green and flavoured with fennel and chilli)

2 bay leaves

a handful of fresh basil leaves, torn by hand, not cut (to prevent them going black)

2 cups chicken or vegetable stock

2 medium potatoes, peeled, cut about dice-sized or chunkier if preferred

salt and pepper to taste (keep in mind *baccalà* imparts some salt to the dish)

Method

- Drain the cod from the water it has been soaking in and gently pat it dry before cutting it into bite-sized pieces. You may then also flour these if desired. (Best to handle the cod gently to avoid it breaking.)
- In a large pot, fry the onions in the olive oil until brown then add in the garlic and floured pieces of cod and fry.
- Add the wine and let it cook down for a few minutes then add in the chilli, tomatoes, olives, bay leaves and basil and cook on medium heat for about 10 minutes. Gently stir occasionally to prevent it from sticking.
- Add the stock and potatoes. Simmer until potatoes are tender. (Alternately the cod may be added at this step with the potatoes, and water instead of stock used – although stock imparts more flavour.)
- Season with salt and pepper to taste and serve immediately.

May be served with fresh bread, rice, polenta or salad.

Mixed Grill

Twentieth-century Greek café style

In cities and towns across Australia, cafés run by Greek migrants
flourished from the 1920s to the 1960s. The 'Mixed Grill' was
one of the most popular items on the menu, cooked 'American
style' to appeal to British–Australian palates of the time.

Ingredients (per person)

1 lamb chop
1 sausage (good quality meat with no cereal fillers)
1 steak (cut of choice)
½ a tomato
1 free-range egg
1–2 bacon rashers (fat left on)
extra virgin olive oil
salt and pepper to taste
optional: lamb's fry or liver

Method

- Pour in some oil and heat a large frying pan.
- Add the sausage and the chop (which take longest to cook).
- After a few minutes add the steak and cook to liking (well done if old style!).
- Add the bacon and cook until crispy.
- *Optional*: when sausage, chop and steak are almost ready, add lamb's fry.

- Next, add the tomato and crack the egg in to cook, leaving the yolk runny.

Best served on a thick ceramic plate with egg sunny-side up,
salt and pepper to taste, toast or buttered bread,
and favourite sauces or condiments.

Egg Flip

Classic milk bar style

Egg flips have been around for centuries and became a popular milk bar drink after the advent of refrigeration. Sought out by manual labourers especially and as a meal replacement or 'pick me up' for those ill with no appetite – don't tell older children there's raw egg in it and they'll love it.

Note: Do not give raw eggs to pregnant women, young children, babies or older adults.

Ingredients

1½ cups milk (full cream works best)
1 free-range egg
dash of vanilla extract (caramel also works well)
2 scoops vanilla ice cream

Adjust ingredients to own taste or preferred milkshake thickness.

Method

- Combine all ingredients in a blender or milkshake mixer.
- Make sure to blend well to ensure the egg is thoroughly mixed in.

Serve straightaway with a paper straw in a
tall glass or in an anodised milkshake container.

Pesche con Crema

Peaches with cream, or are they?

Traditionally for weddings and festivals, especially in Abruzzo and Calabria, these peach cakes are a trick to the eye, to mimic real peaches. This recipe seems complex but is more time-consuming.

Ingredients

Custard cream:
    2 cups full cream milk
    zest of 1 lemon (best in large strips)
    4 free-range egg yolks
    seeds of 1 vanilla bean, scraped out (or ½ tsp vanilla bean paste)
    ¾ cup sugar
    ¼ cup plain flour

Cake dough:
- 3¾ cups plain flour
- 1 tbs baking powder
- 3 free-range eggs
- ¾ cup sugar
- ¾ cup milk
- 115g cooking butter (melted and cooled)
- zest of 1 orange (finely grated)

To assemble peaches:
- ½ cup Italian *Alchermes* or *Maraschino* liqueur (or red *Campari*)
- red and yellow food colouring (natural if possible)

401

- fine sugar for coating (1–2 cups)
- fresh mint leaves

Method

Custard cream:
- In a saucepan, heat the milk, lemon zest and vanilla to a simmer. Turn off heat and leave to infuse.
- In the meantime, in a large bowl whisk egg yolks and sugar until thick and pale yellow; add flour and whisk until well combined.
- Discard lemon zest from milk and slowly whisk hot milk into egg mixture.
- Return to saucepan and on a medium heat stir until cream thickens and starts to boil.
- Transfer custard cream to a large bowl and cover with plastic wrap, pressing down on the surface to prevent a skin from forming. Let cool completely.

Cake dough:
- In a large bowl, stir together the flour and baking powder.
- In another large bowl, whisk the eggs and then add in the sugar whisking further to combine.
- Into the eggs and sugar, whisk the milk, melted butter (cooled) and orange zest until smooth.
- Gradually add flour mixture, mixing with a fork, until the dough is smooth and firm. Let it rest for 5 minutes.
- Preheat oven to 175°C. Line two baking trays with baking paper.
- Take a good tablespoon of the dough and roll it firmly in hands to make a smooth round ball about the size of a walnut. Repeat, keeping all the balls about the same size. Place the balls on prepared baking trays, spacing them a couple of centimetres apart. Flatten tops slightly with fingertips.
- Transfer to oven and bake for about 15 minutes until bottoms are lightly browned and tops are still pale. Transfer to a rack and let cool slightly.

To assemble peaches:

- While the cakes are still warm, use a small, sharp knife to cut a circle about the size of a coin on the bottom (flat) side of each, taking care not to crack the edges. Use the tip of the knife to scrape out enough crumbs to make a hollow to hold about 1 teaspoon custard cream. Set cakes aside.
- Pour liqueur in a small bowl. Add red and yellow food colouring to create a shade of peach. Fill a shallow bowl with sugar. Set aside.
- Fill each hollowed-out cake half with a spoonful of custard cream. Sandwich two together so the filling comes just to the edge, taking care not to break.
- Dip a pastry brush in coloured liqueur and brush it all over the outside of the 'peach' then roll it in sugar to coat. Repeat process with remaining cake halves, liqueur and sugar.
- Store in a sealed container in the refrigerator and chill overnight.

Just before serving, in the top of each 'peach' insert a fresh mint leaf to resemble a leaf and the trickery is complete.

Lasagne con Melanzane

Lasagne with eggplant layers

Lasagne, considered Italy's first pasta dish, was cooked by the Romans long before Marco Polo is said to have brought pasta to Italy from the East in the thirteenth century. While other countries also claim it, lasagne has been embraced, varied and perfected by Italians over centuries and is synonymous with Italy. The original dish used pasta sheets but not tomatoes. This recipe has eggplant layers and is also delicious without the beef for a lighter or vegetarian version.

Ingredients

extra virgin olive oil
1 onion, finely chopped
2–3 garlic cloves, finely chopped
optional: 500g beef mince
optional secret tip: paprika, balsamic vinegar, *colatura di alici*
a handful of basil leaves, torn not cut (to stop them going black)
a handful of parsley, chopped
400g tin diced tomatoes
400g tin crushed tomatoes
1 bottle of tomato passata
salt, pepper
brown sugar
1 eggplant, sliced into rounds about a centimetre thick
400g grated cheddar cheese
250g dried lasagne pasta sheets

Method

- Preheat oven to 180°C. Heat some olive oil in a saucepan and add onion. Cook at a high heat until browned and caramelised but not burnt.
- Add mince (if using) and garlic, and cook at high heat stirring with a wooden spoon until caramelised brown and the juices have disappeared.
- *Secret tip: add ground paprika and a small dash each of balsamic vinegar and colatura di alici or Worcestershire sauce for a deeper savoury, umami background flavour.*
- Add the herbs, tinned tomatoes, bottle of passata and salt and pepper to taste. Reduce heat to medium. Simmer for at least half an hour until sauce thickens, turning down the heat if necessary so it doesn't boil.
- *Secret tip: simmer on a low heat for several hours for a more traditional and tastier sauce.*
- Into a large baking tray greased with olive oil place the pieces of eggplant, sliced into rounds about a centimetre thick. (It is okay to overlap them slightly to fit or use two trays if necessary, depending on the size of the eggplant.) Brush the tops of the eggplant slices with olive oil and season with a little salt and paprika (if using). Bake in oven while sauce continues simmering for about 20 minutes or until eggplant appears soft and cooked.
- To assemble: Grease a large, rectangular lasagne dish with olive oil.
- *Secret tip: a little skimmed sauce in the bottom also helps.*
- Place a layer of the dried pasta sheets over the bottom on the dish (carefully breaking them to fit if necessary). Spoon a layer of sauce mixture over the top, covering all the pasta. Spread a layer of the oven-baked eggplant slices over the top. Sprinkle over a layer of cheese. Repeat layers. Top with remaining sauce and cheese and perhaps a sprinkling of chopped parsley.

- Bake for 40–45 minutes or until pasta is *al dente* and the cheese melted and golden. (Stick a knife in the centre to check the pasta is cooked through.)

After taking it out of the oven, let the lasagne stand for
5–10 minutes and it will be easier to slice and serve.

Zippuli

Calabrian dialect for zeppole

There are many variations (both dialect spellings and recipes) of *zippuli*, a Calabrian word meaning fried dough. Savoury or sweet, they are traditionally served for the *Festa di San Giuseppe* (St Joseph's Day), Christmas, New Year and other celebrations, depending on the town. Mainly cooked in southern Italy, *zippuli* also have an Arabic Mediterranean ancestry.

Ingredients

1kg plain flour
14g (2 sachets) dried yeast
½ tsp salt
750ml (3 cups) tepid water, approximately
olive oil or oil of choice for frying
12 sun-dried tomato halves or anchovy fillets (or six of each) or whatever filling you prefer. A surprise *Piccante Calabrese* chilli or two is optional!

Dough resting time 1–1½ hours

Method

- In a very large bowl, mix the flour, yeast and salt and make a well in the centre.
- Add some of the water into the well a little at a time, gathering flour with your hand as you do and using as much water as

407

you need until all the flour has been incorporated into a sticky dough. (If you accidentally use too much water just add in some flour, a bit at a time, to get the right consistency.)

- Scrape down the sides and leave the dough in the centre of the bowl.
- Cover the bowl with a large tea towel and set aside in a warm place for 1–1½ hours or until the mixture doubles in size.
- Heat the oil in a large, deep saucepan or wok over medium heat. To test if the oil is ready, drop a small piece of dough into the oil and if it sizzles immediately, the oil is ready.
- *Secret tip: Beware of letting the olive oil get so hot it starts to smoke (or use a higher heat oil like grape seed or macadamia instead).*
- Dampen hands with water and take a lump of dough (about 2 tablespoons), stretch it between your fingers and place sun-dried tomato or anchovy fillet lengthways in the centre. Twist the dough to completely encase it, then gently place into the hot oil.
- Repeat with the remaining dough and fillings, making sure you don't overcrowd the pan. Cook the *zippuli*, turning regularly for 3–4 minutes or until golden all over.
- Drain in a colander lined with paper towel and serve warm.

For a dessert version, skip the fillings and simply fry then sprinkle with sugar or honey. Both versions most delicious served fresh and warm.
Buon appetito!

talk about it

Let's talk about books.

Join the conversation:

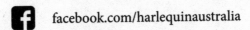 facebook.com/harlequinaustralia

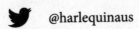 @harlequinaus

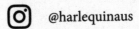 @harlequinaus

harpercollins.com.au/hq

If you love reading and want to know about our
authors and titles, then let's talk about it.